When the Smoke Clears

A Jake Horn Mystery

Gregory Payette

8 FLAGS PUBLISHING

Chapter 1

THE SNOW HAD ALREADY started to stick to the ground outside my office, covering the sidewalks and cars parked along East Broadway. People with heads tucked between their shoulders walked past the window, where I stood inside watching them, each moving as fast as the slick sidewalk would allow. Some perhaps in a hurry to get home or maybe for a good seat at the bar.

Bars and snowstorms were a good match. And I wouldn't have minded a few drinks myself. The last thing I wanted was to be stuck in the office or, worse, in traffic that would no doubt turn my normal fifteen-minute drive home to Milton into an hour. Maybe two, the longer I had to wait.

But I'd promised the woman who'd called me after that morning that I'd wait for her. She mentioned the forecasted storm and promised she'd show up by four.

I glanced at my watch. It was 4:20.

Ms. Connelly didn't share any details about a potential case when she called. It could've been anything: A cheating spouse. A missing child. Homicide. By the sound of her hushed voice, there was something to it.

I turned off the overhead lights, annoyed with one fluorescent bulb flickering from the cold, another buzzing from what was apparently a bad ballast that my landlord swore months earlier he'd get fixed. The light from the lamp on my desk lit up the surrounding area with a yellow glow. The radio was tuned to WBZ. Larry Lapiere said the snow could last a day or two. It didn't sound good, other than to the people locking skis to their car roofs, giddy like kids heading for the mountains. I didn't mind the snow at all, to be honest. But if I was going to be stuck somewhere, I'd rather it be at home, with a fire burning.

It had been a little short of a year since the Blizzard of '78, and nobody I knew of was looking for a repeat.

I wanted to call my daughter at her college in New Hampshire, make sure she was ready for the storm, but didn't want to tie up the line in case Mrs. Connelly tried to call. I checked the soil in the pot of Devil's Ivy on top of the filing cabinet behind the desk, thinking it needed to be watered, especially if I didn't make it back to the office for a couple of days. The soil was dry, but before I made it to the sink in the bathroom, the phone rang. I lifted the handset and answered, "Horn Investigations."

"Mr. Horn? This is Heather Connelly."

"Oh, right. Hello," I said. "Are you still coming?"

"I'm so sorry, but with the snow and all, I—"

"Where are you now?"

"At a payphone. On K Street."

I picked up the phone base and carried it to the window, as far as the line would go without pulling from the wall. I lifted the blinds to get a clearer view outside, and could barely see across the street the way the snow was coming down. "Are you driving here?"

"I was hoping I could walk, from where I'm parked," she said. "It was hard enough finding space."

She had a point. There wasn't any parking available on the street in front of the office. "I can meet you," I said. "Where are you on K?"

"Oh, uh..." She paused. "Oh, there's a place right here. Johnny's Bakery." She had a slight tremble to her voice, I assumed from the cold.

"Is it open?"

"The bakery?" She paused again. I could hear the wind outside coming through the phone. "I... I'm not sure. It might be."

"Well, how about if you go inside, if it's open, and wait for me. We can either come back to my office or we can talk there."

"I'm not sure I want to discuss my business around other people."

"I understand. But you should still go inside. Just wait for me there."

"What if it's closed?" she said.

"Then wait under the awning. Or you can head north on K, toward East Broadway. I'll be there soon."

"Okay," she said. "Thank you."

I grabbed my pea coat from the wooden rack by the door and pulled my wool hat down over my head. My worn leather gloves were still wet from when I'd gone out earlier to clear the dusting off the Nova.

The streets were loud, horns blowing on both sides of the street with anxious commuters trying to get away before the storm got any worse. I had a good feeling as soon as the cold snow hit my face, like needles, it was the kind of snow that wouldn't let up. I was afraid I'd end up sleeping at my office unless my meeting with Mrs. Connelly was short.

I pulled my coat's collar up to block the wind, which seemed to come from all directions. I tried to hurry, but the sidewalk was slippery as ice. I wasn't the only one out there trying to get somewhere, but the normal close-of-business crowd was thin.

I turned left onto K Street. Other than a few kids enjoying the slippery sidewalks, there was hardly anyone outside. I tried to look ahead for Ms. Connelly, but the visibility was poor, the snow now whirling toward my face.

I made it to the next block and could just about make out the buildings on either side of the street. The snow darkened the glow from the street lamp in front of Johnny's Bakery, the payphone Ms. Connelly must've called me from a few steps away. I followed snow-covered footprints up the steps to the plate glass door and pulled on the handle. But it was locked. The lights were off, other than toward the back, through a doorway behind the counter. The chairs were all turned over and placed on top of the six small tables inside.

I turned from the entrance and looked back and forth along the sidewalk. I called out for Ms. Connelly, loud enough for someone within shouting distance to hear. "Ms. Connelly?" I said again, then turned back to the bakery's entrance. Someone was inside, behind the counter, so I knocked on the glass.

It was Johnny DeAngelo, the owner. He barely looked my way, waving me off. "Closed early," he yelled. Or at least I thought that's what he said, the way his voice was muffled behind the glass.

I knocked again, and he appeared frustrated, shaking his head. He leaned a mop he had in his hand against the counter.

Johnny walked to the door, and this time I could hear him. "I said we're closed." But then he smiled, turning the key in the lock to open the door. "Jake? I'm sorry, buddy. I didn't know it was you. What are you doing out in this mess?" He pulled me inside by the arm, then struggled to close the door behind me with the wind coming at us. He pulled it closed and locked it, glancing at my snow covered boots. "I'm not in the mood for another storm," he said. "If I can just get out of here before it gets any worse." He looked me over. You want a drink?"

"No, thank you," I said.

I could still smell the sweetness from Johnny's fresh pies and cakes, although there was a bleach-like odor I guessed was from the tile floor, still wet from his mop.

"I'm looking for someone. She was right outside, I'd say no more than five, ten minutes ago. I told her to come in here."

He shrugged, shaking his head. "I'm sorry, Jake. I closed at four today. Nobody's been in since."

I turned to look outside through the plate glass door, but all I could see was the reflection from the lights in the kitchen. "She called me from the payphone outside, I told her I'd come meet her."

Johnny stood with an expression, like he didn't know what else to say. "Maybe she went home."

I nodded and looked through the glass, then pulled at the handle, forgetting for a moment Johnny had locked it.

"You want to take a coffee with you?" he said.

"No, I'm all right. Thank you, though."

He reached past me and turned the key, holding open the door just enough so I could squeeze through. "If there's anything I can do..."

"Thanks, Johnny." I stepped outside, and a gust of wind almost ripped the door off the hinges as Johnny pulled it closed behind me.

The footprints on the steps in front of me had been covered over.

A sedan drove by, too fast for driving in snow.

I went over to the payphone with the street lamp above it. There were tracks around it, the imprints small. I looked up when headlights shone toward me, but stopped and turned around to go the other way.

I could see the illuminated sign for Sully's General Store at East Fifth and continued on K toward it. I went inside Sully's, and although it was open, there were no customers inside.

Patty Sullivan was behind the counter, a cigarette with a long ash on it in the ashtray, smoke rising from it. Patty had her eyes on the TV on the counter, adjusting the rabbit ears as I approached. She raised her gaze and gave me a nod, picking up her cigarette. She took a drag. "Wicked bad out there, huh Jake? Surprised you stuck around for it."

"I wasn't planning on it," I said, glancing around the store. "Any chance a woman was in here, ten, fifteen minutes ago?"

"What'd she look like?"

"I don't know," I said.

"Young? Old?"

"I wish I could answer that."

Patty just shrugged. "I wasn't watching the clock, but a young woman was in not too long ago. Bought a pack of Newports and left. She wasn't dressed for this weather, I could tell you that much." She drew from her cigarette and turned her eyes back to the TV. "They're saying twelve to fourteen inches." She turned and looked at the clock with an image of the Marlboro man on his horse behind her. "I'm probably closing up early," she said.

I turned for the door. "All right, be safe out there."

"You don't need anything?" she said.

I thought about it, knowing I had nothing more than maybe a six-pack in the fridge at work and nothing to eat at home. "No, not right now." I headed out the door and into the snow, pulling my collar up tight.

I could hear cars in the distance. A horn blew. But otherwise, an eerie quietness had started to envelop the neighborhood.

I headed back toward my office and wondered if Heather Connelly knew the area well enough to take the cut through on Fourth, instead of staying on K to East Broadway.

There were no cars parked on the street now, although a cleared space with hardly any snow and a fresh set of tracks along the curb in front of me showed me there had been.

The temperature felt like it had dropped from when I first left the office, and I wanted to get back before it got any worse. Maybe Ms. Connelly would be there waiting for me.

I turned down Fourth and continued past Hannigan Square. Whatever footprints there might've been ahead of me were fully covered over with snow. It was hard to tell for sure, but I didn't think anybody had recently walked the same way.

By the time I turned onto East Broadway, the snow-covered sidewalks were empty. I stopped and looked around, then stomped my boots on the ground before going back into the office. I pulled them off, along with my gloves and my hat, and placed them by the steam heater. But before I could take my coat off, the phone on my desk rang.

The wet from the snow soaked through my sock. I had to catch my breath after my trek through the storm before I answered: "Horn Investigations."

I listened, but it seemed there was nobody there.

"Hello?" I said. "Are you there?" I waited a couple of moments, listened, then placed the handset down and took off my coat.

Chapter 2

After a mostly sleepless night with the constant sound of the city plows' engines, metal scraping the asphalt under the snow outside, I got up from the couch in my office and went over to the window. I'd moved the Nova to a designated public parking lot the night before, after the mayor called for a parking ban. I did not know if or when I'd be able to get it out.

It had gotten light out, although the sky was gray with snow still falling. But barely. The few cars left parked on the street were covered with a good foot of snow.

Whether or not I wanted to deal with another storm, there was a calmness in the morning I'd admit I sort of enjoyed. It was like everything in the world came to a stop, and the only things left to worry about were shoveling the driveway or walkway, or digging a car out.

I had my wool blanket hung over my shoulders, checking the thermostat. I always kept the heat low at night, whether I was home or stuck at the office. But the morning chill was a little too much, even for me. So I kicked it up a couple of degrees to sixty-five, hopefully enough to keep my landlord off my back for the utility bills he constantly complained about.

After I'd gotten back to the office the night before, I spent a good hour going through the white pages. But I had no luck finding anyone with the name Heather Connelly. There were over one hundred residents in Massachusetts with the last name Connelly, and after calling the first ten, I gave up. And by that time, the snow was too much.

I'd spent the night in Southie, rather than fight the snow-covered roads. The '74 Nova I'd inherited from my grandmother was a horse on dry pavement, but nothing but a sled on snowy streets. After the blizzard hit us the year before, with nearly a hundred people who'd died—some in their cars—I looked at a night on the couch in my office as a decent enough option.

It wasn't like I had anyone to go home to.

My friend Maggie, a Boston cop, worked the 7 a.m. shift, so I thought I could catch her at home before she left. I made a pot of coffee and sat at my desk with my Red Sox mug, and dialed her phone.

It rang about six times before she answered.

"Hello?"

"Hey, it's me," I said, leaning back in my chair. "You got a minute?"

"Maybe two, but I gotta get to work. I'm late. It's a mess out there." She paused. "Where are you?"

"At the office," I said. "I got hung up yesterday waiting for a woman who never showed up."

"A *woman*?"

"A potential client."

I told her about the initial call, and most of what had happened after.

"You couldn't call her?" Maggie said.

"I didn't get her number. She was somewhat secretive when she first called. I asked for her number—I always do—but she said she'd tell me everything I needed when we met."

"So, all you have is a name?"

"Ms. Heather Connelly," I said. "But I don't know what she looks like. I don't know how old she is, where she lives, if she's single or married…"

Maggie said, "And she didn't say anything about why she wanted to meet?"

"No. Nothing."

The line was silent for a moment.

Maggie said, "I'm not sure how much I'll be able to do when I get in. It's kind of crazy out there with the storm. There've already been a dozen accidents. But I'll see what I can dig up."

"I might keep going through the phone book."

"So you don't even know if Connelly's her real name? Or if she's married?"

I sipped my coffee. "Like I said, I've got nothing."

***

By the time I'd cleared the snow from the Nova and got it out of the parking lot, it was almost eight-thirty. The snow had stopped and the sun started to work its way through the gray clouds, reflecting off the snow. I let the engine warm for a few minutes, but once the windows were cleared, I tried to pull it out of the space.

I wasn't the only one in the lot trying to get out, and with the snow everyone cleared from their cars it would be a mess if I didn't leave soon. I slipped the car into drive and eased my foot onto the gas pedal. But at first the tires did nothing but spin. The car wouldn't move. I slapped it into reverse, then into drive, and repeated the process, trying to rock my way out of the snow. The transmission took a beating, but the last thing I needed was to have my car stuck in a lot three blocks from my office.

Lucky for me, a man about my age walked over and knocked on my window. I rolled it down.

"You need a hand?" he said.

I got out and looked at all the other cars buried in the lot. "I've got chains," I said.

The man nodded. "All right, let me know if you need a hand."

It was no secret people in Boston—or throughout New England, for that matter—could be a little rough around the edges, especially to an outsider. But when you needed a hand, you never had to look far.

I said thanks to the man, opened the trunk and pulled out my chains. Once I had them wrapped around the rear tires, it was smooth sailing getting out of there. I pulled over to the side of the street, took the chains off, and headed out of the city.

If there's one thing I'd learned throughout my life in New England, it was to be prepared for the weather.

***

I stopped to see my cousin Raymond in Dorchester. His driveway was already clear and with signs of the blacktop underneath coming through what was left of the packed snow. Raymond, a retired Boston cop, was always up early and out with his snowblower long before the sun had come up. His front steps and covered porch were cleared too.

The sky was bright enough it hurt my eyes, the way it hit the snow. My grandmother used to tell me people with light-colored eyes had more trouble in the sun. I think she was right. In every picture ever taken of me outside, my eyes were usually closed or I'd be squinting so much they'd look that way.

I stepped out of the Nova and slipped on my sunglasses.

Raymond came out the front door and onto his porch with a mug of coffee in his hand. He was a hulk of a man. Six-four and built like a lumberjack. He wore a red sweater with a white turtleneck under it; snow pants and suspenders hung over his shoulders. He looked ready to hit the slopes, but neither of us had skied since we were kids over at Blue Hills.

"I thought it was going to be worse," he said, looking past me toward the piles of snow on either side of the street.

It was cold enough outside that it wasn't likely the sun would melt much of the snow.

Raymond reached into a big bag of salt and tossed a handful of it on a patch of snow by the steps. "You want a coffee?" he said, wiping his bare hand on his pants. He sipped his coffee.

I walked onto the porch. "I could use one."

He walked past me and opened the door, taking his boots off outside. I did the same and followed him in. The house was warm, with the comforting, smoky smell of burning wood from the wood stove.

"Salt's a killer on the hardwoods," he said, sliding his feet into slippers he had on the other side of the doorway. "Beth said I shouldn't use it at all, but I told her it's better than I go out there at night, slip on the ice and crack open my skull." He continued into the kitchen.

His wife Beth was inside. She had her back to the doorway, the weather on the news on the black and white TV. She turned to me, sipping from her mug, and smiled. "Hey, Jake."

Raymond walked past me and grabbed the pot from the Mr. Coffee machine and poured coffee into his Patriots mug. "Here," he said, handing it to me. "You can take this one home with you. I'm done with the Patriots."

I laughed. "You're still upset?"

Raymond shook his head, sipping from his Bruins mug. "You go eleven and five, get blown out in the first round of the playoffs? There's no excuse for that."

"Spring training's right around the corner," I said.

Raymond shook his head. "I already told you I'm done with the Sox too."

Beth rolled her eyes. "Good, so if you're done watching sports maybe you can get everything done around the house you've been promising me."

Raymond gave her a look without another word, then walked out of the kitchen.

I followed him into the living room, where he was crouched down in front of his wood-burning stove. He had the door open, placing a couple of split logs on the fire. The door squeaked when he closed it and turned the knob.

He wiped his brow with his sleeve. "Come on, let's go back outside. It's too warm in here."

It was always warm in Raymond's house, the way he had the stove cranking through most of the winter. But at least he didn't have to burn as much oil.

We both stopped at the door when the phone rang.

Beth stepped out of the kitchen and reached her hand around to grab it off the wall. "Hello?"

Raymond opened the door without looking back. He said to me, "Come on, you're letting the heat out."

I waited, once I heard Beth on the call.

She said, "Oh, hi Maggie. Yes, he is. He's right here. Hang on."

I turned and Beth was holding out the phone. "It's Maggie."

I closed the front door behind Raymond after he went outside, and went over to take the phone from Beth. "You find something?"

"Well, I don't know," Maggie said. "I hope not. A body was recovered this morning, down off of K Street, not far from your office."

A sense of dread flowed through my body. "A woman?"

"Yes. The victim's female. Sorry, I—"

"Has she been identified?" I said.

Beth stood watching me.

Raymond came back in from outside. "What are you doing?"

"He's talking to Maggie," Beth said.

Maggie said, "No. Nothing yet. No identification on her. Appears to be in her twenties, maybe a little older. But I can't say for sure if—"

"How was she killed?"

Maggie paused on the other end. "Her body was frozen, Jake. But there appears to be signs of strangulation. We don't have a full report yet."

"Where exactly was she?"

"K and Eight, behind O'Hara's Meats."

"Two blocks from Johnny's," I said.

Chapter 3

I was back at the house in Milton. When I say 'the house,' I'm talking about my grandmother's home where I'd lived since she left it to me and my daughter Nancy. I never felt quite right calling it mine, since it's a place I'd spent a good part of my life growing up, as did Nancy, while my grandmother was still alive.

And with Nancy being up at Plymouth College in New Hampshire, I had the whole place to myself. It was a two-story house, built in the early 1900s, and probably too much for one man. But it wasn't like I was going to sell it. And with Nancy only a couple years away from graduating college, I guessed she'd eventually move back in with me. Of course, there was a good chance she wouldn't.

Ever since my wife Barbara was killed, nearly thirteen years ago, it has been me and Nancy. The adjustment for me, having Nancy off to college, wasn't easy. I felt an emptiness I didn't enjoy when I walked into that cold house alone every day.

I'd spent the first two hours shoveling the driveway, including the mound of snow the plows left along the street. And by that point my back was sore, and I felt like I'd sweated out ten pounds of body weight.

Everyone else in the neighborhood had already cleared their driveways. I'd never owned a snowblower, but in the past my grandmother's neighbor from across the street, Mr. O'Roarke, would come over with his snowblower. But he and his wife had started going to Florida for the winters a few years back, so I was on my own with the aluminum snow shovel.

When I finally went inside, I could feel the chill in the air, but I had to strip down to my sweat-soaked T-shirt from shoveling. My heart was still pounding in my chest. No wonder heart attacks were so common during snowstorms.

Not that I was weak, but I'd been slacking with the exercise the past couple of months, and after an hour clearing the driveway and steps, I felt it.

Before I went up to take a shower, I went out back and grabbed some wood from the pile. I'd covered it with a tarp a few days before they predicted the snow, and luckily didn't have to deal with trying to burn wet wood.

Once I got the fire going, I went up to shower. I couldn't stop thinking about Heather Connelly, and whether the body they found was hers. Maggie was going to let me know as soon as she had word, but it was bothering me. It made little sense that there was nobody with the name Heather Connelly in Massachusetts.

By the time I'd gotten out of the shower and changed, the fire I'd lit downstairs was roaring. I liked the way it looked, but the downside to an open fireplace, and not a wood-burning stove like Raymond had, was it wasn't very efficient, the heat rarely making it upstairs or even beyond the room where the fire was lit.

But it didn't matter.

I was exhausted, and sat on the couch feeling a fair amount of guilt about the woman's body the police had found. I had a hard time convincing myself it wasn't Heather Connelly, or whoever the woman was who had called me. What if she'd been murdered? It would be my fault. She came to me for help.

I stared into the roaring flames. The burning wood crackled. I could feel the heat on the front of my legs. Leaning my head back, I closed my eyes. But I jumped when the phone next to me rang.

I reached for the handset. "Hello?"

"Dad? It's me."

It was my daughter, Nancy. There wasn't another voice in the world I would've wanted to hear.

"Nance," I said. "I'm sorry I haven't called you. I didn't want to bother you at school."

"I told you, you're not bothering me," she said. "You can call whenever you want. Just leave a message with someone if I'm not in the dorm."

I smiled, staring into the fire. "How was the storm up there?"

"Not as bad as it hit Boston," she said. "I think we only got six inches."

"So you're okay?"

"Of course," she said, sounding as if she wanted to laugh at the question. "I wish we had more snow."

Nancy loved snow as much as anyone. She always wondered how people could live in places without it, but I'd remind her it's more fun when you're young and you don't have to worry about doing things adults have to do. Like going to work, or the grocery store so a family can eat. Or paying for heat.

"Is everything okay with you?" she said. "You sound, uh..."

Nancy was perceptive. She always was, even when she was younger.

"I sound *what*?" I said.

"I don't know. Like something's wrong?"

I was hesitant to tell her what had happened, about the body being found and the possibility it was the woman I was supposed to meet. But Nancy was old enough at that point to understand the truth. I rarely kept anything from her, especially when she could sense something was wrong.

I told her as much as I knew at that point, which wasn't much.

"But you don't know for sure?" she said.

"As of right now, I have no way of knowing whether it was her or not. The police are still trying to find a next of kin, without much luck."

"It's so scary," Nancy said. "The poor woman. Imagine the family, if nobody even knows she's dead."

"Well, *somebody* knows," I said.

Nancy paused on the other end. "What did Maggie say?"

Nancy had already been in the criminology program at Plymouth State for two years. Her interest never wavered. She was always digging into criminal cases, whether or not they had something to do with me. She still hadn't decided what she would do with her life when she got out of college, but it would have something to do with law. I'd hoped for something outside of law enforcement or any kind of investigative work, but the fact was it was already in her blood.

I said, "The police are looking into it."

"Who found her? The woman?" she said.

"A state worker, running the plow," I said.

Nancy gasped. "That's horrible."

I could hear voices in the background, as if someone was talking to her.

"Dad, someone has to use the phone. Can I call you later?"

"You can call me anytime."

Nancy said, "I hope they figure out what happened."

"I do too," I said.

There was a brief silence on the line.

Nancy's voice lowered, almost hushed. "You're not going to get involved in whatever happened, are you?"

I had to think about it for a moment. "I'm not sure. First I need to find out if it's the same woman who called me. I hope it wasn't, not that it'll change what happened to the victim."

"I have a hard time believing you're going to leave it all up to the cops."

She knew me too well.

"I'll wait and see," I said. "I don't know the first thing about the woman who called me. And if her name's not what she told me it was, then we may never have an answer."

"Well, hopefully you get one," Nancy said. A woman's voice in the background came through the phone. "Dad? I've got to get off the phone. Call me at the dorm if you hear anything else."

"I will," I said. "Be safe."

"You too. Love you."

She hung up before I could tell her the same.

I sat quietly, thinking, with the handset resting on my chest before placing it on the base. After a few moments, I stood and went into the kitchen to find something to eat. That's when I noticed a car parked in the street, at the end of my driveway. It was getting dark, making it hard to see who was behind the wheel or what kind of car it was. It appeared to be a yellow sedan, almost the same color as the Nova.

The car didn't move. Not until I went to the front door and opened it. The car took off down Pegoda Street.

I ran outside with my hair still wet, wearing nothing more than my sweatpants and a sweatshirt with slippers on my bare feet. I stepped into the deep snow when I tried to get a closer look at the car or maybe get a plate through the leafless trees. But I was too late. The car was gone.

CHAPTER 4

I'D SPENT THREE HOURS making phone calls to just about every household with the last name Connelly I'd found in the white pages. There were seventeen in Boston alone, and at least a hundred throughout the state. I wasn't sure I was up for calling every single one of them, especially since Maggie also had little luck finding a Heather Connelly through whatever channels she had available. But I had to give it a try.

Out of the thirty calls I made, eleven had a friend or relative with the name Heather. But none with the last name Connelly.

By the time I got through, I'd come to the realization that the woman who called me decided to use a fictitious name. That was the only logical explanation.

What I had no way of knowing was whether the woman who had called me was the unidentified victim of what was being treated by that point as a homicide.

I opened the fridge to see if there was anything to eat. But I found nothing, and decided instead to grab a 'Gansett. I twisted the aluminum tab off the can and drank half the beer before I closed the door.

I stepped to the window when I heard a car outside. A green Plymouth Scamp with a white vinyl roof passed under the streetlight and pulled into the driveway.

It was Maggie.

I went to the front door, opening it as soon as she came up the steps with a brown paper bag in her hand.

"Did you eat?" she said, holding up the bag. "Picked up Chinese."

She walked past me and into the kitchen, placing the bag on the table, then taking off her coat.

"It's one of the coldest winters on record," she said, shaking like she had a chill, running her hands up and down her arms. She wore a sweater over a turtleneck and pulled off her winter hat, her red hair falling down over her shoulders. She threw up her hands. "Damnit, I left the photos in the car."

"Is it open?" I said. She nodded, and I went outside to her car. It felt like I'd been slapped, the way the chill hit me. The moisture in my nostrils froze on contact. I tried the passenger door, but it was locked. Then I went around to the other side. The door stuck at first, as if it'd frozen, but I gave it a good yank and it opened. Reaching inside, I grabbed a large manila envelope, slammed the door closed and hurried back inside.

I opened the envelope on my way into the kitchen and pulled out the photos inside. On top was a picture of a woman's body lying in the snow at night. I stopped in the doorway, glancing at the image. There was a small card paper-clipped to the bottom corner that read, *Jane Doe.*

She appeared to be much younger than I'd expected.

Maggie had already put two plates on the table.

I said, "They still don't know who she is?"

Maggie opened up the bag of food. "No."

I slid the photo back into the envelope and placed it on the counter. "I might've just lost my appetite."

Maggie frowned. "I wish we had more information."

I let out a long sigh and cleared my throat, pointing through the doorway toward the family room. "Do you want to eat in there? By the fire?"

Maggie shivered, as if she had a chill, and nodded.

I grabbed the bag and carried the food along with the envelope into the living room, placing them both on the coffee table in front of the couch. I kneeled on the floor in front of the fireplace and threw a couple of logs on the fire.

Maggie walked up behind me with the dishes and silverware and placed them on the coffee table, then picked up the envelope.

"The medical examiner said she's in her late twenties."

"And they're sure she didn't freeze to death?" I said.

Maggie shook her head. "Didn't you look at the photo?"

"I did, but I thought I'd eat first."

"Strangulation," she said. "But, Jake, we have no idea if this is the same woman. I can see it in your eyes, like you're feeling some sense of guilt about it."

I turned from her and kneeled in front of the fireplace, poking the hot embers to stoke the flame. "I'm just having a hard time believing it was a coincidence. This woman, whose name I don't even know, called me for help. It was the same night. She was in the same area, calling me from the payphone right there, in front of Johnny's."

"No matter what happened, you know there was nothing you could've done. Even if she—"

"I should have hung around longer, instead of running back to my office. I could have looked a little harder for her."

Maggie said, "But you told me you went back hoping she'd be there, then you went out looking again."

I stood as the new logs finally caught fire, placing the poker in the rack next to the fireplace. I took the envelope from Maggie's hand. "Did anyone go over to Sully's? Patty Sullivan was behind the counter, said a young woman had been in there, a little before I went in asking questions."

Maggie nodded. "Detective Carter."

"Carter? Is this his case?"

Detective Nick Carter was old school. He'd been around the block and even knew my Uncle Pat, back when Horn Investigations was in its heyday. I ran into Carter a few times over the years, and may have banged heads with him more than once. But he was a good cop.

Maggie said, "He wants to talk to you."

"To warn me to stay out of this?" I sat on the couch and opened up the bag.

"Most likely," she said. "But he's interested in whatever conversation you had with the woman who called you."

I pulled out the white waxed takeout container and bent the metal handle down to open it. "What'd you get?"

Maggie pulled out the other two containers. "Beef Lo Mein, General Tso's chicken, and hot and sour shrimp."

I said, "You didn't get anything for yourself?"

She laughed. "If you're that hungry, go ahead. Eat it all."

I dumped some of the Lo Mein onto my plate. "I guess you can have a bite." I got up and went into the kitchen to grab two beers, peeling the tabs off both cans before handing one to Maggie. "So, what else did he say?"

"Nick?"

I nodded. "About the woman? Or about me?"

"He's got nothing else going at this point," Maggie said.

"You mean, besides a mysterious woman with a fictional name, who disappeared before my eyes in the middle of a storm?" I took a set of chop sticks from the paper bag and was about to eat with them, but decided I wasn't in the mood. I never really got the hang of them, anyway.

I grabbed a fork and took a bite of the Lo Mein, washing it down with a sip of beer. Maggie and I spent the next couple of minutes eating, without saying much of anything.

I put down my fork and reached for the envelope.

"You don't want to wait until we're done eating?" Maggie said. She was holding a shrimp with her chop sticks.

I didn't answer her, pulling out the photos.

Neither of us was ever bothered by graphic images most normal people would have trouble looking at, especially while trying to eat dinner. We'd both seen enough over the years.

I studied the top photo, and the woman's face, looking closer at the markings on her neck I'd missed the first time.

Maggie leaned into me; I could hear her chewing in my ear.

She said, "You can see the bruise. She also had clear injuries to her larynx and trachea."

"What was the time of death?" I said, flipping through the photos.

"That's a little challenging, with the way she was found," she said. "But it appears to be some time between eight and midnight."

"Is that science? Or is someone basing it on the obvious fact I was supposed to meet a woman in that exact location a few hours earlier?"

Maggie waited to respond while she chewed her food, then wiped her mouth with the napkin. "Detective Carter's using everything he has right now. This is not going to be an easy one."

I said, "Was there anything that could be used to identify her? Jewelry? Or..."

"There was nothing. But there's also a chance somebody else could have taken her jewelry, or any identification, after she was killed. We don't know. Some low life could have—"

"No markings?" I said. "Birth marks? Tattoos?"

Maggie said, "You have to understand, there hasn't been a single call from anyone. No reported persons missing. Nobody's come forward to identify the victim." She took the other photos from me and put them back into the envelope, then placed it aside and picked up her plate. "Everything so far's come to a dead end."

I WAS AT THE office soon after sunrise, watering the Devil's Ivy behind me when the phone rang. I lifted the handset to answer and leaned back against the edge of my desk. "Horn Investigations."

"Jake? It's Nick Carter. I understand you may be able to help me?" he said.

Maggie had warned me he'd be calling. I just hadn't expected it so early, before I'd even gotten a chance to make a pot of coffee.

"Good morning to you too, Detective," I said, considering his lack of salutation. "I don't think I'm going to be much help. All I have is a woman's name. She was supposed to meet me. But the way it looks, I think she'd used a fake name."

The detective said, "Maggie tells me she was in some kind of trouble, so..."

"I can't say one way or the other what kind of trouble she was in. I assumed she wanted to discuss a case."

"What kind of case?"

"We didn't get into it."

"What do you mean you didn't get into it?"

"Exactly what I said. I have no details. She was supposed to meet me. Then it turns out, she's a couple of blocks away when she called. But the storm was just starting to pick up."

"She was near your office?"

"That's what she said when she called. I believe she used a payphone on K. I mean, honestly, I have no idea why she didn't just come right to my office, other than the parking was slim on East Broadway."

Detective Carter paused on the other end. "You mind coming down the station?"

"For what?" I said.

Sometimes I felt the cops had people in for questioning knowing they'd get nowhere with it. Like they had to put on a show for their superiors. And I knew there was nothing Carter could ask me that was going to get him any further ahead than he was getting right then, on the phone.

"I'm telling you," I said. "I got nothing. I have a woman who called me, most likely using a false name, and—"

"Horn," he said. "All I'm asking is for you to come over to the station. What else do you have to do?"

I knew it was only a matter of time before the guy would slip in a dig, like my time had no value. As far as he and just about every other cop in Boston was concerned, private investigators didn't bring much to the table. But when they were at a dead end with nowhere else to turn, they acted like we were best friends.

The fact I'd brought down one of their own a year ago—a crooked detective involved in running guns and trafficking drugs—I couldn't help but think it only made an already rocky relationship somewhat worse. Part of that had to do with my belief that a quarter of the cops in Boston were dirty to begin with. And that might've been on the low end.

My uncle, in his day, got plenty of respect from the cops when he was still around. But that was mostly due to the fact he was at one time a Boston cop himself, until he lost his leg in an accident. He was forced to retire from the only job he'd ever known. But even with one leg, he wasn't about to sit around eating crackers. So he started Horn Investigations. And he grew his agency to a point that residents in and around Boston would call him *before* they'd call the cops.

I said, "If you guys would do your jobs over there, maybe I wouldn't be as busy as I am."

The line went quiet.

Carter said, "Don't make me start digging into this deeper, find out you're holding out, involved in something you're trying to—"

"Involved in something?" I said. "Like what?"

"You get my point. I know how you operate. You like to keep real cops in the dark, just so you can get your glory."

"I think you're confusing me with someone else," I said.

There was no response, and then I heard a dial tone.

Detective Carter had hung up.

I placed the handset down and started over to make a pot of coffee. But the phone rang as soon as I walked away, and I hurried back to my desk to answer. I assumed it was Carter calling back. I answered, "Detective?"

There was a slight pause, before the caller on the other end spoke. "Is this Jake Horn?"

I recognized the voice—a woman's—right away.

"This is, well, I told you my name was Heather Connelly, but..."

"You're alive?" I said, as if I needed to ask.

"Why wouldn't I be?" She let out either a sigh or a slight laugh on the other end. She said, "I'm sorry about not showing up. I was unaware, but my uncle actually followed me down, and made me go home with him. I left my car in a lot overnight."

"Your uncle followed you?"

"He's a bit overprotective," she said.

I paused, confused with what might've been going on. I was annoyed.

"Can you at least tell me what this is all about? I went out looking for you, you know. But you were nowhere. Here I am thinking..." I didn't bring up the body that had been found. "And why would you wait so long to call me?"

"I'm sorry," she said. "I can explain."

"I hope so," I said. "Maybe you can start with telling me your real name?"

"I'm sorry about that too," she said. "My name is Marilyn. Marilyn Green."

"Okay, Marilyn. Thank you for that." I wrote her name down on my yellow legal pad. "So, can you please tell me what this is all about? I'm not a big fan of being lied to."

There was a pause on the other end.

"I said I was sorry." She cleared her throat. "Do you know Larry Green, by any chance?"

"Should I?"

"Have you heard of Green Chrysler? On the Auto Mile, in Norwood?"

"Oh, okay. Yes. That's the place that... The owner used to do those silly commercials from the hot air balloon?" I smiled, thinking about it. I always laughed at those cheesy car dealership commercials. But then I remembered his story from not long ago.

"Larry is or, well... Larry was my husband. He died when his hot air balloon caught fire. The police up there still believe it was an accident, but I'm not convinced they have it right."

"Up there? It was in New Hampshire, right?" I had recalled some details of the case, although I knew little about it.

She said, "His balloon landed in New Hampshire. Or, what was left of it."

"Wasn't it a few months ago?" I said.

"Ten months."

Mrs. Green sounded fairly young on the phone, and as far as I knew, Larry Green was a much older man. How old, I didn't know.

"Okay," I said. "So, you said you think they got it wrong? Are you saying you believe there was some sort of foul play?"

"I do."

"Do you have specific reasons to believe Mr. Green's death wasn't accidental?"

"If you don't mind, Mr. Horn, I was hoping we could meet face-to-face to discuss this further."

"I'm at my office now," I said.

"I was hoping you could come out to see me. I think it's best I lay low for now, until I get some answers."

I had no idea what she meant by that.

"I'd like at least some information before I go anywhere. After the no-show the other night, on top of you providing me a false name, if you can just give me a little more detail about what you're looking for I'd appreciate it."

There was a rustling on the other end of the phone; her voice quiet and almost muffled when she spoke. I pictured her lying down.

"Some things just don't add up in the so-called investigation," Marilyn said.

"Have you spoken to the police about it?" I said.

"Several times. They won't even take my calls any longer."

"What about... Did you and Mr. Green have any children?"

"Larry does, from his previous marriage. They're older, so, I guess I wouldn't call them kids, but..."

"Older?"

"We're the same age," she said. "One son and a daughter."

My initial thought about the age difference seemed to be accurate.

"Okay, so then, do they have anything to say about this?"

"Not really. I brought it up to his son, but he didn't even want to discuss it. We never really had much of a relationship to begin with."

"So, you've gone to the police," I said. "And you've gone to his kids. Now you're looking for someone who'll dig into this a little deeper for you?"

"Yes."

I looked at her name as I'd written it on the pad. Wrote Larry next to her name, and then noted two kids.

"How come you've waited so long? You said it's been ten months?"

"I'm sorry, Mr. Horn. I know you want some questions answered, but I really don't feel like discussing this over the phone."

"Okay," I said.

"Can you come out to my Uncle's house? In Newton?"

"Your uncle? The one who followed you?"

"Yes. His name's Nathan Howell."

"Okay. Why your uncle's house?"

"I live there. For the time being, at least."

"And he'll be expecting me? In case for some reason you're not there?"

"Why wouldn't I be there?"

I didn't need to explain to her that once someone lies to me, even for good reason, I'm going to have a hard time with trust going forward. The fact was, something didn't feel right about any of it. But it wasn't like I had clients banging down my door. I said, "Go ahead and give me your uncle's address. I'll come out at two o'clock, if that's all right?"

Chapter 6

I turned down Eldredge Street in Newton, close to Farlow Park, and parked in front of the stone wall surrounding the Queen Anne Victorian home that apparently belonged to Marilyn's uncle. I looked up at the house and watched the smoke rising from the chimney, smelling the burning wood as soon as I stepped out of the Nova.

I walked up the brick steps and along the shoveled walkway, with accumulated snow on either side of the narrow path leading to the front porch. I headed up the brick steps, and before I knocked an older man with white hair and a thin mustache to match opened the door. He wore a green turtleneck under his red sweater, as if he wasn't quite ready to let go of Christmas.

"Can I help you?" he said, looking at me with a hint of suspicion in his eyes.

"I'm here to see Marilyn?"

The man nodded, as if he had been expecting me. "Come in," he said, stepping back from the open door. He closed it as soon as I stepped inside.

"I assume you're the uncle?"

He nodded and reached out a hand. "May I take your coat?" He didn't tell me his name.

I stepped into the foyer and looked up at the high ceiling, unbuttoning my pea coat. I handed it to him and waited as he hung it in the closet by the door.

Straight ahead was a wide staircase made of wood with a pattern worn onto the edge of each step. To the left was a room where a stunningly beautiful woman with long, curly, dark hair sat in a wingback chair next to the burning fireplace.

It was as if she wanted to put on a show, acting like she didn't know I was there. She finally stood as I stepped into the room and came toward me, her hand extended. A light floral-like perfume hung in the air.

"Jake?" She smiled, with her gaze fixed on mine. "Marilyn Green," she said, then turned to the man. "This is my uncle, Nathan Howell."

She was as young as she sounded on the phone, and I wondered if she'd even hit thirty.

I exchanged a nod with the uncle when he didn't offer me his hand.

A painting over the fireplace behind her caught my eye. I recognized it, guessing Renoir from what little I knew from the dozens of times my wife Barbara dragged me out to every museum in the city at one time or another. Funny, I used to complain about having to go with her.

Marilyn walked over to a couch facing the fireplace and the matching chairs on either side of it. "Please, have a seat." She picked up a teacup and saucer on the side table next to the chair where she was seated. She sipped from the cup, pinky extended. "Would you like a cup of tea?" she said. "Or something else?"

The uncle said, "He doesn't look like a tea drinker." But he didn't offer me anything else, or ask me for confirmation.

"Perhaps you'd like a coffee?" Marilyn said, giving her uncle a look like he was a child with poor manners.

"Coffee would be good," I said.

The uncle cleared his throat and left the room.

"Don't mind him," she said, although I wasn't sure what she meant. "He thinks I'm being foolish asking you to come here."

"Foolish for asking me to come here? Or foolish for hiring a private investigator?"

She didn't answer, placing her tea on the table next to her. She sat and crossed one leg over the other, picking something from her wool pants she flicked toward the fire. A large cat—an orange tabby—came out of nowhere and jumped into her lap.

"Is there a Mrs. Howell?" I glanced at the handful of framed photos on the mantel.

She looked toward the doorway where her uncle had disappeared, then looked to be cautious with her answer. "She's in Florida."

"A snowbird?" I said.

"Well, I guess you could say that. She's been there for a while now." Marilyn lowered her gaze, stroking the cat in her lap.

"Oh," I said, getting enough of the picture, which sounded to be one that Mrs. Howell was perhaps no longer a part of.

Nathan Howell came back into the room with a cup and saucer and placed it on the coffee table in front of the couch where I had sat. The coffee was black, and it didn't appear I'd have an option to drink it any other way.

Mr. Howell sat in the matching wingback chair next to his niece, on the opposite side of the fireplace. The cat jumped down and onto Howell's lap.

"I want to apologize again about leaving without telling you," Marilyn said.

"I was concerned," I said.

"You can blame me," Marilyn's uncle said. "I knew the conditions out there weren't good."

Marilyn smiled at her uncle. "He still thinks I'm a child."

The uncle said, "Well?" and left it at that. I guess I could gather what he meant.

"You said you left your car somewhere?" I said, glancing at Marilyn.

She nodded. "I moved it to a parking garage."

"Must've cost an arm and a leg to leave it there overnight," I said, although it didn't matter to me one way or the other. "Well, it's good to know you're safe. Because, I hate to have to bring it up, but a woman's body was found not far from where you were."

"We heard," Nathan Howell said.

"It's scary to think I was right there," Marilyn said, then turned to her uncle, a worried look replacing the smile she'd had when I first walked in.

I looked from Mr. Howell to Marilyn as I sipped my coffee. "Do you live here?"

Marilyn nodded. "It was supposed to be temporary. I'm thinking about leaving the area entirely. Get out of this wintery mess I've had enough of."

"With your aunt in Florida?" I said.

Marilyn swallowed hard, almost as if she was trying not to, then exchanged a glance with her uncle. "I don't think so. I was thinking more of the West Coast. Maybe San Francisco, or—"

"With no money in your pocket?" the uncle said, as if it was the first time he'd heard it.

"Do you have any other family in the area?"

The uncle jumped in before she could answer. "Her mother is my sister. She died when Marilyn was thirteen, and she's lived with me and Carol ever since."

"Carol? She's your wife?"

Howell gave a nod but didn't appear to want to get into it. His gaze went to the fireplace.

I hoped Marilyn could answer for herself. "And your father?"

"He was killed in the Korean War. I was six, so..."

"I'm sorry," I said, and understood without having to ask more. Clearly, Marilyn's uncle was her caretaker, and the man—along with his wife—who had raised her. At least through her teenage years.

The three of us sat silent for a moment, the only sound coming from the crackling flames in the fireplace.

"Where shall we begin?" I said. "Why don't you tell me about your husband, and what leads you to believe his death wasn't simply an accident?"

"If I may speak my mind," the uncle said. "I am not of the belief his death was anything more than what the police up there had determined. If it were up to me, you wouldn't be here right now, Mr. Horn."

I understood.

"He thinks I'm crazy," Marilyn said. "Paranoid."

Howell rolled his eyes, and the cat jumped down, coming over to the couch and onto my lap.

I didn't dislike cats at all, but they made me nervous. I remember an aunt of mine had one when I was little, and the cat would bite me for no reason at all. Not all cats were like that, but I had a good understanding they did as they pleased with little concern for humans getting in their way.

"I just don't feel there's any reason to take this any further than we already have." He looked at me and said, "I have friends in law enforcement. I spoke to most of them, looking for answers. All indications point to the job they did up there in New Hampshire being the correct call. That's all." He shifted his gaze to Marilyn. "The sooner you can let it go, the happier you'll be."

I petted the cat, since he or she—I had no idea which it was—wasn't going to leave me alone. Luckily, it didn't bite. "So, how long were you married to your husband?"

"Six years," she said.

"She worked for him at his dealership," the uncle said.

Marilyn had a slight smile on her face, as if she were reminiscing. "My aunt got me the job there. She was a good friend of Larry's at—"

"I wouldn't say they were good friends. We both knew Larry, before Marilyn started working there."

I was a bit thrown off by what appeared to be some kind of defensiveness coming from Mr. Howell. "Well, I did make some calls before I came over. It sounds like Green Chrysler was having some problems?"

The uncle said. "The place was barely on life support."

Marilyn said, "After the energy crisis, it was a challenge for the entire automobile industry. Especially for smaller dealerships, like Larry's. He was afraid he was going to lose his dealership. But he was able to keep it afloat. The last few years haven't been easy."

Her uncle said, "Who even wants a Chrysler these days? Certainly not with the price of gas, and the way inflation's going. Imports. That's where it's at. Problem is, Larry never listened to anybody."

There was clearly hostility coming from the uncle. I assumed, which I understood, it had something to do with the fact the niece he raised somehow ended up with a man at least twice her age.

I said to Marilyn. "What did you do for Larry? Your job, I mean?"

"I was his secretary."

"Was he married at the time? When you were working there?"

"What does that have to do with anything?" the uncle said.

"A jealous ex-wife?" I said, as much a question as a statement.

Marilyn looked at her uncle, but his gaze seemed to be back on the fire. His disinterest was becoming apparent.

"I just need to be clear," I said. "I know you've asked me here to potentially have me investigate Larry's death, but—"

"Let's not get ahead of ourselves," Nathan Howell said. "I think the best thing you could do is tell Marilyn there's no real reason to continue with these shenanigans. It's time to face the fact Larry's death was a tragic accident. It's time to move forward."

"I'm not sure I can say that without having my questions answered," I said.

"Well, then I'm saying it. This is a waste of time. I'm sorry..." He stood from the chair.

"If I can just give it to you straight, part of the reason for me being here is the fact she was in the area when the young woman was killed. If, by chance, there might be some sort of connection..."

"You say that as if she was the only person in Boston that evening," the uncle said. "I saw plenty of people out on the streets when I was there."

"All I'm saying is I think..." I paused. "If you'd allow me to, I'd like to mention it to the detective on the case."

"A detective? In Boston?"

I nodded.

The uncle shook his head. "I don't want Marilyn involved in something like that. And we don't need anyone knowing our business."

Marilyn sat in silence, looking from me to her uncle as he walked toward the doorway.

Howell said, "Thank you for coming out, Mr. Horn."

I looked at Marilyn, and she almost looked like she was about to cry. Maybe she *was* crying.

I got up and followed the man walking from the room.

But Marilyn rose to her feet. "Wait. What is your fee?"

I looked from her to the uncle and back to Marilyn again. "Two hundred dollars a day, with a two week minimum."

"Please, Uncle Nathan. I know you don't think this is a good idea. But I need to know the truth."

The uncle walked over to the window and took his time before turning to me. "Can we do this without the police being involved?"

I thought about it. "That's not a problem."

He said, "And I'm not going to pay you an endless amount of money, dragging this thing on and on. I'm not made of money, you know."

From the looks of the house, and the way he acted, I wasn't sure that was true.

"I'll give you a thousand dollars," Howell said. "And that's it."

"That's only going to cover five days of work," I said. "I don't know if—"

"I'm an accountant," the uncle said. "I can do math." He went over to a tall-standing secretary's desk and pulled out a checkbook, leaning over as he wrote it out. "Who do I make it out to?"

I had to make sure I was ready to agree to it. I couldn't see five days being enough time. But a thousand dollar check was hard to pass up. "Make it out to Horn Investigations." I glanced at Marilyn, who had what appeared to be a look of relief on her face.

I had a pretty good feeling the uncle wasn't interested in having me involved, but he had enough in his heart he wanted to do as his niece had wished.

Marilyn went over to the same desk and wrote on a piece of paper, then handed it to me. "I'm going up to New Hampshire tonight. You can call me there if you need to reach me."

"New Hampshire?" I said. "Isn't that where your husband's balloon—"

"We have relatives up there. I have my own space. I like to go up and do some writing."

"You write?"

"Not professionally or anything." She blushed. "Besides, my uncle could use some space."

But he stepped over and put his arm around her. "You know how much I like having you around."

Marilyn reached out and shook my hand. "Thank you, Mr. Horn. Like I said, call that number if you need to reach me."

"And, please, call me Jake," I said.

Nathan Howell opened the closet door and reached in for my coat, handing it to me along with a business card with Howell & Associates Accounting Services on it. "That's my work number," he said. "I wrote my home number on the back."

I felt as if I was being rushed out the door. "I still have questions I'll need to ask," I said, pulling on my coat.

Howell had his hand on the doorknob, as if ready to shove me out. He looked at his watch. "I have an appointment I'm already late for."

I glanced at Marilyn. "I'm just wondering... Did Larry and his son have a good relationship?" I pointed at a glass dish filled with wrapped hard candy on a console table by the door. "Do you mind?"

"Help yourself," the uncle said, holding the dish out toward me.

I took a red piece of candy, unwrapped it and stuck the plastic wrapper in my coat pocket. I stuck the candy in my mouth.

Marilyn said, "Larry and Jason got along just fine."

"*Fine?*"

"Are you asking me if there's a chance Jason had something to do with what happened to Larry?" she said.

"I'm just asking if they had a good relationship. *Fine* doesn't sound like—"

"Other than your typical family arguments here and there, I guess... Sure, got along well enough. I don't know if any of the family was very happy about me and Larry being together."

It sounded to me like the family dynamics were far from perfect once Marilyn entered the picture. "What about the ex-wife?"

She shrugged. "I don't know. She treated me okay. At least in the beginning."

"Were they still married when you started working there?"

"Not happily," Marilyn said. "He was going to leave her, long before I came along."

"He told you that?" I said.

Marilyn looked like she wasn't sure how to answer, but nodded anyway. "I never got the feeling she was too broken up about the whole thing."

The uncle opened the door, and the cold air blasted inside. "I know you have a lot of questions, Mr. Horn, but if we had any answers she wouldn't have called you." He gave me a nod and guided me toward the open door. "Good day, Mr. Horn."

I stepped outside and turned, about to ask for the ex-wife's name, but Mr. Howell had already closed the door behind me.

CHAPTER 7

The First Street Diner was full and loud, with just about every table and booth taken, including the stools at the counter. My cousin Raymond was in the last booth to the left, picking at a plate of french fries, sticking one in his mouth as I sat down across from him.

"Sorry, I couldn't wait," he said. He pushed the plate toward me. "You want some?"

I shook my head. "Got stuck in traffic on the Pike. Should've gone the other way."

"What were you doing up in Newton?"

I had called Raymond before I left the office to meet for lunch, but didn't tell him anything about what I was up to.

"You know the woman I was supposed to meet, the evening of the storm?"

Raymond stopped chewing, nodding. "The dead one?"

I grabbed a fry and stuck it in my mouth. "Yeah, well, turns out she's not dead. It wasn't her."

The waitress, Gloria, stopped over and put a glass of water down in front of me. "Hi Jake. You want a coffee?"

I picked up the glass and took a sip. "No, water's good for now."

"Okay, hon. Let me know when you're ready to order." She hurried away, with almost all the other booths and stools at the counter full.

I went ahead, keeping my voice low, and told Raymond what I knew. Or at least what I knew up until then. "I haven't told Maggie, or anyone else. Not yet."

"I hope you're not going to keep this to yourself," Raymond said. "If there's some connection between this woman you met with, and her being in the same location as the dead girl..."

"I have no idea if what happened to that young woman has anything to do with this case. And I promised her I wouldn't go to the cops. But, don't worry. If I come up with something more, and can make some kind of direct connection, then I'll share whatever I have with them. But, for the moment, I just need to play my hand right."

"Play your hand right?" Raymond rolled his eyes and let out a sigh. "This ain't poker, Jake. You can't just... You gotta at least tell Maggie or let Detective Carter know what you know so far."

"Can you please just keep it to yourself?" I said. "I know how you—"

"You know how I *what*? How I don't distrust the department I served for twenty-five years? I can't look at it the way you and my father did."

"Your father had good reason," I said. "And the road goes both ways. You think the cops would ever share anything with me, that has to do with one of my clients?"

Raymond laughed. "That's not how it works," he said. "There's a reason they wear the uniform, and you wear combat boots and jeans."

"What's that supposed to mean?" I said.

"I don't mean it in a bad way," Raymond said. "I'm just saying, the law's the law. You're a private investigator. Just because you like to freewheel doesn't mean you can ignore the rules that've been put in place."

"Okay," I said. "I don't need the lecture. You're not a cop anymore either."

"But I still abide by the law." Raymond grabbed a fry and took a bite, but dropped the remaining piece on his plate. "They're cold." He looked down at his menu. "Let's just order something to eat. You know how I get when I haven't eaten." He raised his gaze and grinned.

I looked at the plate of fries, or what was left of it. At six-four and well over two-hundred-fifty pounds, Raymond needed a lot of food in his body to fuel his brain. Or it wouldn't work.

I opened the menu and looked it over, although I already knew what I wanted. "There's a retired detective with the New Hampshire State Police who was involved in the Larry Green case. He's a former Boston cop—closed the case in twenty-four hours."

Raymond nodded. "I know all about it. You're talking about Sean McCaffrey."

"You know him?"

"We worked together way back. He retired early. Grabbed the pension from Boston as soon as he could, hooked on with New Hampshire State Police while he was still young enough. He was a detective up there."

"He's retired now," I said.

"Yeah?"

"I guess you don't keep in touch with him?"

"Can't tell you the last time I saw him," Raymond said. "But I was surprised he'd already retired. I don't think he'd been there long enough."

"Maybe I'm wrong," I said. "But is it all right if I ask if he was a straight cop?"

"Not every cop's crooked just because you don't agree with the outcome of an investigation."

I glanced over at the counter, but didn't recognize any of the customers. "I didn't say every cop was crooked. I was just asking about McCaffrey."

Raymond picked up one of the remaining fries on the plate, looked it over and stuck it in his mouth. "You know, it's not that uncommon, a spouse wants to believe there's more to the death of a loved one. It's normal. They can't help but second guess the truth, no matter how obvious it may be."

I said, "So you're already saying she's got it wrong, even though you know nothing about her or the case?"

Raymond grinned. "You're asking it like you've already made up your mind McCaffrey got it wrong. It sounds to me these people you're working for don't have much of a clue to begin with."

"I don't judge," I said. "But it sounds like the cops up there won't even talk to her about it."

"Well, sometimes, in law enforcement, you gotta draw the line."

I laughed. "You ever think about getting involved in PR for some police department around here? You're good at deflecting blame, cover up for all those dirty cops you used to work with."

Raymond growled, "Knock it off, Jake."

"All I'm saying, if you'd let me get back to my point, is I'm not convinced your old buddy McCaffrey did his due diligence. It doesn't mean he's a crooked cop. But he's human, right? People make mistakes. I mean, she claims they wouldn't even take her calls after they'd closed the case. So, can you blame her for not trusting the outcome?"

Raymond looked at the menu, as if he was done with the discussion. "Come on, let's order. You know what you're getting?"

"Turkey club," I said, pushing the menu aside without even look-ing.

Gloria walked over to our table when she saw we were ready and stood with a pad in her hand, a crooked stance, chewing the inside of her cheek with her eyes on Raymond still reading the menu. She said, "Raymond, hon. You need me to order for you?"

He looked up and closed the menu, handing it to her. "Cheese-burger. And another side of fries."

She turned to me. "How about you?"

"The usual. Turkey club. Fries, well done."

Gloria walked away and hung the order slip from her pad on the rack in the pass-through behind the counter.

Raymond had his hands folded on the table. "Did this woman give you any real information?"

I looked around, as if I was afraid somebody would be listening, but the place was loud enough I was sure I didn't have anything to worry about. We still kept our voices low. "Well, I don't know how much you know about Larry Green, but—"

"I remember him from the commercials for his dealership, over there in Norwood, riding in his hot air balloon."

I sipped my water. "I don't have many details yet. And don't know how much the son is going to share with me, but I'm going to talk to him, see what he knows."

The problem with working alone was you have to depend on friends or family to help get your thoughts together. I had Ray-mond. And Maggie was always there to help. My daughter Nancy was starting to be that person too. My fear, if I can call it that, was that she was a lot smarter than me, although still too young to see her own faults.

I said, "So, from what it looks like, the son took over the dealer-ship."

"Does she get along with him? The son?"

"It's hard to say," I said. "I only asked about the relationship with the father. I still don't know if they got along. It wasn't clear. There's also a daughter. She lives in Plymouth with her husband and son. Apparently the mother lives there too."

"The mother? She's Green's first wife?"

I nodded. "I stopped at the library and did some digging through the papers. Came up with this guy, name's Richard Reagan. I found this article by Mike Gorman, with the Globe. He was doing an investigation into dog racing over in Raynham, and Reagan was with Larry Green. They were both interviewed."

"What kind of investigation?"

"For his article, I guess. Had something to do with gambling and organized crime."

"The Mob loves dog racing," Raymond said, pausing for a moment. "You track him down?"

"I haven't had much luck. Found a phone number for him, but the line had been disconnected."

Raymond had a curious look on his face. "And what's the story with your client? She lives with the uncle?"

I nodded. "It sounds to me like she doesn't have the money to be out on her own."

"No life insurance money?" Raymond said.

I shook my head. "I called some contacts. It apparently hadn't been renewed prior to Larry Green's death."

CHAPTER 8

Nick Carter walked me back to a small private office on the third floor at 154 Berkeley, Boston Police headquarters. It had been a while since I last saw the detective, maybe a couple of years, but he seemed more grizzled and gray than I remembered. He had the same disheveled look you'd expect from any good detective, the way his tie was loose and crooked and only part of his shirt tucked in his pants.

"You want a coffee?" he said, closing the door as if he was hoping I'd say no.

I obliged. "I'm all right."

There were two empty desks in the space, each pushed against the brown paneled walls on opposite sides of the room. The floor was carpeted and clean, like the office had hardly been used. In fact, it had an odor as if either the carpet had just been installed, or the gray walls had been recently painted. There were no photos or anything else on the bare walls.

"This your office?" I said.

"Nah, it's a spare. We use it when we either gotta knock someone around, or need to have a private conversation." He grinned.

"Can I assume we're here for the conversation?"

Carter didn't respond, rolling one of the two desk chairs toward me. "Have a seat." I sat in the chair as he grabbed another—a gray metal folding chair without wheels—and turned it around. He sat on it backward. "I appreciate you coming by. Glad you changed your mind."

"Well," I said. "I wouldn't say I changed my mind. But I don't have much to share, but I thought I should at least tell you what I can. I don't want you to think I'm hiding anything."

Of course, hiding something was exactly what I was going to do, at least for the time being. But I didn't want to be accused of ignoring the detective's request to answer his questions, even if I had to hold back most of what I knew.

Carter said, "The latest news I'll share with you is we have a positive ID on the victim found a couple of blocks from your office. Maggie said the woman you were supposed to meet..." He pulled a piece of paper from his shirt pocket and slipped a pair of reading glasses on. "Heather Connelly?"

I nodded, but didn't tell him that wasn't her real name.

He continued, "Well, it wasn't her."

I sat, stone faced, watching him.

"I thought you'd be happy to hear the news?"

I nodded. "Yeah sure. But it's not like there wasn't a victim." I cleared my throat. "What's her name?"

"Gertrude Bailey. Friends called her Trudy. Had enough cocaine in her blood to—"

"An overdose?"

"Strangulation. Maybe a trick gone bad."

I said, "So there's no doubt it's a homicide?"

He looked at me like I had two heads. "I just said she was strangled, didn't I?"

"Yeah, I mean—"

"Officer Donavan tells me you were in the area? Around four or five that afternoon?"

"It's not far from my office." I hesitated, wanting to be sure I understood why he was asking. "I didn't see anything," I said. "There was hardly anyone around."

"But you were out there. Donovan also tells me you went back later that evening?"

I paused, wondering why Maggie had said much of anything to the detective, although I would never ask her to keep quiet when there was an investigation. The last thing I'd do is put her in a position to jeopardize her career, especially as one of only a handful of female officers in Boston.

"I went out looking for the woman, Ms. Connelly, who had called my office. I walked through the snow down K Street, but not as far as 8th or anywhere near O'Hara's, which is where I believed the body was found?"

Carter nodded. "That's right."

"Everything was pretty much closed down by then," I said. "There wasn't anybody around other than the guys running plows."

He nodded, as if already thinking through his next question. "You recognize the name?"

"Of the victim?" I'd started to feel a bit uneasy about where things might've been heading with Carter. "Are you asking me if I hired a hooker?"

"I'm simply asking if you know the name."

"Not at all."

"Well, apparently she was staying at a place in Southie, on a friend's couch."

"I'm sorry," I said. "I guess I'm not following your line of questioning here. What would make you think I knew the victim?"

He didn't answer. "This friend, the one she was staying with, she showed up a couple of hours ago, had heard about what happened, said her friend had been missing. So we took her for a ride, showed her the girl's body. Got a positive ID."

"How old was she?" I said. "The victim?"

"Twenty-six. Up here from New York. No family in the area."

I still wasn't clear why he'd asked me if I knew the name, especially since she wasn't even from Boston. I thought about the photos Maggie showed me, and felt bad about what had happened, considering it seemed I was in the vicinity of the crime. But likely not close enough to do anything about it.

I said to Carter, "Like I told you on the phone, I don't have any real information to help you."

He paused, taking a couple of moments to respond. "I've been at this a long time," he said. "So, don't take this personally. But something's got me thinking there's something you're holding back."

I shifted in the chair. "You think I know who killed her?"

Carter fixed his tie, as if it made a difference. "I know some things about you, Jake. I know you're good at what you do. But I've also heard you're not keen on helping out the men in blue. Not unless there's something in it for you."

"Keen?" I laughed. "I don't know who told you that, but it couldn't be any further from the truth. And, in case you haven't noticed, it's no longer just 'men' in blue."

Carter rolled his eyes. "You know what I'm saying. Don't try to turn things around here. It's not the point. What I'm saying is, if you have knowledge of anything pertaining to this Miss Bailey's homicide, I just hope you're smart enough to—"

"Like I just told you," I said. "I don't know her. And I certainly don't have any idea who killed her, if that's what you're asking."

"I'm asking you to do me a favor and try to be straight with me. If you hear of anything, or if it turns out that call you received has even some minor significance to this case..."

I nodded, but wondered in my mind if I was doing the right thing, keeping Carter in the dark about Marilyn. But the fact was, I couldn't stop myself from thinking there could've been some kind of connection between what happened that night and the fact Marilyn was down there at the same time. It was just a hunch. But it bothered me. Either way, I wasn't in a position to share any of my thoughts with Carter, or anyone else. Not until I did a little more digging myself.

But while I was there, I figured I'd have an opportunity to see if he'd be willing to help me. Even if I wasn't quite ready to share the favor. "Do you mind if I ask you a question about a fairly recent case?"

"What case?"

I said, "Well, it's not even one the Boston Police had anything to do with. At least I don't think you did."

He seemed to hesitate, then shrugged and nodded, leaning back in his chair with his arms folded. "Go ahead."

"The name Larry Green ring a bell?" I said.

"Larry Green? The car guy?" Carter nodded. "He's dead."

"Yeah, I know."

Carter stood from the chair. "What about him?"

"Any chance you know anything about the case?"

He shook his head. "Not really. A former associate of mine here worked on it. But other than what I heard here and there... It was on the news when it happened, but..." Carter's eyes narrowed. "This have something to do with what we were just talking about?"

"No. I was just—"

"Don't lie to me, Horn. Two minutes ago you told me you knew nothing about anything."

"I'm asking. That's all. I understand Larry Green's death was ruled accidental, but—"

"His balloon caught fire. It's not unheard of, the way those things'll go up in flames like that." He shook his head. "You sure as hell won't catch me up in one of those things. I know it was his gimmick. Used to see him in those ads for his dealership."

Part of me wished I hadn't brought it up with him. But the cat was out of the bag.

"I told you, we had an associate... man who ended up doing detective work up there in New Hampshire. State Police. As far as I know, he's retired already. I'm not sure he stuck with it for very long."

"I know who he is," I said. "And from what I've heard, the whole investigation was wrapped up in under a day. Bow on top."

Carter said, "Man burns up in his hot air balloon, I'm not sure how much more time any half-decent detective would need." He sat back down in the chair, eyes squinted with his gaze fixed right on me. "I told you already, I know when someone's not being straight with me, Horn. Whatever you're up to, I don't like how you think you can come in here, look me in the eye and tell me you can't help. Then turn around asking me questions about a case you know has nothing to do with me? How about you stop the bullshit and tell me what this is about."

I looked toward the door and thought maybe it was time to go. I hated withholding information from the detective, but on the other hand, the more I thought about it, the more I felt the chance was just as good there was no connection at all. And the more I thought it through, the more I could see it from both sides.

But I also had in mind I'd promised to keep the cops out of it. And until I had good reason to do otherwise, that's what I was going to do.

CHAPTER 9

THE LAST TIME I'D gone into a car dealership was six years earlier, when it was time for my grandmother to replace her 1961 Plymouth Valiant. She ended up buying a brand new Nova from a local dealer, but when she died three years later, she left me her '74 Nova with just under ten thousand miles on it.

I stepped through the entrance of Green Chrysler and immediately smelled an almost bleach-like odor, but one mixed with a pine-scented air freshener, like the tree-shaped kind hung from a car's rearview mirror. But it was much more potent.

There were a dozen cars parked on the showroom's shiny vinyl floor. But no customers inside, from what I could see. I recognized the Chrysler Cordoba right away, but only because of the recent TV commercials with Ricardo Montalban.

A man with gray slicked-back hair walked over to me almost immediately. He wore a light blue corduroy three-piece suit with a shirt collar opened a few too many buttons, exposing a gold chain tangled up in the curly gray hair on his chest. He nodded at me with his chin and ran his hand over the Cordoba's glossy hood. "She's a beauty, isn't she?"

"Sure," I said, looking around the showroom, hoping I could avoid the sales pitch he was clearly gearing up for.

"You know, the engineers went back to the drawing board on this one," the man said. "They wanted to get the gas mileage up, but not at the expense of the styling." He walked to the driver-side door and opened it. "Elegantly designed. Luxuriously appointed." He slid into the driver's seat and gripped the wheel, taking a quick look at himself in the rearview mirror. "It's an unbelievable value."

"Is it?" I almost laughed at the fact I'd seen the commercial enough times to know the pitch the guy was spewing was almost word-for-word from Ricardo Montalban's script.

The man stepped out and gestured for me to sit inside. "See for yourself how comfortable she is. Rich Corinthian leather."

I pushed the door closed. "Is Jason Green here, by any chance?"

The man paused before he answered, eyebrows raised. "Jason? Uh, well, I'd be happy to assist you, sir, if..."

"I appreciate that. But I'm not here to buy a car," I said.

The man laughed. "Oh, I've heard *that* line before. But I can assure you, if you're looking for a deal—"

"I'm really not," I said. "I'm here for Jason."

He looked past the other cars toward the back of the showroom, where a young woman with a powder-blue bow in her hair sat behind a metal desk. She focused on the typewriter in front of her, tapping the keys and sliding the carriage over each time the type-writer's bell rang.

The salesman's smile disappeared once he realized I wasn't going to be the one to pad his commission check. "I'm not sure he's available right now." He pulled a handkerchief from his pocket and wiped a small area on the hood in a circular motion.

"Can you find out?" I said. "If he's available?"

The man cleared his throat and nodded. "Wait right here." He went over to the woman and leaned with his hands on the desk, glancing my way as he spoke to her, his voice low enough I couldn't make out what he'd said.

She had looked up at him from her typewriter, then shifted her gaze my way.

The salesman came back over to where I was waiting. "As I'd said, he's not available right now. But if you want to talk to Kathy over there, she can set you up with an appointment."

I started toward her, but first stopped and turned to the salesman. "What's your name?"

He reached inside his suit-jacket's pocket and pulled out a business card, handing it to me. "Gary Holden. I'm sure Jason will take care of you, but if you decide you want to take her for a spin, or you know someone in the market for a Chrysler, give me a call."

I looked over the card and then slipped it into my pocket. "Thanks Gary. I will."

The woman behind the desk watched as I approached her, the sound of my boots echoing off the vinyl floor with each step. I stopped in front of her. "Hello."

She gave me a nice smile. "I understand you'd like to make an appointment to see Mr. Green?"

"Unless he's available now?" I said.

She looked over her shoulder toward the closed door, then shook her head. "Not right now."

"I can wait," I said. I checked my watch. It was almost two o'clock.

"Well, it's better if you made an appointment. I'm not sure he's—"

The door with the PRIVATE sign on it opened. Two men stepped out, both younger, with one in a suit and tie, the other wearing a blue and red ski jacket with jeans and snow boots, like he was heading for the slopes.

The woman behind the desk looked at me, then shifted her gaze to the man in the suit. "Jason? This gentleman is here to see you?"

Jason came around to where I stood and looked me over. He was about my height, maybe an inch or two shorter, but certainly younger with dark hair fixed neatly on his head. He adjusted his tie. "How can I help you?"

"My name's Jake Horn," I said, handing him my business card.

He took it and looked it over. "What's this about?" Before I answered, he turned to the other man and shook his hand, but in a friendly way, like they were buddies. "I'll see you there as soon as I'm done here."

The woman, Kathy, watched the young man in the ski jacket leaving, a sense of admiration in her eyes. She smiled when he looked back at her. "Bye, Sean."

The man continued across the showroom, giving a thumbs-up to the salesman holding the door for him. "Later, Gary." I watched him until he walked out of sight.

Jason said, "Mr, uh..." He grabbed the card he'd put on the desk and gave it a quick look. "Mr. Horn? Are you going to answer my question?"

I nodded, turning to him. "Do you mind if we speak somewhere in private?"

He hesitated, then looked toward the open door he'd just come out of and nodded. "Right this way." He stepped around the desk, and I followed him through the door. He closed it behind me, then continued down a hallway with six small, empty offices on either side with the lights turned off on all but one.

At the end of the short hall, he walked into a much larger office, with *Jason Green, President,* etched in a gold placard on the door.

There was a black leather couch on one side of the room, a huge cherry-wood desk with two chairs in front of it and an over-sized black leather chair behind it. He sat in the leather one. "Have a seat," he said, closing an open folder on his desk. "So, are you going to keep me in the dark here, or—"

"I'm here about your father," I said, taking a seat in one of the two wooden chairs across from him.

"My father?" He sighed. "Please don't tell me... Did Marilyn send you here?"

I wasn't sure I should answer, but it clearly wasn't a secret what she was up to.

"Listen, some of us have accepted, well..." He paused, a look on his face like he had to think hard about what he wanted to say. "Accidents happen. Marilyn just can't seem to accept that fact."

I waited, wondering if there'd be more.

There wasn't.

"How's business going?" I said, looking at all the wood and gold plaques on the wall of his office. I couldn't exactly read what they were from where I was sitting, but there were plenty of them. Awards of some sort.

"It's hard to compete with the big boys around here," Jason said. "Especially guys like Johnny Bachman, who saw the opportunity with foreign cars before anyone else did. I told my dad that's where we needed to go, but he wouldn't listen to me."

"Where you needed to go?"

"I just mean, where he should've made changes a long time ago. People don't want these big cars anymore. And now Chrysler's looking for the government to bail them out." He reached for the magazine he had on his desk and opened it to a page he had book-marked with a blank piece of paper. He turned the magazine so I could see. "See this? Dad *hated* these Datsuns. But that's where the market is now. We're hoping, in six more months, to be selling these exact cars right here."

The picture on the page he showed me had an ad for a green Datsun hatchback, with a family of four somehow squeezed into the vehicle. I understood the future of automobiles was in smaller cars, with trouble ahead, the way we were all sucking up oil from the earth, like it would always be there.

But I also couldn't see myself driving a tiny car I could barely squeeze into.

"Why didn't your father want to sell them?" I said.

"He was stubborn. Swore he'd only ever sell American cars. It really upset the people who helped him get this place off the ground. The investors didn't like that he refused to change."

"Investors?" I said.

"Well, I call them investors. But really, they're mostly friends of his. Or in some cases former friends. These are people who expected this place to give them a solid return, and it never happened. Back ten years ago, you could open a car dealership and make money hand over fist without even trying. Everything changed after the energy crisis. Especially for smaller dealers like us."

I wondered if I was about to get somewhere. "So, these so-called investors were upset that your father wouldn't sell Datsuns?"

"Who wants to lose money? Or course they weren't happy. The truth is, they didn't care whether it was Datsun or Toyota, or... Something needed to change. And anyone with half a brain knows the Japanese make a better car."

"Was Richard Reagan an investor who might've been upset?" I said.

Jason looked surprised I threw out Reagan's name. "How do you know Richard?"

"I don't," I said. "But I know he had something to do with this place?"

Jason waited, then nodded. "Mr. Reagan was one of the original investors. He was a friend of my dad's. Made a lot of money in the sixties and like a lot of people thought the automobile business was the place to invest. But once the oil crisis hit..."

"Was he involved here? Or—"

"Just the guy with the money. From what I know he was involved in a lot of different businesses. I know he did well enough whenever my dad needed money he'd call Mr. Reagan. He helped get this place off the ground. And if it wasn't his own money, he'd get it from someone else."

I had to think about what he'd said. "So, he acted like some kind of banker?"

"You could say that."

"And what about now?"

Jason Green stared back at me, shaking his head. "He's flat broke. Lives in some crummy triple decker in Taunton. Whatever he had left he blew at the dog track."

"Were they friends? Your dad and Reagan? I mean, toward the end?"

Jason paused before he answered. "They had a falling out."

"Over money?"

Jason Green nodded. "Isn't that what it's always about?"

I shifted in my seat. I never understood how people let money rule their lives, but that's just how it was. The American dream. I said, "What about the other investors? You made it sound like there were others who may've lost money?"

"Everyone did. But it wasn't like there were a lot of them. Really, just four. All friends."

"Of your father's?"

"Yes. He'd convinced them all to invest to get the business off the ground. Things were looking good, although not exactly profitable. But then four years ago, late '75, my dad needed more money or he was going to have to close down. They were all reluctant, but gave him what he needed. My dad was a good salesman. He could convince anyone to do just about anything."

"So, what happened?"

"It didn't work out. That's when everyone told him to shift gears. Go with a different manufacturer and move away from Chrysler. But he gambled. He was convinced these big boats nobody could afford to drive would make a come back." Jason shook his head. "Never did. And now I'm dealing with how to clear out this showroom, try to break even by getting rid of inventory. In fact, I'm hearing there's a good chance we'll have another crisis—an energy shortage—this year. This place will be dead in the water." He pointed at the picture of the Datsun in the magazine. "This is the only thing that'll save this dealership. If my father had only made the move six months ago, we'd be back on track."

"So, the investors lost out again?" I said.

"They lost their shirts." He opened a drawer on his desk and pulled out a hard-pack of Merit cigarettes, reaching toward me with the top flipped open. "Cigarette?"

I waved my hand, shaking him off.

He pulled a smoke from the box and stuck it in his mouth, lighting it as he spoke through his teeth. "All four investors all wanted out. They each demanded their money back if he wasn't going to change. But there was nothing to give back." He drew from his cigarette and blew a stream of smoke in my direction.

I turned my head to avoid breathing it in. "So, now what?"

"Well, they know the only way to recoup what they lost was to help us do what we need to do going forward. Two of 'em are on board." He cleared his throat. "I hate to say it, but with my father gone, as much as I miss him. Hopefully— maybe by the summer—we'll be changing the sign out there to read *Green Datsun*."

"What about the others?"

"The investors?" He nodded, taking a drag from his cigarette. "Well, I said they were all friends. But my grandfather gave up what I hear was his life savings as an investor. He had a stroke, and was dead a year later."

I wasn't sure what to say. Clearly these investments that were made hadn't paid off for anyone. "Who else was involved?"

"As investors?" Jason shrugged. "He had smaller investors who put up cash." He studied the burning tip of his cigarette. "Under the table."

"Under the table?" I said. "What does that mean?"

Jason exhaled. "Off the books."

"I see." I watched him, expecting more. "And what about Reagan? Isn't he looking for payback?"

"Yeah, of course. He calls me every once in a while looking for some cash, but I'm not doing much better myself. I mean, I can put food on the table, but we're not exactly rolling in dough here. And we're running out of time." He drew from his cigarette, then with his index finger flicked the top of it over the glass ashtray on his desk, knocking a long gray ash into it.

Jason appeared smart enough when it came to the situation he was in. But it seemed to me he wasn't exactly broken up about his father's death.

I said, "Did you go to college?"

He gave a proud nod. "BC."

"And you came here to work, after you graduated?"

"I didn't graduate. Couldn't pay the tuition."

"So you came to work here?" I said.

"I'd work here weekends, doing sales. But it was tough. By the time I got here nobody wanted these boats."

I glanced at the magazine and the picture in the Datsun ad on Jason's desk. "Were you working here when Marilyn first started?"

He let out a quick snort. "Yeah, I guess I've known the gold digger a long time."

"Gold digger?" I guess I understood where he was coming from, the son of a man who married a woman half his age. But the pot at the end of the rainbow was clearly empty by the time she got to it. "Do you two get along?"

Jason leaned back in his chair, put his feet up on his desk and looked up, blowing a long stream of smoke toward the ceiling. "No comment."

"I'll take that as a no."

"I wouldn't say we don't get along. There's just nothing there. We have no relationship. Never did."

"Even when she was working here? You must've had to interact at some point?"

He said, "I'm always cordial."

"And what about after they were married. Did she keep working?"

"Here? Not as the receptionist. I don't know what she did, to be honest. She was on the payroll, but after my father was gone, I cut her off. There was no money to pay her to begin with, never mind by that point."

"So, you fired your father's widow?" I said.

He crushed out his cigarette, and wouldn't look me in the eye. "It was a business decision."

I nodded as if I understood. Even if I didn't. "She doesn't have any piece of ownership?"

He'd already pulled out another cigarette. I started to wonder if the guy's nerves were getting the best of him.

"Luckily, no. She did not," he said, dropping his feet from the desk. He straightened up in his chair. "Her uncle will take care of her, like he always has."

Even if he denied it, there was no hiding the fact that Jason Green held some kind of resentment toward Marilyn. And perhaps toward her uncle.

I looked at the framed photos on his desk but couldn't make them out, the way they were turned and facing Jason. "Are you married?"

"Why?" He seemed to be somewhat offended by the question.

I raised my hands, palms toward him. "I'm just asking."

I actually already knew he was.

"Is your wife part of the business?"

He seemed hesitant to answer, taking his time before he finally nodded. "She's legally an owner now, yes," he said. "Minority owner."

"So your wife owns a piece, but your own father's widow—"

"Hey, I had to make some changes to the business, or we wouldn't have survived another day. We still might not, if things don't fall into place the way I hope it will." Jason put the unlit cigarette on the desk. "It's not my fault my father wasn't much of a planner."

"Do you mean—"

"You ask me, Marilyn's doing all because she's upset he left her with nothing." He cracked a sly smile. "If you're trying to figure out if someone killed him, maybe you should talk to her."

The phone on his desk rang, and he picked it up on the first ring. "Hello?" He listened, nodding, then looked at his watch. "Yeah. I said I'd be there. I got held up. Give me fifteen minutes." He placed the handset down and stood up from the chair. "Sorry, Mr. Horn, but I gotta head out." He nodded once toward the phone. "Hoping to go get some good news about getting some Datsuns in here."

"Who's Sean?" I said. "The guy who was here earlier? The skier?"

Jason didn't respond right away, grabbing his long camel coat from a rack by the door. "You'd never know it looking at him, but he's got money. And a lot of connections." He opened the door and held it for me.

I followed him out and stepped into the showroom. The receptionist turned and looked at us over her shoulder. Gary, the salesman, was leaning on the desk. The two had been laughing, but Gary straightened up and his expression turned, like some kind of slacker caught doing nothing.

Jason said, "Kathy, I'll be back later. You can reach me at Marcello's in Foxboro if you need me." He turned to Gary. "Why don't you go outside and put some salt down on the ice. The last thing we need is another slip and fall injury to deal with."

Gary nodded and walked over to a coat rack by the door, taking down a dark leather jacket.

I followed Jason outside into the cold. I said to him, "Did you say something about a slip and fall?"

Jason nodded. "People try to take advantage of businesses when they're desperate, as if we have all this money to hand out."

"Have you been sued?" I said.

"More than once. But one thing Dad always had was a decent lawyer to squash frivolous lawsuits."

CHAPTER 10

MAGGIE WAS BEHIND THE wheel of the Boston Police cruiser parked on the street when I pulled into the driveway in Milton. She drove in behind me and got out as soon as I did, still in uniform.

"You get off early?" I said, pulling one leather glove off of my hand with my teeth.

"I'm not off for another hour," she said, following me to the front door. "Detective Carter asked me to come talk to you."

I gave her a quick look over my shoulder and slid my key into the door lock, pushing it open. I waited for her to walk in ahead of me, then stepped in after her.

I flicked on the light, and right away checked the thermostat. As cold as it was outside, walking into the house wasn't much warmer.

"Do you have the heat turned off?" Maggie said.

I didn't answer, but turned up the heat a couple of degrees and the furnace kicked on right away, with a quiet boom coming from the basement.

"Carter's concerned you're withholding information about the Trudy Bailey murder."

"Concerned?" I said, hanging my pea coat on the rack. "Tell him I said thanks for his concern."

Maggie unzipped her coat but kept it on. "What's going on, Jake?"

We went into the kitchen, and I grabbed a 'Gansette from the fridge, holding the can up for her. "You on the clock?"

She had a look on her face like she didn't appreciate my hospitality, as if I was making an attempt at making light of her uniformed visit. She stood in the doorway. "He thinks you're lying about something."

"I'm not," I said, pulling the tab off the can of beer. I took a sip. I hated the idea he'd send Maggie over to see if I'd tell her more than I'd told him, which wasn't much at all. "You want a coffee?"

"No, Jake. I want you to tell me what this is all about."

"I don't know what it's all about. It's all speculation right now."

"Speculation about what?" Maggie said, a slight sense of frustration in her voice. She walked to the sink, where she grabbed a glass from the drying rack and helped herself to some water. "He's working this homicide investigation, Jake. As good as you are at not showing your cards, I know you. There's something... And if you have information that's going to help solve his case, then—"

"There's nothing to it," I said, pulling a chair out from under the table. I sat down.

"I don't believe you."

I paused, thinking. I knew I could trust Maggie as much as anyone. But she wore the badge, and had an obligation to the law. I didn't think it was right to put her in a position where she'd have to lie about something I'd said, just because I'd asked her to.

I said, "Carter didn't tell you anything?"

"He said you were working on something, had to do with a case in New Hampshire, but hinted at you knowing something about what happened to that poor girl."

"Well, he's wrong. But..." I thought about how much to hold back from her. "Do you know the name Larry Green?"

"Carter told me you were asking about him."

"Well, his widow is the one I'm working for. At least for the next five days. And before I actually met with her, she was in Boston, about a block from my office. She called me from a payphone that was maybe a hundred yards from where that body was found."

Maggie's eyes widened. "And you didn't tell Carter?"

"I don't think there's anything to tell him," I said. "She didn't do it, if that's what you mean."

Maggie gave a slight tilt of her head. "You told me her name was Heather Connelly?"

"I did. She didn't use her real name when she called me."

"Why not?"

I shrugged. "I guess she was just being careful."

"Of what?"

"I don't know. She's nervous about..." I thought about it a little more. "I guess I don't know."

We both stood in silence for a moment. I could hear the oil burner rumbling beneath us, which to me was the sound of money burning. But it felt good to get some heat going through the house.

Maggie pulled out a chair across from me and sat down, hands flat on the maple-topped table. "She was married to Larry Green?"

"Yes. Her real name is Marilyn. Marilyn Green."

"And she's hired you? To do what? I don't know a lot about the Larry Green case but as far as I know the fire was accidental."

"She suspects the cops got it wrong."

"Based on what?"

"A hunch, I guess." I grinned. Maybe a part of me was embarrassed for taking the job.

"This was in New Hampshire, right? Where the balloon caught fire?"

"Yes."

"So why would you ask Carter about it?"

I leaned against the counter and sipped my beer. "It just hit me to ask, when I was there with him."

"About a case that took place in another state?" Maggie shot a sharp gaze my way. "I don't understand what makes you think there could be some connection between your client and the victim?"

"I didn't say there was."

"I know you didn't. But I can see it. You have that look."

"What *look*?"

Maggie shrugged. "Your wheels are turning."

"Well, whatever's on my mind I'm just trying to come up with some ideas," I said. "It's an odd situation."

We both remained silent for a moment.

"Did you work with Sean McCaffrey?" I said.

Maggie paused, then nodded. "I know the name."

"Did you know he was a detective in New Hampshire?"

"Carter told me you asked about him."

I looked toward the window when I saw headlights out front drive by, but the car kept moving. "Raymond knows him. But you know how he gets—like I can never question another cop's work."

Maggie rolled her eyes.

"Apparently McCaffrey is the one who investigated the fire that killed Green. Found nothing, other than the fact it was accidental."

She gave me a look like she didn't know what else to say. "Why don't you talk to him?"

"McCaffrey? I'm planning on it." I tipped my head back and finished my can of beer.

"But, you know by asking Carter about it you've opened a can of worms, right? He didn't tell me this, but I wouldn't be surprised if he called McCaffrey."

I got up, tossed the empty can into the can under the sink, and grabbed another one from the fridge. I peeled the tab off the top and looked it over.

I remembered when I was a kid, some man my mother was dating at the time peeled the tab off his can of beer as I had, and told me he could make a duck call out of it. He played around with the tab, really working it, making it look, to me, like he was going to come up with something worth seeing.

After a good minute or two, he raised the tab to his mouth, and put the circular part of it to his lips. He said, "Here ducky ducky. Heeeerre ducky ducky." He laughed so hard he almost fell off the couch. My mother did the same, but I'm not sure how she could've found it funny. I didn't.

I remembered staring back at the guy, the dozen or so empty beer cans on the coffee table between us, wondering how soon it'd be before my mother would move on from yet another clown she'd brought home.

Maggie got up from the table. "Can I use your phone?" I nodded, and she lifted the handset from the wall. She walked through the open doorway, turning the corner with the cord stretched as far as it would go into the other room.

I poked my head through the doorway. "Are you afraid I'm going to listen?"

She shook her head and covered the mouthpiece with her hand. "I'm calling Detective Carter. It's cold in the kitchen."

I went over to the phone on the table by the couch, lifted the handset and carried it over to her with the base. "Here." I handed it to her, then took the phone from the kitchen out of her hand and hung it up on the other side of the wall, then went into the same room with Maggie.

She said into the phone, "Can you put me through to Detective Carter?" She paused. "Yes, it's Officer Donovan."

I grabbed some newspapers from the pile on the hearth, rolled them up and stuffed them under the grate in the fireplace, piling kindling and wood over the top of it. I lit the edge of the paper and crouched, watching the flames grow.

Maggie had the phone against her ear and came toward me, carrying the phone's base in her other hand. "I'm not sure Carter's in."

"Why are you calling him," I said, watching the flames.

"Because he's waiting to hear from me. I thought I'd tell him what you want me to," she said. "That you don't know anything."

I grinned at her. "I appreciate that."

Maggie put the base back on the side table next to the couch and hung up the phone. "He didn't answer."

She sat on the couch and watched me finish lighting the fire. She still had her blue Boston PD winter coat on. But she stood up a moment later. "I need to get back to the station." She headed for the front door.

"What are you going to tell him?" I said, following her.

She stopped, her hand on the knob, and turned to me. "I just told you what I'm going to tell him. Nothing. Problem is, I'm not sure he's going to believe it. He's suspicious of everyone, and will assume I'm covering for you."

"But you're not."

She nodded, opening the door.

I stood watching her head down the steps. "Careful. It's slippery out there."

She looked at me, her brown eyes glowing under the light over the porch. "If it's all right, I'll take a raincheck on that beer."

CHAPTER II

I LEFT WITH THE sun still rising and made it out to Newton early enough in the morning that I'd avoided the normally heavy traffic heading into the city. Stopping on the way, I called to let Marilyn and her uncle know I was coming out to see them, but nobody answered. I was afraid she had already left for New Hampshire.

But when I finally arrived at the house, Mr. Howell led me into the kitchen, where Marilyn was seated at a table by the window having a coffee, the Boston Globe spread open in front of her. She didn't appear to be in any kind of rush or look as if she was concerned about much of anything.

"Good morning, Jake," she said, rising from the chair. She wiped her hands on a cocktail napkin, then reached out and shook my hand.

I glanced past her out through the double French doors leading to the backyard. The snow back there was almost untouched, except for the footprints leading to two bird feeders hanging from a gray leaf-less tree. There were a handful of squirrels on the ground with four or five blue jays fighting over the feeder.

"Aren't the birds just beautiful," she said, following my gaze toward the yard.

"Blue Jays are mean," I said.

"But beautiful," she said, her gaze fixed through the glass on the door. The daylight coming through the window reflected off her face.

"Would you like a coffee?" Howell said, already pouring a cup before I could answer. He handed it to me in a small china cup.

"Thank you," I said. I had to hold it like a glass, because my finger barely fit through the tiny handle. But it was hot enough that it burned my hand, and I placed it on the table.

Marilyn gathered up the newspaper and folded it over, tossing it on the counter.

"I take it you had an uneventful night?" I said, sitting in the chair across from her.

Howell walked out of the kitchen and came back a moment later with a revolver in his hand. It was a .38, and he placed it on the table in front of me. "Do you know anything about guns?"

I looked the thing over, but didn't pick it up. "I suppose so."

"Well, I don't," Howell said. "I want Marilyn to hold onto it, for protection."

I looked at Marilyn.

She said, "I think someone's been following me."

"Recently?" I said.

She nodded. "I went to the store yesterday to get a couple of things. When I drove away, another car got behind me and followed me home."

"Here?" I said.

"Not all the way," she said.

It was hard to say if she had it right. "Did you get a look at the vehicle?"

"Not really. It was dark out." She smiled. "Honestly, I thought it was you for a moment."

"It wasn't me, I said. "But are you saying it looked like my car?"

Marilyn shrugged. "I think it was yellow. But it wasn't hard to say for sure." She picked up the gun and pointed it at me. "I wouldn't even know how to use this thing."

I pushed the muzzle away, moving her hand so she pointed it downward. "First rule is don't point it at anyone. Unless you're going to shoot the person, of course."

"Sorry." She placed the gun on the table.

"Was that the only time you've been followed?" I said. "Or that you *suspect* you've been followed?"

"Well, I told you already I thought someone was behind me when I drove into Boston to see you. Turns out I knew who it was." She glanced at her uncle and smiled, as if she found humor in it.

"Listen," I said. "If you're truly concerned, why not go to the police?"

The uncle made a sound, sipping his coffee.

"They're no help," Marilyn said. "I already told you they refuse to believe Larry was—"

"I mean the local police. About you being followed."

"The Newton police?" her uncle said. He laughed. "Incompetent."

I didn't ask why he felt that way, but I also wasn't the person to argue his point. "I have a good friend with Boston PD. I know we're not in Boston here, but—"

"No!" Marilyn snapped. "They're worse than any of them."

"It's not a secret that department's full of dirty cops," the uncle said.

Marilyn held her teacup in front of her, as if preparing to take a sip. "I don't trust the police," she said. She turned in her chair to look out the window toward the backyard. "And definitely not anyone from Boston."

I looked over at Howell taking an English muffin from the plastic sleeve, tearing the muffin in two after working it with his fingers. He dropped it in the toaster and looked toward Marilyn. "Maybe you should tell him?"

She turned from the window, glancing from me to the uncle, her mouth as if it wanted to move, but she wouldn't let it.

"Tell me what?" I said.

Marilyn placed her cup on the table and folded her hands in her lap. "Larry wasn't my first husband."

She seemed too young to have already been through two marriages. But who was I to judge? "Okay," I said, and waited for more.

"My first husband was a police officer," she said.

"You were married to a cop?" I said. "Really?"

She seemed to hesitate. "A Boston cop."

I felt my eyes widen. "That's a small piece of information you probably could've shared with me before now. No?"

She lowered her chin. Her hands on her lap, gripping a cocktail napkin she tore to pieces that dropped on the floor. "He was killed. Shot, while off duty."

I looked from Marilyn to Mr. Howell, both remaining quiet, at least for a good handful of seconds. I thought about Raymond, assuming he had to've known the officer. Maggie too, I guessed. "What was his name?"

Marilyn said, "Charles. But his friends called him Chuck. Chuck Johnson."

"Oh." I had to think for a moment. The name didn't sound familiar. The news she'd shared had shifted every thought in my mind. I had made some assumptions that might turn out to be wrong.

She said, "We weren't actually still together when he was killed. We were divorced."

I bit my tongue at first, trying not to make light of it or say something stupid about how it must've been different losing an ex-husband compared to losing a husband she was still married to. "If you don't mind me asking, did your divorce from Charles, er, Chuck, have anything to do with you and Larry getting together?"

She swallowed hard, then shook her head. "There were other reasons."

"*Other* reasons?" I said. "Does that mean it might've been *one* of the reasons?"

"The man was a real son of a bitch," Howell said, eyeballing the .38 on the table.

I glanced at Marilyn.

"He pushed her," Howell said, once again not even letting her answer for herself.

Marilyn stood and turned to the glass doors, looking toward the snow-covered yard.

"Did you report it?" I said. "That he laid his hands on you?"

She didn't turn to look at me, but shook her head. "I couldn't."

I tried to do the math in my head, hoping to understand the timing of her marriages to both men. "Forgive me for asking, but just so I understand... Did you say you were married to Larry for six years?"

She nodded, and when she turned I saw she had tears in her eyes. She reached for another napkin from the stack on the table, dabbing the corner of each eye. "Sometimes I wonder if I'm cursed, the way people in my life don't seem to stick around this earth for very long."

Howell and I exchanged a glance.

I didn't know what to say.

I said, "I want to make sure I have everything straight."

She sniffled, nodding her head.

"You had divorced your first husband. How many years ago?"

"Seven," she said.

"And, then, he was killed... around the same time you remarried Larry?"

"We had a June wedding. Chuck was killed in May, 1973. May fifteenth."

I gave her a moment to catch her breath. She was clearly emotional, something I felt she might've been holding back all along, the way she held her chin high, her smile as if it'd been painted on her face the whole time I'd been around.

"So, you don't suppose or... You're not trying to say that what happened to your husband, Larry, could've possibly had something to do with your ex-husband, right? I mean, I'm not insinuating anything at all, but—"

"No!" Marilyn snapped, shaking her head. "You didn't know Larry. He was a sweet man."

"Was he?" the uncle said, buttering his English muffin on the counter, his back to us.

Marilyn gazed at him. "He wasn't perfect. But..." She sniffled again, wiping her nose with the napkin.

I said, "Is that why you didn't want to go to the police? I mean, you think they're not going to help you, because you were married to a cop who was killed? Besides, if your ex was a cop in Boston, I can't imagine why you couldn't at least go to the cops here in Newton, just tell them you're concerned for your safety?"

The uncle said, "I'm a little confused why you're so adamant we go to the police."

"I'm not. I'm just asking questions."

Marilyn said, "Chuck had some friends, fellow officers, who drove by the church the day of my wedding. We were married at Trinity Church. Back Bay."

"They ticketed half the guests' cars," the uncle said.

I was starting to understand—right or wrong—the fear was there might've been some within the Boston Police Department who knew Marilyn's first husband and possibly held something against her, as if it was her fault he was killed.

On the other hand, I guess I didn't know enough to say one way or the other.

"I told you, I have a couple of friends over there. My cousin's a former officer with Boston, and a good friend of mine… She's a good cop. I can talk to her, if you'd like. See if she can—"

"No!" Marilyn said, pounding her fist on the table with a touch of rage I hadn't picked up on before that point. "I do not want to talk to anyone over there. I don't care who you know."

I said, "I'm just trying to make sure we do this the right way. Especially when it comes to your own safety."

Howell looked at his watch. "Speaking of… We should get going. They're expecting us."

I'd almost forgotten she was supposed to be leaving.

"New Hampshire?" I said.

He nodded, his eyes on his niece. "We have to get going."

I still had plenty of questions for Marilyn. More than I did when I first arrived. "What about the detective in New Hampshire who investigated Larry's so-called accident?"

"Detective McCaffrey?" Marilyn said.

"Yes. I'm just wondering if there's any chance he was a friend of your first husband?"

"I didn't even know until recently that Detective McCaffrey was a former Boston cop." she said.

I pulled at my chin. "And what about your first husband and Larry? Did they ever meet?"

"Chuck suspected something was going on." She carried her teacup and dish over to the sink. "He actually showed up at the dealership and threatened Larry, told him if he ever saw him out on the streets, he'd kill him."

The uncle cleared his throat and looked at his watch again. "All right, Marilyn. We're running late." He reached out to shake my hand. "Thank you for coming by. I'm sorry we can't continue this conversation right now."

"How can I reach you?" I said to Marilyn. I was just getting started.

Marilyn pulled a small piece of paper out of the drawer and wrote on it, handing it to me. "Here's the number up there."

I took the paper, folded it over and stuck it in my pocket.

I stopped at the door and turned to Marilyn. "Did they ever find who killed him? Your first husband?"

She shook her head. "It was a convenience store robbery. He was there buying cigarettes."

"No witnesses?"

"Chuck and the clerk were both killed," she said. "There was nobody else there." Opening the door for me, she grinned, looking me in the eye. "I'm sorry I wasn't more upfront with you. But if you need to reach me…"

The uncle came around the corner. "Marilyn, we're late."

I opened the door and stepped outside, the cold air blowing into my face as I headed down the steps. "I'll be in touch."

Marilyn closed the door.

Walking along the shoveled, yet somewhat icy brick pathway, I looked ahead at a yellow sedan driving slowly on the street. It sped up and took off as if whoever was behind the wheel had noticed I was watching.

I hurried to the Nova, being careful with each slippery step. Jumping into the driver-side, I started the cold engine and took off after the vehicle. Continuing on Eldredge, I stopped at Church Street and looked straight ahead toward Grace Church. I turned to look at cars coming from the right, then looked left toward Farlow Park.

But the car could've gone in either direction, and I realized I was already too late.

CHAPTER 12

ACCORDING TO THE POLICE officer working the phone at Boston Police headquarters, Maggie was out on a traffic detail. He told me she was working around the building of the soon-to-be-built John F. Kennedy Library and Museum on Columbia Point in Dorchester.

I didn't know much about the new library, other than it was supposed to open at the site of an old garbage dump in the upcoming fall. I'd read in The Globe how it had taken a long time to get to where they could finally start the work, especially after the original plan to build it in Cambridge got nixed. Apparently, the residents didn't want crowds filling their streets.

I filled my thermos with coffee before I'd hit the road, knowing after I caught up with Maggie, if I could find her, I'd head to the South Shore to talk to Larry Green's daughter and his first wife in Plymouth.

Driving along Columbia Point around the construction project, I passed at least a dozen cops around the site. None, however, were a tall, attractive, red-headed female. I stopped to ask one officer on detail, but he tried to wave me along. I rolled down my window, and a rush of cold coming off the Dorchester Bay blasted me in the face.

"Officer Donovan around?" I said, having to raise my voice.

The cop appeared to be young, but built like an ox. He gave me a stare through his sunglasses sitting on his bright-red nose. "Who are you?"

"Jake Horn," I said. "A friend."

"Horn, huh?" He put his hand out. "You got some I.D.?"

"For what?" I said.

The cop lowered his sunglasses and looked at me over the top of them. "You got a problem, buddy?"

I knew how some Boston cops liked to play games. "No, sir. I don't have a problem." I wanted to push back, but instead, I raised myself from the seat and took my wallet out of my back pocket. I handed him my license.

He looked over it, then put the two-way to his mouth. "Donovan, you read?" His teeth chattered as he waited, holding the two-way near his ear.

A couple of moments later, Maggie's voice came over the radio: "Donovan."

"I have a gentleman here looking for you," the officer said, white mist coming from his mouth as he spoke. "Jake Horn. You know him?"

The two-way squawked, Maggie's voice coming through again: "Yes. Send him my way."

The young cop pointed straight ahead. "She's round the corner, quarter mile that way. You'll see a sign for the construction entrance. She's right after it." He handed me back my license. "Gotta be careful nowadays, never know what someone's up to around here."

I gave him a nod and slowly pulled away, driving along the uneven, unpaved road. The Nova bounced and squeaked with each hole the wheels dropped into.

I spotted Maggie up ahead, standing just outside the chain-link fence enclosing the construction area. She gave me a wave as I drove closer, and I pulled the car over to the side of the road as far as I could go without driving against the plowed piles of snow. I walked toward her.

"What are you doing here?" she said, bundled in her black, mid-length leather jacket, sunglasses on. She wore black leather gloves and held a Dunkin' Donuts cup in her hand.

The late-morning sun reflected off the snow covering most of the ground, other than what looked like frozen mud on the road.

I said, "You haven't said anything to Detective Carter, have you?"

"About Larry Green's widow?" She had her collar up, shaking her head as she straightened her wool hat. "All I told him was you didn't know anything. I don't think he believes it, but he trusts me enough not to push me too hard."

"Well," I said. "I found out why Larry's widow won't go to the cops." I told her about Marilyn's first husband, Chuck Johnson, and how she was afraid there was still some hostility toward her with not only the Boston police, but perhaps other surrounding departments.

"But this was how many years ago?" Maggie said.

"When he was killed? I think she said six years."

"I really don't know anything about him," Maggie said. "And I've never heard a word about her, until you. But if you're saying she won't ask the cops for help because her husband was a Boston cop, then I guess I don't understand the situation."

"Well, the thing is she believes someone's been following her."

"Then she should report it to the police, don't you think?"

I nodded. "I know. That's what I'm trying to tell you; she won't go to the police. Not even the locals, where she lives with the uncle."

Maggie remained quiet until she turned and stepped into the middle of the hard but muddy road to stop a dump truck driving toward her. She put her hands up and blew her whistle to stop the driver, then walked over to the driver-side.

I was tired, and hadn't really been able to wake myself up since I climbed out of bed. So I headed back to the Nova and grabbed my Thermos of coffee to take a sip from it.

After Maggie finished talking to the driver of the truck, she let him continue through the gate. Maggie watched, then turned and saw I wasn't where I was a moment ago, then headed over to me standing outside the Nova.

The cold breeze came across the water again, the temperature so low I could feel the burn on my cheeks.

Maggie said, "When did you find out?"

"About Chuck Johnson?"

"Yes. You didn't mention it when—"

"I just found out about it. She was hesitant to tell me anything about it. Her uncle was the one who pressed her, as if she didn't like the idea she was keeping it from me."

I couldn't see Maggie's eyes but, if I could, I imagined she'd be rolling them.

"Something's not right," she said.

I took another sip from the thermos. "There's something odd about both of them."

"Both of them?"

"Marilyn and her uncle, Nathan Howell."

Maggie was quiet, thinking. "And Carter never mentioned anything to you about her first husband?"

"No, but I was thinking about it. Once I mentioned Larry Green, don't you think he would've brought up how his widow was married to a Boston cop?"

Maggie shrugged. "Maybe he doesn't know?"

"Maybe," I said. But I wasn't buying it. "Would it surprise you if he was holding back from giving me information? Considering he expected something from me first?"

Maggie stared back at me through her sunglasses.

I said, "So what else do you know about him?"

"Who?"

"Chuck Johnson."

"Not much at all," Maggie said. "There's a portrait of him in one hall at headquarters, with other slain officers. But if he's who I'm thinking of, I'm not sure he was a cop for very long."

I glanced over at the construction area, wondering how much they could actually get done, with the ground frozen solid, and the cold whipping through the half-constructed building.

I said, "What about when Larry Green got fried in that balloon? You never heard anyone mention his widow was once married to Boston a cop? Someone must've brought it up at some point, don't you think?"

Maggie gave me a look, as if she wasn't happy with my questioning. "You're making it sound like you think I'm lying to you."

"I don't mean to," I said. "But, Detective Carter, on the other hand..."

"You're going to have to stop this," she said. "I'd tell you if I had something that would help you, Jake. You know that. But the way you're talking... You have to remember, Larry Green's case took place in New Hampshire. Boston Police had nothing to do with any of it."

I again glanced toward the construction site. "Nothing seems to make much sense."

Maggie said, "If I can be honest with—"

"I thought you *were* being honest?" I smiled, my cheeks feeling like they were going to crack from the cold.

Maggie continued, "When Larry Green was killed, it wasn't exactly big news for us. I mean, I know it was on the news and all, but for us—the Boston PD, I mean—we had almost 27,000 violent crimes last year. Over 200 murders. The only reason I even remember it is because of the way it happened, the owner of a dealership who was fairly well known locally, died in a burning hot air balloon. But other than that..."

"*Allegedly* burned in the balloon," I said.

Maggie stared back at me. "Jake, you have to admit this is going to be a real challenge for you. What little I looked into it, the evidence certainly points to it being purely accidental. How could you possibly explain how it wasn't, or why someone would go through all the trouble to kill someone in such a fashion."

I said, "For the reason you just stated: It looks purely accidental. There's no physical evidence so it's easy for everyone to make the same assumption. I guess it's like burning someone alive in their car or house, but someone might've decided to take it to another level."

CHAPTER 13

It was already getting dark out by the time I made it to the South Shore a little before four o'clock. I turned off Route 3 and headed into downtown Plymouth. I thought about me and Barbara, when we took Nancy to the Thanksgiving Day Parade. Nancy might've been one or two years old, and slept through the whole parade.

I drove down Court Street, through the downtown on Main, then slowed enough to get a good look beyond the tall grass toward the harbor. The view was hard to beat.

I continued on Sandwich Street into Chiltonville, where Larry Green's daughter lived.

Chiltonville was a woodsy area in Plymouth with homes having a decent amount of space and just a stone's throw from the water.

I recalled the time Barbara and I drove through the area and the rest of the South Shore, looking at houses, with Nancy asleep in the back. We spent a lot of weekends doing just that—looking at houses in the different areas throughout New England whenever we could, if I wasn't busy working a case. We could never decide if we wanted to stay in Boston or move farther away. And as I drove, I couldn't help but think that if we'd moved out of the city back then, Barbara would likely still be alive.

It's not only the choices we make that impact the rest of our lives. It's also the ones we *don't* make. Her death ate at me every single day. Of course, I can't help but blame myself. I should have stopped her from leaving the house that morning, even if I had no reason to.

I pulled over and opened up the map, folding it to check the address I'd written. Realizing I'd already passed the street I was looking for, I continued ahead and stopped where the road forked, in front of a red saltbox between the two roads. I banged a uey and started back in the other direction, my tires spinning on a patch of ice I hit.

Dwight Avenue—the road I'd missed—was on my left where I turned into a neighborhood of colonials, ranches, and Cape Cod homes. The yards were big and surrounded by a mix of bare gray oak trees and green-covered pines. Smoke poured out of just about every chimney.

I pulled into the driveway of a two-story, white-clapboard colonial. There was a Volkswagen Bus, what some might call a "Hippie" van, parked at the front of the driveway next to the home's side entrance. There was no garage.

I parked behind the VW and tried to see inside through the windows, wondering if anybody was home. I got out and stepped onto the driveway covered with packed snow. The crisp air had the smell of burning firewood, with plenty of snow on the ground, although seemingly less than Boston.

A wooden Flexible Flyer sled was on its side and sticking out of the snow a few feet from the front steps. It reminded me of the days I'd take Nancy sledding on Boston Common.

Standing at the front door, I could hear music inside. I wasn't sure at first, but recognized Barbara Streisand's voice. She was singing

"You Don't Bring Me Flowers," her new duet with Neil Diamond. Not a horrible song, but not exactly my cup of tea.

I rang the doorbell and watched the wooden door behind the white metal storm door open almost immediately, as if the person behind it already knew someone was out there.

A woman looked out through the glass between us, looking me up and down. She pushed open the door and poked her head outside into the cold. "Can I help you?"

She was older than me by a few years, hair graying but pulled back into a long ponytail behind her head. She wore a long green sweater over a pair of bell-bottom jeans with furry slippers on her feet. I guessed the VW Bus was hers.

"Sorry to bother you," I said. "My name's Jake Horn, I'm a private investigator from up in Boston, and—"

"Oh," she said, nodding. "I was told I might be meeting you."

"Oh yeah?"

"My son Jason called me earlier."

"Oh," I said. "I guess that means you're Karen?"

She nodded and smiled. "I didn't expect you'd drive all the way down here from Boston without phoning first?"

"Sorry," I said. "It's not always easy getting in front of someone, especially when you try to set up something over the phone. Usually, once I say I'm a private investigator, I either get hung up on or the person promises to call me back. But never does."

"I understand," she said, again looking me over. "Do you have some kind of identification? You never know who's telling the truth about who they are."

I pulled off my glove and reached into the inside pocket of my coat, taking out a business card I handed to her.

She took the card and looked it over, giving me a quick glance before she pushed the door open wide. "Come inside."

After stomping my boots on the concrete landing outside the door to shake the snow off, I stepped through the doorway. There was a sweet smell in the air, like someone had baked something. It was warm inside, almost too warm, with the glow from a fireplace lighting up the room to the left of where I stood, just inside the door. The stairs straight ahead of me led to a lighted hallway, and I wasn't sure if anyone else was there.

"Would you like me to take off my boots?" I said, praying she didn't say yes. I knew I had wool socks on, but couldn't remember if they were one of the many pairs with holes in the toes.

"No, that's all right," she said. "Just wipe them on the mat." She turned into the room with the fireplace but stopped and walked toward me, her hand out. "I'll take your coat."

I handed it to her, and she hung it on a rack by the door. I followed her into the room with the fireplace.

Barbara Streisand was still playing loudly from two tall speakers on either side of a closed cabinet with a record player spinning on top. Karen opened the cabinet doors and turned the knob on the stereo, lowering the volume.

As far as I knew, the house belonged to her daughter Brenda. But then I wondered if the information I had was wrong. So I went ahead and asked her.

"Actually, it's my daughter's home," she said. "I live here with her and my son-in-law. They're both at work now. My grandson's upstairs taking a nap." She grabbed a paperback from the couch and placed it on the coffee table. "Can I get you a drink?"

I could have used one. But I had a good drive ahead of me. "No, I'm all right. Thank you."

She gestured toward the couch. "Please, have a seat."

I sat facing a console TV encased inside a cabinet with rabbit ears sticking up from the top of it.

She sat in a recliner in the corner, facing me. "I'm not sure what you're expecting to get out of me. Larry and I haven't been married in quite a few years." She looked down at her hands. She had rings on her fingers, but none that would indicate a second marriage. "So, Jason said the gold digger hired you? I'm not sure why she's going through this. Maybe she's upset Larry didn't leave her any money when he died."

There was an understandable sense of hostility toward Marilyn.

I said, "Well, the police don't always get things right."

She looked me over. "Do you have a reason to believe it wasn't an accident?"

I didn't really have an answer. "I've only just started."

Karen appeared to be waiting to see if I had more to say. "Are you sure you don't want a drink? I like to have a glass of wine in the afternoon, when the little one goes down for a nap. Sometimes grandma needs to relax." She laughed as she rose to her feet and left the room.

Even with her graying hair, she appeared younger compared to her dead ex-husband. I wondered if at one point, before Marilyn, Karen had been the younger woman.

She came back holding a glass of wine. "If you change your mind about a drink, just let me know. We have wine. Beer. Bourbon..." She sat back down in the chair and sipped from the glass.

"Thanks," I said, sitting toward the front edge of the couch cushion. "Are you okay if I ask you some questions?"

Karen shrugged, then nodded. "As long as you don't try to pin anything on me." She laughed.

"Well, I guess for starters, do you want to tell me about your relationship with Larry?"

She took another sip of wine before she answered. "Well, I don't hate him like I used to. Or, I guess I should say I *didn't* hate him like I used to, up until..." She cleared her throat. "I barely spoke to him over the past few years. I'd say, once the divorce was final, we probably only had maybe a dozen conversations. Of course, we had the kids, so..."

"And did they both have a normal relationship with Larry?"

"Normal?" She chuckled. "Nobody had a 'normal' relationship with Larry."

"What do you mean by that?"

Karen pulled at her lower lip. "He was oblivious to things around him. If you had asked him about his relationship with his kids, he probably would have said everything was great between them. Or he'd say he was a good father."

"He wasn't?"

She paused, as if she had to think about it. "I guess he was fine. He was more interested in that dealership than his own family."

"Would your daughter say the same thing? That he might not've been the best father?"

Karen shrugged. "I guess you'd have to ask her."

"How old is she now?"

"She's twenty-five. When Larry left me, she was still in high school. Do you know what something like that does to a teenage girl? When her father leaves?" She took another sip of her wine.

"I know what it's like to no longer have a parent present," I said, but didn't go into details.

"It was Brenda's senior year. That just shows you how self-centered he was. He couldn't even let her enjoy the most important year of her life." She looked down into her glass. "Brenda had a lot of resentment through the years. Of course, it wasn't easy when he died."

"And what about you?"

"What about me?" Karen said.

"How did you feel about it? When you found out he was dead? Did you believe, from the beginning, that it was an accident."

"Did I believe it was an accident?" She repeated my question in a way that said she found the question odd.

"What I mean is, did it make sense to you that Larry would go up in a balloon like that, and... It catches fire?"

Karen said, "He was always somewhat of a showman. The fact he went down in a burning hot air balloon is almost fitting."

"Fitting?" I said.

I was clear there was little love lost between the two, and that Karen had little sympathy for what happened to her ex-husband.

She placed her wineglass on a small side table next to her chair, and seemed to ponder the question a little longer. "Well, like I said, he could sometimes be oblivious to trouble around him. Even when everything in his life seemed to be falling apart, and he was close to losing what little he had left, he would just go about his days like everything was fine. Maybe that's how he was inside that balloon's basket, watching everything burn around him, as if everything would be all right."

"I'm not sure what else someone is supposed to do at that point?" I said.

Karen sipped her wine, her gaze toward the fire.

"I don't know either," she said. "It must have been awful."

We both sat in silence for a couple of moments.

I said, "Would you believe there's a chance someone was responsible for what happened to him?"

"Would I believe it?" She shrugged.

"Okay, let me ask it another way: Could you see him having someone out there who wanted him dead badly enough to do something like this?"

"Why not just shoot him?" she said.

I had the same thoughts, of course. It was a lot to go through to kill someone.

She sat as if she were thinking, almost in a daze, staring at nothing at all. "Well, the gold digger must not've been happy they ended up broke. But if she's the one who's hired you..." She paused. "There were plenty of people depending on Larry to make some money with that dealership."

"Your son mentioned a few who invested in the business?"

Karen pushed a few loose strands of hair back from her face. I could tell she had something to say, but was maybe thinking it through first. Looking toward the floor, she raised her gaze to me. "I know I said I hadn't talked to him in a while. But he actually came here to Plymouth to see Brenda and the baby not too long ago. The way he talked, it was as if the business was doing better. But I already knew the truth. We actually talked for a little while, for the first time in a long time."

I watched her, waiting, in case she had more to say.

"Did you get the feeling he was in trouble? I mean, beyond the fact his business was falling apart? Any mention of any threat, or—"

"Like I said, Larry always made it appear as if everything was fine," she said. "But I could always see through it. It had to've been wearing on him... all the pressure from the business. And I know those investors—some who were friends of his—were begging him to take the dealership in another direction."

"They blamed him for the failures?" I said.

She took a moment to answer. "Larry wasn't one to change his mind. And he believed the best cars were made right here in America."

I thought about her son, Jason, doing all he could do to make the change he'd wanted to make all along, but apparently only had the power to make it once his father was out of the way.

I said, "Is there anyone you can think of who was hurt more than others by the dealership losing money?"

Karen was holding her glass, about to take a sip until she stopped. "Richard Reagan."

It was the name I had in mind.

"He was a friend of Larry's. At one time was a fairly wealthy man. He lived in a beautiful six-bedroom colonial on the water, in Scituate. Last I heard he's in a run-down three-family in Taunton."

"But he didn't lose all his money because of the dealership, did he?"

"No, I don't believe so. He went through a divorce of his own, and had other investments I understand didn't quite work out."

I said, "I understand he spends a lot of time at the dog track?"

Karen nodded. "He's always been a gambler. Maybe that's why he wasn't afraid to give Larry the money he needed." She finished what was in her glass. "I wasn't around by the time things started falling apart at the dealership. But I knew enough to know there was trouble brewing, not only with the energy crisis but the whole economy." She rose from her seat. "Richard believed gambling would solve his problems."

She appeared to be a caring woman, not only somewhat saddened by her ex-husband's death, but perhaps also about the alleged downfall of Richard Reagan.

I said, "Would you say Richard and Larry remained friends? Until the end?"

Karen waited before she finally shook her head. "I don't think so."

CHAPTER 14

I UNDERSTOOD MR. REAGAN had run into some bad luck over
the past few years, but I wasn't expecting he'd live in a rundown
triple-decker in Taunton. Cars parked along the street were stuck
in the mounds of snow the plows had pushed up against them.
Ignoring a parking ban is never a wise choice.

After a good minute, I rang the doorbell again, then stepped
down off the steps to look up at the second floor. It appeared the
lights were on up there, but nobody answered.

I figured there'd be a chance Reagan wasn't there, assuming that
was the case as I walked back to my car parked at the end of the
driveway. But I stopped when I heard the door open behind me.

I looked back at a man with a sweater that looked too small, his fat
belly hanging out from the bottom. The scarf tied around his neck
and a knitted hat with a pom-pom on his head looked like something
a boy would wear.

"Who are you?"

I didn't answer. "Are you Richard Reagan?" He was, for the most
part, what I pictured he'd look like. Or maybe a little worse.

He narrowed his eyes and rubbed what looked like at least a good week's worth of growth on his face. "Who's asking?"

"My name's Jake," I said, glancing past him and into the building toward the dark-stained stairway that curved around the rounded wall and disappeared.

"Jake who?" he said.

"Horn."

He looked out toward the street, as if he was making sure I was alone.

"What do you want?" he said. "You selling something?"

I was close enough, on the top step now, that I got a whiff of booze coming from his breath. "I'm a private investigator. I'd like to ask you some questions about an old friend of yours, Larry Green."

Reagan raised his eyebrows. "Private investigator, huh? Who you workin' for?"

A cold breeze came up from behind me that sent a shiver up my neck. "Do you mind if I come inside?"

"Yeah, I mind. We can talk right here."

I heard a door open from somewhere inside, and Richard turned and looked to his right.

A woman I couldn't see yelled, "Shut the door, you idiot!"

A door slammed, and Reagan turned to me, burped, then excused himself. "You want a beer?"

I was going to say no, but thought maybe the guy'd trust me more if I didn't turn down the drink. I nodded. "Sure."

He waved for me to follow. "You know what? You can come up. Don't mind the mess."

I followed him in and closed the door, then headed up the stairs behind him.

There was a hint of cat urine odor hanging in the air.

"You have a cat?" I said.

"Not me. The old lady on the first floor does. She's the landlord. Cat pisses all over the place, and she has the nerve to yell at me for leaving the door open." He continued ahead of me.

The door to the apartment on the second floor had been left open.

I followed him in and noticed he had a slight limp when he walked. But I didn't think much of it.

The place wasn't as messy as he made it sound, although the coffee table in that first room we entered from the stairs had dozens or maybe even hundreds of newspapers and books stacked at least a foot high on top of it. Other than the coffee table and a leather recliner in the corner that looked similar to the one at Karen Green's house, the place appeared to be nearly empty. There was hardly any furniture. The walls were bare.

I could smell cigarettes and some kind of fried meat.

Reagan left his scarf and hat on, which made sense since it was almost as cold inside as it was outside.

He left the room and came back with two cans of Black Label. He handed me one, then went back into the kitchen and came out with a folding chair he placed by the coffee table. "I told you the place was a mess," he said, straightening up some of the papers. He moved a stack of books to the floor by the recliner and exposed a small space on the coffee table.

"Looks like you do a lot of reading?" I said.

He shrugged and nodded at the same time. "Try to keep the brain sharp, you know?" He picked up one of the books, looked at the back of it, then went and sat in the recliner. He used the handle on the side of the chair and reclined back with his feet up, the worn soles of his shoes facing me.

I left my coat on but took off my leather gloves and tucked them in the pockets before I sat down in the folding chair.

"So," Reagan said, "His widow hired you, huh?"

"How'd you know that?"

Eyebrows raised, he shook his head, then put his beer to his mouth, taking a few loud gulps before he let out another burp. "Word gets around."

I paused. "Larry was a friend of yours, no?"

"Sure, you could say that."

I wasn't convinced.

He said, "Obviously, you've met Marilyn. She's a little out there, don't you think?"

"Out there?"

"The girl's nuts. Cuckoo." Reagan turned his finger, making a circle next to his head.

I gazed back at the man in his undersized sweater, the red, blue, and green scarf around his neck, and what looked like an old hat with half the pompom missing. With the way he had all the newspapers and books, I thought maybe he was some kind of hoarder who was a little more off-center himself than I'd imagined before I got there. I wondered who he thought he was, calling someone else crazy.

"Are you saying you don't believe her?" I said.

He appeared to have to think about it for a moment. "Man like Larry, has a lot of pride, you know? Always thought he could fix things himself. But he might've got to a point he just couldn't handle it."

I stared back at him, taking a minute to understand what he was suggesting. "You're not saying you think he took his own life, are you?"

Reagan tipped his head back and finished the rest of his beer. "Just a thought."

I wondered if the guy was on to something. The thought hadn't even crossed my mind, and I hadn't heard anyone else suggest it, either.

Richard Reagan said, "I know you're a private dick or whatever you call yourself. But, the thing is, I can't see how you or anyone else will ever know. So, if we're left to guess, it would make sense, wouldn't it? Larry goes up in the air on a Saturday morning, sets off into the air and torches himself?" He huffed out a small laugh, shaking his head. "What a way to go, huh?"

I didn't know what to say.

Reagan continued, "Larry was at a point he was out of answers. Even if he'd done what everyone else wanted him to do, I'm not sure it would've made a difference." He shook his can and sipped whatever was left at the bottom. "I gave him a lot of money, you know. I got to a point where I knew I wasn't going to get it back. Like most people, I'd pretty much given up on Larry."

We both sat without a word for a few moments, the only sound coming from what sounded like plows outside, dropping salt.

Reagan reached for the handle on the side of the recliner and got himself upright. Wiping his chin with his sleeve, he said, "It got to a point I had to let my lawyer do the talking. At least back when I could still afford one. So Larry and I stopped communicating."

"How did you two meet?" I said.

He took a moment. "Larry's old man helped me get my first business off the ground. In fact, Larry worked for me. He managed one of my stores."

"A car dealership?" I said.

Reagan shook his head. "Furniture. And let me tell you, I did all right. I made good money. But I saw the writing on the wall when these factories started opening up in the south. Times were tough, nobody wanted to pay the price of real wood anymore. People no longer cared if their furniture was made here in New England. Next thing you know, these big warehouse stores start opening everywhere, selling that garbage from the south. I'm talking veneers, furniture made of plastic. Absolute garbage. But that's what people wanted. Thing is, I was lucky enough to see the writing on the wall, and cashed out before it was too late."

"So, then what'd you do?" I said.

"Well, I invested in other people's businesses. That's what you do, you want to make real money. So when Larry wanted to open a car dealership—he was always a car guy—he had some money. But he needed more. He tapped into his friends for investment." Reagan pointed to himself. "Larry started one of the first Chrysler dealerships outside of Boston. None of us saw the energy crisis coming. By the time we did, it was too late. I don't know. His kid wanted him to jump into the Japanese market, but it's not like you just flip a switch. He had a lot of inventory sitting on that lot. Now it's Jason's problem, and I'm not sure he has the answers either."

I finally took a sip from the can of Black Label I'd been holding.

Reagan started for the kitchen. "You want another one?"

I hadn't even put a dent in the beer I had. "I'm all right."

It was hard to tell if Reagan held a grudge against Larry or not. It seemed he did not. But I couldn't understand how he couldn't. Anyone losing a quarter million dollars, ending up in what looked to be the poorhouse, was reason enough to want revenge.

But I really just couldn't see it. And maybe he wasn't far off base with his suggestion Larry Green could have taken his own life. It wasn't at all far-fetched.

Reagan walked back into the room with a new can of Black Label and peeled off the tab, tossing it onto the small area of bare wood on the coffee table. Walking over to the window, he pulled up the shade and looked out. "You like your Nova?" he said, looking back at me. "Love the yellow. I don't know why they stopped making that third generation. The Chevy X-Body."

I turned in my chair to face him, his back to me while he continued his gaze out the window. "It's a good car," I said. "Not exactly made for driving in the winter around here, but..."

"That's one thing about those Japanese. They got the front wheel drive right." He turned to me, tapping his temple with his long finger. "They're smarter than us. They make their cars smaller, more fuel efficient..." He turned back to the window. "Larry was so damn stubborn... I told him, if you won't go foreign, at least maybe look at other manufacturers. Even Chevy might've been a better option." He walked back to the recliner and plopped into it, some of his open beer spilling on his sweater. "Who knows. Maybe Jason'll work out a deal with Nissan to sell their Datsuns. I'm not counting on it though."

"Would you get your money back? If he can turn it around?"

Reagan shrugged but said nothing else.

I said, "What about this friend of his, name's Sean? Do you know anything about him?"

Reagan sat up straight. "Sean Ranier."

"You know him?"

"I know of him. Kid's got money. Cocky bastard. Rubs a lot of people the wrong way. But he's connected."

"Connected? As in—"

"He's got money." He took a good drink of beer, then his expression changed, as if something had suddenly occurred to him. "So, are you here because you think I had something to do with what happened to Larry?"

I waited before I answered. To me, I had very few answers. And as far as I was concerned, everyone was a suspect. "You certainly have a motive," I said.

Richard struggled to push himself out of the recliner, but finally got to his feet and walked toward the door, opening it. "I lost a lot of money. But I told you already; I never blamed Larry for what happened to me, living in this rat infested..." He shook his head. "I don't blame other people for my own misfortunes. But I assure you, next time—if there ever is a next time—I won't be so foolish."

CHAPTER 15

I PARKED AT THE corner of the lot at Trucchi's Supermarket on Tremont Street to use the payphone and call Raymond.

Beth answered on the third ring. "Hello?"

"Hey Beth, it's me. Is Raymond around?"

"Jake? Where are you? He's been calling you."

"At home?" I said. "I haven't been there."

"I don't know. Hang on." The phone became muffled on the other end, and Beth yelled for Raymond before she came back on the line. "He's coming."

It took half a minute before Raymond picked up. "Jake? Where are you?"

"Taunton."

"What are you doing in Taunton?"

"I met with a friend of Larry Green's."

"Yeah, well that's why I've been looking for you. We need to talk." There was a touch of irritation in his voice.

I said, "Is everything all right?"

"I'm not sure. How come you didn't tell me your client was married to a cop?"

"You say that like I was hiding it from you," I said. "I was going to ask if you knew him."

"I did," Raymond said. "We were in the same precinct. I remember the night he was killed."

I waited, wondering if he was going to have more to say. "Why would you be mad at me about any of it?"

"I was just surprised you didn't tell me your client was his ex-wife, once you found out."

"I'm running around trying to piece this thing together," I said. "I haven't had a moment to piss. And I only had one dime." I had to think. "Who told you? Maggie?"

"No, I haven't talked to her. You want to know who told me?" He waited, as if to create unnecessary suspense. "Sean McCaffrey."

"McCaffrey? Detective McCaffrey? He called you? Why?"

"Because he knows you're my cousin. He knew my father too. He got wind you've been digging into the Larry Green case... He just wants to know what's going on."

"And he brought up Chuck Johnson?"

"Uh huh."

I paused, trying to get a feel for what Raymond had in mind. "What else did he say?"

"He wants to talk to you," he said. "He asked if I could get you to meet him."

"Where?"

"This place called Mickey's. It's north of Boston."

"How far north?"

"Over the line. New Hampshire."

I looked at my watch, using the streetlight in the parking lot to see the time. "It's kind of late to go up there now, isn't it?" The drive would be at least an hour. But if it meant meeting the detective who investigated Larry Green's death, it would be worth it. "You sure he'll still be there?"

"It sounded like he's there all night," Raymond said.

I thought about it for a moment. I didn't want to miss the opportunity. "Are you coming with me? Or—"

"I'll have to check with Beth," Raymond said. "You won't be here for, what, half hour?"

"I'll drive fast."

***

All eyes were on the TVs behind the bar when Raymond and I walked into a smoke-filled bar called Mickey's. A few heads turned to look our way, with the cold air that followed. A fireplace burned, and combined with the warmth and dark wood on the walls and the low lights, it appeared to be a decent place to have a few beers. And other than skiing, there wasn't much else to do in New Hampshire.

Most of the stools were taken, voices raised with everyone trying to talk over each other. The volume high on the game on the TV, I looked around for a guy who looked like a retired detective. I didn't know what McCaffrey looked like. And most of the male-leaning crowd of older, blue-collar patrons could've fit the description I had in my head.

Raymond had his gaze fixed at the far end of the bar from where we stood.

The bartender, a thin gray-haired man wearing a white buttoned shirt and tie with his sleeves rolled up past his elbows, gave me and Raymond a nod. "What are you gentlemen having?"

Raymond answered without asking me. "Black Label and a 'Gansett."

A lot of eyes were still on Raymond, with his size that gave him a presence most people couldn't claim.

The bartender nodded toward the empty table in the far corner. "You want to sit down over there, I'll bring them over."

Raymond slapped me on the arm. "Go grab a table." He walked past all the men at the bar and down to the far end, where the bar turned a corner and finished into the wall.

I went over and sat at the only empty table, watching Raymond go over to a man I suspected might've been McCaffrey. They shook hands, then both turned and looked over at me. The man tipped his head back and finished his mug of beer.

Raymond came over to the table and sat down across from me. "I think he's had a few."

I looked at the loud, crowded bar. "Is there anyone here who hasn't?"

Raymond smiled. "Yeah, me. But give me some time."

The bartender came over with a draft beer for Raymond and a 'Gansett bottle for me. "You boys want something to eat? Got corned beef tonight"

Raymond shook his head and said, "Go ahead, Jake. I already ate."

I was hungry, but also hesitant to order food until I talked to McCaffrey. The last thing I needed was a couple of beers on an empty stomach. "I'll have the corned beef."

The bartender said, "Cabbage and boiled potatoes?"

I nodded as he walked away, my mouth already watering.

I glanced over at the end of the bar where former detective Sean McCaffrey had been seated, but his stool was empty now.

I said to Raymond, "Where'd he go?"

But before he answered, McCaffrey walked out of the restroom and headed toward our table. He looked like he'd had more than a few, the way he stumbled, squeezing between the tables and the seated patrons.

With a stoic look on his reddened face, the man was shorter and older than I'd expected. He had a thick and bushy head of gray hair with a mustache just as full.

Raymond pointed at me when McCaffrey made it to our table. "Sean, this is my cousin, Jake."

McCaffrey shook my hand and pulled up a chair between me and Raymond. "I've heard your name around a bit," he said. "More so recently."

"I hope you don't hold anything against me," I said. "I get hired to do a job, and—"

"Yeah, no. Of course. We've all got a job to do, right?" His words were slurred. "As long as you don't try to make me look bad. I'd hate for anything to come back to bite me." He laughed and looked around the table and appeared as if he'd lost something, but then turned and looked back toward the bar. "Hang on. I forgot my beer." He went back over to the bar and picked up his empty pint glass, looking it over like he didn't realize he'd already finished it.

I watched him hold up the glass for the bartender. "Another one, Dicky?"

I said to Raymond, "I can't talk to the guy like this—three sheets to the wind."

Raymond sipped his beer. "Don't worry, he can handle it."

"Handle it?" I watched the bartender fill McCaffrey's glass from the tap and hand it to him.

Raymond said, "I don't know what to tell you. You want to get up and leave? We drove all this way, might as well talk to the guy." He took another sip of beer, his eyes toward the Bruins' game on the TV behind the bar.

McCaffrey walked back our way with his own fresh pint and placed it down, a splash of beer spilling over his hand and onto the table. He sat in the chair, then turned to look at the TV when the crowd at the bar and most of the patrons at the tables cheered.

Bruins right-winger Terry O'Reilly was trading punches with one of the Flyers' players, the linesmen trying to get in to break it up. Fred Cusick could be heard giving the play-by-play.

Or, blow-by-blow.

McCaffrey turned back from the TV. "Once in a generation you get an enforcer who can score the way O'Reilly does." He sipped his pint and leaned with his arms folded on the table.

I liked hockey, but I wasn't there to socialize. "Listen," I said. "I just want to make it clear... It's not my job to make law enforcement look bad. But it *is* my job to get to the truth, when that's what my client's looking for."

McCaffrey had a confused look on his face. "I'm not following. Unless... Are you trying to say I did something wrong?" He glanced at Raymond.

I shook my head. "That's not what I'm saying at all. But I know there wasn't much to the investigation. I mean, from what I understand, the case was closed fast."

"Fast?" McCaffrey leaned in closer to me, looking me right in the eye. "When something's as clear as this one, we don't need to dick around, keep looking for reasons to prove ourselves wrong. The man's balloon caught fire, and he fell to his death."

"It wasn't the burns?"

McCaffrey shook his head. "Autopsy showed it was the fall. I mean, being stuck in there while the thing burned didn't help him, but..." He looked like he wanted to smile as he lifted his glass and took a few good gulps.

"So you ruled everything else out?" I said. "There was no possibility there could've been foul play?"

McCaffrey shook his head without hesitation. Even though the guy had clearly had a few beers, and certainly had an Irish Whisper, he didn't come off as being incoherent.

He said, "We looked at all possibilities."

"Then I assume you know he had a lot of people out there who were upset with him," I said. "And that includes members of his own family."

McCaffrey held his stare on me, eyelids heavy. He waited a moment, like he was thinking. "Upset about what?"

I glanced at Raymond, and couldn't believe what I was hearing. "Didn't you talk to any of them? About his business? Or about the people that he owed money to?"

McCaffrey remained still, as he wasn't sure what to say. "Of course we spoke to his family. I mean, come on now, what kind of question is that?" He held his half-empty glass of beer against his sweater. "The man was having a hard time with his business. That was no secret, but—"

"Did you know his son had been gearing up to take over his dealership?" I said. "And that he was likely even working behind the scenes to make some changes his own father would have resisted?"

McCaffrey had a surprised look on his face. The guy clearly hadn't gone the extra mile to dig into anything other than what he saw on the scene. He said, "I don't know what you want from me. I have no doubt it was accidental. What else do you want me to say?" His tone had turned more defensive.

Raymond put his hand on McCaffrey's arm. "Listen, Sean. Jake here... He's just doing what his client's asking him to do. I told him you wouldn't take any of this personally."

McCaffrey pulled his arm back. "I get it. But I don't like the idea of being questioned about something as simple and straight-forward as this case had been. If there was someone else involved—if that's what you're implying—there would have been some evidence. But that balloon was completely destroyed by the time it landed. The man who owned the building said he came out and saw what was left of it burning on the ground. The gondola was nothing but ashes."

I turned and looked up at the hockey game on the TV, but it was intermission. I said to McCaffrey, "What if he was already dead? You ever think of that?"

"Already dead?" McCaffrey shook his head. "I'm sorry, but you're reaching. I mean, all the time that's passed, it's easy now to make these wild assumptions. But the fact is, there was hardly any evidence to begin with. I told you, the basket, or the gondola—whatever it's called... it was clear as day nobody would've survived."

He leaned his head back and finished the beer in his glass and placed it on the table, wiping his thick mustache with his hand.

I just stared back at him, straight-faced, giving Raymond a quick glance, like I wanted to say out loud: *I thought you said this guy was a decent detective*?

"Who's the witness?" I said. "The man who saw it land?"

"He didn't see it land. He was working in his shop, went outside and there it was on the ground. Or what was left of it."

"Does he have a name?" I said.

McCaffrey at first appeared hesitant, but finally responded. "Bill Pearson. He's a woodworker up there. Went outside and saw it hanging from the building."

"I thought you said it was on the ground?"

McCaffrey's Adam's apple jumped in his throat. "The envelope—the part people call the balloon—was hung up on some part of the building. What was left of the gondola, whatever hadn't completely burned, was smoldering on the ground. Bill called the fire department first. All that wood in his shop would all go up in flames. A big concern, of course."

I said, "So, this guy, Pearson... Just so I'm clear, you're saying he didn't see it fall from the sky?"

McCaffrey gritted his teeth and slammed his fist on the table. "Who the hell do you think you are?" He gave Raymond a quick glance, then shifted his gaze back to me. "You could go through every case of mine, going all the way back to my time in Boston, and... I'm not going to try to tell you I haven't made mistakes in my career, like every cop out there. You know how many cases I've investigated in my life?"

"I think what Jake's asking," Raymond said, "is if there's a chance Mr. Pearson knew more than what he'd let on at the time? Isn't that possible? That there could be more to it?"

McCaffrey laughed, shaking his head with his gaze on Raymond. "I think you're both hoping there are answers that don't exist." He stood up from the chair and grabbed his empty pint from the table. "I've got nothing else to say here." He walked over to the bar, tossed a few bills on it and grabbed his jacket from the coat rack on the wall and slipped it on. He walked out the door of the bar and into the darkness outside. A rush of cold air blew in before he closed the door behind him.

I turned to Raymond. "You think there's a chance he was this liquored-up during the investigation?"

Raymond shook his head. "No, that's not like him. But, like most detectives, he doesn't like being questioned about a case. Would you?"

I didn't have to respond. Raymond knew the answer.

CHAPTER 16

IT WAS ALMOST MIDNIGHT by the time I made it back into Boston, after dropping Raymond off at his house. Before heading home myself, I drove over to Maggie's apartment.

I knocked on her door and stood in the hallway of her apartment building waiting for what felt like five minutes until Maggie finally opened the door.

"Jake?"

Dressed in gray sweatpants and a matching crewneck sweatshirt that had Boston Police printed on the front, her eyes looked heavy. Her red hair hung past her shoulders and appeared curlier than normal. She looked me over. "What are you doing out so late?"

"I would've called first," I said, "But I didn't have change."

"It's okay." She pulled me in by my sleeve. "Come in." Her cat Max came over and rubbed against my leg. He was bigger than a small dog and at least twenty pounds. "I fell asleep on the couch."

A light came from the TV in the other room, the volume barely audible. A candle burned on the counter in the small kitchen, and smelled like a Christmas tree.

"You fell asleep?" I said. "With the candle burning?"

"I dozed off." She blew out the candle. "You want a beer?"

"No thanks," I said. "I just got back from New Hampshire. Had a couple already, at this place called Mickey's. Up in Salem."

"With who?"

"Raymond went up there with me. We met with Sean McCaffrey."

"McCaffrey?" she said. "You had beers with him?"

"I had a couple. But he had plenty more."

"But he talked to you? About Larry Green?"

I said, "He didn't like me questioning the investigation."

"Well, can you blame him?" She filled the kettle with cold water from the sink.

I pulled a chair out from under the table in front of the refrigerator and sat down. "I get the feeling I'm right about the fact that he didn't do much investigating with this one. Or he just got sloppy."

"Did you say that to him?"

"Well, he looked like he'd been drinking all evening. Long before we got there. So it wasn't what you'd call a smooth conversation. Either way, he couldn't answer most of my questions. Or didn't want to. Of course, he got a bit defensive. But apparently there was only one witness who saw the balloon. He wasn't clear about what the man saw."

"No?"

"Well, first he said the balloon landed on the building. The guy owns some kind of wood shop up there. But then it sounded like it was on the ground. And the man—the woodworker who owned the shop where it went down—apparently didn't see much of anything. At least not according to McCaffrey."

Maggie stood, leaning against the counter with her arms folded in front of her. "So, it doesn't sound like he was interested in helping you?"

I shook my head. "Not at all."

The kettle's whistle blew and Maggie took the water off the stove. She opened the cabinet. "I hear he could be a little gruff." She pulled down two mugs. "Are you going to have some tea?" She nodded toward the closed door to the pantry. "I can make you coffee. I have Folgers."

"Coffee wouldn't be bad," I said. I needed caffeine.

She opened the pantry and reached in for the jar, dropping a couple of spoonfuls into one mug.

I told her about the rest of what turned out to be a brief conversation with McCaffrey, although there wasn't much to it.

She poured the water into the mugs.

I got up and reached for the one with the coffee and accidentally bumped into Maggie as she was picking up her tea. Boiling hot water came up out of the mug and spilled onto her hand.

She didn't say anything or even make a noise, but grabbed her hand, squeezing it. "Shit, that hurt."

"I'm sorry, I..." I turned on the faucet, sticking my finger under to check for cold water. I grabbed her wrist and moved her hand so it was under the faucet. "Keep it there." I could see her fair skin was bright red around her hand. "Are you okay?"

We both stood close, up against each other. I tried to help her, close enough I could smell the sweet smell of her hair.

Maggie glanced back at me with her green eyes glowing in the light over our heads. "It's fine." She kept her hand under the running water.

I stepped away and moved both mugs to the table. "Maybe I should just stay out of your way."

She turned from the sink and smiled, wrapping her hand in a cloth from a drawer.

"Are you sure it's okay?" I said.

She nodded and sat at the table. "Are you saying you think there's a chance this woodworker might've seen something more?"

"I don't know. But he's the only one who saw much of anything. If I can talk to the guy, maybe get some answers."

Maggie said, "But what about the other witness who saw the balloon?"

"Someone saw it in the air, somewhere over 93. There might've been others, but supposedly nobody else came forward. I'm guessing the cops up there didn't spend much time looking for more witnesses either. If I can talk to this guy up there—Bill Pearson—maybe I can get the details of what he witnessed. If all he did was come outside his shop and see the balloon hanging off his roof, I'm not sure what he'll know."

Maggie unwrapped her hand from the towel, held it up and looked it over. "No blisters."

I smiled, sipping my coffee. "I'm going to go up there in the morning. To New Hampshire."

"You mean, to where the balloon landed?"

"Yeah. It's right over the line. The field Larry used to take off from, where he stored his balloon, was in Boston. I didn't know they could go that far, but I'm not some hot air balloon expert."

"What about Larry Green?" Maggie said. "Did he know what he was doing? As the pilot?"

"I suppose so," I said. "You must've seen him in his commercials, right?"

Maggie nodded, lifting her mug to her lips. She blew on it, the steam dancing off the top.

I said, "But it's a fair enough question, wondering how the balloon could make it all the way to New Hampshire?" I sipped the coffee. "I don't have the answer."

Maggie remained quiet, looking into her mug of tea for a moment before raising her gaze. "Are you starting to think he might've already been dead? Before the balloon took off?"

"It's a theory," I said.

"But, without anything left of the balloon, and no real physical evidence... How would you ever prove any of it, no matter what might've happened?"

"I think that's what McCaffrey was trying to say. There was nothing else available to prove it could have been anything other than an accidental fire."

"Don't you think he would've kept a fire extinguisher or something in there?" Maggie said.

"I don't know. You would think so, considering fires aren't exactly uncommon."

"Do you know exactly where his body was found?"

I shook my head. "I don't. Not precisely."

"Maybe have a look around the area?"

"Yeah, of course," I said, for a moment feeling somewhat annoyed with her having to make such a suggestion. But I knew she was only trying to help. "The fact is, physical evidence simply may not exist. I guess I'm hoping to come up with some real motives, if any exist."

She reached across the table and put her hand on top of mine. "This is why clients love you," she said, then pulled her hand back, acting almost as if she didn't mean to do it. She cleared her throat and stood from the table. "What about Trudy Bailey?"

"What about her? I don't know if—"

"No. I mean, when are you going to tell Detective Carter you think there could be a connection? If it turns out whoever killed that poor young woman might've been after Marilyn Green... It won't look good, Jake. If you didn't come forward with—"

"Are you worried about me? Or are you worried because I told you about it, and you're keeping quiet for my sake?"

Maggie paused before she answered. "Well, I guess it's both. I'm just being honest. You've put me in an awkward position, Jake. I can't even look the man in the eye right now. It's almost like he knows I'm holding something back."

"Would you rather just tell him?" I said.

"Me?" She shook her head. "It needs to be *you*. I already told you I don't want to be in the middle of it. And now…"

"I'm sorry I told you in the first place, then."

Maggie let out a sigh. "Don't you think if you tell him what you've come up with so far, there's a chance he might do what he can to help you with Larry Green's case?"

"I don't want his help. I just need more time," I said. "I want to go up to New Hampshire first, talk to the only witness, see what he saw that morning. And, while I'm up there I'll go see Marilyn."

"She's in New Hampshire?"

I wanted to smack myself. As much as I trusted Maggie, it made no sense for me to tell her where Marilyn had gone. Nobody needed to know. I said, "I just meant, on my way back. In the morning. I can't help but think there's a piece I'm missing."

Maggie said, "A piece you're missing? Or a piece your client's keeping from *you*?"

I shrugged and took another sip of coffee. "I haven't actually spoken to her one-on-one, without the uncle around. He likes to step in and answer her questions, like she's still a little kid."

Chapter 17

I rushed down the driveway, dragging the trash can behind me after seeing the garbage truck four houses away. The packed snow on the asphalt made it slippery, and I almost wiped out when I got to the street, but caught myself before I hit the ground. I avoided a nasty fall, but dropped the can. The lid fell off and rolled into the middle of the street. The two garbage bags ended up in the snow.

By the time the truck had stopped in front of the house, I'd gotten things cleaned up, both bags in the can with the cover on top. "Morning," I said to the two collectors as I tried to catch my breath in the cold air without breathing in the rotting odor floating out from the back of the truck.

I was already behind schedule and had increased the chance I'd get caught in rush hour traffic going through Boston.

But just as I opened the door, the phone rang. I rinsed my hands in the kitchen sink and grabbed the phone off the wall. I couldn't imagine who would call so early. "Hello?"

"Jake?"

I recognized the voice. "Who's this?"

"Detective Nick Carter," he said. "I'm following up on our discussion from the other day. I was hoping you could stop by headquarters again?"

I had to think through what to say. "Today?"

"I was thinking perhaps this morning," he said.

I didn't respond.

"Horn? You there?"

"Yeah, I'm here. I just... I'm kind of in the middle of something."

I was certain Carter growled through the phone. He said, "You do understand I'm in the middle of a murder investigation, don't you? And, to tell you the truth, we can't afford another unsolved case to start the year. We're not even out of January, and we're—"

"Okay," I said, checking my watch. "How about this afternoon?"

"How about being straight with me, huh? I'm hearing you've been hired by Larry Green's wife? Is that why you were asking about him?"

I didn't ask how he'd heard. I wondered if Maggie had said something, even if it wasn't intentional. "I assure you, I'm not trying to keep anything from you. In fact, if you want to know the truth... You might as well know I'm heading to New Hampshire this morning. I want to talk to some woodworker up there who allegedly owns the property where Larry Green's balloon landed."

Carter said, "But you didn't answer my question. Is that who hired you? Marilyn Green?"

I had promised Marilyn I'd keep it from the cops. But the cat was clearly already out of the bag. "All right," I said. "How about if I tell you what I know, but off the record? Is that possible?"

The other line went quiet, other than a whistle-like noise coming from the phone. I wondered if the man had a cold.

"This'd better be good," Carter said.

"Is it off the record?" I repeated.

It took him a moment to respond. "Sure."

"Okay, well, the story is that Marilyn Green was out there that night, down on K Street. And I don't know if there's a connection or not. There's a possibility someone's been following her. At least she's afraid that might be the case. And, well, I can't help but think there's a chance someone might've thought Trudy Bailey was Marilyn Green."

"What? That's what you've been keeping from me? Are you serious?" The line went quiet. "Just because she was in the area?"

"I don't know," I said. "Maybe, if it turns out Larry Green's death wasn't accidental, the fact she contacted me raised some red flags for whoever's responsible."

Carter said, "I don't understand."

"I told you I didn't have anything to share with you yet. I don't have any answers. But, what I do know is your buddy in New Hampshire didn't give the investigation much attention. I don't know if he had retirement on his mind, or..."

"McCaffrey? Did you ever hear me say he was my buddy?"

"Well, no, but—"

"Just because McCaffrey's a former Boston cop, doesn't mean he has anything to do with me."

"I know that. I'm just telling you something I—"

"Who the hell are you to decide whether or not a police investigation is thorough enough. It sounds to me you're not even sure your client's telling you the truth."

I looked at the clock on the stove. "Listen, I'm not trying to play games with you, detective. And if I had more information, I'd share it."

"You know, I could bring Mrs. Green in here for questioning."

"Questioning about what?"

"That young woman."

"You can't be serious," I said. "And didn't you say this was off the record."

Carter stayed quiet on the other end.

"Well, she's not around right now anyway," I said.

"What's that supposed to mean?"

"Exactly what I said. She's not around."

"Where is she?" Carter said.

"I don't know. She said she had to leave town. She didn't tell me where she was going."

There was *some* truth to that statement.

"Listen," I said. "I gotta run. When I have more to share, I will."

"Am I supposed to believe that?"

"You can believe what you want, detective."

"Watch it, Horn."

I was getting ready to hang up.

Carter said, "Can you tell me again why you're going to New Hampshire?"

I thought I'd made it clear, but perhaps Carter wasn't a listener. I said, "To talk to the man who allegedly saw what was left of the balloon that landed on his property. If I have any information or have reason to believe any of this has anything to do with the Trudy Bailey case, I'll let you know."

But all I heard from the other end was a dial tone.

***

Sure enough, the forty-minute ride to the New Hampshire line ended up taking an hour-and-a-half with traffic, thanks to my fiasco getting the garbage out to the curb and the call from Detective Carter.

I got off of 93 and turned onto Cross Street looking for a gas station and payphone, finally spotting Zeke's Exxon a half mile from the highway. I pulled the Nova next to the pump, and a man bundled up in a hooded coat came out of the building and over to me.

I handed him a five. "Hopefully that fills it up. I'm going to go use the phone."

He gave me a nod without saying a word, and I hurried over to call Nancy. I figured she was in classes anyway, but being that I was in New Hampshire—even if it was over an hour away—I'd feel bad if I didn't at least give her a call.

I dropped a dime into the slot. The phone in her dorm rang six times before one of her dorm mates finally picked it up.

"Hello?" The young woman who answered sounded like she'd just woken up.

"Hi, this is Nancy's dad. Is she around?"

"Oh, hello Mr. Horn," she said, but didn't tell me her name. I'd met a lot of Nancy's friends, but never knew who was who by the voice. "Nancy's at class right now. Do you want me to leave her a message?"

"Maybe just tell her I called. I'm just checking in. I'll try her again later. You don't know when she'll be back, do you?"

"Sorry, I don't," the girl said. "But I'll tell her you called. Maybe try her in a couple of hours?"

"Okay. I'll do that," I said. "Bye." I hung up.

I was disappointed. But I hoped she'd call me back at the house or the office.

I put another coin into the phone, then pulled the paper with the number to the house where Marilyn Green was supposed to be staying. I didn't even know the address—and hadn't asked for it—although I knew she was somewhere in New Hampshire.

The phone rang three, four, five times while I hung on the line, expecting someone to answer. But by the ninth or tenth ring, I hung up. I stuck my finger in to grab my dime, then dug into my pockets for more change, and counted eighty-five cents. Enough for a toll call into Massachusetts.

I dialed Nathan Howell's house in Newton, hoping he'd answer. It took two rings for him to pick up. "Hello?"

"Mr. Howell? It's Jake Horn."

"Oh, Jake. Yes... I was wondering if I was going to hear from you."

"I'm in New Hampshire," I said. "I just called the number you gave me for Marilyn and nobody answered. So I was wondering if you've spoken with her?"

"I don't think it's smart for you to go see Marilyn. Do you? What if someone—"

"I'm not up here to see Marilyn. But I thought I'd call her. I'm going to talk with the man who owns the property where Larry's balloon landed."

"Bill Pearson?" Howell said. "I remember the name."

"Did you ever speak to him?"

There was a brief pause. "We tried," he said.

"But you never spoke to him?"

"Marilyn drove up to his workshop one time. She was alone, and whoever she spoke to said he wasn't there, but she felt whoever it was, was lying."

"Maybe I'll have better luck." I was curious, however. I said, "What made you want to talk to him?"

"Well, I guess I'm not exactly sure. He seems to be the only person who saw anything. We just thought maybe we could get a better understanding of what he saw. The police up there didn't seem to have much to report, other than the obvious."

"Well, I'll see what I can find out. I'd also like to find the other witness who saw the balloon. I find it odd there was nobody else."

"I agree," Nathan Howell said. "But the person—a woman—didn't see it on fire or see it going down. So, apparently she wasn't much help."

"Well, I'll try to talk to her," I said. "I'm interested in hearing what Mr. Pearson has to say, and whether he actually saw the balloon land."

"Why would that matter?" he said.

"Well, I'm just thinking out loud here, but if there's a chance the balloon was placed there, like it was staged..."

"You think so?" Howell said.

"Just some ideas I'm thinking through, that's all." I looked at my watch. "Listen, I need to get moving. I'm not far from Pearson's shop now. But, if you talk to Marilyn, can you tell her to give me a call at my office? I should be back sometime this afternoon."

Chapter 18

I drove past the sign for Pearson's Woodworks and continued slowly on a narrow road covered with a mix of hard-packed snow and frozen mud. The two-story barn ahead was surrounded by tall pine trees with power lines running high along the road.

The sky was gray and overcast, the lights inside the building glowed from between closed curtains on the windows. Heading for the entrance, I walked past a Ford pickup truck parked near the door. A brass bell hung on the exterior wall above the sign with the hours of business listed.

I went inside to the faint and whirring sound of a power saw that seemed to come from another area of the barn. The smell of fresh-cut wood and chemical smells surrounded me.

"Hello?" I said, standing by a counter made of a half-sawn tree trunk with a phone and cash register on top. An aluminum coffee can filled with carpenters' pencils had 5 CENTS EACH written in pencil on masking tape stuck to the can.

The area at the entrance was small, with an open doorway a few feet from where I stood. A curtain hung across it.

I called out, "Hello? Anybody here?"

The sound of a saw grew louder as I pushed the curtain aside and stepped through the doorway. I'd entered another room filled with wood furniture, from tables and chairs to dressers and cabinets, some finished and stained, others raw wood.

But there was nobody there.

I went through another doorway, this time with an actual door that was closed. I opened it. "Mr. Pearson?" There was a sign—carved, of course—that hung on the closed door: DO NOT ENTER. To the right of the door was a plain piece of wood hanging from a piece of leather nailed into the wall. Written on it, in black marker: *No customers allowed in the workshop without permission from the owner.*

I knocked on the door. "Mr. Pearson? Are you in there?" The power equipment made a high-pitched whirring sound that hadn't stopped. I turned the knob and opened the door. I poked my head in to look, noticing a table saw amongst the machines and power equipment, toward the back of the area.

The saw was running, there didn't appear to be anyone using it.

"Mr. Pearson?" I said, my voice raised. Looking back and forth and toward the sawdust-covered wood floor, I continued toward the running table saw.

I was five feet away from it when I saw two boots on the floor, toes up, sticking out from behind the large wooden box-like structure the table saw sat on top of.

I stepped around, looked down and saw a body. An older man was lifeless on the floor. He had blood on his chest and coming from his forehead, the blood pooled up under him.

I killed the power and kneeled down next to the man, feeling under his bloodied jaw for a pulse.

There wasn't one.

He had all his limbs and fingers, from what I could see. Looking at the blood on his clothes, my first thought was he'd been shot.

I ran through the door I'd just come through and grabbed the phone at the front counter by the entrance. But when I picked it up, there was no dial tone. I clicked the switch numerous times, tapping it to see if I could get a connection, but no luck.

It had started to snow outside. I needed to find a phone, but there didn't appear to be any neighbors or other buildings anywhere in sight, from what I could see.

I jumped in the Nova and took off down the driveway and drove for a little less than a mile, to where I saw a small, white Cape Cod home with blue shutters set back from the road. I jumped out of the Nova and ran for the door, ringing the doorbell. It took a couple of moments, but an old woman came to the door.

Before she asked, I told her what had happened. "Call the police," I said.

***

I was outside Pearson's Woodworks when two police vehicles arrived, one a Ford Bronco, the other a sedan, lights flashing, followed by an ambulance and an unmarked vehicle behind it.

The officers got out of the cars, one holding his hand on his holster, as if ready to draw his gun as he came toward me.

"You the one who called?" he said. The officer was tall and wide, built like a bear, his stomach hanging well over his belt. "Can I see some identification?" He glanced at the Nova. "Is that your vehicle?"

"Yes, sir," I said, my nerves acting up a bit, considering I didn't know many New Hampshire cops.

The officer nodded at the door I'd left open and said to the other cop, "Why don't you go take a look. I'll be right in."

The second officer, young and tall with a thin build, nodded, but I could see by the look on his face he wasn't looking forward to it. I didn't know what the crime rate was in the small town of Derry, but I imagined the cop was young enough he might've been walking into his first fatal scene.

"You know Bill?" the older of the two said, looking over my driver's license.

"Actually, no," I said. I was hesitant to tell him why I was there, but I likely didn't have much of a choice. "I'm a private investigator. From Boston."

The man looked up from my license. "You have some kind of business with Bill?"

"Sort of," I said, and decided not to go into specifics.

But it didn't work.

"What's 'sort of' mean?" he said.

"Well, uh, to be honest..." I thought about making up a story, but knew it would only get me in trouble. "There was a hot air balloon accident, the balloon that landed right here on Mr. Pearson's property?"

The cop nodded. "What about it?"

"Well, I'm just working on something," I said, hoping I didn't have to go into more detail about it.

The officer looked at my license one more time, then handed it back to me. "Let me go in, see what the story is." He opened the door and held it open for me. "You want to give me the details of what you found when you first got here? Maybe walk me through it?"

"Sure, I can do that," I said, following him inside.

"I'm Chief Williams," he said, holding the door. "So, what'd you do when you first walked in here?"

I told him every step I took, and how I heard the saw running, called for Mr. Pearson, and didn't get a response. "I walked back there, knocked on the door to his shop, where the power tools are. Hearing the saw running, I just assumed he was in here doing some work."

The chief continued ahead of me, through the open door to where the other officer stood, with two paramedics over the body.

One paramedic looked toward us. "Dr. Harper's on his way."

"Who's Dr. Harper?" I said.

Chief Williams crouched down next to the body, looking it over. "County medical examiner." He fixed his gaze on the other young officer, who appeared to have lost some color in his face. "Why don't you go outside and get yourself some air." He stood up and turned to me. "So, what is it you were hoping to learn from Bill about that balloon, beyond what we already know?"

I didn't really have a good answer, because I hadn't exactly thought it all through. "I just wanted to ask him what he saw that morning, with the hot air balloon. I imagine it was pretty rough."

"That it was," the chief said. "A freak accident."

"Was it?" I said, wishing I had kept my mouth shut as soon as the words left my mouth.

"The detective on the case, Detective McCaffrey... he's from down your neck of the woods. I think you'd be making a mistake if you're suggesting he did something wrong."

"He's human," I said. "We all make mistakes."

The chief laughed. "So, you think coming up here all these months later, you'd find some kind of clue that'd crack a case that's already closed?"

"Honestly?" I said. "I don't know what I would have found. You never know what someone'll say, you ask the right questions."

"Thanks for the advice, Mr. Horn," Williams said, almost a snort coming out his nose.

I had some theories rolling around in my head, but none of them were any more than a hunch. The chance of a balloon landing on what looked like a tiny piece of land, with very little clearance, seemed odd to me. But if this turned out to be staged, what would be the reasoning for not only choosing a woodworker to help, but to do it all the way up in New Hampshire?

"With all due respect, Chief," I said, "I can't really explain much of anything right now without making it sound like a bunch of hogwash."

I'd never used the word *hogwash* before. I wasn't even sure how it came out of my mouth.

The chief said, "I'm just trying to decide why you think you had a good enough reason to come all the way up here from Boston to see Mr. Pearson when, you ask me, a simple phone call could've done the trick."

"You think I'm lying?" I was sure the look on my face came off as a bit smug. "Why would I call you to report he was dead, if I had something to do with what happened here?"

The chief said, "Just like you were saying, I also have some questions I'm going to need to have answered. The thing is, Mr. Horn, when a stranger shows up in my town like this, without good enough reason, and one of our citizens ends up dead, well..." He looked toward the door and yelled for the other officer.

The young man poked his head in the door. "Chief?"

The chief looked over at him. "Why don't you take Mr. Horn here outside and get a written statement from him, huh?" Chief Williams gave me a nod with his chin. "You're free to go, after he's done with you." He took my business card from his coat pocket and looked it over. "But you can expect I'll be in touch over the next day or two."

CHAPTER 19

By the time I made it back to Boston, the spaces on both sides of East Broadway were all taken, with no parking in sight for at least two blocks in either direction from my office. I drove slowly, hoping someone would leave and open up a space. But the drivers behind me didn't like it, horns blowing every time I tapped my brakes.

I finally turned down Emerson for at least a couple of blocks to where a friend of my Uncle Pat's owned a place called Jerry's Dry Cleaning. His building backed up to an alley where he had a couple of spaces, and he was usually okay with me parking there.

Lucky for me, at least there was an available space where the snow had been shoveled, between the dumpster and the back door. I went inside into the hot and steamy back room of the building with the industrial washing machines roaring. Two middle-aged women were folding clothes.

"Is Jerry around?" I said.

Both women nodded and one answered in broken English, "In front."

I walked past them and poked my head out through the doorway to the front. Jerry, short and bald with white hair around the sides of his head, stood behind the counter helping a customer.

I said, "Hey, Jerry?"

He looked over his shoulder at me. "Hi Jake. What are you doing back here?"

"I hope it's okay, I parked the Nova by the dumpster. East Broadway's full. Traffic's a mess."

"Yeah, yeah, of course Jake. No problem at all. As long as you get it out of there by morning?"

"No problem," I said. "I'll only be at the office a couple hours."

Jerry gave me a wave and went back to helping his customer on the other side of the counter.

I walked through the back room and out the door into the alley, making sure the Nova was locked up before I started the long walk to my office.

Paths were cleared through the piles of snow, from the back doors of each shop to the narrow pathway going down the alley. The snow piles took up most of the space, with ice formed on the asphalt making it slippery. Someone had put down sand. I had gloves on, and kept my hands out of my pockets, in case I had to catch my fall.

There was a cut-through at the far end of the building, which was better than walking out the way I drove in. Once I got out to Emerson, I knew of a few other shortcuts to get me to my office quicker than if I'd stayed on the streets.

I was maybe fifty yards from the cut-through between the two buildings on either side, and turned to look back when I had a weird feeling someone besides me was in the alley.

A man wearing a knitted black winter hat with dark sunglasses—there wasn't any sunlight in the alley—and a long, dark coat, unbuttoned with the hem swinging the more he picked up his pace.

At first, I thought—or *tried* to think—nothing of it. I continued toward the cut-through from the alley, my gaze on the opening between the buildings.

But then another man, dressed in similar fashion to the other but somewhat smaller, stepped out from the opening I was headed for, and stood there as if waiting for me.

I glanced over my shoulder, and the one behind me had picked up his pace, almost into a jog. I looked ahead again, and the other man had started toward me.

I knew it wasn't good, looking around the snow-covered ground for something—anything—to make what I guessed was about to be a fight a fair one.

I looked back and forth from one man to the other, knowing I had nowhere to go. "You sure you want to do this?" I said, and decided my first move was going to be to choose one or the other.

I picked the bigger one, spun around as soon as he was close enough and threw a punch before he even had a chance to react. The sunglasses flew off his face and landed in the snow. The big man stumbled back, but caught his footing on a mound of snow and came right at me, taking a couple of wild swings.

I got a good look at his face as his fists were flying, but I'd never seen him before.

One of his wild swings came inches from making a connection, but I ducked out of the way at the last second and hit him with an uppercut, catching him square under the chin. I'm sure his feet came off the ground when I hit him.

He spun around as he fell, landing face-first in the mound of snow.

But just as I turned to deal with my other friend, I felt cold, hard pain shoot through my brain. Cracked with something hard on the back of my head, I caught a glimpse of the man's hand coming toward me again. He had a pistol in his grip.

With the warmth of my own blood dripping down my ice-cold ears, I lowered my shoulder and charged the man, striking him in his chest. I drove him across the alley to the other side, over a mound of snow and into the brick wall.

But even though the man was shorter than me, he was built like a bull. I was sure he'd cracked the back of his head against the bricks, but his thick muscular body bounced from the wall. He grabbed me and spun me around like a small child, tossing me onto the ice-covered asphalt.

I had landed on my stomach. My chin bounced when it hit the cold, hard ground. More warm blood.

Before I could push myself up, the first man I thought I'd taken care of was already up on his feet. He pulled a gun from the back of his waist and had it pointed at me, breathing heavily as he walked toward me, wiping the blood from his mouth with the back of his black leather glove.

He stood over me. "Turn around," he said. I looked away and stared at the snow beneath me. I felt the gun's muzzle pressed against my skull. "Close your eyes."

"For what?" I said. "If you're going to shoot me, what's the difference?"

The other man—the bull—was on the other side of me. I could see his boots coming close to my face, and feared I was about to get kicked in the mouth.

The tall one said, "You need to learn to mind your business."

"Mind my business?" I said. "I *was* minding my business. You're the one who just showed up and—"

"Shut your mouth," the man yelled, placing his boot on my back, the gun still pressed against my skull.

My face was numb, touching the snow now. I wanted to get a look at either one of the two, but moving my head didn't seem to be an option. The boots that were next to my face were no longer there, and I wondered where the short and stocky one had gone.

But I found out when he drove his boot into my ribs. I couldn't breathe, coughing. "What... What do you want? My wallet? It's in my front pocket."

I didn't have much cash.

"I told you," the tall one said. "You are going to mind your own business uh? Larry Green's death was an accident. There's nothing else you need to know about. You understand?"

"I don't know what you're talking about," I said. "Who's Larry Green?"

The heavy boot pressed against my back.

The tall one said, "Do I make myself clear?"

I coughed again, causing my ribs to hurt even more. "Honestly?" I said. "I wouldn't say so."

I wasn't sure I deserved another kick, but that's exactly what I got. At least it wasn't in the ribs, although I was sure I'd ruptured a kidney.

"All right, all right," I said. "I get it. You don't want me to investigate." I had a feeling, by that point, they weren't going to shoot me. I hoped I was right, and tried to get another look at either of the two men, turning my head, praying there were no more kicks coming. "Who sent you?"

The two men lifted me by my arms, throwing me into a brick wall I bounced off of and landed deep into a mound of snow. And when I tried to push myself up, my hands sank. When I finally got up and turned around, both men were gone.

CHAPTER 20

I WAS IN THE kitchen at my grandmother's house back in Milton looking into the empty fridge. Raymond walked in the front door, carrying a six-pack of Narragansett beer. He pulled a can from the plastic rings and handed it to me.

"I figured you could use a drink," he said, pulling another one off for himself. He put the four remaining cans in the fridge and looked me over. "They got you pretty good, huh?"

I sat down at the table with the beer and a bag of frozen peas. I moved the bag from the back of my head to my ribs, unsure which needed it more.

Raymond said, "You sure you don't need x-rays?"

I shook my head, and felt pain on my side when I did.

Raymond went over to the sink and looked at the bloody towel I left. "You've never seen these guys before?"

"Not that I could see. Just a couple of hoodlum Italians, from what I could tell."

"Mob?" Raymond said.

"No idea. One of 'em was tall though, about my height. Which of course is odd for an Italian."

Raymond said, "What about you? You're tall."

"I'm only half Italian, as you know." I took another sip of my beer. I was hesitant to say what was on my mind, but Raymond wasn't dumb. "The only other people besides you and Maggie who knew I was going up to talk to Bill Pearson was Sean McCaffrey and Detective Carter."

"You told McCaffrey you were going up there? I didn't hear that."

"I think it was implied," I said.

"Well, either way. Probably too soon to be jumping to any conclusions," Raymond said.

"What are you, going to defend them now?" I said. "Just because they wear—or wore—the badge? And, besides. He was dead when I got up there. At least an hour before. So someone wanted to make sure he'd shut up before I got there."

Raymond sipped his beer and stood from the table, strolling over to the window where he stopped and looked out toward the street. "You think these two were the ones in that yellow sedan you said had been following you?"

"I didn't see a vehicle," I said.

"And you never got the make, when you saw it at your client's house?" Raymond turned from the window.

"I never got close enough," I said. "But if I had to guess, it was an Impala."

The phone rang, and I winced from the pain that shot through my ribs when I turned to get up and answer it. "Hello?"

"Hey Jake. It's Maggie. I got your message. I went by your office to see if you were there, but, obviously you're not. Is everything okay?"

"I guess so. I was jumped by a couple of thugs in the alley behind Jerry's Dry Cleaning."

"What? Are you okay?"

"Sure."

"What were you doing in the alley?" she said.

"Parking. Maybe I should've been a little more patient looking for a spot on the street."

Maggie paused on the other end. "And you're sure you're okay?"

"I'm fine."

Maggie paused again, almost as if she was doing something else. "Are you going to file a report?"

"With the police?" I said. "For what?"

"Because it's illegal to attack another human." I expected her to laugh when she said it, but she did not.

I went ahead and gave her the brief rundown of my morning, going up to New Hampshire, finding the man dead, and ending up face down and bloodied in the alley.

"And now, I'm having a beer," I said. "With Raymond."

"You're drinking?" Maggie said.

"Yeah, why not? Calms the nerves, you know." I took a drink from the can. "I'm surprised you hadn't heard about what happened in New Hampshire."

"I've been running around all day," she said. "It's my day off. I haven't even been home. I'm a little out of the loop."

"Well, I'll fill you in on who knew I was going up there," I said.

Raymond murmured, "Here he goes again, blaming the cops..."

"What did he say?" Maggie said, clearly hearing Raymond's deep voice through the phone.

"He doesn't like that I brought up the fact Nick Carter knew I was going up to Derry to see that man. I spoke with him in the morning. And, the night before, I told you I met with Detective Mc-Caffrey. If that's simply a coincidence that both men knew, then..."

"I"m going to have to side with Raymond here, Jake. Just because you brought down one detective doesn't mean you need to make it your M.O. to after the whole department."

"I never said it was my M.O. But you have to admit..."

Maggie said, "Carter's one of the best detectives we have. Don't you remember he was behind taking down two fellow officers himself, about ten years ago? He's not a crooked cop, if that's what you're trying to imply."

"I'm not. But it doesn't mean I shouldn't ask questions when he knew I was going up there to talk to Mr. Pearson."

"I get what you're saying," Maggie said. "But, I promise you Carter had nothing to do with it."

"You promise?" I let out a slight laugh, but could tell by Maggie's serious tone she didn't find any of it funny.

She said, "How long are you going to be at the house?"

"I don't know. I need to go get something to eat. I might head into the office."

Maggie paused. "Then how about I pick up sandwiches and meet you there? Is Raymond going with you?"

I pulled the handset from my ear and asked him, "You want to come with me to Boston?"

Raymond looked at me funny. "You're going there now?"

"I need to get back to the office," I said.

He shrugged, then nodded. "Okay, I'll take a ride."

I said into the phone, "We'll be there in twenty."

"Give me time to get sandwiches. I'll see you there." Maggie hung up, and I stood still, thinking for a moment, before I hung the handset on the wall.

I said to Raymond, "What I don't understand is why these two men didn't just shoot me dead. Why bother with a warning? If these guys are killers..."

Raymond said, "You should feel good about the fact you're alive, no?"

"Yeah, yeah, of course. But don't you think, there's got to be a reason?"

We both sat quiet. "We should leave in a couple of minutes, in case we hit traffic."

The phone rang again, and I jumped up, thinking maybe it was Maggie again.

"Hello?"

"Dad? Hey…"

A smile landed on my face. "Nancy, how's it going? You got my message?"

"I did. But I was in class. But then I had to go find some change."

"Didn't I give you a few rolls of quarters to take back with you?"

"It doesn't last long," she said.

"But I gave it to you for phone calls. Not the soda machine."

Nancy laughed, then her tone turned serious. "Is everything all right?"

"Yeah, of course. Good. Why?" I didn't want to worry her.

"I don't know. Your voice sounds a little… Like something's wrong."

Nancy was intuitive, always able to read emotions, sometimes just by someone's actions, or by the sound of a person's voice. She could easily sense someone's mood, or if something was bothering someone.

"I'm in the middle of a case," I said, hoping that was enough of an explanation, in case she had picked up something in my voice. "You know how it goes."

Nancy said, "I was in class a little while ago, and the teacher told us about a murder in Dover, New Hampshire. It happened this morning."

"Your teacher knew about it?" I said.

"He's a former trooper with New Hampshire State Police. He keeps a police scanner in the classroom."

"Oh, uh…" I was surprised she already knew about it. "But you didn't get the details yet?" I said.

"No, not really. He didn't say." She said, "Did you know about it?"

I was hesitant at first to tell her the truth. But I also needed her to be careful. And she was of course going to ask questions. That's just how she was.

"Actually," I said. "I was there. I'm the one who discovered the body." I paused. "I want you to be careful. Keep your eyes peeled, like I always tell you. And if you see anything you don't like, call security or the police right away."

The line went silent.

She said, "But you said nothing was wrong. Now you're telling me to..." I could hear in her voice that she was worried.

"I don't want you to worry. Just pay attention out there. That's all. Same as always."

She took a moment before responding. "Are you in some kind of trouble?"

"It's got to do with this case I'm involved with."

"The man who died in the hot air balloon?" she said.

I realized there was little I could keep from her, especially the older she got, and the more she understood. So I gave her more details about Bill Pearson, and how he was the one who had originally reported the balloon landing—on fire—on his property.

"Is everything going all right with school?" I said, trying to ease her worry and change the subject.

"It's going well," she said. "But I want to know more about your case. Do you have any idea who might've killed this man?"

"I don't know anything at all right now. I wish I did." I felt a sense of regret come over me, like I was far from having any answers.

Another young woman's voice was in the background saying something I couldn't make out.

Nancy said, "Can I call you later? I have to get to class. Someone needs the phone."

"Of course," I said. "Call me anytime you want. But just do me a favor, like I said, keep your eyes peeled."

"But you haven't really said why," she said.

I said, "I just want you to be careful. Always."

I could hear her sigh through the phone.

"Okay," she said. "I'll be careful. Love you." She hung up.

Raymond was standing by the sink, looking out the window. He turned to me. "Is she doing okay?"

"Nancy?" I nodded, picking up the can of beer I didn't feel like finishing. Raymond was retired. Having an afternoon beer was part of his day. For me, it didn't seem to help me relax the way it used to.

I walked to the sink and pushed the blood-stained towel aside, dumping my beer down the drain.

"What are you doing?" Raymond said, his eyebrows raised. "That's perfectly good beer."

"I'm sorry," I said. "All it's going to do is put me to sleep."

Chapter 21

Maggie showed up at my office with a greasy brown paper bag she handed to me as she walked in the front door. "I picked up some spuckies," she said.

Not everyone in Boston called an Italian sub a *spuckie*. But born and raised in the city, Maggie never thought to call it anything else.

I carried the bag over to the folding table with the coffee maker on top and a mini-fridge underneath, along with some mugs and a stack of paper plates.

Raymond was behind my desk, on the phone.

"Who's he talking to?" Maggie gave him a nod when she walked past him.

"A statie he knows up in New Hampshire, trying to get some information on Bill Pearson's murder."

"I made a couple of calls myself before I came over," Maggie said. "Words already out about what happened up there, and there are whispers about a connection to Larry Green."

"I'll be honest," I said. "I was starting to have doubts about it myself, until I saw Bill Pearson dead."

We were both quiet while Raymond was talking a few feet away on the phone.

I opened the bag of sandwiches, each rolled in waxed paper, and placed them on plates. I handed one to Maggie. "We can eat at my desk." I carried the other two plated sandwiches. We walked over to the two chairs across from Raymond, who was seated in the big leather chair that actually belonged to his father. "Here," I said, sliding the plate in front of him.

Raymond gave me a thumbs-up, the phone still to his ear.

Maggie and I both sat down with plates on our laps. It wasn't the best setup in the office for dining.

I kept my voice low so as not to disturb Raymond's call. "The one person I thought about, as soon as I walked into that workshop and saw all this really nice, custom wood furniture, was Richard Reagan."

"He's the friend you spoke to?"

"A friend of Larry Green's," I said, just to make sure it was clear.

Maggie held her sandwich and turned her head, about to take a bite.

I nodded, unwrapping my sandwich and sticking a loose sliced pickle in my mouth. "Reagan's the man who seems to've lost the most, with the dealership failing."

"But he wasn't any kind of owner?" she said.

"An investor," I said. "He was supposed to get the money he sunk into after so many years. He'd been hoping the dealership would get turned around."

Maggie said, "Did he indicate he felt there was a better chance of it with Green's son taking over?"

I took a bite of my sandwich and nodded, trying to finish what was in my mouth so I could answer. "It's certainly a motive."

I guessed we were making it hard on Raymond to hear on the other end of the phone when he stood up from behind the desk and stretched the phone's cord to get away from us, to the other side of the partition, a tall and wide paneled wall that divided my work area from the client seating area.

The client seating area was nothing more than an old leather couch and a coffee table left from the old days when my uncle was still around. On some late nights, I used the couch as my bed.

I said to Maggie, "Reagan used to be in the furniture business, but got out of it about ten years ago. After he sold it, he invested the money he made in Larry Green's business."

"But what's the connection between Reagan and Bill Pearson?"

I shrugged, taking another bite of my sandwich. "All I know is that Pearson made custom furniture. I had no reason to ask at the time if Reagan knew Bill Reardon. But I'm going to ask. It would make sense, wouldn't it?"

"It can't be just a coincidence," Maggie said.

"No more than a coincidence Detective Carter knew I was going up to New Hampshire."

Maggie was chewing what she'd just bitten off, finished and wiped her mouth. "You have to get off that idea."

I put my sandwich on the desk and stood. "You want a cola?" I didn't wait for an answer, grabbed three glass bottles of RC from the mini-fridge and placed them on the desk.

Raymond came back around from the other side of the partition. He hung up the phone. "There's a problem," he said.

"What's that?" I stopped chewing and exchanged a quick glance with Maggie.

"Somebody claims to've seen your car up there, earlier than when you'd told the police you arrived."

"My car?" I said, shaking my head. "That's not possible."

"Word just came through when I was talking to my buddy up there."

I thought for a moment, but then it hit me. "What about the Impala? It had to've been them; the two goons who jumped me. It makes sense, they got up there in time to kill Pearson before I got there."

"I didn't say anything about that," Raymond said. "The guy I spoke to's a trooper. He's not involved in the investigation. Derry Police are running the show."

I didn't want to panic, but I was worried this was going to come down on me harder than I'd expected. I said, "I met the chief of police up there, and he was acting a bit suspicious for no other reason than I was the one who happened to find the body."

"And you're not from Derry," Maggie said. "Small town like that, an outsider shows up and there's a dead man…"

"Exactly," I said. "But, now, someone claims they saw a yellow vehicle? And the chief even asked me about my car. But that was before they'd started talking to witnesses." I glanced at the phone on the desk. "I'm surprised he hasn't called me yet."

***

I dropped Raymond off at his house after we left the office and headed to Taunton. Maggie didn't think it would be a good idea for her to join me, but promised me she'd swing by the station and see what else she could dig up.

There was a bit of traffic on Route 44, and by the time I got to Reagan's apartment, the sun had already disappeared. There were flurries hitting the windshield, and I turned the radio to WBZ to make sure there wasn't some kind of storm coming I wasn't aware of.

It was the last thing we needed.

When I pulled into the driveway at the triple-decker, the only lights on inside were on the first and third floor. Richard's apartment appeared dark inside.

I walked up the steps coated with a dusting of snow, and saw the building's door cracked open by an inch or two. I didn't bother knocking and instead pushed it open. I closed it behind me, being careful not to make a lot of noise. I tried to be quiet going up the curved stairs, but they creaked with each step.

When I got to Reagan's door, it too was open. I knocked. "Hello?"

I heard something. A groan, perhaps. But it was hard to tell.

"Hello?" I knocked again.

The same sound came from somewhere in the apartment. I eased the door open. "Reagan?" Taking a step inside, I felt around for the light switch on the wall. "Are you home?"

Again, more groans, but louder this time.

I felt around for at least another minute and found the switch on the wall, flipping it to turn the lights on in the first room I'd entered.

"Richard?" I walked toward the dark kitchen, the glow from the front room enough that I could just about see where I was going. I felt around and found another switch on the wall. "Are you here?" I said, and Mr. Reagan had his head down on the table, arms folded under it like a pillow. At least a dozen empty cans of Black Label beer were on top of the table and on the floor.

I tried to move him. "Reagan? Are you all right?"

He moaned, but wouldn't lift his head.

I pulled the chair back and pulled his upper body back. He was just about limp, but he opened his eyes.

The man had dried blood on his chin, one of his eyes half closed.

"What happened?" I said, trying to lift the man from the chair and bring him to the front room. I could only guess he'd been beaten up, but there was also a chance he'd fallen down, as drunk as he appeared, and cracked his face on a piece of furniture.

I slipped my head under his arm and helped him from the chair, dragging the man—nothing but dead weight—down the hall where I plopped him into the leather recliner.

He had his eyes open, looking up at me like he wasn't sure who I was. Or where he was. "What are you... I didn't do nothin'," he said, mumbling and slurring his words.

"It's Jake," I said. "Jake Horn. The private detective."

The man cracked a small grin, nodding. "Okay." He closed his eyes, and his head slumped forward.

"Mr. Reagan," I said, pushing him back. But he wasn't with it enough to get a full sentence out of his mouth. I went into the kitchen, got him a glass of water from the sink, and brought it back. "Here, drink this." I had to take his hand and wrap it around the glass.

He took it, had a few gulps with most of it going down his chin and taking some of the dried blood on his face with it. His eyes opened, then closed.

I went back into the kitchen and looked for a coffee machine, but he didn't seem to have one. Opening the empty cabinets, I couldn't even find any coffee to make for him. Not until I got to the last cabinet, and inside found a jar of Taster's Choice.

There was an empty stainless steel pot on the stove, so I boiled some water in it. I checked on Reagan, and he had fallen asleep in the recliner. Once the water boiled, I rinsed a stained cup from the sink and brought a coffee out to him.

Reagan was upright in the recliner, snoring, but when I woke him, his eyes popped open. Staring straight ahead with one eye open, he looked at me like it was the first time he'd ever seen me. "Who are you?"

"Jake Horn." I handed him the cup. But I was afraid he was going to drop it. "You got it?"

He grabbed it from me, nodding, and took a sip. "You're that P.I. from Boston, right?"

I nodded.

"How'd you get in here?"

"Both doors were open," I said. "What happened?"

He sipped the coffee again, then cleared a space on the coffee table so he could put the cup down. "Nothing."

"Nothing?" I stood over him. "It doesn't look like *nothing*. Did somebody do this to you?"

He waved his hand at me and coughed, fixing the red scarf he had around his neck. He touched his head. "Where's my hat?"

I looked around the room and saw a knitted hat with a pompom sticking out from under a newspaper on the floor. "Tell me what happened," I said, handing the hat to him. "Who did this to you?"

He pulled the hat on. "Nobody did anything," he said, mumbling.

"You have to tell me."

He looked at me, a lazy grin on his face. "Nope. Nothing happened." He closed his eyes, then opened them a moment later, raising his gaze to me. "You need to leave," he said. "You're the one who..." He cleared his throat and sipped his coffee.

"I'm the one who *what*?" I said.

He closed his eyes again, and his head rolled around before his chin dropped onto his chest. I thought he was dead.

"Reagan," I said, shaking him.

His eyes opened wide. "What? What?" He looked around, startled.

"Okay," I said. "If you're not going to tell me what happened, then why don't you tell me what you know about Bill Pearson?"

This time, he looked up from the chair. "Bill? Why?"

"Because he's dead."

Reagan raised his eyebrows. "Pearson? He's dead?"

"Someone killed him," I said. "And I can't help but think that either you had something to do with it, or you know whoever did it. It was no coincidence Larry's balloon landed on his property."

Reagan turned from me, looking out the window into the darkness outside.

"Does what happened to you here have anything to do with what happened to Pearson?"

"Nobody did anything. I fell," Reagan said.

I could tell the man was lying. And was possibly scared.

"Did they threaten you?" I said. "Did they tell you not to talk to me?"

"I'm not talking." He shifted his way to the front edge of the recliner's cushion and pushed himself up, grabbing the wall for support. He tried to get his footing. "I need to go to bed. That means you gotta leave."

"I'm not leaving until you tell me what you know. And what whoever did this to you said."

Reagan hobbled into the kitchen, barely able to walk. He used the wall in the short hall to keep him from falling over. "I'm going to bed. If you don't leave, I'm calling the cops."

He walked into a dark room and slammed the door behind him. I glanced around at the mess, then locked the door to his apartment and left.

CHAPTER 22

It might've been a little too late to show up on someone's doorstep unannounced, but I was fairly close to Plymouth after leaving Richard Reagan's apartment. Outside of a few random names I still had on my list, Larry Green's daughter and her husband were the two from his immediate family I had yet to have a conversation with. And there was no sense in waiting.

The lights were on inside the two-story colonial when I pulled into the driveway. A pickup truck was parked behind the VW bus, but no other vehicles.

By the time I got out and followed the walkway, the front door had already opened. A thin young man with a plaid flannel shirt poked his head out, watching me approach him.

He gave me a nod with his chin. "Yeah?"

"Are you Matt?" I said.

He looked me over, but didn't respond.

Larry Green's first wife, Karen, walked up behind him and nudged him aside. She smiled. "Jake? What are you doing out this way so late?" She held the door open for me. "Please, come in."

The man stepped back and I walked into the warm home. It smelled like dinner had just been cooked, reminding me of when my grandmother was still around, when her house—the one I lived in—always smelled like something was on the stove or in the oven.

Karen closed the door behind me. "Matt, this is Jake Horn. He's the private investigator I was telling you about."

I extended my hand to shake his, but he ignored it, crossing his arms across his chest instead. "This about Larry?" He looked at his watch. "It's almost nine o'clock."

"I know it's late," I said. "I'm sorry. I was in the area and thought it'd be all right to stop by." I watched Karen walk away and into the other room, where the only light appeared to come from the flames in the fireplace and the TV, with the volume all the way down.

"Come on in," she said. "Can I get you a drink? Matt? Do you have a beer for Mr. Horn?"

Matt hadn't stopped staring at me, arms still crossed, making it clear he wasn't overly excited to have his night interrupted by a stranger.

I walked into the other room, and Karen went into the kitchen, coming out a moment later with a can of Stroh's, handing it to me. "I'm sure Matt won't mind," she said, side-eyeing her son-in-law.

She hadn't noticed the bruises on my face when I first walked into the house, but stepped in closer as I ripped the tab off the beer. "What happened to your face?"

On one hand, I wasn't sure I needed to tell her. On the other hand, there was no reason not to let her know what I'd run up against. "I ran into a couple of goons," I said. "And was warned not to investigate Larry's death."

She gasped, eyes wide open as she covered her mouth with her hand. "Is that really true?"

Matt walked over to us with a look of interest in his eyes.

I looked at the two. "Do either of you know anyone who drives a yellow Chevy Impala?"

Karen shook her head right away, but Matt didn't bother to answer.

"Why are you asking us?" he said.

"Because it's a car I've seen around. I'm sure it's the vehicle being driven by the men who attacked me."

Matt said, "You think we had something to do with you getting your ass kicked?" He laughed, shaking his head. "I'd do it myself, if—"

"I'm just asking the question," I said, realizing there was a slim chance this guy would be hospitable. "A man was shot and killed in New Hampshire. A yellow car was spotted in the area earlier that morning."

Matt walked to the window and pulled aside the curtain. He looked outside. "*You're* driving a yellow car, aren't you?" He stepped back. "You sure it wasn't you?"

I stared back at him, his gaze on mine. I didn't bother answering his foolish question.

Karen said, "Did this man—the one who was killed—have something to do with what happened to Larry?"

"Well, that's what I'm trying to figure out," I said. "The victim, Bill Pearson, owned the building where your ex-husband's balloon landed."

Karen and Matt both glanced at each other.

"I remember the name," Karen said. "I mean, Bill, uh, what was it?"

"Pearson," I said.

Karen pulled at her chin, nodding. "He owned some kind of furniture making business, didn't he?"

"Pearson Woodworking," I said. "He built custom furniture. And there's the point where I start to wonder if there's some kind of connection."

"Connection to who?" Karen said.

"Well, I understand Reagan was in the furniture business. Do you know anything about that?"

"You mean, his furniture stores? That was a long time ago, before they started producing the cheap stuff in the South." She went over to the fireplace and placed a log on the fire. "Did you talk to Richard?"

"I just came from his apartment," I said. "And it looked like he was knocked around by someone. Possibly the same people I bumped into in Boston."

"He was beat up?" Karen said, her hand to her mouth.

"He wouldn't tell me anything about it," I said. "But I know what it looks like when a man's been pushed around."

She reached for a glass of white wine from the table by the leather recliner that reminded me of the one at Richard Reagan's. "The poor man," she said. "Is he all right?" She sipped her wine.

I said, "He was drunk enough he may not've been feeling much pain. He went to bed while I was there, so I let myself out. I'm hoping I can catch him sober in the morning."

I heard steps on the stairs and turned to see a woman who looked like Karen, but younger and with long blond hair.

She stopped on the stairs and gazed at me, then looked at her mother and husband. "What's going on?"

"Brenda?" I said. "I'm Jake."

"The private investigator," her mother said, before I had a chance to.

Brenda gave me a quick grin as she continued into the room.

Matt said to Brenda, "Is he asleep?"

"It took a long time," she said. "He didn't want me to leave him. He was scared."

"He needs to learn to put himself to sleep," Matt said. "Or he'll never grow out of it."

The more this guy opened his mouth, the less I liked him.

"He's just a little boy," Karen said, chastising her son-in-law. "I'm sure you weren't big and tough when you were his age."

I didn't think the young man looked big or tough at his present age, never mind when he was a baby.

Brenda walked over to the couch and collapsed, letting out a deep sigh. "Is there any wine left?" She looked straight ahead at the TV.

"Of course," her mother said, and disappeared into the kitchen.

Brenda looked up at me. "So, why are you here?"

"As I told your mother and husband, I was in the area. I'm sorry if I've disturbed your—"

"It's fine with me." She got up from the couch and changed the channel on the TV. "Charlie's Angels is on." She glanced my way again and sat on the couch, one leg tucked under the other. "You must like shows like Charlie's Angels, huh? Being a detective?"

"I don't watch a lot of TV," I said.

Karen walked into the room and handed her daughter a glass of wine.

I said to Brenda, "I was just asking your mother and husband if they know anyone who drives a yellow Chevy Impala. Any chance you do?"

"We don't," Matt snapped, answering before his wife had a chance to.

But Brenda looked like she was still thinking, looking at Matt, then finally shaking her head. "Why?"

"Just somebody I'm looking for," I said. She got up from the couch and sat on the padded arm, facing me. "So, do you really think my dad's death wasn't an accident?"

"From what I've found so far, it's likely there's more to it than the police initially believed."

Karen said to her daughter, "The man where Daddy's balloon landed was killed."

Brenda appeared surprised, but didn't respond at first.

"He was shot," Karen said, before her daughter had even asked.

The daughter's husband said, "How do you know this has anything to do with what happened to Larry?"

"I don't," I said. "I would've liked to have had a chance to speak to Mr. Pearson. But he was already dead when I arrived at his workshop."

"So you've never spoken to him?" Matt said.

I shook my head. "But it doesn't make it any less suspicious."

Matt just stared back at me without a word.

"And it's not just me," I said. "In case you're wondering. The cops up there are involved, of course."

The three all looked at each other.

Brenda said, "I'm sorry, but I guess I'm confused. Why did you go up to talk to him?"

"Because I wanted to know if he actually saw the balloon land. Or at least get the details of what he found that morning, and if it aligns with what the detective on the case claimed to have found."

"Oh, so now you think the police are lying?" Matt said, a smug look on his face. "Is that where this is going? The police killed Larry?" He laughed, shaking his head.

I had no doubt right then that I didn't like this guy at all. "That's not what I said. What I did say was that there are... I have some questions about what might've happened that morning, and how the balloon ended up where it did, on Pearson's property."

The three all looked at each other again, and I almost had a feeling they were keeping something from me. Or perhaps knew something nobody appeared ready to share.

Karen said to her daughter, "Mr. Reagan was beaten up when Jake went over there."

Brenda gasped. "Oh no. By who?"

"I'm going to find out," I said. "And why I was hoping one of you would know something about a yellow vehicle. Besides mine, of course."

Matt said, "You said Reagan wouldn't tell you what happened."

"Someone must've threatened him."

"Are you saying this all has something to do with what happened to my dad?" Brenda said, getting up from the couch and stepping over to stand with her mother.

"He has no idea." Matt stared back at me. "He sounds like all he's doing is making assumptions, taking guesses."

I couldn't make sense of the man's hostility toward me, but one thing for sure is he needed to be smacked. "The way you're acting," I said, "I'm going to start getting suspicious you have something to hide."

Matt shook his head. "I've got nothing to hide. And even if I did..."

"How did you and your father-in-law get along?" I said. "Should I go ahead and assume not very well would be the answer."

Matt stared at me, eyes narrowed.

Brenda said, "Matt used to work at the dealership," she said.

I turned to her. "Used to?"

"The dealership wasn't making enough money," Brenda said.

Matt said, "You don't always have to stick up for him like you do. He kept other people there, even after he said he couldn't afford to pay me. "

Karen spoke up. "Matt, do you really think Larry would have laid you off if he didn't have to?" It was as if she was sticking up for her dead ex-husband, and I wasn't exactly sure why. Karen hadn't taken her eyes off Matt, and she appeared to be annoyed with him. "I never thought it was a good idea for you to work there in the first place."

Brenda said, "Do we have to get into this again?"

Matt stared at the two, turned and grabbed a coat from the back of a chair as he headed out of the room. He opened the front door and walked outside, slamming the door behind him.

"What just happened?" I said. "Is he leaving? Because my car's parked behind the truck."

Brenda let out a sigh. "Matt's had a hard time finding work."

"What kind of work?" I asked.

Brenda looked at her mother, almost as if she wasn't sure what she should say. "He does odd jobs here and there. He's a body man, but those jobs are hard to find right now."

"Body man?" I said.

Karen nodded. "Matt does body work. On cars."

Brenda said, "My father wanted to help us out, and thought he could expand the business by offering to do body repair at the dealership. He hired Matt, but it just didn't work out."

"He seems to still be upset about it?" I said. "It's been a while, hasn't it?"

The truck engine revved outside, and when I looked toward the picture window with the curtains closed, a sliver of light shone through the small opening from the truck's headlights.

Karen went to the window and opened the curtains to look outside. The truck was driving through the snow on the lawn, the back end sliding until it hit the pavement. "What is wrong with that man?"

"He's under a lot of stress," Brenda said. "We all are."

I looked from Brenda to Karen, but neither seemed ready to give me more details.

I thought about Matt and his father-in-law. "Did those two get along? Matt and Larry?"

Karen and Brenda exchanged a glance, and it seemed neither one was sure they wanted to answer.

But Karen spoke up. "They had stopped speaking. Ever since Larry told him he couldn't afford to keep the body work service going."

CHAPTER 23

I AWOKE FEELING SOMEWHAT concerned about Richard Reagan, after leaving him the way I did. No matter what actually happened to him, I was sure he'd wake up with a good headache, and thought I should be there when he did.

But when I rang the middle doorbell outside, there was no answer. I walked along the shoveled path back to the driveway where I'd parked and realized there was a small parking area around the back.

There were two cars. One was a two-door Dodge Dart with a white vinyl roof and rust on the lower part of the passenger side. The other vehicle was a Volkswagen Beetle. I didn't know what kind of car Richard Reagan drove, or if either belonged to him.

I looked in both vehicles, guessing that if one was his, I'd find a stack of newspapers and magazines, the way he had them piled in his apartment. But neither car did.

I heard a knock from inside the first-floor window, and saw an old woman with white messy hair yelling something at me, but I couldn't make out what she was saying.

I pointed to my ears and yelled, "I can't hear you."

I guessed she wanted to know why I was looking in the cars, and when she lifted the window I learned that's exactly what it was.

"Get away from my car," she said. "Before I call the cops."

"I'm sorry," I said, raising my hands, palms out, so she could see them. "I was wondering if one of these cars belonged to Richard Reagan?"

She shook her head. "The Dodge is mine. The Bug belongs to Danny."

"Who's Danny?"

"He lives on the third floor. He owns the building. And if he finds out you're snooping around his car, he'll—"

"I'm not snooping. I'm just trying to find Richard. He didn't answer the door."

"I saw him leave early this morning," she said.

"Do you know where he went?"

"How would I know? I hardly talk to the man."

A cat the size of a dog jumped up on the windowsill and blocked the woman's face. She moved it out of the way. "I suggest you get out of here," she said, then slammed the window closed.

"Wait!" I walked to the window and knocked in the glass. The woman opened it once again and I said, "What kind of car does he drive?"

"Who? Richard? I don't know. What do I look like, some kind of car expert?" She slammed the window closed, and this time pulled down the shade.

I walked around to the front of the building but stopped when I saw a yellow vehicle driving along the street. When I saw it was the same Impala, I ran down the driveway to the Nova and jumped behind the wheel. I started the engine and slapped the stick into reverse, the tires spinning on the wet pavement from the melting snow.

Backing up onto the street without looking, I pointed the car in the direction of the Impala and slammed my foot on the gas. The yellow Impala turned ahead, picking up speed as I raced to catch up with it.

I followed behind it for another mile, both vehicles going well over the speed limit and passing cars in the opposite lane. Once we hit Route 44, the Impala picked up speed. I passed three or four cars and was only two back when the vehicle spun around, cutting off oncoming traffic, and drove past me heading in the opposite direction from where we came.

I jerked the wheel and tried to follow, but another car pulled out of the Bank Boston parking lot and cut right in front of me. I slammed on my brakes, and the Nova spun out of control on the wet pavement. I tried to cut the wheel, but it was no use. Swerving, I veered straight across to the other side of Route 44, smashing into the snow piled high on the side of the road left behind by the plows.

The front end of the Nova was off the ground, the nose buried in the snow. I put the car in reverse and tried to back out, but all the wheels did was spin. Slamming my fist on the steering wheel, I turned to my left at a man standing outside my window.

"Are you okay?" he said, his voice muffled on the other side of the glass.

I rolled down the window. The man was small and thin, dressed in a suit and tie.

It was the person who had cut me off.

"Didn't you see me coming?" I snapped, even though I knew I was driving too fast.

"You spun around from the other side of the road," he said. "How was I supposed to know you—"

"I'm sorry. You're right." I stepped out of the Nova. The rear-end of the Nova was sticking out into the road. Traffic was backing up as drivers tried to cut around me. In the distance I could hear sirens, and within a moment blue lights came from over a hill. I said, "Shit" under my breath.

The man said, "Do you want me to help you?"

I looked him over again, with his pressed suit and wing-tipped shoes. "I think I'll be all right," I said, nodding toward the police vehicle coming our way. "If you have somewhere to be, maybe you should just get out of here, before you get held up."

"Are you sure?" the man said.

"Yeah, I'm sure. Thanks for stopping. And sorry about what happened. I hope you're all right."

The man gave me a nod, turned and hurried to his vehicle across the road. He took off in his car, going in the direction opposite the traffic the Nova had created.

The police vehicle siren rang a couple of times, enough for the cars to move aside and let the officer get through.

I had the tire chains in the trunk, but waited to get started.

The cop stopped the oncoming traffic and yelled over to me. "Are you all right?"

I nodded, but wasn't actually sure. "It's stuck in the snow." I was afraid to see the damage to the Nova's front end.

The officer blew his whistle to hold up the traffic that had been moving freely on the opposite side of the road, putting his hand up to stop it. He then directed the cars that were stopped—blocked by the Nova's rear—to go around it and into the lane he'd opened.

It took him a good ten minutes to clear most of the cars while I got the chains wrapped around my rear tires. But even with the chains and clearing some of the snow under the rear tires, the car wouldn't move. The drive wheel in the rear was not only stuck in the snow, but raised off the ground enough to keep the tires from touching the pavement. The snow under the car—hard packed snow that had been plowed and piled to the side of the road—was hardened enough I couldn't even put enough weight in back to get the tires to touch the ground.

The cop came over. "You might need a tow," he said. "You want me to call one out?"

I was so mad at myself for being in that position. All I could think about was the Impala once again getting away.

The cop said, "Can I see your license?"

"What for?" I said. I didn't mean for it to come out the way it did.

"Listen, buddy. I'm trying to help you here. I'm calling dispatch so we can get a truck out. They're going to need your information."

"Oh, right." I reached for my wallet in my pocket and gave him the license.

"Be right back," he said, without looking at it.

Another police vehicle arrived and pulled off to the side of the road ahead of the first officer's car. The two spoke for a few moments, and the second officer took over, directing traffic around my so-called accident.

I was embarrassed, being the fool who couldn't handle the common obstacles of winter driving.

I continued trying to get the Nova free, having no luck at all. When I stepped out of the driver's seat, the officer walked over to me. I could see from the look on his face that something wasn't right.

"Mr. Horn, please turn around and put your hands on your head."

"Excuse me?"

"There's a warrant out for your arrest, for the murder of William Pearson of Derry New Hampshire."

"Are you serious? I'm—"

"Mr. Horn. Please put your hands on your head."

A third police vehicle arrived on the scene, and two officers had drawn their weapons.

I did as the officer had asked. And as he read me my rights, I had a hard time focusing my thoughts. My mind was going in fifty different directions, wondering how I was possibly going to get out of what was turning out to be a terrible situation.

CHAPTER 24

Massachusetts State Police transported me to New Hampshire, where I was met at the border by Chief Al Williams, the cop I'd met the morning I'd found Bill Pearson dead in his workshop.

I sat in the back of his car and pleaded with him, to no avail. I said, "What proof do you have? Besides the fact I drive a yellow car?"

Williams didn't answer my questions, quiet with his eyes on the road until we pulled into the Derry Police Station parking lot. The building was nothing more than a small Cape Cod house with a big antenna on the roof and a Derry Police sign over the door.

I said, "Are you going to tell me what this is all about?"

The chief walked me in through the front entrance of the building and straight into a holding cell down a short hall. "You'll be waiting on the judge, who'll decide whether or not you can be released on bail. Considering this is a murder case..." He looked at his watch. "We may not hear until morning."

"But what I'm asking," I said, "is what makes you think I killed Bill Pearson? I've never even met the man."

The chief stepped into the cell and removed the handcuffs from my wrists, then stepped out and slammed the door, turning the key inside the lock. He looked in at me through the bars. "If I was to listen to my gut, then I'm probably going to have to admit I'm having a hard time believing you killed that man. But there's just enough evidence right now I'd be foolish to ignore. The fact your car was at Bill's shop that morning, earlier than you had claimed, has me wondering why someone who's innocent would lie about something like that. You had to've had a reason, but—"

"I'm the one who called you when I found him!" I said. "Why would I call you if I killed the man? Why wouldn't I just leave?"

"Because you suspected somebody saw your car, and your only option was to cover it up. You were there at 7:30 in the morning, but you told me you'd arrived much later."

"I know whose car it was," I said. "It wasn't mine. Yeah, it's the same color, coincidentally. But mine's a Nova. Did you ask this alleged witness what kind of car it was?"

He nodded. "I showed her a photo of your vehicle. She's sure it's the one she saw in the parking lot, an hour before you told me you were there. Right after Bill arrived, the same time he does every morning."

"Do you even have a murder weapon?" I said.

"Well, now there's the other piece that pretty much tied things up, Mr. Horn. See, we found the murder weapon in the woods behind the building. It's a Smith & Wesson .357 Magnum. You familiar with that kind of gun?"

I knew from the way he asked that I was in trouble.

"I own a .357," I said. "But..." I had to think about it. I hadn't checked under my seat. I stared back at him, but didn't know what to say. I couldn't imagine someone taking it from the Nova, where I thought I'd left it.

"The gun is registered to your name," he said.

And there it was.

I'd been set up.

I gripped the bars. "I didn't... Why would I leave it at the scene? You can't be serious? Do you even believe any of this yourself? It's a joke!"

"I'm sorry, it's just how things are going to have to work right now."

"Where's my car now?" I said.

"Still in Massachusetts, I believe. Taunton. I already had a man down to go through it. Found nothing else inside it, so..."

"I didn't kill that man!" I took a deep breath and slowly exhaled, shaking my head. I knew I had to keep it together. "Don't I get a phone call?"

Chief Williams nodded. "Of course." He pulled the key from his belt and slipped it in the lock, pulling open the jail door. "Right over there," he said, nodding toward the small wooden desk pushed against the wall, ten feet from the jail cell. I walked toward it, but he grabbed me and turned me around. He took the cuffs from his belt and put them back on my wrists.

"I'm not going to run," I said.

"That's what they always say." Chief Williams gripped my arm and helped me, hands behind my back, easing me onto the wooden chair next to the desk. He lifted the phone from one side of the desk and placed it down next to me. "What's the number?" he said, lifting the handset with one finger on the rotary dial.

I wasn't sure who to call. I'd need a lawyer, but my first step was just to get out of there. Maggie could help, but I wasn't sure if she was on duty, or if I could even get in touch with her. It had crossed my mind for a second to call Nancy, since she was already in New Hampshire, but really not much closer to Derry than Raymond was in Boston.

I thought about calling Nathan Howell, since there was no answer when I'd called the number Marilyn had given me. I didn't even know where she was. But as part of the contract I had them sign—a contract my uncle created long ago—was the stipulation that any legal fees incurred during an investigation, when no fault of the investigator on the case, would be covered by the client.

"I have a phone number in my pocket," I said. "That's the number I'd like to call."

I stood from the chair and turned my hip, my front pocket toward the chief. "Can you get it?"

"Your pockets were emptied," he said, reminding me, then walked down the short hall into the main area of the station, by the front entrance. I heard him call out for the other officer, then came back a moment later with a large yellow envelope. He opened the clasp and dumped the contents onto the desk. My wallet, a handful of business cards, my watch, and a folded piece of paper fell out onto the desk.

"Right there," I said. "That's the number. Hopefully someone answers. Ask for Marilyn."

The chief looked at the paper and dialed the number, then put the handset against my ear. I used my shoulder to hold it there. He said, "It's your phone call, not mine." He walked away, down the short hall toward the front of the station.

The phone rang three or four times before a man finally answered. "Hello?"

"This is Jake Horn. I'm calling for Marilyn Green. Is she there?"

There was a pause on the other end. "Who is this again?"

"Jake Horn. I'm a private investigator. I'm working for Marilyn on her—"

"She gave you this number?"

"Yes," I said. "Can you get her on the line? I really need to talk to her. It's—"

"Well, she's not here right now," he said.

"She's supposed to be there, isn't she?" I said.

"She does as she pleases. It's really none of my business what she does," the man said.

"I'm sorry," I said. "I didn't mean it in the way you—"

"She left a little while ago, went out to get something to eat. At least that's what I was told."

I didn't understand the purpose of her going up to New Hampshire to stay safe—or if it even made sense. But it didn't seem like that was even the case. It sounded to me like she was on more of a break or a little getaway than anything else.

I said, "Do you expect her back soon? It's... Actually, can you tell me where you are? Where I'm calling?"

"My house," the man said.

"No, I mean, where's your house? What town?"

The line went quiet.

"Hello?"

"I'm really not comfortable sharing that information with a stranger."

I closed my eyes and took a deep breath, trying to remain somewhat calm. "I just need to know if... Listen," I said. "I'm in Derry right now. At the police station. I've been arrested. I need Marilyn's help."

There was a long pause.

I said, "Please. I need to get in touch with her. Is there any way you can find her? Tell her where I am?"

The line went quiet, and I wondered if he was still there. "Okay. I can try."

"Thank you," I said. "Have her call the station. The Derry police station. Or tell her to come down, if she's not too far away. Can you do that?"

There was another long pause. "I'll do what I can, sir," the man said.

***

I'd somehow dozed off on the cold wooden bench, but I opened my eyes when keys clanked against the bars on the jail cell. Chief Williams was on the other side, opening the door. "You've got a visitor."

I looked past him at Marilyn Green, standing in the hall between the holding area and the front of the station, wearing a long fur coat and gloves she pulled from her hands as she watched me.

I wasn't even sure what time it was when I stepped out of the cell.

"I guess you got the message," I said.

She gave me a nod, her lips tight together.

I looked at the chief. "Has bail been set?"

He nodded, shifting his glance from Marilyn to me. "To be honest, I'm a bit surprised. I didn't expect you'd be leaving so soon. But the judge can be a bit lenient sometimes..."

"Maybe saw how thin the evidence is," I said.

The chief fixed his gaze on me, eyes narrowed, then turned and walked past me and Marilyn.

We followed him to the front of the station.

"Got a few things I need you to sign," he said, and pulled a clipboard out of a drawer.

"Are you going to tell me what this is all about?" Marilyn said, her voice low.

The chief said, "Your friend here is suspected of murdering a local man, who—"

"Bill Pearson," I said. "And I didn't do it."

"Bill Pearson?" Marilyn's eyes opened wide. "Larry's balloon landed on his property," she said.

The chief looked up from the paper he was filling out with a pen. "You're the wife," he said. "I knew I recognized you."

Marilyn said, "We met, when I came up here with my uncle, right after it happened."

I said to her, "So you knew Bill Pearson?"

She shook her head. "No. We'd never met."

There was something new I'd learned every time Marilyn opened her mouth.

The chief placed a clipboard and pen in front of me. "Sign this," he said. "And you're free to go. For now."

I skimmed over the document and signed on the line at the bottom. Looking the chief in the eyes, I said, "Do you seriously think I killed that man?"

Williams paused before he answered. "You wouldn't be in here if I didn't."

CHAPTER 25

IT WAS ALMOST MIDNIGHT, and after the twenty-minute drive east of Manchester in New Hampshire, Marilyn turned the red Ford Bronco she was driving down a narrow dirt road with deep snow piled on either side of the entrance but dug around a mailbox. We continued through a dark wooded area, with thin slivers of moonlight cutting through the snow-covered trees above.

Outdoor lighting reflected off the white exterior of the house I could see in the distance. And once we arrived in front of the L-shaped ranch, Marilyn parked the Bronco away from the lights and in front of a barn set back to the left of the house. Stepping out of the vehicle and into darkness, the air felt so cold the moisture in my nostrils froze. A dog's deep bark echoed in the distance.

"We'll have to be quiet," Marilyn said. "Art and Claudia are likely asleep."

I followed her into the house through a side door and into a room with a wood-burning stove and shelves filled with plenty of books. There was already a lamp on in the small room, giving off a dim yellow light. It sat on a small table between a couch and matching chair with an ottoman in front of it.

To the left of the door—the door we'd just used—was a small writing desk with a closed leather-bound book on top. A gold pen stuck up from a black marble block.

"Is this where you sleep?" I said.

She laughed quietly, shaking her head. "Claudia calls it the reading room."

The curtains on the windows were closed, warmth from the cast-iron stove filling the room. Vertical pine boards covered the walls, giving the room a country home feel.

Marilyn continued, "But the last two nights, I've fallen asleep on the couch. It's not easy going upstairs, trying to sleep."

There were three windows—one to the left of the door, over the desk; the other two on the adjoining wall on the front side of the house. I stepped to the window on the left and pulled the curtain aside, looking out toward the driveway and the red Ford Bronco hidden in darkness by the barn. The glow from the tiny crescent moon and bright stars reflected off the snow-covered ground.

"So," she said, removing her fur coat and draping it over her arm. She pulled her hat off and fluffed her hair with her free hand. "Are you sure you're okay staying here tonight? You can have the couch, or there's a spare bedroom upstairs."

I really didn't want to end up staying there at all, especially knowing the cops—I wasn't sure which ones—were going to show up with a warrant to search my grandmother's house. But I knew I didn't have much of a choice.

"Are you okay?" she said. "You look like you're unsure."

"I'm having a hard time getting my head wrapped around what transpired the last couple of days. I wasn't expecting to be the prime suspect in a murder I had nothing to do with."

She didn't seem to have a reply, and reached her hand toward me. "Can I take your coat?"

I hadn't even unbuttoned it, but finally took it off and handed it to her.

"I'll be right back," she said, nodding toward the thirteen-inch TV on what looked like a small, wooden crate. "Claudia hates having that in here. Art was the one who wanted it... But he never used this room anyway. If you want to put something on..." She turned for the door, the light from the lamp filling the dark hallway. Marilyn turned on another light, and I could see the kitchen across the hall. She turned to me, her voice hushed. "Can I get you a drink? Bourbon, or..."

I didn't drink much bourbon. Not like I used to when I was younger. But at that point, it didn't sound like a bad idea. "Sure, whatever you make."

"You want ice?"

I shrugged, then nodded. "Sounds good." She pulled the door closed, leaving me in the room. It felt a little strange being there with my client, in the situation I was in. I liked the room with its comforting feel. I glanced at the phone and thought about calling Maggie or Raymond. But it was too late for either of them, although they'd both wonder why I hadn't called at all, once they got word I'd been arrested.

I looked over the books on the shelves. There were hundreds of them. Novels. Encyclopedias. Books on farming and bird watching. I went to the window again and looked out at the snow and the silence surrounding us. I understood why it made sense to be all the way up here, out of harm's way.

I went over to the desk. A draft came through the door. I flipped open the leather-bound book filled with handwritten notes and long verses. But I turned, somewhat startled, when the door from the hall opened and Marilyn walked in with one short glass she carried over to me.

She grabbed the book and slipped it into the desk's middle drawer without saying a word, then left the room again. She was back in a couple of moments carrying another glass for herself, that she raised to me before taking a sip. "Cheers."

I found it odd.

"What are we toasting?" I said. "That I've been arrested, rather than having any answers?" I took a sip anyway.

She showed what looked like a forced smile, her lips tight, and turned to the wood-burning stove. With her back to me, she held her free hand over the stove, as if feeling the warmth from it. "I'm sorry about what's happened," she said, turning back to me. "But I don't understand what you were hoping to find, talking to that man."

"Who? Bill Pearson?" I said. "Well, I wanted to know what he saw that morning, when the balloon landed on his property."

Marilyn nodded. "I understand. What I meant was, why would someone kill him? What is it he could've told you? Obviously somebody knew he had something he could have told you, am I right?"

"I think you might be," I said. "It only makes me think my initial presumptions were correct."

"Which is what?" she said. "That he knew what happened to Larry?"

I had to think it through. I had some ideas in my head that may not've been ready to share. But I wasn't sure it would hurt to tell her some of what I had in mind. "Larry allegedly flew the balloon out of Boston, lands all the way up in New Hampshire? And from what I saw, there was hardly enough space for it to make it past the trees."

She put her glass down on the small table under the lamp. "You think the whole thing was staged?"

I didn't want to lead her down a path I wasn't sure of myself. "I have no proof it did or didn't happen the way it appeared. But something doesn't add up. And now they've got me framed for murder of a man I've never even met."

Marilyn sat on the couch and reached for her glass, leaning forward on the edge with her elbows resting on her knees. "I'm sorry," she said. "But I don't understand how you think... Why would anyone go through all the trouble to do this to him? Burning his balloon? With him inside it?" Her eyes filled with tears glowing in the dim light from the lamp.

I finally took a sip of the bourbon. The heat filled my chest after a slight burn at the top of my throat.

It had been a while.

I wasn't sure I had a good enough answer for why someone would kill her husband the way it was done. I said, "If what happened to Larry truly wasn't an accident, then whoever did this wasn't an amateur. It was planned out. Maybe Bill Pearson was paid to be involved. I don't know. My guess is whoever is behind it is... They're professionals."

"What kind of professionals?" she said.

I didn't think I had to explain that part, but apparently, I did. I couldn't figure out Marilyn. She seemed, on the one hand, to have it all together. On the other hand, there was something naïve... something innocent about her that almost made me question which part of it all was an act.

I said, "I was attacked by two men, the two I assume are the ones I've seen more than once driving around in a yellow car similar to mine. Similar, at least, to someone who isn't familiar enough with the different makes and models out there. I don't know if they'd planned to set me up from the start, or if once they realized I wasn't going to listen to their threats..."

"What *threats*?" she said.

"To stop investigating the case." I glanced at her. "That first night in Boston, when you got off the phone with me, did you see a yellow car?"

She shook her head. "No. Just a man, walking toward me, and—"

"You haven't said anything about seeing someone out there."

She was still. Quiet. "There were still people out and about. Honestly, I didn't think much of it at the time."

"And then what?" I said.

"My uncle showed up. He made me park my car in the garage, and we drove home."

There was no way of saying whoever she saw that night was after her or not. Or if it could've been whoever had killed that young woman. Of course, there was also a chance it was one of the two men I'd run into in the alley.

"What about the gun the police found?" she said. "Was it really yours?"

She had a look on her face like she wasn't sure what to believe, and perhaps wondered if I was being completely straight with her.

"Yes, the gun is mine. I rarely carry it."

"But you had it that morning? When you went to see Mr. Pearson?"

"I left it under my seat."

"In your car?"

I knew how foolish it sounded. "I do my best not to use it. I rarely take it with me when I leave the house. Normally it's locked away at my grandmother's house."

She cocked her head. "Your grandmother's house? She lets you keep your gun at—"

"I live there."

Her face had a confused, twisted look to it. "You live with your grandmother?"

"Well, no. She passed away some time ago, left me her house. I can't help think it's still hers, even though she's gone. It's just always been her house, for as long as I've been alive."

Marilyn held her gaze on me for a moment and quietly sipped her drink until the ice at the bottom rattled in the glass. She rose from her seat. "Would you like another?"

I thought about it. Being in the middle of New Hampshire, in what felt like an ideal getaway if the timing was better. But I really didn't need a second drink. "I think I'll pass," I said. "Thank you."

She left the room.

I went to the window and stared out at the snow-covered ground, waiting.

She came back in a couple of minutes later and sat down on the couch with a fresh drink in her hand.

"I have something to tell you," I said, sitting in the easy chair across from her. "I know you wanted me to keep everything you told me from the police, but I had no choice. That woman who was murdered that night... if these same two guys who were after me, and who were likely after you that night have anything to do with her murder, I really can't keep the detective on the case in the dark."

She rested her drink on her thigh. "How am I supposed to trust you if you can't keep your word?"

I had already changed my mind about having a second drink. But it was likely too late to ask for a refill.

"Listen, I think we both understand if there's someone out there who might want to cause you harm, then it could've been you who was killed that night. I understand you're not comfortable with the police in Boston, after what happened with your ex-husband, but..."

Marilyn sat without a word for a couple of moments until she finally cleared her throat. "I'm afraid the cops suspected Larry had something to do with what happened to Chuck."

"What? Why?"

She sipped her drink, then lowered it to her thigh, her gaze shifting toward the glass. "They questioned both me and Larry when it first happened. But nothing ever came of it. But like I said, I always wondered."

"Wondered what?"

Her gaze went to the window, and she took a moment before she spoke. "Larry threatened to kill him. It was in jest, of course. He was never the type to do something like that. But, it was just that, when Chuck was first killed..."

"Wait a minute," I said. "Are you telling me you think Larry killed your first husband?"

She wouldn't look at me. And didn't seem to want to respond.

"Then what about the cops?" I said. "If they believe Larry had something to do with your ex-husband's death, then..."

Marilyn rose from her seat. "I don't know what I'm supposed to believe anymore."

Chapter 26

After a sleepless night on the couch in the so-called reading room at the house where I stayed, Marilyn drove me back down to Taunton to pick up my car from impound. There was damage to the front end, where I'd crashed into the mound of snow. But at least I could drive it out of there.

Marilyn followed me when I stopped at a payphone to see if I could get in touch with Maggie. I knew I was going to need all the help I could get, now that I was the one who was in trouble.

Maggie didn't answer at her apartment, and when I called the station, I was told she was likely on her way in. I didn't leave my name or a message, but dropped another dime into the slot and dialed Raymond.

Beth answered on the first ring. "Hello?"

"Beth, it's me."

"Jake?" she said, her voice filled with concern. "Where have you been? Raymond's been looking for you. He said you've been arrested?"

"Word travels fast," I said.

"Sean McCaffrey called him."

"Is he there now?"

"McCaffrey?"

"No," I said. "Raymond. Is he there?"

"Sorry. No. He's out with Maggie. They're both trying to find you."

"Oh," I said, glancing over at Marilyn parked behind the Nova in her red Ford Bronco, the visor down in front of her. It looked like she was putting on lipstick.

I said, "If Raymond calls, tell him to try me at the office. I'm not sure I'll be there, but—"

"Can you tell me what's going on?" Beth said. "Why did they arrest you?"

"There's a lot to it," I thought about Sean McCaffrey, and how he had known about what happened. But the fact that he called Raymond to tell him told me something. I just wasn't sure what. "When I know more, I'll let you know. But I gotta run."

"Okay," she said. "Be careful, Jake."

I could hear the worry in Beth's voice, which wasn't exactly her thing.

I hung up and went up to the Bronco's driver-side window. Marilyn rolled it down. "I have to go to my office," I said.

"Should I come with you?"

I didn't think there was any reason for it. "You should either go to your uncle's, or go back to New Hampshire. I wasn't sure, at first, if you had anything to worry about. And I don't want to alarm you, but you need to keep yourself safe. I don't know who's behind what's going on here. But I'll find out. For now... I know you don't want the cops involved, but if you're in danger and you can't reach me at the office or the house, you're going to have to reconsider your stance."

"Even if they're the ones behind it?" she said, a worried look on her face.

I thought about it. "You can't distrust everyone."

***

Before I left Taunton, I headed back over to Richard Reagan's apartment, hoping he'd be there this time. I couldn't help but think he knew something, considering the fact he was clearly knocked around the night I saw him.

When I pulled up on the street, I parked behind a sporty Datsun 280Z. I'd only seen a couple around. It was a two-seater with metallic brown paint, the hood and trim painted gold. I liked the look of it, but couldn't see how it would be comfortable for a man over six feet.

I walked up the driveway, wondering who the car belonged to. A man walked out of the apartment. I recognized him right away as the man in the ski jacket who I saw at the dealership. He continued toward me, wearing the same jacket he wore the first time with the collar up, sunglasses over his eyes and his hair slicked back. His boots went up to his knees with a little fur on top. I thought they looked like women's boots. But who was I to judge?

"Hey," I said, gently grabbing him by the arm to stop him as he walked by as if I wasn't there. "You're Jason Green's friend, aren't you?"

He pulled his shades down low enough so he could look me over. "Do I know you?"

He clearly didn't recognize me from the dealership.

"I don't think so." I looked toward Richard Reagan's apartment. "You here visiting Richard?"

He paused, sliding his shades back over his eyes. "Who are you?"

"Just an acquaintance," I said. "Your name's Kip, isn't it?"

He didn't look to be sure he should answer. "Kip Rainier."

"So, you're involved in the business with Jason? You the money-man?" I said. "I understand you're the one who's supposed to help turn that dealership around?"

"I don't know where you get your information, but…"

I looked over at the 280Z parked on the street. "So, you've got some big contacts in Japan, huh? Must be nice, have those kinds of connections, at such a young age?"

He stared back at me like he didn't know what to say.

I turned and walked away from him, starting back up the driveway and onto the porch. I pushed the doorbell for the second floor and looked back at the man.

He hadn't moved, looking my way, until he started toward me. "What do you want with Richard?" he said. "Are you the one who's been bothering him?"

"I was going to ask you the same thing."

He stepped onto the porch. "Why don't you leave him alone?"

I looked back at Kip, but didn't respond. I rang the doorbell again. "Am I supposed to believe you had nothing to do with him getting knocked around?"

"Who was knocked around?" he said. "Richard?"

"Weren't you just up there?"

"Yeah, but—"

"You didn't notice his face was a little banged up?"

"He told me he fell."

I looked down at the man's hands. His knuckles were red, but it could have been from the cold. "Is that what you told him to say?"

Kip removed his sunglasses. "Excuse me?" he said. "What are you trying to say?"

"I'm just asking a question."

He said, "In case you weren't aware, Richard likes to have a drink or two. It's not the first time he's fallen and smashed that ugly mug."

I heard footsteps on the stairs, from the other side of the door.

When it opened, Richard was on the other side, looking from me to Kip. "You two know each other?"

"Not exactly," I said.

"Jake?" Kip said. "You're Jake?" He laughed. "The one Jason's crazy step-mother hired?"

I hesitated to answer, but nodded. "What's that supposed to mean?"

"What's *what* supposed to mean? That money-hungry... She's been stirring things up ever since those two got married. And now she's doing it again."

I thought I understood what he meant, but didn't push him to explain. I didn't need to.

Richard started to close the door. "You're letting the cold in!" He actually looked better than when I'd left him, although his face was still black and blue with a small bandage under his eye.

Before he could close the door all the way, I stuck my foot in to stop it. "Wait," I said. "How do you two know each other? I assume, through Larry? Or the son?"

Richard said, "I used to do business with Kip's father, bless his soul. I've known Kip since he was a little kid." He looked past me at the young man. "Imagine if your father saw me now... living like a pauper."

"I told you," Kip said. "We're getting it all straightened out."

Richard appeared to roll his eyes. "Well, unless one of you wants to pay for the heat in this place, I'm closing the door. Old lady Agatha will start yelling at me." He slammed the door closed.

I said to Kip, "I don't understand the story. Or how Richard's life fell apart. All because of the dealership?"

Kip shrugged. "Well, it was the start. Like a lot of people, he put too much faith in Jason's father. And then it was all downhill from there. But I'm going to help him."

"How so?" I said.

"By helping Jason get his business back on track, make him the biggest Datsun dealership in New England." He cracked a crooked smile. "I know people."

"Then why didn't you help out when Larry Green was still around? Before his business collapsed."

He laughed. "You never met Larry. That stubborn old man. The last thing he wanted was a dealership selling cars made by the Japanese." He looked toward his 280Z. "He fought in the war, you know."

"World War Two?"

Kip nodded. "He used to talk about it all the time, at least whenever Jason and I tried to convince him to change to a Datsun dealership. He wouldn't buy anything made in Japan. Not even a camera." He took a step off the porch. "I think you're wasting your time."

I watched him walk down the driveway and toward the street. "It seems to me a few of you are going to benefit in a way that wasn't possible when Larry Green was still alive."

"What's that supposed to mean?"

I shrugged, looking at his clenched fists as he started back toward me.

He clenched his teeth. "If you're going to stand there and tell me you think I had something to do with Mr. Green's death…"

"I was just making a point," I said. "And I know you'd like to act like nothing happened to Richard the other night, but somebody knocked him around. Someone tried to make sure he kept his mouth shut."

"I know nothing about it," he said. "But what I do know is Mr. Green's widow has a few screws loose. Everyone knows the only reason she keeps bringing this up is because she never got any money out of the deal."

"The deal?"

"Being married to Larry Green."

I paused, waiting. He seemed to know more about the situation than I'd suspected.

"I think you came here to make sure Richard keeps his mouth shut about something," I said. "I'm just not sure what that something is."

He held his hand with a grip, as if he was getting ready to throw a punch. "You're asking for it, old man!"

"Don't even think about it," I said. "I'm not looking for a fight. I'm looking for answers."

But Kip didn't seem to want to listen. He came at me with his head down, trying to drive his shoulder into me. The way he came up the stairs, his face was positioned in line with my boot. With his next step, I grabbed him by the back of his coat and drove my knee into his chest.

He flung his arms into the air and fell down the steps, stumbling back into the snow on the other side of the shoveled walkway. But he jumped to his feet and came at me again.

Grabbing my legs, he wrapped them up like a linebacker making a tackle.

I fell back against the door. The weight of us both knocked it open, splintering the wood around the latch. We both fell and lay at the bottom of the stairs inside. I was lucky I didn't crack my head wide open on the step.

I had him in a headlock, turning him over in a wrestling move I hadn't used since high school. I had him pinned now, his legs kicking. He wasn't strong enough to get free.

I heard a door swing open upstairs, looked up and saw Richard.

"Hey! Get off him!" he yelled. "Knock it off! Both of you!"

I eased up my grip and got to my feet.

Kip stayed on the ground, then got up on one knee, breathing heavy. He touched his bloody mouth and looked at his fingers, backing up through the doorway and onto the porch. "We're not done here," he said, pointing at me. "Next time I see you..." He wiped his mouth with the back of his hand, then turned and left, walking down the driveway without another word.

"Look at what you did to the door!" Reagan yelled. "Who's going to pay for this?"

The door opened to my left, and the same old lady I had seen the day before was standing there, a broom in her hand. "What's going on out here?"

"It's fine, Agatha," Richard said. "Just go back inside. I'll take care of it."

"You'd better," she said. "You're always making a mess... You and your loser friends." She slammed her door.

"Richard," I said, feeling the back of my head where it'd knocked into the door before we busted it open. "You need to tell me what's going on here."

He shook his head and pulled a gun from his pants. "I'm sorry, but you need to leave. You have no idea who you're dealing with."

I put my hands up. "What are you doing?"

"I'm warning you, for your own good. Don't come back here. Stay out of this." He pushed me out onto the porch and slammed the door, even though it wouldn't close all the way.

"Reagan!" I said, and was about to push open the door, but thought better of it. I heard sirens in the distance, and couldn't be sure they were for me.

I stood, waiting, then decided I'd come back at another time.

Chapter 27

I walked into my office and could see my breath. After I locked the door, I turned on the heat and left my coat on until it warmed up enough. I kept the blinds closed.

I had no way of getting in touch with either Raymond or Maggie, but hoped they'd show up or at least call. I was going to need some help.

The first thing I did before I sat down was water the Devil's Ivy. With the energy costs rising again, my office stayed cold throughout the winter. I wondered if it would be better to keep the plant at my grandmother's house, even though I spent so much time at the office. I couldn't let it die.

Somehow I'd kept the plant alive beyond its normal lifespan. My daughter Nancy joked I took better care of that plant than I did of myself.

She might've been right.

I'd brewed a pot of coffee and carried a cup over to my desk with the yellow pages in front of me, open to Green Chrysler. The person I wanted to talk to was Jason Green, and had little doubt he already knew about my run-in with his buddy at Richard Reagan's apartment.

But when I called and told the woman who answered who I was... she said he'd just left.

I couldn't help but think it was more than just a coincidence he wasn't there to take my call.

The next call I made was to Detective Nick Carter. I was put right through to his desk. Even after I said my name.

Carter picked up on the first ring. "Horn?"

I sat on the edge of my desk, nodding. "Yeah, it's me."

"I thought you were locked up?" he said.

"I was lucky I got bail, from what I was told," I said. "What have you heard?"

"Well, nothing good, if that's what you're hoping to hear. You were at the scene of a murder, your car was spotted by a witness early in the morning, and your gun ended up in the woods. And, well, I'm sure you already know it appears it was the same weapon used on the victim."

"I get the feeling, by your cordial tone, you don't believe I did it?" I said.

Carter cleared his throat. "I don't think you're that foolish. I don't know you that well, but it'd take a little more to convince me you're the prime suspect. Not that my opinion matters up there. Live free or die, right?"

"Even the chief of police up there, Chief Williams, seemed to have his doubts. But he was honest with me, and said with the evidence they had, he had little choice but to obtain a warrant for my arrest."

"Funny how the law works isn't it?" Carter said.

"I'm not sure 'funny' is the word I'd use, but..."

Carter paused on the other end. "I actually spoke with Chief Williams. Just a little while ago."

"You called him?"

"Your cousin, Raymond, called me in the middle of the night. See if there was anything I could do. He was going to head up there himself, but he was told someone had already posted bail for you."

"My client," I said. "Can you tell me what Chief Williams had to say about the case? I'm in trouble here, if they can't find whoever killed that man."

"We didn't talk for long," Carter said. "But the fact is, they don't have any other suspects right now. I'm sorry."

I was hesitant to tell him what had happened over at Richard Reagan's apartment. I wasn't even sure how I'd explain it.

"I know the two men who did it," I said. "At least I *think* I do. The problem is, I don't actually *know* who they are. But, I know the car. It's a yellow Chevy Impala. That's why whoever said they saw my car, clearly made a mistake."

Carter was quiet for a moment. "Okay, I could see that. But what about your gun? How do you explain that one?"

"These two men know enough about it. Where I live. Where I work. They've been following me all over New England. They must've taken it out of my car."

Carter said, "You left your gun in your car?"

"I rarely do. I hardly ever use it, to be honest. But I'm sure I had it, probably ran in somewhere and..." I sipped my coffee, without feeling the need to finish my thought.

"So, any chance you've met these two supposed suspects, face to face?" Carter said.

I gave him the details about being jumped in the alley, and how I could probably I.D. both men if I saw them again. "But now I'm afraid they won't show up again."

"What makes you say that?"

"I'm not sure. My guess is they're hired guns, and now that I saw them both, they'd have to assume the heat's about to get turned up."

Carter was quiet on the other end. "Here's the thing," he said. "I'm not sure what I can do right now."

"How about looking into who these men are?"

More silence filled the line.

"Maybe I'll talk to Williams," he said. "Although the last thing any town cop up there wants is some city detective getting involved in a crime that has little to do with him."

I said, "But if these two men were involved in what happened to Larry Green, this could potentially tie into the Trudy Bailey murder." I explained what I knew about Bill Pearson, and why I had gone up there to talk to him. "If Pearson didn't know anything about what really happened to Larry Green, he'd still be alive."

"You seem to make a lot of assumptions," Carter said. "With little evidence to back it up. In my business, assumptions lead to mistakes."

"I'm not just pulling things out of my—"

"It's all just a little too far-fetched," Carter said.

I was quiet. I couldn't deny it made little sense. But I couldn't let it all slide either. "There's something there," I said. "I'm telling you. I just don't know what it is. Not yet."

I could hear Carter breathing on the other end.

I sat in the chair behind my desk. "Do you have any other leads in Trudy Bailey's death?"

"We're working on a few things," Carter said.

He didn't sound very convincing.

"Okay, then what I'm telling you is if we find these two men..."

"We?" Carter laughed. "There is no 'we' so I'm not sure you—"

"What if I can make the connection between what happened to Larry Green and Trudy Bailey's murder? Don't ignore the fact there's a chance the same men who killed him, killed your victim. But they thought she was Marilyn Green."

Again, Carter went quiet.

"You haven't even told me why someone would want to kill Marilyn Green," he said.

"I *have* told you. Because she's the only one who believed Larry's death wasn't an accident. There's not another person out there who suspects anything."

"Besides you," Carter said.

The line went silent.

"You there?" I said.

"Yeah, I'm here. I'm just not sure what... I don't know what you expect me to do."

"How about tell me you'll help me get a better understanding of what happened to Larry Green? Or see if your buddy Sean McCaffrey will open up about it?"

"McCaffrey called me already. Mainly, he doesn't like the idea his name's being dragged into this. But he made it clear Larry Green's case was open-and-shut. He found no reason to believe it was anything more than an accident. A malfunction."

"Malfunction?"

Carter didn't respond.

"You know what else McCaffrey told me?" he said. "That the relationship between Green and his wife—his widow—wasn't as peachy as she might lead you to believe."

"What's that supposed to mean?" I said.

"I'm just telling you what he said. In fact, I've said enough already."

The man frustrated me. But I was used to it, from dealing with cops all my years in the business. They always saw me as someone on the outside looking in.

I said, "You ask me, it feels like you're more interested in protecting your buddy than—"

I knew as soon as the words left my mouth I'd crossed the line.

"You'd better watch your step, Horn."

He was right. I had to be careful. I didn't need more cops lined up against me than I already had. And before I could say another word, the next thing coming through the phone was a dial tone.

CHAPTER 28

THERE WERE BALLOONS FLOATING in the air, tied to the antenna of just about every car marked for sale in the Green Chrysler parking lot. A banner hung on the building over the entrance that read, Clearance Event. I didn't notice any vehicles in the customer parking lot, but saw the salesman, Gary Holden, standing outside the entrance smoking a cigarette.

He appeared to be watching me park the Nova and started walking toward me. But he stopped when I stepped out of the car, did a one-eighty and made a beeline for the entrance.

I walked inside and didn't see Holden anywhere, assuming he thought I was a potential customer until he saw who it was. The woman I recognized from the first time I was there sat behind the reception desk with a phone to her ear, watching me as I approached her.

Before I said a word, a door opened toward the back, behind the desk, where the offices were. Gary Holden walked out and started past me.

I said, "Usually car salesmen run toward someone walking in, not in the opposite direction."

Holden shook his head. "I wasn't running from you."

"No? If I had to guess, I'd say you wanted to warn somebody I was here."

Holden cleared his throat. "Jason's not here, if that's who you're looking for."

The woman behind the desk hung up the phone. "Can I help you?"

"Well, I've just been informed that Jason's not here. I was hoping to talk to him."

"I'm sorry," she said. "He isn't available today."

"He's not available? Or he's not here?" I looked from Holden to the woman looking nervous behind the desk.

I found out for myself and headed for the same doorway Jason Green had taken me through a couple of days earlier.

"Sir!" the woman snapped, following me. "You can't go in there."

Holden hurried toward me and stepped in my path before I made it to the door I already knew went to Jason's office. He crossed his arms. "You can't go back there."

I stood face-to-face with him, the smell of his gas station cologne burning my nose. "I don't know what the big deal is," I said. "Is he afraid to talk to me?"

I looked past Holden when the door opened at the end of the hall behind him. Jason Green stood dressed in a pin-stripe suit and gave a nod.

"Gary," he said, holding up his hand like he was calling off the dog. "It's fine"

The woman said to Jason, "Do you want me to call the police?"

Jason shook his head. "That won't be necessary." He waved for me to follow him.

Gary Holden waited a moment before he finally stepped out of my way, eyeing me as he walked over to the reception desk with the woman, both watching me.

I followed Jason into his office. He sat behind his desk and pulled a cigarette from a pack in front of him, offering it to me before sticking one in his mouth.

"No, thanks," I said, taking the seat across from him. "I hear they're bad for you."

"Says who?" he said, lighting a match under the tip of his cigarette, until smoke rose and an orange glow formed.

"Let me just get something clear," he said. "First, I want to assure you I have nothing to hide. But I also don't feel I should allow my friends and family to be bothered. Especially by the prime suspect in a murder case."

"Give me a break," I said. "I've been set up. So why don't you tell me what you know about it?"

"About what?"

"About me being set up. The man who coincidentally owns the property where your father's balloon landed is dead. You don't think I should be a bit suspicious?"

Jason drew from his cigarette. "I'm sorry. I don't know anything about it." The smoke left his mouth with his words. "I'm trying to run a business here. I'm focused on turning this place around. And there are a lot of people depending on me to do so. To me, it seems all you're doing is getting in the way with this nonsense."

"Nonsense? Don't you care there's a chance what you've been told happened to your father is a lie? And, I'm sorry, but I can't help but think someone close to him had a good enough reason for wanting him dead."

Jason stood from the desk, ripping the cigarette from his mouth. "Don't you dare try to tell me I had something to do with what happened. Do you really think I wanted all this responsibility on my shoulders?"

"I didn't say I thought it was you, did I?" I said. "But, now that you mention it…"

The phone rang on his desk, and Jason picked it up. "Hello?" He nodded. "Already? Okay, send her back." He hung up the phone. "I'm sorry, but we're done here. I have a visitor."

"Who? Your buddy with all the money?" I said. "I'm sure you heard we ran into each other at Reagan's place?"

Jason stared back at me without an answer, placing the cigarette in the brown glass ashtray in front of him.

The door opened, and his mother, Karen, walked in. She wore a long skirt and a powder blue trench coat she unbuttoned as she stepped through the door. Her hair was up. I had only assumed the VW Bus I saw parked at the house was hers.

She glanced over at me and smiled. "What a surprise." She shifted her gaze to Jason. "You didn't tell me you were meeting with Mr. Horn."

"I'm not," he snapped. "And he's leaving." He stepped around his desk and reached for my arm, but I yanked it away.

"I'm not done," I said. "And since you're both here…"

Jason aggressively crushed what was left of his cigarette in the ashtray. "No," he said. "We're done here. If I have to, I'll call the cops. I'm sure they'd love to know a suspected murderer won't leave my dealership."

"Jason, stop it," Karen snapped, as if scolding him. She sat down in the other chair next to where I stood, looking me over. "You don't look like a killer."

I said, "As I was telling your son, somebody set me up."

She looked at Jason. "I'm sure there's a simple explanation for what happened up there."

"Yeah, it's simple," I said. "Someone's afraid the truth about what happened to Larry is going to get out." I looked from Karen to her son. "What happened up there in New Hampshire, and with someone trying to stop me from doing a job, is a clear indication Larry's death wasn't what you've all been led to believe."

Jason stood behind the desk and pulled out another cigarette. "Well I sure as hell didn't kill my own father."

I said, "I've made it clear, I'm not saying you did. But, you have to admit you and your friends..."

"What friends?" Jason said, acting like he had no idea what I was talking about.

"What's this about?" Karen said.

I nodded at Jason. "Ask him. I'm sure he knows all about it."

Jason just stood there, smoking his cigarette, watching me.

I said to Karen, "I went over to see Richard Reagan and Jason's buddy Kip was there."

Karen crinkled her nose. "Kip? What was he doing there?" She turned to her son, waiting for an answer.

"He's trying to help Mr. Reagan," Jason said. "He's trying to help all of us."

"He's the one with the money, is that right?" I said. "Are you going to use him the same way your father did with Richard?"

"My father didn't use Richard. They were friends."

I nodded. "Yeah, I get that. But the guy's a mess now. And someone showed up at his place and knocked him around. He wouldn't tell me why."

"It wasn't Kip, if that's what you're saying."

I nodded. "If you say so."

Karen was watching me, silent, waiting for more.

"Here's the thing," I said. "I can't shake the feeling that just about everyone I've talked to so far seems to have had something to benefit from with Larry being out of the picture."

Karen shook her head. "I hope you're not insinuating you think Jason or I had something to do with it. That's ridiculous."

"It might be," I said. "But don't you still have ownership in this business?" I waited, eyeing Karen.

She paused, as if she had to think about it. "I was there when Larry started this place. He was the one who insisted I be a shareholder. And I'm sure he regretted that decision once he laid eyes on the gold digger."

Jason pointed at me, the cigarette between his fingers, eyes squinted with the smoke rising into his face. "I don't like what you're trying to imply. I told you already, I did not kill my father. Neither one of us did."

Karen's voice was calm, her gaze on me now. "Is that what you're saying? You think one of us had—"

"I'm not pointing any fingers," I said. "And I prefer to believe a man's own family wouldn't be responsible for his death. But, the fact is, I fully believe Larry was murdered. Too many things have happened since I took this case to indicate otherwise."

Karen's voice was soft and almost shaken. "But I just want that to be clear. There's no way anyone from his own family would—"

"What about Kip?" I said. "What's his deal?"

"His deal?" Jason said.

"Why was he at Richard's apartment?"

Jason shrugged.

"And then, after he was gone, Reagan warns me to stay out of it."

Jason and his mother looked at each other, neither saying a word. Karen's eyes widened.

Jason said, "Mr. Reagan's not well. The man lost his marbles long ago, in case you haven't noticed."

"I'm not sure," I said. "I have a feeling he knows more about what's going on than it appears. He was pretty clear with me about how he lost all his money investing in this place."

Jason had a crooked smile on his face. "He didn't happen to mention all the money he blew at the dog track? From what I've heard, it wasn't just a couple of bucks either."

"What's your point?" I said.

Jason shrugged. "You make it sound like he was knocked around because of whatever you claim might've happened to my father. You ever think his gambling is what got him in trouble?"

Karen nodded, as if agreeing with her son. "He could owe money. Gambling ruins people, and they're always looking for someone else to blame." She gave Jason a look, as if she was hoping for some reassurance that the theory made sense.

"So, then why was your buddy at Reagan's apartment?" I said.

"I told you," Jason said. "He wants to help him." He took a deep drag of his cigarette and exhaled, walking around from behind the desk. He went over to a window and looked out. "Maybe he was just giving him reassurance we're all doing what we can to turn this place around. Everyone knows Reagan needs the money as much as anyone."

I wasn't sure I could believe a word coming out of the man's mouth.

Karen looked at her watch, then eyed her son.

Jason said, "Well, Mr. Horn, I'm sorry, but we have some personal business to discuss. So, if you don't mind..." He walked toward the door and opened it, gesturing for me to leave. "Good bye, Mr. Horn."

CHAPTER 29

I STOPPED AT A payphone and called Raymond's house. With barely a ring, he answered.

I said, "It's me."

"Where are you?" he said. "We looked everywhere for you."

"I've been busy."

"I heard," he said. "How'd you get yourself wrapped up in something like this again?"

"Well, I didn't do it," I said.

"Yeah, well it doesn't look good. I hear you left your gun in the car again?"

"I'm not sure how they got it. I suppose I might have."

Raymond raised his voice. "How many times have I told you not to—"

"I don't need it right now, Raymond. I'm in trouble here. Unless I can find those two men. But I have a feeling they're long gone now."

"Maggie's been looking for that Impala," Raymond said. "There are four registered in Massachusetts. Four yellow Impala's. Hopefully she can get the information we need that'll help track them down." He paused. "So how come you didn't call me or Maggie when they took you in?"

"I only get one call," I said.

"And you used it to call your client?"

"She bailed me out. And she was already in New Hampshire."

Raymond sighed on the other end. "So they let you out? Then where'd you go?"

"To the house where she's staying."

"Oh no... You didn't."

"Come on, Raymond. Give it a break. I slept on the couch. How could you even ask?"

"Where are you now?" he said. "We should get together, figure out how we're going to get you out of this mess."

"That would be good," I said. "I just left Norwood, the car dealership to talk to Larry Green's kid."

"Kid?"

"Well, not a kid, exactly. He runs the show at the dealership, now that the father's gone."

"Oh, right," Raymond said. "What'd he say?"

"Not much at all, but there's something about him I can't quite put my finger on. I got there, this salesman who works for him, I swear he ran to tell him I was there when I first showed up. Like they were looking out for me."

The line went silent.

I watched a car pull up and park next to mine. "So, McCaffrey was the one who told you I'd been arrested?"

"He got a call from someone up there. I think he was just trying to be helpful, even though you're trying to make him look bad."

"Make him look bad? That's not what my goal is here, Raymond. You know that."

"Well, I think he'd like to avoid getting pulled into anything. The guy's retired. The last thing he wants is someone digging up dirt on him, trying to say he's a crooked copy or was involved in something he—"

"I never said he was a crooked cop. But something doesn't smell right up there. The man who was only one of two people who witnessed Larry Green's balloon is now dead." I looked out from the phone booth toward the traffic flying by on Route 1.

Raymond didn't respond, and I got the feeling he was only half listening at that point. I could hear the TV in the background. He said, "Did you eat yet?"

"No. Nothing. My ears are ringing, I'm so hungry."

A woman stepped out of the car that had parked next to mine and stood nearby, waiting for the phone.

Raymond said, "You want to meet me at the diner? I'll call Maggie, see if she can meet us."

"Isn't she working?"

"Yeah, but she'll be down that end."

I thought about it. "I don't know. You know how she feels about discussing my business when she's in uniform."

"This is more than business. You've been arrested for murder, Jake. There's no chance you're going to be able to do this yourself. You cross the wrong line, you're going to end up doing thirty-to-life in some Podunk prison in the Granite State."

"Either way, I need to run by grandma's house first," I said. "I'm sure they've already got the search warrant."

"You haven't been there yet?" Raymond said.

"I'm on my way now."

"I hope they haven't busted down any doors without you being there. I already made some calls myself, but didn't get much information about it."

"I appreciate it," I said.

"Well, don't thank me yet. I'm not sure I have much pull. I heard Mass State Police are assisting the locals from up there in Derry, besides Milton PD, of course."

I said, "I'm not sure what else they think they'd find anyway. They already have my gun." I turned from the phone and looked past the woman watching me. "I should get going, head over to the house now. I'd hate to miss them going through my underwear drawer."

Raymond didn't seem to find that funny. "What about the witness who allegedly saw the yellow vehicle," he said. "Did you get any details?"

"Well, I haven't spoken to the person, if that's what you mean. Female, that's all I know so far. But the last thing I need is to end up being charged with witness tampering."

"I'm not saying you should talk to her. Just wondering what kind of information she gave them. What else did she say, besides she saw a yellow car?"

"I don't know," I said.

"And what about the second person who claimed to've seen the balloon in the air? Any details on her?" Raymond said.

"Only what I saw in the paper when it first happened. But I haven't had much luck tracking her down. She's not even from around here."

"Where's she from?" he said.

"Vermont. She was allegedly in Boston visiting a friend when it happened. My plan was to find her, or at least try to have a conversation after I met with Pearson. For obvious reasons, I had a change of plans."

"You know I'd ask McCaffrey for more information," Raymond said. "But I'm not sure he'd be up for it."

"No, don't bother," I said. "I have the woman's name, I just haven't been able to track her down."

"You want me to see what I can find?"

"I'll give you her info when we meet up. It's at the house." A gust of wind blew across the parking lot, sending a chill through my body. "Let me run, get over to the house. I'm afraid of what I'm going to find when I get there."

"You want me to go there now?" Raymond said.

"I don't know if it's a good idea," I said. "You don't need to let them see you involved in this. I appreciate it, though. I'll call you when I see what's going on. Hopefully the front door's still on the hinges."

***

I could see the police vehicles in front of the house as soon as I turned off Blue Hill Ave. Two of the vehicles were Mass State Police, another a town of Milton Police car, and one with Dover Police on the door.

The front door to the house was wide open.

I parked on the street, noticing my neighbors in their windows looking out at the scene. I hurried up the driveway and walked past the two Mass State vehicles, one parked behind the other.

Once I was on the shoveled walkway, I could see the lock had been busted off the door, splintered where someone had cracked the latch. I felt anger boil inside me, and had to talk myself out of losing my cool when I stepped through the opening. But it wasn't easy to stay calm, the way the frustrations of the past couple of days were slowly building inside me like boiling lava.

I stepped through and felt no difference in the temperature inside the house compared to the outside. I heard the furnace running in the basement and yelled, "You people can't even keep the door closed?" I glanced through the doorway to the kitchen, where two officers looked over at me.

Both men reached for their holstered guns, but I put up my hands before either drew his firearm. "I live here," I said. "Can you show me your search warrant?"

"Mr. Horn?" one of them said.

"Yes. Now, if you'd just tell me what you're looking for, it'd make things a lot easier for all of us." I grabbed a chair from under the kitchen table, carried it to the front door and closed it, sticking the back of the chair under the knob to keep it from opening. The latch was on the floor. "So who's going to fix my door?"

One cop pointed toward the stairs behind me. "Chief Williams, from Derry PD, has the warrant."

I went to the stairs and stood at the bottom, looking up. I could hear voices up there. "Hello?" I yelled. "Chief Williams? You up there?"

Nobody answered, so I ran up and stood at the top, in the hallway. I first checked Nancy's room, and was thankful there was nobody in there. That would have set me off. I turned and went down the hall to my bedroom.

A male officer stepped out wearing a Derry, New Hampshire police uniform. "Who are you?" he said, his hand, like the other two, as if going for his holstered gun.

"I live here." I raised my hands to show him I was unarmed. "Where's Chief Williams?"

Williams walked out of my bedroom. "I'm sorry about this, Jake. We tried to reach you, called your office several times. We called you here at your home at least a dozen times."

He introduced me to the uniformed officer, but I was more focused on everything going on in the house than catching his name.

I said, "You guys couldn't have figured a better way in? On top of breaking my door, you leave it wide open with the cold? I don't make the big bucks like you do... And in case you haven't noticed, oil's not cheap." I looked past him at two other men in the bedroom, neither in uniform. One was going through the writing desk next to my bed. "What exactly do you think you're going to find? My diary, with my murder confession?"

Williams looked like he wanted to crack a small smile, shaking his head. "It's procedure, Jake. I think you know how this stuff works."

The phone rang downstairs. There was one in the bedroom, but I hurried to grab the one down there by the couch. "Hello?"

It was Maggie. "Jake? It's me. You're home?"

Normally I'd say something in response to her calling me at the house, then asking if I was there. But it wasn't the time for it. "Yeah. I just wished I'd gotten here a little sooner, before the cops kicked in my door."

"Oh no," she said. "I was afraid that might happen. I talked to Detective Carter. He knew it was going down."

"I guess he didn't bother trying to help?" I said.

"I don't think he wants to be involved in something outside of the city"

I looked up the stairs at the two plainclothes officers walking toward Nancy's room. "Hold on," I said to Maggie, and covered the mouthpiece on the handset. I yelled upstairs, "Hey! Stay out of that room!" I didn't see Chief Williams in the hall.

I put the phone back to my ear. "Are you coming over here at any point?"

"Raymond said you hadn't eaten all day, and might meet him at First Street?"

"I don't know. I'm not going anywhere any time soon. The only thing I see myself doing is running to the hardware store to buy a new lock for the front door."

"That's a shame," she said. "But you know how it goes."

"Sadly, I do." I looked up the stairs at the cops going in and out of rooms. "I gotta go. Let's talk later."

I was about to hang up, but Maggie said, "Did Raymond tell you I'm digging for owners of yellow Chevy Impalas?"

"Yeah. Any luck?"

"I'm out on patrol now, at a payphone. I'll continue looking when I get back to the station. Hopefully I can find something."

Chapter 30

IT WAS DARK OUT by the time the cops had finally left the house, leaving empty-handed, as far as I could tell. Chief Williams at least showed some courtesy, apologizing more than once for someone breaking in the door.

I'd seen enough warrants served when the person of interest wasn't home, and knew there was always one cop in the bunch who couldn't wait to kick a door in. Most of the time, especially if it was someone in my shoes—not exactly a law man but someone in, at least, the same crime-solving industry—they'd try to get in while doing as little damage as possible.

It clearly didn't go that way.

I still hadn't eaten, but had to run out to the hardware store to get some things to fix the broken door lock. On the way back, I made a quick stop at the corner store and grabbed a can of tuna and a loaf of bread. What I needed as much as anything was something in my stomach, and a few hours of real sleep.

I'd finally gotten the door repaired when Raymond showed up with a pizza box in his hand. "I got you this. I ended up eating at home, and know you probably have an empty fridge, as usual."

I didn't mention the can of tuna on the counter.

Raymond had a six-pack of Narragansett beer hanging on his finger, one can missing. "Here, you look like you could use a couple of these." He shivered. "It's cold in here."

I took the beers from him. "I appreciate it," I said. "Who knows how long they had the door open."

Raymond held up the pizza box. "I assumed you didn't get to eat?" He went into the kitchen and put the box on the table. "I know how you get when you're hungry."

I went over to the fire I'd lit a little earlier trying to warm the place up. I stared at the orange flames, thinking about all that had happened, and how it wasn't going anywhere near what I'd expected.

Raymond came out of the kitchen. "You all right?"

"I guess so. I was thinking... wondering why I walked away from a fairly lucrative client—the insurance work—so I could take on more challenging cases."

"Because you get bored," he said.

I nodded. Raymond was right. "I'm just not sure it's all worth it. Do you know what it's like being arrested for murder?"

He laughed, shaking his head. "Uh, not exactly." He reached into his coat pocket where he had the sixth can of beer, still unopened, placing it on the coffee table in front of the couch. He took off his coat and tossed it over the backrest. "Did you call a lawyer?"

I shook my head. "No."

"You probably should."

I took the six-pack—five-pack, actually—with me into the kitchen and stuck it in the fridge, then grabbed a piece of pizza and took it back into the other room.

"It's not that I think I can do it on my own, but I'd rather wait, see what I can figure out first." I folded the slice over and had half of it in my mouth, the grease from it dripping down my wrist.

"A lawyer would at least be able to give you some guidance," Raymond said. "You know?"

"I'll call him when I'm ready, all right?"

He nodded with a big grin, picking up his beer. He cracked the tab on the top of the can and took a few gulps. "I just don't want you to think you can do this all alone. This is a big deal, as I'm sure you know. I'm going to help you—whatever you need—and make sure you get out of this mess. But, still... You're going to need legal representation."

"I know."

Raymond was always there for me. Always. But, the fact I was wrapped up in a murder case that could send me away made it a bit more personal for both of us. And I could tell he was worried.

He had always wanted to be a cop, ever since he was a little kid. When he retired, I had approached the idea of him helping me out in the business. After all, it was his father's agency to begin with. I only took it over when my uncle died because Raymond wanted nothing to do with it. Not while he was still a cop in Boston.

I'd even once suggested to Raymond he get his private investigator's license once he retired. But he knew there wasn't much business coming through the door. Horn Investigations wasn't half of what it was when my Uncle Pat was in charge.

But I'd noticed Raymond liked to discuss my cases. He wanted to help. I wondered if he was just bored sitting around the house in retirement or doing yard work all day.

I assumed he liked the idea of doing what he could to help me without having to commit to being a part of the business.

I finished the slice of pizza so fast I'm not sure I tasted it, then went in the kitchen and got another.

I looked through the doorway and watched Raymond looking over the repair work I did to the front door.

"You like my work," I said. "You should've seen what a mess it was when the cops broke in."

"It's still a mess," Raymond said, crouching down studying the repairs I'd made, replacing the entire knob. "You're going to have to do better than this, no?"

I bit the second slice of pizza and dropped it on the plate, leaving it on the table. I went out to see what the problem was. "At least it locks now. It wouldn't even stay closed after the cops left."

"Look at all this glue!" Raymond touched the wood I'd glued on, where the door had splintered.

"I'll sand it tomorrow," I said. "Touch it up, nobody'll even notice."

Raymond glanced back at it, a crooked smile on his face. "Don't worry. I got a guy, can come out tomorrow and fix it up for you. This is a solid door. You don't want to just put it back together with Duct tape."

"I used screws. And glue. That's a brand new knob. I should have made the damn cops fix it."

Raymond huffed, shaking his head. "Too bad it doesn't work that way." He sipped his beer, and we both looked toward the headlights from a car coming up the driveway.

The streetlights reflected off the Plymouth Scamp's green finish. Maggie was behind the wheel and parked next to Raymond's LeBarron. She didn't get out right away.

I shifted my gaze to Raymond's Chrysler. "Where did you buy your car?"

"The LeBarron?" He seemed to think for a moment. "Oh, uh, Hunt Chrysler. In Pawtucket."

I said, "Why'd you go down to Rhode Island?"

"Buddy of mine used to be a cop, was working over there. In sales."

"He's not anymore?" I said.

Raymond shook his head. "Nah, I don't think he was making any kind of money. Gave deals to all his buddies, but there was nothing left for him."

"American cars aren't selling like they used to," I said. "Not the big vehicles."

Raymond cracked a sly smile. "What are you, the car expert now?"

I shook my head. "It's what I was told, talking to Larry Green's family. That's why that dealership had been losing money all these years."

"What's wrong with big American cars? I like mine," Raymond said, like he was offended.

"That's the issue with Green Chrysler," I said. "They got hurt in '73 during the energy crisis, never recovered. The son wants to turn it into a Datsun dealership."

"Datsun? Are you serious?" Raymond shook his head. "You'll never see me driving anything but American."

"And you're not alone. But, the thing is, foreign makers understand the need for fuel conservation. We haven't quite figured that out yet over here."

"You sound like one of those hippies I see downtown," Raymond said.

I laughed. "I'm just saying, think about it. We keep making these American cars, ignoring the fact we have to depend on foreign energy, what do you think's going to happen? The Carter administration's already warning of an oil shortage. It'll be '73 all over again."

Raymond waved me off. "I'm not going to fall for that alarmist BS. I don't know how—"

"Let's not get into the politics of it," I said. "What we're talking about is Larry Green's car business. From what I understand, he wasn't able to even *give* his cars away. They've apparently been losing money for quite a few years"

"Then why are they still in business?" Raymond said. "Why not close the place down?"

I shrugged, glancing out the window as Maggie walked up the steps. I opened the door for her and said to Raymond, "I guess because it's the family's business. The son claims he didn't even want it, but he doesn't look like he's ready to walk away."

Maggie walked in, taking off her winter hat, brushing her long, red hair with her hand.

I closed the door, and Maggie said, "What a mess."

"What is?"

"The door." She ran her hand over the wood I'd glued back on, then looked at her hand. "Is that glue?"

"I thought I did a good job on it," I said.

She cracked a crooked smile, glancing over at Raymond. The two seemed to get a kick out of my handyman skills. Or lack thereof.

Raymond laughed. "His next business, he's going to be a handyman."

"Like you're some skilled carpenter?" I said.

He tipped his head back and drank from his can. "I never said I was."

I helped Maggie with her coat and hung it on the rack by the door. "Raymond brought a pizza over," I said. "It's in the kitchen. Sorry I didn't wait. I was starving."

"I had a late lunch," she said, eyeing Raymond. "Have you got an extra beer?"

"They're in the fridge," he said.

I went in and got her one, pulling the tab off the can. I handed the can to her and pulled another plate down from the cabinet, placing it on the table. "Help yourself if you're hungry."

I thought about what Raymond had said about the dealership in Rhode Island, and followed Maggie into the other room by the fire. "You know what?" I said, looking over at Raymond. "I might go down to Rhode Island tomorrow, go see Gautieri."

Raymond had turned on the TV and sat on the couch. He didn't respond, and I wasn't sure he heard me.

Maggie said, "Why exactly would you go see New England's most corrupt politician?"

"He's not a bad guy," I said.

She rolled her eyes and sipped her beer. "I'm not sure I buy that, but..."

"Maybe he'd know something about those two goons that jumped me."

"Why?" Raymond said. "Because he has his own goons?"

"Maybe," I said. "He knows a lot of people. He's always got his ear to the ground."

"You mean he knows a lot of crooks," Maggie said.

I shrugged and gave a slight nod. "It's worth a shot. You never know. He knows people all over the Northeast, obviously on both sides of the law. I'm pretty sure the two men were Italian. You never know if they're connected in some way."

"Connected?" Maggie said.

Raymond appeared to have stopped listening, his gaze instead fixed on the TV. "Guys?"

Maggie and I both walked over to him just as he got up from the couch and turned the volume up on the TV.

"Look at this," he said.

"What is it?" I said.

"Shhh!" He put his hand up, palm toward me.

The three of us stood watching Tom Ellis on channel four.

I looked at the scene they were showing on the news, a building in flames. It was an inferno, firefighters spraying water from their hoses on a building without making much of a difference.

"What is it?" I said.

Raymond's eyes went wide, his eyebrows raised. He looked at me, without a word. "It's Green Chrysler," he said. "The building's on fire."

CHAPTER 31

THE NIGHT SKY SURROUNDING Green Chrysler was filled with a color-wheel of lights. Black smoke poured from the orange flames shooting from the building. Blue and red flashing lights came from at least a dozen police, fire, and rescue vehicles. Firefighters were on ladders with hoses shooting water into the flames and at what was left of the roof. They appeared to have the blaze under control compared to the images we saw on the news. The glass on the front of the building was gone, and it appeared that most of the vehicles inside had become blackened piles of steel.

We weren't allowed to get close to the dealership. Officers were on Route One turning cars away and redirecting traffic down a side street. But there were plenty of onlookers out of their cars parked on the side of the road, watching Green Chrysler go up in flames.

Maggie drove as close as she could, parking where we could get a better view. The three of us, including Raymond, watched until an officer came over to us.

"You gotta clear out of here," he yelled.

"What happened?" I said, as if expecting a straight answer.

The man was a local Norwood cop. "What's it look like?" he said, a look of annoyance on his face.

I said, "I'm asking if they know how it happened?"

Maggie pulled me back and showed her badge to the officer. "Sorry," she said. "My friend knows people who work there. He's just concerned."

The arrogant cop glanced at her badge, then scowled. "Does this look like Boston, sweetie pie?"

Raymond stepped around from the other side of the car, where he'd gotten out of the passenger side, and looked down at the cop barely tall enough to reach Raymond's chin. "Hey, show some respect to a fellow officer," he said. "I'm retired, but you think I'd ever show that kind of disrespect to you, if you showed up in the city?"

The cop looked up at Raymond—all six-four of him—but just stared without a response. He didn't seem concerned. "I want everyone to move out of here. Now!" He walked away, continuing to the other cars where people stood watching the scene.

"What an ass," I said.

Maggie shook her head. "He wouldn't have said that if I was a man."

"Sweetie-pie?" I said, trying to make light of it. "Probably not."

Maggie opened the driver-side door and was about to step inside.

I watched the cop, making sure he was far enough away. "I'm going to go see what I can find out. Do me a favor..." I pointed toward the side street where most of the cars were turning. "Park down that road, I'll be right back."

Raymond said, "They're not going to let you get close."

I gave him the thumbs-up, then made sure the cop wasn't watching me and ran across the road, staying low in the darkness and under the blue and red lights cutting through the air. Walking onto the lot, I had the collar of my pea coat up to block my ears from the cold, although I was almost certain I could feel the heat coming from the building.

With my hands in my pockets, I acted like I was just going for a stroll, keeping my head down as I walked past the vehicles from the Channel 4, Channel 5, and Channel 38 news vans.

I made it as far as the customer parking lot, where only a handful of cars were parked. I spotted Jason Green standing with the dealership's receptionist. She was wearing a fur coat and heels. Jason wore a long wool coat.

"What happened?" I said, walking up behind them. They both appeared startled by my sudden appearance.

"What are you doing here?" Jason said.

"I saw the fire on the news," I said. "Came right over." I watched two firemen, each on their own cherry picker, controlling the hoses with water being sprayed down onto the burning building. "So, is this a good thing for you? Or a bad thing?" I didn't know what kind of reaction I would get to my question. Arson was often used as an easy way out of a crumbling business.

"Are you serious?" Jason said. "This is my father's legacy. Our family business. It's all gone now."

I couldn't get a good feel if he was putting on an act or not.

I looked at the woman, her arms folded in front of her like she was cold. She glanced at me but seemed like she didn't want to make eye contact, and hadn't said a word. It was hard to say for sure, but it appeared the two were together, as a couple. I wanted to laugh at Jason, apparently following in his old man's footsteps, dating the receptionist.

I asked again, "Does anyone know what happened?"

Jason shook his head, his gaze fixed on the building. He looked like he might've been genuinely upset, but it was hard to tell in the darkness and the lights and glow from the fire on their faces.

The man had already thrown out mixed signals from the moment I met him. First, he told me he didn't want to own the business. Then he appeared to act as if he'd wiped a tear from his cheek as flames ripped through the building.

Neither seemed to say a word to each other, nor wanted to talk to me. They both just stared, as if in shock. But Jason finally turned to me again. "What do you want?" he said.

I shrugged and didn't answer him. I said, "You think it could've been arson? I'd imagine for a place like this, unless I misunderstood where the business was, financially, a pile of ashes would be worth a lot more than what it was, right?"

Jason said, "You really expect me to say this is a good thing? The last thing I ever expected was to see something like this happen." He shook his head, closing his eyes for a moment. "When I find out who's responsible..."

"I thought you said you don't know what happened?" I cleared my throat, watching him for an answer. "Are you already saying it's arson?"

He seemed to need a moment to think through his answer. "What I'm saying is if it turns out someone made a mistake, or, okay, let's say someone did do something like this on purpose. I'm going to see to it that this person pays the price."

"What if that person was you?" I said, just to get his reaction.

I didn't expect it to go over well.

The woman with him, now under his arm, opened her eyes wide.

He took his arm away from his female friend and turned to me, getting a little too close to me for comfort. "I don't like these accusations you seem to enjoy throwing around." He had a hint of booze on his breath. "What is it with you?" he said. "You can't find any answers to whatever it is you want to believe, so you go around pointing fingers, taking shots at people, see if someone will confess to something?"

"It's more effective than you might think," I said with a grin, keeping my gaze on his. I was afraid he was getting ready to throw a punch, from the look in his eye. "So, seriously. What if they determine it's arson? Who would get the insurance payout?"

"This is none of your business," he said, then changed his answer. "I don't know."

"There's no way that was true," I said. "You'd think that would be one of the first things you'd do... make sure whatever money's left in this place is safe."

"This business wasn't worth ten cents," he said.

"Yeah, I get that. But, the building... All the cars in here. Had to be worth quite a bit. And, I understand you own the land too, so..."

He closed his eyes and took a deep breath, as if trying to control himself from losing his cool. "Listen. I don't know why you're here. But I suggest you leave. Or I'm going to get a cop to drag you out of here for trespassing. And if you don't think I know enough of them to ask for a favor..."

"I get it," I said, holding up my hands. "It's nice to have connections. Especially when you need to cover something up."

Jason Green charged at me.

The woman screamed as he tackled me and we both fell to the ground, wrestling on the cold asphalt.

He threw a couple of punches, but before I had a chance to give one back, we were pulled apart by two cops.

"What the hell's going on here?" one of them said.

The other cop pulled me away from Jason and held my arms behind me.

Jason brushed his coat with his hands, pointing at me. "This man was harassing me. He's already been arrested for a murder up in New Hampshire. Go ahead, ask him about it."

The two cops turned to me, as if waiting for an answer.

The flames on the building had somewhat subsided, although there was still plenty of smoke pouring into the air with a strong smell of burning rubber and plastic, which I imagined was toxic.

The bigger of the two officers said to me, "Is what this man just said accurate?"

I gave a slight shrug. "Well, technically, it might be."

"It *might* be?" The cop hadn't let go of my arms.

I heard Raymond call out from somewhere behind me. "Hey! He's all right..." He walked over to the Norwood police officers and smiled when he made eye contact with one of them. "Mikey?"

The bigger cop, with an inch or two on me, let go of my arm and turned to Raymond. "Hey, Raymond! What are you doing here?" They shook hands. The cop pointed at me with his thumb. "You know this guy?"

"He's my cousin," Raymond said. "Whatever happened here, don't worry. He's all right."

"You sure he's all right?" the cop said. "He just admitted he'd been arrested for a murder up in New Hampshire."

Raymond grabbed me by the collar and pulled me toward him. He said to the cop, "Well, it's a bit of a mix-up."

I looked at Jason and said to the cop, "If anyone was potentially involved in a murder..." I paused, realizing my accusation had crossed the line.

The cops both turned to Jason, then back at me and Raymond.

"What's that supposed to mean," the shorter of the two cops said.

"Don't listen to him," Jason said. "This guy's a troublemaker."

The cop who knew Raymond said, "Your cousin and Mr. Green were wrestling on the ground, like a couple of high school kids."

"Who's Mr. Green?" Raymond said, his gaze on Jason. "You?"

Jason straightened out his coat but didn't respond.

"He's Larry Green's kid," I said.

Raymond said to his buddy, the cop, "If you can maybe just forget any of this happened. Sounds to me this is just a minor scuffle. Right?"

"Scuffle?" Green snapped, pointing at me. "This man assaulted me!"

"Give me a break," I said.

But before the argument grew into anything more, Raymond pulled me toward Route one. He looked over his shoulder at the cop. "Mikey, I'll catch up with you again soon. We'll grab a beer one night." He hadn't let go of my arm, squeezing it with his enormous hands. He said through gritted teeth, "What's wrong with you?"

I yanked my arm from his grasp. "The guy attacked me. All I did was ask what happened."

We both continued our walk toward Route One and tried to stay out of sight of the cop directing the traffic.

"Where'd Maggie park?"

Raymond stopped and looked back and forth, as if he wasn't sure where she'd gone. "She's the one who said I should go check on you. Was afraid you'd get yourself in trouble. As usual, she was right."

CHAPTER 32

I'D FINALLY FALLEN ASLEEP after tossing and turning for most of the night. The house was chilly—the way I preferred it for sleeping. I was comfortable enough under a few layers of blankets. When the phone next to my bed rang, I jumped up immediately, my heart racing as I came out of a short but deep sleep.

The red lights on the clock radio glowed in a blur until my eyes finally focused. It was 4:13 am.

I reached for the phone next to the bed and cleared my throat. "Hello?"

"Is this Jake?"

"Yeah?" I couldn't place the voice.

"It's Chief Williams. In Derry."

I sat up on the edge of the bed and turned on the lamp. I listened without a response.

He said, "I'm sorry to be calling you so early, but I wanted to reach out to you right away. The charges against you are being dropped."

I wiped my hand down my face, followed by a sigh of relief. "You mind telling me why?"

"You don't sound very happy for someone who's off the hook for—"

"I'm jumping for joy," I said. "You just can't see it."

There was silence on the line.

The chief said, "It turns out the tire tracks we found in the snow around Bob Pearson's shop, where someone had apparently turned around, don't match the tracks from your Nova. We actually got some cooperation or, a tip, from the Londonderry police. Next town over..."

I sat still, my head in my hand with the phone to my ear, wishing the chief would spit it out.

"The Texaco owner over there, in Londonderry, said he had a customer that morning who gave him some trouble. Turns out he was the driver, with someone else in the passenger seat, of a yellow Chevrolet Impala. We matched the tire size to that type of vehicle. It's wider than the Nova. The owner of the station didn't get the plate, but said it was a New York registered vehicle."

"What about my gun?"

"We're not quite there yet," he said. "But I know what I know, Jake. And aside from what we've found, I personally don't believe you killed Bob Pearson."

I stopped myself from asking why they jumped the gun with my arrest in the first place, before they'd had their case buttoned up a bit tighter. Maybe it was just the fact that he was the chief of a small-town police department with limited resources. As angry as I could've gotten, I didn't have time to take it personally. "I appreciate the call. But are the charges officially dropped?"

"You should be cleared within twenty-four hours," Chief Williams said.

"Then I'll feel a heck of a lot better when it's official."

"We'll try to find these men," the chief said. "But my department doesn't have a lot of manpower. Not enough to send someone out to New York looking for them, assuming they didn't stick around."

"I have a feeling they didn't," I said. "But I have someone in mind who might be able to help."

***

I left the house around seven in the morning and headed into Providence. I was undecided as to whether I should stop at a payphone and call Tony Gautieri, the mayor of Providence, before showing up at his door unannounced. It had been a good year since I first met him, back when I was on a case and without a doubt was sure he was behind a man's murder.

It turned out he was not. And in fact he played a role in helping me find the killer I was looking for.

Gautieri lived at the Biltmore Hotel, in downtown Providence, a few steps from the entrance to his office at City Hall.

I rode the hotel elevator up to the 13th floor, stepped off and headed down the hall toward the double doors at the end.

I stood back so that whoever looked out the peephole couldn't see who it was. I didn't want any surprises.

The locks clicked on the other side, and the door opened.

Tony Gautieri's graying hair was slicked back on his head. He wore a pressed white dress shirt, and pin-striped suit pants held up with suspenders. "Jake! My friend!"

Tony appeared happy to see me. He reached out and shook my hand, pulling me in and wrapping me up with a hug. He led me into his room. "What a surprise, kid." He stepped back and looked me over. "You look good."

"Good to see you too, Mr. Mayor."

"Come on now. How many times I gotta tell you? It's Tony, to my friends." He smiled and gestured toward the couch.

The sunlight from the tall and wide windows overlooking the city of Providence lit up the room, reflecting off the crystal glasses and liquor bottles on the wet bar.

The room was warm and cozy with the gas fireplace burning.

I never understood why he lived in a hotel, but I guess it made sense for a single man.

"You want some espresso?" He walked into the kitchen area. "I was just about to make myself a cup."

"No, thank you," I said. "I don't want to take up a lot of your time."

He was around the corner, on the other side of the wall that divided the living room area from the kitchen, but stepped out with a small cup and saucer in his hand. "Have a seat." He sat down on the couch a few feet in front of the window, his back to the sun.

I sat on the couch across from him, a coffee table between us, and had to squint, the way the sun came through the windows at my face.

Tony noticed. "You want me to close the curtains?"

"No, I'm all right."

Tony had been the mayor for a few years at that point, winning his reelection in a landslide. Few cities in America would hire a man with rumored Mafia connections, but Tony Gautieri loved his city. He was a man of the people. At least that's what he'd say in his speeches.

Tony extended his arm over the top of the cushion. "So, how have you been?"

"I'm actually hoping you can help me find someone."

Tony leaned forward and picked up his espresso, looking at me over the rim as he took a sip. "Anything's possible. I guess it depends exactly what you're referring to."

I thought about how much I should tell him. "Somebody tried to set me up for murder."

"Tried? Does that mean this person was, uh, unsuccessful?"

"As of this morning, it looks that way," I said. "But I'm not out of the woods yet. I'm working on a case, a man up in Mass was killed in a hot air balloon that allegedly caught fire."

"I heard about this," Tony said. "The car guy, right?"

I nodded. "His name was Larry Green."

Tony placed his cup on the table and stood up from the couch and walked around it, looking out the window overlooking Kennedy Plaza and most of downtown. "What do you want to know?"

"Well, the man's widow hired me to find out what happened. She doesn't believe it was an accident."

Tony turned from the window. "No?"

I stared back at him, my eyes still squinted but getting used to the sunlight blasting through the glass. "There are these men I've run into..." I told him about what happened in New Hampshire.

The look on Tony's face told me he might've known more about the story than I might've realized before I showed up at his door.

"So, what I need to do is track down the two men."

"You got names?"

"No. And I barely got a good look at either one," I said. "But I'm almost certain they were of Italian heritage. One was tall. Maybe my height. The other one was short and stocky."

Tony said, "Not a lot of Italians out there as tall as you."

"Well, I'm *half* Italian," I said.

He cracked a smile. "You know what I'm saying. I'm five-ten, and I'm tall compared to most Italians around here." He stepped around the couch and picked up the cup and saucer, taking another sip, his pinkie out as he did. "So, you think I know every Italian in the Northeast?"

"I'm pretty certain they're hired help."

"Yeah?" He nodded, quiet for a moment or two. "You want to know if I can find out who it was?"

You didn't have to beat around the bush with Tony.

"I've hit a lot of dead ends," I said. "I thought I'd give it a shot, see if you could help."

"You don't know anything yet, right? You're going around asking questions, thinking maybe someone lit that thing on fire, right? And then, these two goons show up? They knocked you around?"

"We knocked each other around," I said. "But I got out of there before it got out of control, without finding out who they were."

"But you're not dead?"

"I don't think so," I said. I smiled.

"You know what I'm saying. I mean, they didn't kill you. So, clearly, it was some kind of warning. Right? Sounds to me someone's playing games with you."

"Not just games," I said. "They tried to set me up for murder. The cops up there took me into custody, and it was only this morning, a few hours ago, I got word the charges would be dropped."

"No shit?"

"And they stole my gun. From my car."

"You leave your gun in the car?" Tony said.

I rolled my eyes. He wasn't the first person to question a foolish decision on my part. "They used it to kill this man in New Hampshire who might've known something about what happened to Larry Green."

"Ouch. They didn't hold you?"

"I posted bail."

"They took you in on murder and you got bail?" He nodded, impressed. "Someone must like you up there."

"It's complicated," I said, thinking about Chief Williams taking me in, when he knew something wasn't right. "These two men drive a yellow Chevy Impala. You remember my car, right?"

"The Nova?" he nodded. "Ohhh, so these two... Someone saw the yellow car. Cops figure it's you? Then they find the gun? That's all they need."

"Exactly." I stood up from the couch and walked over to the fireplace. It didn't seem to throw off much heat. Most gas fireplaces didn't. But the room was still warm without it, or at least it felt that way with the low winter sun coming in through the windows.

I said, "The car had a New York registration, according to the call I got this morning."

"New York?" he said. "You didn't say they were from New York. That's a different story."

"Why's that?" I said. "You know plenty of people in New York, don't you?"

"Of course I do. I'm just saying, I thought you were telling me these two guys were from around here. Rhode Island guys."

"I don't know. They might be. All I can tell you is they had New York plates. Could've been stolen for all I know."

Tony folded his arms, pulling at his chin with his free hand. "So, two Italians guys, one tall, one short, driving a yellow Chevy Impala with New York plates?" He narrowed his eyes, as if he was thinking it through. "All right. I'll tell you what. I'll make some calls, put some feelers out. But you're not giving me much to work with."

"I know that," I said. "I wouldn't have come to you if I had some kind of leads. I've got nothing right now."

"On top of investigating a murder you're not even sure was a murder?" He looked at his watch. "Listen, Jake. What's your timing like? I got meetings all day today. There's a lot of work to do in this city, you know? To make Providence what I think it could be. This is the best city in the world, you know." He stepped to the window again, quiet for a couple of moments as he looked out, a glow around him from the sun in the bright blue sky straight ahead of him. "Can you give me a couple days?" He turned from the window.

He must have seen it on my face that waiting wasn't an option.

"All right," he said. "Here's what I'll do. Give me a few hours. I got a meeting at nine. Hope to be done at ten. I'll put a couple of my guys on it, see what they can dig up."

CHAPTER 33

MAGGIE, DRESSED IN STREET clothes, leaned against the brick wall outside my office. She straightened up when she saw me coming from where I'd parked the Nova a couple blocks away.

She wore big sunglasses and a winter hat, her coat open in front with the temperature in Boston close to fifty degrees. It was warmer than it had been in at least a few weeks. Her milk-white Irish skin glowed in the winter sun.

She said, "So, it's good news, right?"

"I'm not out of the woods yet," I said.

"But what did he say?"

"Chief Williams?" I unlocked the door to my office and let Maggie in ahead of me. "Apparently there are still some questions. And, of course, the fact they used my gun doesn't help."

We walked inside, and I opened the blinds on all the windows, letting the sun that clipped past the buildings across East Broadway into my office.

"What about your friend?" she said. "Is he going to help?"

"Gautieri? It sounds like it. He actually seemed like he knew something about the Larry Green case, but wasn't letting on."

"Why's that?" she said. "Did he say something that—"

"Just the way he acted. He knew what had happened to him. I might've been reading too much into it, but—"

"It's not like it wasn't in the news," she said. "A lot of people knew Larry Green from his silly air balloon commercials."

"Have you heard anything else about the fire? At the dealership?" I went over to the coffee machine to brew a pot.

Maggie said, "I'm hearing arson."

"Not a surprise."

"But these are just rumors at the department. Boston PD's not involved in any way. I don't even think Norwood police will have any indication of what happened until the fire marshal completes his investigation. It could take weeks."

"I know. But I'm moving on the assumption somebody burned that place down." I said, "Maybe the only way anyone was ever going to get money out of the place was to pull something like this off, and collect whatever insurance money they had coming."

Maggie said, "Jason Green?"

"I don't know. Would he have done it, showed up at the scene, standing outside watching it burn like he was seeing a show? He took over as CEO after his father's death. There's a good chance he'd be the one to put a chunk of change in his pocket. Don't you think?"

I could see Maggie's wheels were turning. "Or it could be the opposite."

"Opposite of what?"

"You said yourself, it seems a few people might've had it in for Larry Green. Or maybe someone who wanted to take down the whole business, hoping to get some money out of it."

"The list might be long," I said. "There were quite a few employees laid off too, especially after Jason took over. His father, it seemed, did what he could to keep people working. Maybe not a good business move, but it seems like he did what he could to keep people employed. But after he was gone, even his own son-in-law was fired."

"A bit ruthless," Maggie said.

I dumped water into the coffee machine. "I guess. But the place wasn't bringing in money. They have one sales guy, and the couple of times I've been there all he does is stand around. I've never seen a single customer in the place. He can't be making much money."

Maggie stood silent, then walked over to the window at the front of the office, looking outside at East Broadway. "The way you're explaining it," she said, "is that somebody would have killed Larry Green for one reason, but burned the building down for another?" She turned to me. "So you're not even sure it's the same person, right?"

I said, "That's what makes me think someone wanted Larry gone to change the business, or build it back from the ground up."

The phone rang, the bell louder than I needed it to be. I hurried over to my desk, leaving the brewing pot of coffee, and answered the phone on the second ring.

"Horn Investigations."

"Jake?"

"Speaking."

"It's Marilyn."

"Where are you?" I said. "I tried calling your uncle's house a little earlier, but—"

"We were out," she said. "But I'm actually back in New Hampshire now. I'll be here for the next few days." She paused. "I'm sure you saw what happened?"

"The dealership? Of course," I said.

I told her about the good news I got from Chief Williams."

"So, you think you'll be cleared?" she said.

I gave Maggie a look as she stood watching me on the phone as I said to Marilyn, "I don't think it's official just yet, but I'm feeling better about it than I did when you bailed me out." I leaned on my desk and saw someone in sunglasses and a baseball hat walk by the office and peek through the open blinds on the window, but whoever it was didn't stop. "What do you know about the fire?"

"I only heard about it this morning," Marilyn said. "It was on the news."

"I was actually there last night."

"At the dealership?"

"As soon as I saw it on the news," I said. "We drove over. They were still trying to put it out."

"We?" she said. "You don't work alone?"

I didn't need to explain anything to her about Maggie or Raymond. "I do."

She said, "What did you see?"

"The fire was pretty bad. The building's destroyed. And I saw Jason, watching it burn. He was there with his receptionist, which also surprised me. I guess those two are a couple?"

"I don't know anything about her," Marilyn said. "What's her name?"

I felt foolish, considering I'd never even asked. "I actually don't know. I would've asked, but things got a little rough between me and Jason last night."

"Rough?" she said.

"I guess he didn't like me accusing him of burning the place down."

"Oh," she said, and left it at that without asking for details. "So did you talk to him?"

"I did," I said, glancing over at Maggie, watching me. "But they don't even know if it's arson at this stage, although I'd be shocked to hear it wasn't. My two theories, if it was arson, is that either someone wanted to destroy the business, or wanted revenge. I guess it also could've been a disgruntled ex-employee, taking it out on—"

"Jason fired a few people," she said. "So that wouldn't surprise me at all."

"But that also might mean it may not be the same person who—assuming someone *did* kill him—was involved in what happened to Larry."

"Why do you say it like that? Like you don't believe he was killed?"

"It's not that I don't believe it," I said. "I'm just trying to avoid making assumptions. The problem I have right now is I still need some kind of evidence that's not just circumstantial."

"But what about those two men? And that poor man shot and killed up in New Hampshire? Don't you think there's enough to point to—"

"It's not all physical evidence, and I'm afraid that's what I'm going to need as proof." I had to think for a moment. "It doesn't mean we can't determine what happened to him," I said. "Circumstantial evidence is *still* evidence. And there's enough that's occurred at this point, anyone with half a brain knows there's a lot more to this story compared to what the police initially determined had happened to Larry."

The line went quiet.

"Marilyn?"

"Yes," she said. "I'm here. I just... I had so much hope you'd find something by now. But it doesn't sound like that's the case. I can't tell for sure if you're trying to tell me I may never know the truth? Or if you're more confident than how you're coming across."

I waited several seconds before I responded. "I don't mean to come off that way. But I need to be straight with you. The simple fact is we're not going to find a Polaroid of someone lighting that balloon with a match."

Marilyn made a noise, like a cry or some kind of squeal, and I realized my approach, the way I'd said it, was a little rougher around the edges than it needed to be. "I'm sorry. I just want you to understand…"

I was afraid she might've started crying into the phone

"Listen," I said. "Can you get me some names of employees who you feel were loyal to your husband? But maybe not so much to Jason? There must've been some people like that, no? It seemed the two were on opposite sides of how that business should've been run. And, maybe—I can't make a promise—maybe that's what happened."

"Do you mean, with the fire?" she said.

"Well, that, and—"

"But, we didn't hire you to find the person who burned down a building. I hired you to find my husband's killer." Marilyn's voice was raised as if she were mad. "If you don't think you can do what we've paid you for, then maybe I should look for someone who can."

It happened often. More than I liked. A client—usually the ones who came from some kind of money—didn't get the answer he or she was hoping for during an investigation. And soon the threats would start if the answers didn't come soon enough.

Even when I prepared a client ahead of time and made it clear that it's only in the movies where investigations get wrapped up in a day or two, my investigations never seemed to move fast enough for clients who expected answers with the snap of a finger.

Most cases rarely followed a straight path. I spent my days looking for puzzle pieces and knocking on doors. Sometimes it was pure luck I'd find whatever it is I was looking for.

I learned over the years to take it all as it came, and to do what I could to give my client peace of mind. My Uncle Pat used to say that half the job of a private investigator was keeping clients from losing their heads.

Maggie watched me with a crooked smile on her face.

I said to Marilyn, "They don't even know if it was arson. I'm just trying to get ahead of it. My hope is it will lead us toward the answer you're looking for. I'm trying to find the truth behind what happened to Larry. I promise you, I am. But right now I need to work my way around this. The answer's out there. It always is. It's just going to take more time."

She seemed to calm down somewhat. "What do you want me to do?"

"Like I said, give me some more names. You don't have to do it now. Just list out the employees, especially those who may have been more loyal to Larry, and maybe not so much to Jason."

"I can do that, but I still don't understand why—"

"Please, just trust me," I said.

It took her a moment, but she finally answered. "Sure, yes. Okay. I'm sorry. It's just been emotional for me. And seeing that dealership he worked so hard for burn to the ground..."

"Can you think of anyone, off the top of your head?" I said.

She cleared her throat and blew her nose into the other end of the phone. "Gary Holden is the only salesman who is still there. At least, until last night. The three others who used to work for Larry were fired."

"By Jason?" I said.

"Yes, of course. Larry didn't like to let anyone go, unless he had to."

"But didn't he fire his own son-in-law?" I said.

Marilyn took a moment. "Matt? Well, yes, that was different."

"How so?" I said. I didn't tell her I'd already heard about it.

"Larry was a good person. But, well, he and Matt didn't exactly see eye-to-eye. The work for him just wasn't there. And it's not like Jason hired him back," she said.

There was a pause on the line.

"I have to go now," Marilyn said. "You know where to reach me."

Before I could say another word, the dial tone buzzed in my ear. I placed the handset down and collapsed into the chair behind my desk.

Maggie walked over and put a hot coffee in front of me. "Here," she said, sitting down in the chair on the other side of my desk. "Didn't sound like a good call?"

I looked into the mug of coffee. "I thought I was about to get fired. I don't have any answers."

"Do you really think it's worth going to talk to every former employee of the dealership?" she said. "I mean, it sounded like your client didn't understand why you wanted to investigate that fire. I might have to agree with her."

"I can't ignore it."

"You might have to. At least until they've determined the cause of the fire. You said it yourself, if someone did burn it down, why would that same person kill Larry Green?"

"How do you expect me to answer that?" I said. "I have no idea."

We were both silent for a couple of moments, other than Maggie sipping her coffee.

She said, "Then, why not just focus on what you *do* know."

I leaned back in the chair, my head back, eyes on the stained tiles on the ceiling. "Maybe Gautieri can come up with a name, or somehow figure out who those two guys are. If I can find them—"

"It just seems like a longshot," Maggie said. "You said it yourself, just because he's Italian doesn't mean he knows every Italian on the East Coast."

"I bet if they're involved in crime he does." I picked up the mug and took a sip. The coffee was still hot.

We both sat there, wheels turning.

"What about Richard Reagan?" she said. "He basically admitted to you he knows something, didn't he?"

"All he did was warn me."

"And you don't think the fact Jason Green's friend was over there should tell you something? Have you spoken to either since?"

I shook my head. "It crossed my mind to go to the kid's house."

"What's his name?" Maggie said.

"Kip Rainier."

"And how does he know Richard Reagan? Did they say?"

"Apparently Reagan and Larry Green were both friends with the kid's father. He's the one who had all the money."

"The father? I know the name, Rainier. Wasn't he some kind of businessman?"

I nodded. "Have you heard of him?"

Maggie took a moment to answer. "There's a Rainier who did time, back when I had just started. I only remember because it was my first exposure to a real white-collar crime. I think the FBI got involved."

"You sure it's the same guy?"

"I think his name was Sal," she said. "Sal Rainier? He died in prison."

"What was the crime?"

"Tax evasion, I believe. Or something along those lines. From what I know, he used to go into businesses that were struggling, buy them out from under ownership. He'd strip them down to nothing so they'd appear profitable, then sell the business to another investor."

"Dirt bags," I said. "But the father's dead. I don't know if the son is involved in that type of business or not."

Maggie folded her arms while pulling at her chin. "So, then, what exactly does he do?"

I had to think about it. I didn't know as much about him as I would have liked. "I'm not sure. He's the one who was supposed to help turn Green Chrysler into a Datsun dealership. Allegedly, he had some kind of connections to make it happen. I didn't think they were far off from it."

"Far from what? Selling Datsuns?"

I nodded.

Maggie said, "I assume this guy, Kip, had money he was investing?"

"Unless he was doing it as a friend, to help Jason Green. I can't imagine that's the case, but..."

"Have you checked the corporate papers?" Maggie said.

"For Green Chrysler?"

"Yes, to see who the officers are, of the corporation. If Jason Green slipped right into the role of CEO after his father's death, then there must've been a succession plan already established."

I said, "And could Jason have made changes from there?"

"What kind of changes?"

"To whoever else is part of the corporation?"

Maggie nodded. "You mean, the other officers? The board would have to vote. But it depends on who the majority shareholders are."

"Oh," I said. "How do you know so much about this?"

She grinned. "I took a corporate law class in college."

Maggie was one of the smartest people I know. "I still don't understand why you're not a detective." She stood up from the chair. "Ten years ago female cops didn't even get to wear a uniform, or carry a gun." She rose from her chair. "I'm heading out. But I can take a ride by the Secretary of State's office, get a copy of their corporate filing if you'd like?"

"Thank you," I said, nodding. "Whatever you can do to help, I'd appreciate it."

Chapter 34

Yellow police tape ran across the Route One entrance to Green Chrysler. I parked the Nova along the road and could see three people walking around the building and the rubble surrounding it. Ducking under the tape, I headed across the parking lot. The parked cars were covered in soot from the fire and many appeared damaged.

By the time I was close enough, I realized it was Jason Green and his mother Karen, wearing sunglasses and a long wool coat. Kip Rainier was there in his colorful ski jacket, all standing outside looking over what was left of Green Chrysler.

It wasn't much.

The roof had caved in, the sales floor covered in water and glass and blackened building materials. The cars in the showroom were nothing but charred piles of steel.

The three all turned to me, and Jason said, "Take another step closer and I'm calling the cops."

"I'm not here to cause trouble," I said, looking at Karen, who looked away as soon as I caught her gaze.

Jason's buddy, Kip, said, "Call the cops. He's trespassing."

I put both hands up in front of me. "I'm just trying to get some answers." It wasn't helpful having either of them against me. "The fact is," I said, "when something like this happens to a business that's failing—as you've made it clear this dealership was—it's going to raise serious questions about those who may benefit from such a tragedy. I'm sure you know that."

"Larry built this place from nothing," Karen said. "If you're trying to say any of us had something to do with what happened last night, I'd—"

"I said no such thing. I'm only stating the obvious. I know how insurance companies work."

"But this has nothing to do with you," she said.

"No?"

Jason said, "When are you going to come to the realization, like the rest of us, that my father's death was an accident? We all worried when he went up in that thing. It was old, you know. And it's not the first time a hot air balloon has caught fire."

"Hot air balloon fires aren't that common," I said. "If you'd like to know the facts..." I shook my head. "I'm sorry. I'd like to believe you. But I just can't."

"Believe me about what?" Jason said.

"The fact you're not willing to admit someone killed your father, well... That alone makes me suspicious."

Jason said, "So, you're not only saying I burned this building down, but that I killed my father?" He started toward me, but his mother grabbed him by the arm.

I nodded at Kip. "How's Richard?"

Kip just stared back at me without a response.

"Have you seen him?"

After a pause, he shook his head. "Nope."

I glanced at the debris around the building. "Does he know about this?"

"How should I know?"

"But I thought he was your buddy," I said. "You promised him you were going to take care of everything. Is this what you meant?"

Rainier didn't respond.

I shifted my gaze back to Jason and his mother. "So, is this the end of Green Chrysler?"

Jason said, "Once again, it's none of your business."

I said to Karen, "So, what's your role here? Supportive mom? Or do you all benefit from this?"

"Excuse me?" she said, removing her sunglasses.

"I'm just wondering what you're doing. You were here the other day with Jason. You're here now. I'm trying to figure out if you were more involved in the business than you led me to believe. Is that the case?"

She stared back at me. "This is still a family business. I was the one who helped Larry in the beginning. You don't think it upsets me to see it all gone?"

"I don't know," I said. "Does it?"

Kip took a step and gave me a shove with both hands. "Time for you to go, buddy."

I was about to take a swing, but Karen stepped between us. "Stop it! Both of you!" She looked me in the eye with a hint of anger in her gaze. "You need to leave. This is upsetting enough."

I backed away, knowing that throwing a few punches at Kip would not solve anything, even if it might make me feel better for a moment. "I think I'll go talk to Reagan," I said. "See what he has to say."

I told them that only because I wanted to see what kind of reaction I'd get.

Kip said, "Why don't you just leave the old man alone?"

"Richard's not well," Karen said.

"Not well?" I said, although I knew what she meant. Clearly, the man had hit rock bottom in more ways than one.

She gazed at me as if I'd asked a foolish question. "The poor man doesn't have any money. He's living in that rat-infested apartment, all those books and papers everywhere like a damn hoarder."

"I didn't know you'd been there," I said. "You didn't give me the impression you were close enough to pay him a visit."

She slipped her sunglasses back on, but didn't break her gaze. "Can't you just leave us all alone? We didn't ask for any of this."

"Well, I'm sorry. But somebody did. And if you think threats are going to stop me..." I gazed at Kip. "You came right out and told me you were there to help Richard get his money back. Did you forget you told me that?"

"It's the truth," he said, turning to look at the pile of rubble. "But, now, I'm not so sure. No car manufacturer is going to want to be involved in this mess."

"What?" Jason said. "What if we rebuild? I thought you said—"

"I'm sorry." Kip turned from me to his friend. "The deal I was working on... This isn't good. It's likely any deal I could pull off is going to fall through. The Japanese are serious businessmen. They're not going to be sympathetic to what happened here. I'm sorry."

Jason was clearly agitated, and upset to a point either he was a talented actor, or the conversation I'd witnessed really did unfold right before my eyes. He said to Kip, "Are you kidding me?"

I felt as if I was watching something staged by a couple of Hollywood actors. But maybe I was wrong.

"I'll do what I can," Kip said. "But I already let them know what happened. The reaction wasn't good, of course."

"Wait a minute," I said, turning to Kip. "You're saying that this building burning down is going to ruin whatever plans you allegedly had?"

Kip took a step toward Jason, reaching out to shake his hand. "I'm sorry."

Jason knocked it away. "How could you do this?"

"It's not me," Kip said. "I swear, I... I'm still going to talk to them. I'll do what I can. But I'm afraid it's not going to be what we were hoping for. If I can keep it alive, it'll be another year or two before anything happens. Maybe more. They're going to move on to something else."

Something didn't jibe. But I wasn't sure what it was.

"I'm sorry," Kip said once again. He walked past me and headed toward the customer parking lot, where his 280Z was parked next to a Chrysler LeBarron—the same model Raymond had.

"Great friend," I said, eyeing Jason.

The 280Z started up. Kip revved the engine before he took off, tires squealing. He went around the back of the building where I couldn't see the car until it appeared a moment later, buzzing by heading north on Route One. I didn't know there was a second entrance to the dealership behind the building.

"I think it's time for me to go, too." I turned and headed for the road saying nothing else. I was more confused with the situation than I'd already been.

I wasn't sure I could rule out Jason being responsible for burning down the building, and he clearly wasn't aware of the repercussions if he was in fact the one behind it. But it didn't mean he—or the other two—had nothing to do with killing Larry Green.

***

I pulled into Sam's Sunoco in Walpole to use the payphone, and called Gautieri. I'd hoped he had some answers for me.

The woman who answered the phone at City Hall put me on hold, and it took another few minutes before Tony finally picked up.

"Jake?"

"Tony. I hate to bug you, I was just curious if you've heard anything about my two friends in the yellow Impala?"

"As a matter of fact," he said, "I called your office a couple of times but nobody answered. I put the word out, like I said I would, and it's possible I know who these two men are."

"No kidding?" I said. "I really appreciate the help. I know how busy you are, and—"

"There's a *but*," he said. "I don't have their names."

"What? Why not?"

Gautieri said, "Well, because they're somewhat connected with someone my family is associated with, and, uh... that's just how we work. All right?"

"But I thought you said you could help me?"

"I am going to help you. But I'm not going to give you every detail."

I leaned my forehead against the cold steel payphone, the handset up to my ear. "Come on, Tony. What am I supposed to do without names?"

"Isn't that what you do? The private investigator thing? I'm sure you'll figure it out. What I can tell you is that, as you'd mentioned, that these two are, well, they're freelancers."

"Freelancers?"

"Yeah. They're uh—"

"Hired guns?" I said.

"That's right. And, from what I hear, not the brightest bulbs."

"What can you tell me?" I said. "How can I find them?"

"I'll tell you where you can find them, all right?"

I nodded, holding the phone. "I appreciate it, Tony."

"No problem, my friend." He cleared his throat. "Now, you know Shrewsbury Street? In Worcester?"

"Is that the Italian section?" I said.

"Yeah, it's the heart of the Italian community out there. I used to spend a lot of time there, when I was a kid."

"But the car had New York plates," I said. "You sure it's the right—"

"I'm not certain about the car. Plates probably'd been stolen. Maybe the car was stolen. I can't answer that."

"Okay," I said, waiting.

"Now," Gautieri said, "there's a place called Rossati's Restaurant. Good food. Small place. But these two men you're looking for, they frequent the place. Mostly in the evening, from what I've been told. You should be able to find them hanging out at the bar. You know what I'm saying?"

"Yes, I do. Of course. Thank you. This is really—"

"I have your word," he said. "You never got this from me?"

"Of course. Yes. You have my word. You never told me a thing."

"This phone call never happened," he said. "Capiche?"

"Yes, absolutely. Thank you, Tony." I hung up the phone.

CHAPTER 35

Raymond opened his front door as soon as I pulled into the driveway and stepped out onto his porch. Slipping his jacket on, he yelled something into the house behind him as he pulled the door closed.

The Nova's headlights shone on him hurrying down the steps, zipping his jacket. He came over to my side of the Nova, and I rolled down the window. The frozen mist came from his mouth.

I said, "You getting in?"

He shook his head. "No, let's take the LeBarron. They know your car, obviously."

"I thought of that," I said. "But it's not like I'm going to park it near the place."

"I don't care," he said. "Let's go. I'll drive."

He turned, the hem of his jacket caught on the pistol he had tucked into the back of his pants. I hoped we could make it through the night without a shot being fired.

I locked up the front door of the Nova, but popped the trunk. "Should I move it to the street? In case Beth has to get out?"

"Nah, she's not going anywhere," he said.

I pulled the rope, duct tape, and two black canvas bags from the trunk and handed them to Raymond. He opened the lid of the LeBarron's trunk and tossed them inside.

"Hang on," I said, and went up to the front door of the house.

Raymond stood between the driver-side door and the car itself watching me, his elbow casually resting on the roof. "Where are you going?"

"To give Beth my keys. You never know." I knocked on the door.

Beth opened it and said "Will you tell me where you two are going? Raymond told me not to worry, but..."

I handed her my keys. "He's driving, so why don't you hold onto these, in case you have to move my car. Or, you can drive it if you need to." I turned and headed down the steps.

"Jake!" she said. "Why won't you two tell me where you're going?"

I kept going, acting as if I couldn't hear her raised voice, although I'm sure even the neighbors could.

"Please, be careful," she said. "Both of you."

Raymond had already started the engine when I stepped into the driver's side. The leather seats were hard and cold.

He started to back up before I'd even closed the door. Cutting the wheel, he whipped the front end around in the street, slamming down the gas as he took off ahead, the tires spinning on the sand and salt on the asphalt. He reached into his jacket pocket and pulled out a small revolver, handing it to me. "Here," he said. "My old reliable Saturday Night Special. Careful. It's loaded."

I looked it over, then put it in the glovebox.

Raymond drove over to Morrissey Boulevard and headed north to Columbia Road, where he picked up 93 and took the exit for The Pike.

It was an hour-long drive, and neither of us said much of anything for the first few miles.

The Bruins game was on the radio, but I paid little attention to it. The volume was low, although I could make out Bob Wilson's play-by-play, with Glenn Ordway doing the color. I had enough on my mind to worry about the score.

"So how come you didn't tell Maggie?" Raymond said. "I almost slipped when she told me she was trying to reach you."

"When was she trying to reach me? About what?" I thought about the corporation papers she was going to get before she went in for a night shift she'd picked up from another officer who needed the evening off.

"I wasn't thinking," he said. "She didn't sound like it was important."

"Well, I'm thinking it might've been." I told him about the corporation and how she thought it would be a good idea to see exactly who was an officer in the business, and who wasn't. Something must have changed after Larry Green had died.

Raymond was quiet for the next few miles, but I could feel him glancing at me every few moments, the glow from the display on the dash the only light inside the car. He finally said, "You ever wonder if maybe this guy took his own life?"

I had my eyes on the dark highway ahead. There were few other cars on the road, other than one that would pass by every few minutes. I took a moment before I answered. "I thought about it. But it doesn't make much sense. Who would light himself on fire? Why not just jump?"

Raymond nodded, as if he agreed with my line of thinking.

I said, "I told Marilyn, his widow, there's always a chance we may never know the truth for sure. But after all that's happened, I'd be a fool to think your old buddy did his job."

Raymond gave me a look. "McCaffrey?"

"Yeah. But in his defense, he had little to go by."

"He was a good cop," Raymond said. "I can't tell you what happened up there, but I'm not going to believe he was tied up in any of this. I mean, maybe he got a little lazy, knowing retirement was right around the corner."

"Well, you know me. Every cop is crooked until I see proof otherwise."

"That's a shitty way to go through life, don't you think?"

I thought Raymond would've understood I wasn't being serious. But when it came to defending his fellow boys in blue, he always took it personally.

I said, "I'm just hoping we get some answers tonight."

"That's assuming they're where Gautieri said they'd be," Raymond said. "What are we going to do if they're not? We don't even have names."

"It's a crapshoot. But I'm just hoping we find some luck. I could use it."

Raymond laughed, but I wasn't sure why.

I said, "What's so funny?"

He gave me a quick look out of the corner of his eye, repositioning himself in the seat, stretching his back. "You talk about the cops being crooked, but here you are, somehow became good buddies with a mob-connected mayor? And now he's helping you catch up with a couple of hoodlums?" He laughed again. "You know what that means?"

I waited without a reply.

Raymond said, "You think it's different, you getting tips from a mob guy?"

"He's not technically a mob guy," I said.

"If that's what you want to tell yourself, then..."

"Everybody needs someone in the know," I said. "And Tony knows a lot of people. In this case, it could work out in my favor."

"It could," Raymond said. "Let's just hope we're not walking into a bees nest of some sort."

I waited, wondering if he'd explain what he meant.

"You ever worry if Gautieri'd set you up?" he said.

I laughed. "Oh, now who's the one going through life with such skepticism?"

Raymond gave me a quick glance. "There's a difference between a mayor with mob ties and the boys in blue. Do I really need to explain that to you?"

I turned and glanced out the passenger window at the moving dirt-covered piles of snow built up along the edges of The Pike. "He's not setting me up," I said. "What would be the purpose?"

Raymond waited. "You said it yourself, he seemed to know something more about Larry Green's death than he let on."

"Maybe. But I trust him," I said.

"Yeah? You two are that tight, huh?" Raymond chuckled, his eyes ahead on the road.

I didn't respond, and had to think about it a little more to make sure I hadn't overlooked something that could put me and Raymond in some kind of danger. At least more danger than we were expecting.

We both stayed quiet for the next five miles, at least until the headlights cut through the darkness on The Pike and shined on the sign for Route 9. I grabbed the paper from my pocket with directions I'd written from the map, and turned on the dome light. "Take this exit," I said, turning off the light so Raymond could see.

He hardly slowed down when we hit the exit, the tires squealing on the off-ramp before he finally let up on the gas.

"We stay on this for nine miles," I said. "Then take a right on Shrewsbury."

Raymond reached for his .38 resting on the seat between us. He controlled the steering wheel with his wrists and rotated out the pistol's cylinder. He used the glow from the dashboard lights to examine the gun, then closed the cylinder and placed the .38 back on the seat.

"I'm kind of hoping you won't have to use that," I said.

"We're definitely going to use it," he said. "But I assume you mean, you're hoping one of us doesn't have to pull a trigger."

I took the Saturday Night Special out of the glovebox and held it in my hand. It was small, but did the job when needed. I was never a big fan of guns, although I wasn't afraid to use one. The only gun I ever owned was the one my uncle had given me, and I knew I'd have to get it back. My uncle would be rolling in his grave knowing I left it under the seat and someone allegedly used it as a murder weapon.

Chapter 36

RAYMOND AND I BOTH wore baseball caps walking into Rossati's Italian Restaurant, as if that was enough of a disguise for someone who knew exactly who I was.

His was black and gold with the spoked Bruins emblem on the front. Mine was a red and blue Red Sox hat.

We were greeted by an old woman standing by the front door with menus in her hand. "We're going to the bar," I said, and continued past her.

There were stairs that went to the second level, but the lights appeared to be off up there. The sign at the bottom step said Private Parties Only.

The dining tables were spread out in a few different small rooms, rather than the restaurant being one open area. One space looked to be the main dining area, the others smaller rooms where I could see through doorways into them, with fewer tables. But all were full, most of the people somewhat dressed up, at least more so than me and Raymond.

The dimly lit bar area was as full as the dining room, the bar long with three sides and at least twenty-five stools. The only two stools available were at the far end.

We had a lot of glances coming our way. Which was normally the case with Raymond at six-foot-four and me just a couple of inches less, it was never easy to blend in with the crowd. We were also the only ones with hats on.

I tried not to make eye contact with anyone as we took the two remaining seats at the bar.

The bartender came right over, placing a cocktail napkin in front of each of us. "What'll it be, gentlemen?"

I looked at the line of beer bottles along the back wall behind the man, then over at the tap. I knew I probably shouldn't have a drink, but I also didn't want to stand out like a sore thumb, sitting at a bar with nothing to sip on. "You have Narragansett?"

"Of course." He gave Raymond a nod with his chin. "You?"

"I'll take a bottle of Black Label."

The bartender gave one more quick nod and walked away.

I had kept my head somewhat low without making it obvious I was trying to look around. It appeared to be mostly men at the bar, other than a couple of nicely dressed women down the other end from where Raymond and I were seated.

Some patrons continued watching us.

I didn't recognize anyone as either of the two men we were looking for.

"You see 'em?" Raymond said, his voice hushed.

I tried to get a look at each customer at the bar. I wasn't 100 percent certain what these two guys looked like after our meet up in Boston, but I had a pretty good idea.

The bartender brought over our beers and reached under the counter, placing two menus on the bar. "My name's Angelo. When you're ready to order something to eat, give me a shout." He walked away.

Raymond took a good swig of his beer. "I hope this isn't a waste of time."

I didn't respond. "Maybe we should eat?"

Raymond started peeling the label off his bottle. "I guess I shouldn't have more than one, huh?"

I tried to listen to some of the conversations around me.

Raymond kept his voice hushed and said, "I know I asked you this already, but you sure you can trust Gautieri."

"And I already told you; I don't think he'd steer me wrong. Not on purpose. So you can stop worrying. We just have to hope these guys show up, if they're not already here." I leaned on the bar, arms folded. I hadn't touched my beer.

Raymond and I both turned and looked over our shoulders when a side door opened behind us and a cold draft filled the area around the bar. The sign over the door said EMERGENCY EXIT.

A man walked in, bundled up a long black jacket and knitted hat. I recognized him right away from the alley. He was the taller of the two. I made sure not to make eye contact, but saw enough of him that I knew I had it right. I leaned toward Raymond and whispered, "It's him."

We both turned and looked straight ahead, the man no more than a couple of feet behind us. Sipping our beers, we tried to look normal, like just a couple of guys at the bar having a drink. My heart raced, but I did all I could to remain calm.

What I really wanted to do was jump up, stick the gun in the guy's ribs and drag him outside... beat him until he spilled his guts. But that wasn't a reality. Not in a place he likely knew half the crowd. And there were already more people there than I'd expected.

I took a quick look over my shoulder and saw the guy hanging his jacket on the rack. He walked toward us and stood two feet away.

"Hey, Angelo," he said, talking over us, to the bartender. "You didn't save me a seat?"

More than half of the patrons seated at the bar gave him a nod or a quick wave. But nobody got up or offered him a seat, so it wasn't like he was some kind of boss anyone feared.

He was so close at that point, I could smell the man's cheap cologne. I didn't want to turn my head or look at Raymond, fearing the guy'd recognize me. I had no idea how long he'd been following me, or how long he'd had an eye on me over the past week.

I wondered where his shorter buddy was. The way Gautieri made it sound was that he knew who these guys were because they were some kind of duo. If he was right, the other guy could've been outside, or not far behind.

I pulled the brim of my hat down tight over my eyes and lowered my head. The man hadn't moved from behind us. The bartender walked over with a drink in his hand, said excuse me and reached between me and Raymond to hand the man the glass.

The guy behind me said, "Excuse my reach, gentleman." He took the glass from Angelo.

The bartender looked around the rest of the bar. "Sorry, Louie. Hopefully a seat will open up soon. You want me to get you a chair from the dining room?"

The man laughed. "Are you serious? What am I going to do, go sit in the corner, like some kid at school?" He walked away and went down the bar to talk to a couple of men who looked to be deep into their own conversation. He shook hands with each one, then the two laughed, as if he'd said something funny.

I tried not to stare or make it look obvious we were watching, but I caught a glimpse of him looking our way.

"Shit," I said, under my breath.

Raymond had his hat pulled low too. He leaned toward me. "What if I get up and leave, tell him to sit down right here."

"Then what?"

"You stick the gun in his ribs, get him to go outside."

"No way," I said. "Someone'll see it. I'd rather wait, get him in the bathroom or—"

"What if he doesn't have to pee?"

"He's at a bar," I said. "Who goes to a bar and doesn't hit the head at least once." I gave Raymond a quick glance, then sipped my beer, shifting my gaze back toward the man. And it looked, at least for a moment, like he was looking our way once again.

"I got an idea," Raymond said. "How about I grab his coat and hat, make sure he sees me. I'll go out the same door he just came in."

"It's an emergency exit," I said. "We don't want to set off an alarm."

Raymond shook his head. "It doesn't look armed."

I looked at the door again. "If you think it'll work…"

He finished whatever beer was left. "I wish I could have another two or three," he said, reaching back for his wallet. He pulled it out and threw a couple of bills up on the bar.

I said, "What if he's not the only one who runs out after you?"

"I guess that's a possibility. But at least we'd get him outside. Then you come out right after him. You don't think it'll work?"

I thought for a moment, keeping my chin down. "Let's give it a try."

The bartender came over. "You want a couple more?"

Raymond stood up. He took his own jacket off the back of the chair and slipped it on.

I pulled out a couple of ones and slid it toward Angelo. "I'll have one more." I didn't want it to look like I was leaving. "All right," I said to Raymond, loud enough so anyone around us could hear me. "I'll see you later." I wasn't sure why I said it the way I did, but it's what came out of my mouth.

Angelo brought over another 'Gansett and slid the bottle toward me, put a Black Label in front of Raymond's seat, and took my money to the register. He rang me up for the two beers and brought back some change.

I lifted my gaze just enough to catch the man, Louie, looking toward Raymond walking away from the bar. "Oh," the man said, his voice raised. "Big guy, you leaving? That seat available?"

Raymond didn't turn back or answer. He instead grabbed the jacket from the coat rack and took off out the side door.

This guy, Louie, yelled at Raymond. "Hey! What the..." He buzzed past me and out the door after Raymond.

I waited before I got up.

Everyone at the bar looked to see what was happening. But nobody moved.

Angelo was at the other end of the bar. I got up from the stool, and instead of going out the side door, I headed toward the entrance. I walked past the woman at the door, gave her a nod and a smile, then once outside ran around to the side of the building.

I spotted the yellow Chevy Impala parked in the street, and could hear yelling from the other side of the building. I ran around the corner to see this guy Louie going after Raymond, who ran fast for a man his size.

But the man caught up to Raymond.

"Give me my jacket, you son of a bitch, before I—"

Raymond stopped, threw the jacket in the man's face, and had his .38 raised.

When the man took the jacket off his face, his eyes opened wide, staring back at Raymond's gun. "What the hell?"

I stepped up behind the guy and jammed the Saturday Night Special into his spine. "Let's go for a ride, Louie."

CHAPTER 37

RAYMOND TURNED THE LIGHTS off and drove slowly around to the back of the United Screw Machine Products building off Shrewsbury Street. He stopped the car and slipped it into park. The manufacturing facility appeared to be closed, with only a single streetlight shining in the distance at the back of the lot.

We both stepped out and went around to the rear of the LeBarron. I held up the gun, pointed it at the trunk, and Raymond slipped his key into the lock. The lid popped open, and our friend looked up at us and tried to move, but didn't have much luck the way we'd used duct tape to tie his hands and his feet.

I ripped the single piece of tape from his mouth, and he started yelling at us in what I guess was Italian.

"I don't speak Italian," I said. "So if you have something to say…"

"You sons of bitches," the man yelled. "Do you have any idea who I am?"

Raymond and I both shook our heads.

"We actually don't," I said. "But that's what we'd like to find out." I had the wallet I had taken from him earlier in my pocket, and pulled it out to show him. "So far, we know your name's Louie Ricci. We'd love to hear more." I looked through the wallet. "I also know you don't have that much cash."

We reached into the trunk for our friend. I grabbed his arms, and Raymond grabbed his legs. The man flailed, tried to kick both feet at once, which did little for him. But he wouldn't stop kicking, so we dropped him onto the cold hard ground.

He screamed in pain when he hit the asphalt with a thump.

It took the man a minute—he apparently still hadn't recognized me—until his eyes opened wide and he finally realized it wasn't the first time we'd met. "Hey, you're the... You're that private investigator!" He squinted his eyes. "How'd you find me?"

"It's what I do," I said, smiling.

Raymond pulled his gun from the back of his pants and stuck it in the man's face. "We want names."

"What names?" The man eyed the gun inches from his cheek.

"Who are you working for?" I said.

He lifted his head and glared up at me from the ground. "I don't know what you're talking about."

I put my boot on his chest. "Listen. I know someone sent you after me in that alley. You don't know me. And I don't know you. But I know you didn't do it on your own, just for fun. So, all you have to tell me is who hired you."

Louie Ricci didn't answer.

There was a case not too long ago when I was being threatened by a man—an ex-cop—who I thought was going to pull my teeth with pliers. It didn't happen, but the threat of it gave me an idea before we left Raymond's house.

I reached into my coat's inside pocket and pulled out a pair of pliers. "Hold his head," I said, stepping closer while moving the pliers toward his mouth.

Raymond kept the gun pressed against Louie's face and grabbed a bunch of the man's hair, yanking his head back.

"Open wide," I said, moving in closer with the pliers held open.

"Wait! Wait!" he said. "What are you doing?"

"What's it look like?" I said, putting more pressure on his chest with my boot. "I'm going to take out your teeth. One at a time, until you tell me who you're working for."

Ricci had nice white teeth to go with his bright, wide eyes filled with fear. He tried shaking his head, but Raymond had a pretty good grip on him.

He had his mouth closed, but Raymond cocked the hammer on his .38. "Open your mouth."

Louie opened right away, and I tapped his front teeth with the tip of the metal pliers. "Should I start with the front? Or the back? The front's probably easier, right?"

"No! Stop!" he cried. "I don't know any names. I never get them. It came through a contact in Boston. The man who hired me."

"And *what* were you told to do?" I said. "To get me to stop investigating Larry Green's death? And to kill an innocent man in New Hampshire?"

"And the girl," Raymond said. "The hooker?"

Ricci cried, "No, stop! I didn't kill nobody."

I hadn't taken my boot off the man's chest, wondering how I could get this guy to talk.

"You're going away for murder," I said. "So you might as well tell us who you work for."

"Who's your boss?" Raymond yelled, lifting the guy like a rag doll from the ground and swinging him around, slamming his limp body against the car. He pushed the muzzle of his .38 against Louie Ricci's temple and gave me a quick nod. "Go ahead. Start with the front teeth."

"No-no-no!" Louie said. "The guy I work for... I'll tell you what you want to know. I just do what I'm paid to do. I don't ask questions."

"You said that already," I said. "I want a name."

I raised the pliers and said to Raymond, "Hold his head still."

Raymond pressed the muzzle against Ricci's cheek. "Open your mouth."

"No! Please... I'm telling you the truth. That's just how we... That's how I work. No names. No information. Just tell me the targets, I do what I'm paid to do."

"Kill innocent people?" I said.

The man didn't respond.

"Did you kill Larry Green?"

He shook his head, or at least tried to. "No."

"And why didn't you kill me?" I said. "You had the chance, didn't you?"

He shrugged. "If I was hired to kill you, you would be dead. I was only told to scare you off. It's not my business to make the decision whether you live or die. Unless I have no choice." He looked, side-eyed, at Raymond with the gun to Louie's head.

I said, "I need a name. The client. Your contact. One or the other."

"I told you, I don't know the name. I do not work for them. I work for my contact."

I laughed, but more out of frustration. "Then tell me *his* name."

"I don't know." Ricci was shaking. Maybe from the cold, maybe from all Raymond breathing in his face with the .38 pressed hard into his cheek.

"Where's your buddy?" I said. "The short one you were with in the alley?"

"How should I know?" he said. "He's not my buddy. I don't even like him. We run jobs together here and there. That's all."

I said, "So now you're going to tell me you don't know his name, either?"

Louie Ricci held his gaze on me for a moment or two, then shook his head. "I can't tell you his name."

I was losing patience.

"You can't tell me?" I took a deep breath and exhaled in frustration, then surprised him with a punch to the gut. I didn't like the way I had to go about my business with this guy, but he was a dirtbag. I'd get over it.

Ricci coughed, wheezing, and fell to the ground as Raymond let go of him. But I picked him up myself, slammed him against the car and had the gun's muzzle under his chin. "You think you're leaving here without talking?" I glanced at Raymond. "Hold his head. I was hoping to avoid this."

I had the pliers out again as Raymond grabbed Ricci by the head, his .38 pressed against his skull.

"Okay, okay," he said. "I'll tell you my contact's name. But you have to swear you won't tell him where you got it from."

"Oh, okay," I said, as if it was going to matter. "Give me the name."

"Bruno," he said. "Johnny Bruno."

"Who is he?" I said. "Your contact?"

He nodded. "Please, don't tell him I told you. He'll kill me."

Raymond gave me a look. "We good?"

I thought about it for a moment, then nodded. "Get the rope."

CHAPTER 38

IT WAS PAST MIDNIGHT by the time we'd made it back to Raymond's house. Maggie's Scamp was in the driveway, parked behind the Nova. A curtain opened, and Beth peeked out through the window, and a moment later the front door opened.

Beth stepped outside, arms folded, squeezing herself in the frigid air. "Where have you two been? I've been worried sick!"

Maggie, at least half a foot taller than Beth and standing behind her, stood in the doorway looking at me and Raymond from behind as we walked up the steps.

The smell of the fire burning cut through the frigid air.

I said to Maggie. "What are you doing here?" I looked at my watch.

"I've been calling you all night. Your house. The office. I finally called Beth, and she said you wouldn't tell her where you guys went."

"I didn't want you to worry," Raymond said, kissing Beth on the top of her head as we stepped inside. He closed the door and put his arm around her.

Maggie glanced from me to Raymond. "You could have at least called. Beth was worried. We both were."

"I'm sorry," Raymond said. "We would have called if we saw a payphone. You know how it is between here and Worcester, on The Pike for the whole ride."

"What were you doing in Worcester?" Maggie said. She turned to me.

I looked at the two gazing at me and Raymond, waiting for answers. I was hesitant to say anything at first. But then I went ahead and told them most of the story about what we'd done, and how the night unfolded, and how ultimately we got Johnny Bruno's name as the man who allegedly hired Louie Ricci.

"But you didn't call the cops?" Beth said.

Raymond and I both glanced at each other and shrugged at the same time..

I said, "We tied him to the lamp post in the parking lot, taped a sign to him to call Chief Williams *and* Detective Carter."

Maggie ran her hands down her face. "Are you serious? It's freezing out there."

Raymond and I both nodded.

"I actually did call the cops, let them know," I said. "And we made sure our friend kept his hat on his head, so he stayed warm." I turned to Maggie. "Why were you looking for me?"

She was clearly upset with me and Raymond. I wasn't sure if it was because she hated when I'd break the rules, or because we didn't include her in on the fun.

"It was about those corporate documents," she said. "I found some things. There were a lot of changes before and after Larry Green's death."

Raymond put a log on the fire.

"What kind of changes?" I said.

"Karen Green and Kip Rainier were both added to the corporation, as officers. It happened a week after Larry Green's death."

I said, "And neither were part of it, when Larry was still alive?"

Maggie shrugged. "They may have been involved, but they weren't corporate officers. Jason Green became the President and CEO after his father's death. Then he adds his mother back. And hires his buddy."

Raymond was poking the fire and looked back at me and Maggie. "What exactly does that tell you? He added his mother and his rich friend? I'm not sure there's anything strange about that."

"It may not be strange," I said. "But it's certainly more than a coincidence the changes are made as soon as the father's gone."

Maggie said, "Something else I found, which dates back prior to Larry Green's death. Richard Reagan was at one time an officer. Vice President."

I said, "I thought he was just an investor?"

Maggie said, "I spent an hour at the Secretary of State's office, going through old records and notes. They have to record every move the corporation made throughout its brief history."

"That's interesting," I said. "So, Reagan was an officer in the business, and an investor? But he was removed?"

"He apparently resigned," Maggie said. "Marilyn Green took his place as Vice President."

"She was vice president? I wonder why she never mentioned that," I said. "Or that she had replaced Richard Reagan?"

None of us had an answer.

"So," I said. "They get rid of Larry, they change the company to how the kid wanted to, and—"

"Are you really thinking Jason Green killed his father?" Maggie said. "To take over a business you said he didn't sound like he wanted in the first place?"

"I'm not saying one way or the other. But it's no doubt suspicious, all that seems to have happened once the father was out of the picture."

"What about the ex-wife?" Raymond said. "She jumps right back into the company, they get your client—the widow—out of there…"

I didn't respond, because I wasn't sure what to think. "I can't see them all collaborating, to get rid of Larry Green by having him killed? It just doesn't make sense."

Maggie said, "So what about this guy, Johnny Bruno? Do you have any other information, other than a name? Or are you going to just go knock on his door? And what do you think's going to happen when they find his friend tied to the utility pole?" She looked around the room and said to Beth.

"We don't even know where to find him," I said. "Or where to find him."

Maggie turned to Beth. "Where are your White Pages?"

Beth went and opened the doors under a cabinet-like side table next to the couch. She pulled out the phone book and handed it to Maggie.

Maggie sat on the couch and flipped through the pages.

Raymond said, "What about asking your best buddy down there in Providence if he knows who this Bruno guy is?"

I shook my head. "He would've mentioned it, if he had more he wanted me to know."

"It wouldn't hurt to ask, would it?" Raymond said. "He doesn't seem to mind helping you out, so—"

"That's the problem," I said. "I'm not sure I want to go there, get wrapped up in owing him too many favors. I'm already in the hole, after this last one. Besides, what if he *does* know who he is? And he's got some kind of connection to the guy. Then what? I end up on the wrong side of the fence."

Maggie said, "You're afraid of being on the wrong side, against a mob-connected mayor?"

I had to think about it before I responded. "Why would I want to be on his bad side?"

Raymond said, "If he knows this guy, Bruno... Maybe as soon as you mention his name, he tells you what he's all about, where to find him."

I didn't like the idea of going to Gautieri. "I'd rather try some other avenues first." I glanced over at Maggie, running her finger down a page inside the White Pages. "Any luck?"

She looked up from the phone book, shaking her head. "I get what you're saying. About Gautieri. The way guys like him operate. You keep going back to the well, you're going to have to replenish it at some point. And, besides, how involved do you want him to be? He pointed you in the right direction. Next time might be different. I'd leave it at that."

Beth sat in the wingback chair by the fireplace and yawned. I thought for sure she was about to fall asleep. But she straightened up in her chair. "Can someone explain to me who this Bruno guy is?"

Raymond stepped toward her, resting his hand on her shoulder. "The less you know, the better."

She pushed his hand away. "How do you know I can't help? I've been around this city since the day I was born. You don't think maybe I know a person or two?"

"We don't even know if he's in Boston?" I said, the three of us watching her.

Beth sat in silence for a couple of moments. "Actually," she said, "I went to school with a kid with the last name Bruno. Michael Bruno. He had a sister, Sophia. They lived with their cousins in an apartment on Church Street, right near the school."

"No Johnny?" I said.

"Not that I remember. But it could've been the cousin. I'm not sure if that helps at all. I mean, we were maybe twelve years old at the time. It was a long time ago. I remember their parents had split up, so the kids moved in with the cousins. But then they moved away, and I never saw them again."

We were all quiet, waiting for more.

"Well, it's more than anything else we have," I said, turning to Maggie. "Is there a Michael Bruno listed? Or maybe Sophia?"

Maggie looked down at the White Pages again, running her finger along the page. Then she raised her gaze, eyes open wide. "There is! Michael Bruno. Right in Hyde Park."

"A little late to call now," I said, looking at my watch. "But maybe I'll take a spin by in the morning. You never know."

Beth got up and opened the secretary desk by the front door, came back with a pad and a pen. "Here," she said, handing it to Maggie.

Maggie wrote on the paper and handed it to me.

Raymond stepped over and took the piece of paper from my hand, looked it over and handed it back. "What are you going to do? Just show up and ask if he knows a man named Johnny?"

I thought about it, then nodded. "I'm not sure what other options I have."

CHAPTER 39

I PARKED ON THE street in front of the Cape Cod-style home in Hyde Park, the number matching the address we'd gotten from the phone book. I walked up the driveway, slipping on the patches of ice left over from the cold night, after an unseasonably warm day where a good amount of the snow around had melted.

The problem with melting snow in New England was that it normally dropped below freezing at night, no matter how warm or sunny it got during the day. And what remained was patches of ice on roads, driveways and sidewalks. I assumed it was a busy time of the year for ER doctors, with all the broken arms. Not to mention lawyers waiting around, hoping someone had forgotten to put down sand or salt before a customer slipped and fell.

There were two doors. One at the center of the front of the house, the other at a breezeway between the main house and the garage.

I went for the door to the left, stepping onto the slate-topped porch at the breezeway's entrance. I looked at my watch. It was 8:05.

Ringing the doorbell, I knew there was a chance this could be a quick visit, with the possibility this guy would have no idea who Johnny Bruno was. To say it was a longshot was an understatement.

A middle-aged woman opened the door wearing a robe and slippers with curlers in her hair. She had a coffee mug in her hand. "Yes?"

"Hi, I'm looking for Michael?" I said. "Am I at the right house?"

A man yelled from somewhere in the house. "You think we live in an igloo? Shut the door! You're letting all the heat out!"

The woman rolled her eyes and held the door for me. "You'd better come in," she said.

I stepped inside the enclosed breezeway, furnished with a padded steel couch and a couple of matching chairs made for the outdoors. The door to the rest of the house, to the right, was up two concrete steps and still open behind her. I could see into the kitchen.

She again looked me over. "So, who did you say you were?"

I hadn't actually told her yet. She hadn't asked. "My name's Jake. Jake Horn."

The woman was very attractive, even with the curlers in her hair. She wore sweet perfume.

"Does Michael know who you are?"

"He may," I said. "Was that him yelling?"

She paused, then nodded. "I'll have to get him," she said. "He's not a morning person."

"I really just need to ask him a question," I said.

"Yeah? What about?"

The woman came across as having a bit of an edge to her, which wasn't exactly uncommon around Boston.

"I'm looking for someone he may or may not be related to. Name's Johnny Bruno."

The woman appeared to lose color in her face as her eyebrows raised. "Johnny?" She cleared her throat, but didn't respond.

The man inside the house yelled out, "Angie! Where the hell are my blue socks!"

The woman—Angie, apparently—pointed toward the open doorway and into the kitchen with her thumb. "Why don't I go get Michael."

"If by chance he's not able to come to the door," I said, "I get the feeling you'd be able to help. The look on your face has me thinking you know who Johnny is?"

She gave a small grin. "I think it's best if you talk to Michael."

But as she turned for the door, a man in suit pants and a dress shirt with slippers on his feet and a tie hung around his neck stood at the top step, looking out at us from the kitchen.

"Are you Michael?" I said.

He didn't answer me, but glanced at his wife. "Who the hell's *this*?"

She replied, "This is, uh..." She turned to me. "What did you say your name was again?"

"Jake Horn," I said, gazing at the man in the doorway.

He was older. Hair pepper gray. He appeared tall, but it might've been because he was standing up a few steps from the enclosed breezeway inside the house, looking down at us.

The woman said, "He wants to know where your cousin is."

"Which one?"

She seemed to hesitate, and I noticed the jump in her throat as she swallowed. "Johnny."

The man stared back at me, appearing somewhat perplexed, then stepped down to the breezeway. He pulled the door closed behind him.

"You're looking for Johnny, huh?" he said.

I wasn't sure if I should come up with a better reason than it was nothing more than a crapshoot. "Honestly, I'd heard he might be your cousin, so I thought I'd—"

"What is it you want with this guy… Johnny?"

"Well," I said. "He's a friend of a friend. I got his name, and—"

"I'm sorry," he said. "But I don't know anyone by the name of Johnny." He gave his wife a nod. "Go inside, babe."

She gave me a look, maybe one like she was sorry, or that there could be trouble, then went into the house. She glanced back at me as she started to close the door.

"Oh, babe," the man said, pointing toward his feet. "I can't find my blue socks."

She closed the door without a word, and then it was just me and this guy, Michael, standing in the chilly breezeway.

"So," he said. "What line of work are you in?"

"What line of work?" I said.

"Is that a difficult question?" he said.

I could've made up a story about being in some other profession, but told myself it wasn't necessary. "I'm a private investigator."

"A private dick, huh? And you show up at my house, thinking I know this guy Johnny?"

"Well," I said, "I was hoping he might've been a relative, or…"

The man pulled at his untied tie, hung around his neck. "So you don't know where, uh, this Johnny guy lives?"

"Well, honestly, I guess I wouldn't be here if I knew where he was."

The man laughed. "You a wise ass?"

"Not really." I was starting to think this maybe wasn't going to be as easy as I'd hoped the night before. "Listen," I said, "If you don't know who he is, or where I can find him, then, well…" I'd admit the man was making me nervous, the way he was acting. "I'm sorry to waste your time. I guess I'll have to look elsewhere."

The man turned and looked up at the closed door leading to his kitchen. "You know what?" he said. "I might actually be able to help you. How about you come on inside, I'll have Angie make you a coffee."

"No, I think I'm okay," I said. I turned for the other door.

But he grabbed my arm. "No, please. I insist. Come on in, have some coffee. You can tell me what it is you want with this guy, and..." He shrugged. "Like I said, perhaps I can help you."

I pulled my arm from his grasp. I knew right then the best thing I could do was get out of there. It was too late, but I realized it was a mistake to come alone. "Thank you for the offer," I said, "But—"

The man pulled a small revolver from the back of his pants. "I told you, I insist." He gestured with the barrel of his gun for me to walk up the steps. "Go ahead. Let's go inside where it's warm. Have ourselves a nice chat."

I had my hands up where he could see them. "Uh, the thing is," I said, shaking my head. "I didn't come here looking for trouble. So maybe I should just leave, get out of your way so you can get on with your day?"

He laughed, shaking his head. "Nah, you're not in my way." He glanced at his watch. "In fact, I think I'm going to cancel my meeting." He turned me toward the step and poked the gun in my back. "Go 'head, open the door. Angie'll make you a nice cup o' Joe."

Another mistake I made was leaving the Saturday Night Special Raymond gave me at the house. Even though he'd told me to hold on to it, I didn't like the idea of getting him in any kind of trouble if something had gone down.

I turned the knob, and we stepped into the kitchen. There was a breakfast smell in the air. Bacon and syrup, along with a coffee machine with an empty carafe.

"Angie!" Michael yelled. "Come make our friend some coffee!"

There was a black-and-white TV on the counter with aluminum foil wrapped around the rabbit ears. Jane Pauley was on the Today Show.

"Have a seat," he said, giving me a nudge toward a dark brown, grain-finish round table with four chairs.

I didn't have a choice at that point, and did what he said. I sat, watching him. "Listen," I said. "I told you, I'm not here looking for trouble, I just—"

"Yeah, I heard you the first time," the man said. "And I'd like to think there won't be any trouble, although I'm not sure I'm in a position to make any promises."

Angie walked into the kitchen. "Oh," she said, her eyes wide, her gaze going to the gun. "What's going on?"

"Didn't I tell you to make us some coffee?" he said.

The woman appeared nervous, handing Michael his socks. "I only have two hands," she said, taking a can of Chock Full O'Nuts from the cabinet. She pulled the yellow plastic top off the can and glanced over her shoulder at the gun in the man's hand. "Do you have to have that thing out?"

"Do you have to ask stupid questions?" he said, turning back to me with a nod. He gestured for me to stand. "You carrying?"

I shook my head, but he didn't seem to believe me, patting me down and checking inside my coat.

"I'm not trying to cause any trouble," I said. "I just wanted to find a man named Johnny Bruno. But if I—"

"Okay," he said. "You're going to have to stop repeating yourself. You made your point. You're not here to cause any trouble. But, like I just told you, I think I'm going to have to be the one who decides whether you're causing trouble or not."

The coffee maker hissed, steam coming off the top, then slowly dripped dark liquid into the carafe.

Angie walked out of the room.

The man said, "You want something to eat?"

I shook my head. "No. I'm all right."

He lifted the phone off the wall and dialed, watching me, the gun still in his other hand. "Yeah, it's me," he said. "Listen. I got someone here you're going to want to talk to." He paused. "Yeah, I think you know who he is."

It was clear this guy Michael Bruno knew exactly who I was.

He continued his phone conversation while keeping an eye on me. "The private detective. Yeah, I have no idea. I was just about to ask you how he'd..." He listened, nodding into the phone. "Yeah, I guess I can do that. Give me a half hour. Traffic's probably not too good right now."

He hung up and turned to me. "Get up. We're going for a ride."

"I'm not going anywhere," I said.

He cracked a grin and glanced at the gun in his hand. "I'm not sure you have much of a choice."

He might've been right.

"What about my coffee?" I said. "I could use a cup before we go anywhere."

Michael Bruno looked at me, like he wasn't sure I was being serious, his eyes slightly squinted.

Angie walked into the kitchen, curlers out of her hair now, wearing jeans and a sweater. She looked good. "You want me to pour that coffee?"

"No," Bruno said. "We're leaving."

"I'd like a cup, if you don't mind," I said.

He rolled his eyes and with a nod, said to Angie, "Jesus. Get the guy a cup. Make it quick."

She pulled a cup from the cabinet and filled it with hot coffee, steam rising off the top of it.

She handed it to me, and I took a sip. It was hot enough it just about burnt my lips. I was standing at that point, Michael with the gun down, like he'd relaxed a bit. I turned to him, about to raise the cup to my mouth, but tossed the full thing in his face.

He screamed, and I drove my shoulder into him, knocking him backward into the sink. He tried to get to his feet but slipped on the coffee on the floor and landed on his back.

I was already on my way out the door, running down the driveway toward the street, where I'd parked.

I heard the door of the house crash open, but when I turned to look, I slipped on a patch of ice. My feet came out from under me, and I landed on my back, knocking my head on the asphalt.

But I jumped to my feet and made it to the Nova. Just as I ducked into the driver-side, a shot was fired my way.

Michael Bruno ran toward me as fast as he could go, considering he still had slippers on his feet. He had the gun raised and fired another shot, but I had the engine started. I slammed the pedal down, going in reverse away from the driveway. If I'd gone forward, I would've given him a perfect shot.

As soon as I was away from the front of his yard, I slammed on the brakes and spun the car around. There was barely enough room on the narrow street, and I almost clipped a station wagon parked in front of the neighbor's house.

But I got away from Bruno without another shot being fired, looking in the rearview at him in his suit and slippers, watching me from the middle of the street.

CHAPTER 40

I WAS LUCKY TO find a parking space three spots down from the door to my office. But that's as far as my luck had gone. When I stepped out onto the sidewalk, I spotted a blue Ford LTD parked across the street. And I had a good feeling I knew who it belonged to.

I started to unlock the office door and looked to my left. Maggie was walking toward me, and I shifted my gaze across the street to Detective Nick Carter stepping out of his LTD. "What's this all about?" I said, looking at Maggie as she approached.

Carter stepped onto the sidewalk and came up behind me.

Maggie said, "Jake, officers were called to a home this morning. The man who called... His name is Michael Bruno. Do you know the name?"

I glanced at her and the odd look she was giving me. She already knew from the night before at Raymond and Beth's that I was going to Michael Bruno's house in the morning. But I had a feeling she had no choice but to put on a show for Carter.

"Michael Bruno?" I shook my head. "Doesn't ring a bell."

Carter said, "A neighbor called in shots being fired at the Bruno's home in Hyde Park. A couple of officers were sent over there, and apparently Mr. Bruno claims you broke into his house. He said you were harassing his wife."

I said, "And you believe this load of—"

"Are you telling me you weren't there?" Carter said, crossing his arms.

I unlocked the door to my office and held the door open. Maggie walked past me, giving me a look with her eyes wide, like she wasn't sure what she was supposed to do.

Carter followed Maggie inside and I hung my coat on the rack. I said, "I didn't say I wasn't there, but..." Neither Maggie nor the detective removed their cruiser jackets.

"I know what you were doing there," Carter said, pulling down the zipper on his jacket. He rested his hands on his hips.

I looked at Maggie, wondering if she might've given him any details. I hoped she hadn't, but it felt like some kind of a game, and I wasn't convinced I knew which side she was on.

Carter said, "Don't look at her. She didn't tell me anything. I told her to meet me here, hoping maybe you'd be a little more truthful with her than you'd be with me."

"Why would I lie to you?" I said.

Carter didn't bother to respond. "It's time you come clean, Horn. I've been out in Worcester since four in the morning, and I'm getting cranky."

"What's in Worcester?" I said, sticking with the game playing for as long as I'd have to.

But Carter glared at me, a look on his face like he wasn't in the mood for any of it.

"I guess you got my note?" I said, grinning.

"You tied a man to a phone pole in the middle of thirty degree weather."

"How'd you know it was me?"

"Who else was with you? Raymond?"

"Raymond had nothing to do with any of it."

"No? Then how come witnesses at a nearby restaurant, where we found the yellow Impala, claimed Ricci ran after a tall, large man, saying he had to be six-six?"

"Sounds like a mix-up to me. Raymond's only six-four."

Carter said, "He's going to get himself in trouble. Not only is he a retired cop, but he's not a licensed private investigator either. And I'm not saying that gives you the right to do what you did, but—"

"Raymond wasn't there," I said.

Carter knew I was full of shit.

He took a long, deep breath before letting out a sigh. "Are you going to at least tell me what the story is with you going after this Louie Ricci character? I can only assume it has something to do with whatever it was you were doing at Michael Bruno's house this morning."

"Didn't you talk to Ricci?" I said, hoping to find out what he knew before I spilled my own guts.

"He wouldn't say a word," Carter said. "Clamped down like a clam. Of course, what I'd like to know is if he had anything to do with Trudy Bailey's murder."

"I can't say if he did or not," I said.

Carter looked around my office, his eyes going right to the stained tiles on the ceiling

"What about Chief Williams? Did he show up out there?"

Carter nodded. "He was busy looking at the tires on the yellow Impala, back at the restaurant, hoping to match them to the scene at that wood shop in New Hampshire."

Maggie was quiet, leaning against my desk now. She said to me, "Do you want to tell Detective Carter why you were at Michael Bruno's house?"

I turned to her, accepting the fact that she was still going to act as if she knew nothing about it, which made sense from her standpoint. The last thing she needed was for Carter to find out she was helping me out behind his back.

I turned to Maggie, then to Carter. "Louie Ricci gave me a name."

"What name?" Carter said. "Micheal Bruno?"

"Johnny, actually. Johnny Bruno. Michael wouldn't admit he knew him. My initial guess is they're related, and Bruno—Michael—is protecting him."

Carter pulled at his chin. "Why's that name sound so familiar?" He glanced at Maggie. "You know that name? Johnny Bruno?"

Maggie shook her head. "Sorry. No."

I walked around to the other side of my desk and collapsed in the chair. I needed a nap.

Carter said, "So what did Ricci tell you? This Johnny Bruno... Is he someone he works with?"

I had to think about how much to tell Carter. But the more I talked to him, the more I realized we were on the same team.

"I tracked him down because he was one of two men who tried to shut me up. I needed to know who hired him. Of course, at first he wouldn't talk. But we... I mean, *I* put a little bit of pressure on him. He threw the name Johnny Bruno out there as some kind of middle man, who takes orders from someone else but puts like Ricci to work as a heavy. I don't really know who else is involved, or what this guy Michael Ricci's role is. I know he's got a gun."

Carter said. "What do you mean, a heavy? Are you saying these guys are hit men?"

"Hit men. Tough guys. Heavies. I don't know what they are, exactly. My best guess right now is Louie Ricci, working for Johnny Bruno—and perhaps this guy Michael—can likely be traced back to Larry Green's death."

I wasn't sure Detective Carter was even listening, the way he looked around the office.

"You got a bathroom in here?"

I pointed toward the back. "Down that hall."

Carter walked away, and I waited until I heard the bathroom door close. I kept my voice hushed and said to Maggie, "Is it really a big deal if he finds out you knew about Michael Bruno?"

Maggie gave me a sharp-eyed look, like she didn't want to discuss it.

"It's not like you did anything wrong," I said. "All you did was look through the White Pages."

"I gave you his address," she said, her voice in a whisper. "That would certainly be considered crossing the line." She glanced toward the hall, where the bathroom was. "But just so you know, I've had no luck finding Johnny Bruno. Nobody anywhere around here. No John. No Jonathan. Not a single person in Massachusetts with that name."

I thought about it, and remembered the call Michael Bruno had made. "Michael called him while I was there, told whoever it was on the other end we were coming out to see him. When he got off the phone, holding the gun on me, he said we were going for a ride. Unless I'm mistaken, I'm almost certain we were going to see Johnny."

"Is that what he told you?" Maggie said.

The more I thought about it, the less sure I was. "I... I don' t know."

The door opened down the hall and Detective Carter walked out of the bathroom, rubbing his hands on his pants. "So, here's the problem I haven't told you about yet; Michael Bruno had told one of the officers he wants to press charges."

"Against who?" I said, although I was pretty sure I knew the answer."

"Against you."

I laughed, shaking my head. "Who the hell does this guy think he is? This is crazy."

Maggie said, "He needs to make it look like he's the victim, that he did nothing wrong. What do you expect he'd do?"

"I guess I'm surprised," I said. "Wouldn't it have made more sense if he didn't even mention my name?"

Carter said, "What we have is a homeowner who fired his weapon, and when the police show up he needs to come up with a good enough reason for doing so. He claims you broke into his house. And, of course, there are witnesses... neighbors who saw a yellow Nova driving away when the shots were fired. The fact you disappeared from the scene isn't going to help you."

"The man held me at gun point, then fired shots at me. Should I have stood there and taken one in the chest?" I said. "I'm not sure why you're coming across like you believe this guy's telling the truth."

Carter let out another sigh. "You need to come clean with me, Horn. How did you end up at this guy's house? You said you were looking for this guy, Johnny Bruno. So how'd you end up at Michael Bruno's house, getting yourself into all this trouble? Just because he has the same last name? I would think any crackpot investigator could at least make sure he's going to the right house, no?"

"It's obvious he knows him. Why the hell do you think he pulled his gun? They know I'm close."

"Close to what?" Carter said. "Getting yourself killed?"

I was hesitant to go into anymore details, mainly because I was afraid he'd find out not only that Raymond and Beth had helped me, but Maggie too.

"I figured I'd take a chance," I said. "And it's obvious I've tapped into something."

"I don't think you have any idea what you've tapped into," Carter snapped.

I wondered if he knew something he wasn't telling me.

"Micheal Bruno's clean," he said. "At least from what we've been able to find. No criminal record of any kind. Got in a little tax trouble in '72, but that was with the feds. Nothing ever came of it."

"What's he do?" I said.

"For work?" Carter shrugged. "He's in some kind of import-export business. Of course, that could mean a number of things."

Maggie and I both glanced at each other.

"That right there sounds a little shady, don't you think?"

Carter didn't respond.

"What about the woman?" I said. "Her name was Angie, but I wasn't sure if she was his wife or not. No ring on her finger, so—"

"She *is* his wife," Carter said. "But just so you understand, I haven't spoken directly to Bruno myself. I'm only here because, well..." He glanced at Maggie. "If *she* trusts you, then..." Carter turned and looked at the framed photos on the wall. My Uncle Pat was in all of them, posing with mostly famous Bostonians, from politicians to athletes from around the town. "Your uncle was a good man."

I nodded in agreement.

Carter sat in a chair across from my desk. "Did you actually speak to Bruno's wife?"

"She's the one who gave it away, at first, when I asked her if she knew Johnny Bruno," I said. "She seemed surprised by the question, but told me they were cousins. That's when she went in the house to get Michael"

"You were outside?" Maggie said.

"We were in the enclosed breezeway. But Bruno's in the house—the main part of the house—yelling out at her about letting the heat out. And his missing socks. Next thing you know, he comes out into the breezeway through the door from the kitchen, has his gun pulled as soon as he realizes why I'm there."

"So they let you in the house?" Carter said.

I held my gaze on him for a moment. "The way you're asking, it's like you need me to confirm I didn't break in."

"I just want to make sure we've got the story straight." He stood up from the chair. "I'm on your side, Jake."

I stood up from the desk after him. "He told me to go in the house. I didn't have a choice, with a gun at my back."

We were all quiet for a couple of moments.

"So, what do we do from here?" I said.

Carter started toward the door. "Let me talk to the two officers who went to Bruno's house. In the meantime..." He gave Maggie a nod with his chin. "You on patrol today?"

She nodded. "All day."

Carter pulled at his chin, like his wheels were turning. "Would you mind helping me out? See what else you can dig up on this Michael Bruno? And this alleged Johnny Bruno, whoever the hell he is?"

I knew she wasn't about to tell him she'd already done that, and had no luck at all finding a Johnny Bruno.

"Sure," she said. "But I'm supposed to be—"

"Don't worry. I'll make sure Lt. Mason knows you're helping me out. It's no secret in that building you should make detective one day. Maybe before I retire, I can see what I can do to push you in that direction."

Carter reached for the door but looked my way before he opened it. "Listen, you may want to be careful, keep your eyes open until we have some idea what this Bruno—either one of 'em—is all about. If they didn't know who you were before you showed up, they do now."

"Oh, that's the thing," I said. "He knew *exactly* who I was."

CHAPTER 41

I WALKED INTO MY grandmother's house and felt an immediate chill inside, even after I'd closed the door. It was more than the usual draft, coming from somewhere else in the house. I went into the family room and over to the fireplace to check the flue to make sure it was closed. But the cold air—more than just a draft—came from somewhere at the back of the house. I went into the dining room, a room I rarely entered, and walked around my grandmother's long chestnut table.

The source of the cold air was a window left open by a couple of inches. I looked through it and into the backyard. It was clear by the way the wood on the sill had splintered that someone had popped the lock to get the window open.

I closed it and remained still, with a nearly certain feeling in my bones that I wasn't the only one in the house. And when I turned around, I saw I was right.

A man I vaguely recognized stood inside the doorway, a gun in his hand that looked to be a .45 with a long wide barrel.

I raised both hands. "Are you here to kill me?"

It was the other man from the alley, the shorter one, who was with Louie Ricci at the time outside the dry cleaners. He stared back at me, shaking his head. "All you had to do was listen."

"Listened to *what*?"

"You were warned. More than once. You've caused a lot of trouble."

"Trouble?" I said. "*I've* caused trouble?" I put on a smile. "Listen, I've got a client paying me to find out what happened to her husband. And, obviously, you've got someone paying you to make sure I don't. I guess we both answer to other people, right? But killing me? The cops already know who you are. Your buddy gave them your name."

I didn't know if that was true, but it was worth a try.

He stared back at me, then slowly shook his head. "I'm sorry, buddy. I don't make the decisions here."

"Who does?" I said. "Johnny Bruno?"

"Johnny?" The man appeared perplexed. "Where'd you hear that name?"

"Your buddy Louie. Isn't that who you work for? Johnny Bruno?"

The man laughed, shaking his head. "Nobody calls him Johnny, other than a few close friends. He don't even like it."

"Wait," I said. "Then who is he? If his name's not..." It hit me, like a wet bag of sand. "Michael Bruno? Is that who... Is he—"

"Like I said, nobody calls him Johnny. Got me, why the hell Louie would even use the name. He's never been too quick on his feet, to be honest with you." The man looked me over. "I don't know what else Louie told you, but he's got himself in a bit of hot water as it is. To be honest, he's better off staying in jail. Not that he'll be much safer there, but..."

"You're not bullshitting me?" I said. "You mean to tell me I've been after a guy named Johnny but he doesn't actually exist? It's not even his name?" It didn't make sense.

"Why would I lie about something like that?" the man said. He kept the gun on me.

"Can you just put that gun down?" I said, staring at the muzzle of the .45 pointed at me.

"I'm sorry, pal. I got a job to do. It wasn't supposed to come to this. The person who…" he cleared his throat. "The intention, at the request of the client, was for you not to be killed. But, that's not here nor there…"

"A person?" I said. "Not Johnny? Or Michael? Who the hell hired you?"

He cocked the hammer. "I'm sorry, buddy, but—"

"Wait!" I said, trying to think through what I could even say to stop this man from doing what he was sent there to do. "Listen, how about—"

"You have no idea who you're dealing with," the man said. "He's a powerful man."

"Who is? Bruno?"

The man didn't respond.

I thought for a moment. I said, "Is he as powerful as Tony Gautieri?" I knew as soon as the words left my mouth I might have made a mistake. And the last thing I wanted to do was throw Gautieri's name out there. But for obvious reasons, I didn't have many options.

The man's eyes opened wide. "You know Mr. Gautieri?"

"He's a good friend of mine," I said. "A *very* good friend. I could go pick up that phone, call him right now, tell him I need a favor, and—"

"You serious?" he said. The man kept his gun on me, but looked to be thinking things through as he lowered it a bit.

"Serious as death," I said. "And that's what you'll be dealing with when he finds out you were the one who killed one of his good friends."

The man swallowed hard. "Does Mr. Bruno know you know Tony Gautieri?"

"I have no idea what he knows. Maybe you should ask him?"

It appeared I at least had the man thinking through whether he wanted to pull that trigger or not.

"How much is Bruno paying you to kill me?"

"That's none of your business."

"Well, it kind of is, considering I'm the one on the wrong end of that gun. But, what if I told you I'd put in a word with Tony? I know he could use a good man like you down in Rhode Island."

I could see through the man's dumb look he was at least thinking it through.

I said, "Does this guy Bruno even respect you? How long've you been doing this? Have you ever gotten a promotion or anything? A pay raise? Or does he just keep you at the bottom, doing all the dirty work?"

I had a feeling I was getting through to the guy, even though I was sure his skull was pretty thick. Words just kept coming from my mouth, since I figured the more I talked, the more time I had to figure out a way to get out of that dining room alive.

"I'm sorry," the man said. He raised the .45.

A shot fired.

I closed my eyes, squeezing them tight. I felt no pain, and slowly opened one eye. Then the other.

The man, who a moment earlier was standing in front of me, was now on the floor. He seemed to be alive, looking at me like a scared little boy. Blood came from his chest onto the rug and the hardwood flooring underneath him.

I crouched down and picked up the gun he'd let go of, then turned with it, looking out the window. I didn't see anybody.

Someone pounded on the front door.

I stepped over the bloodied man and rushed to see who it was, opening the door.

Detective Nick Carter was on the top step outside. He ran past me and into the dining room where the man whose name I never got lay on the floor, bleeding.

Carter crouched down and put his hand under the man's jaw.

"Is he dead?" I said.

He looked up at me and nodded. "I told you to keep your eyes open."

"I had them open. But I was facing the wrong direction. He was here when I got home." I nodded toward the window where the glass had shattered from Carter's bullet. "He came in through that window."

Carter had his two-way radio out. "His name's Joey Carmelo. An associate of Johnny Bruno."

"Johnny?" I said. "This guy just told me his name's not Johnny. Michael Bruno is Johnny."

"I'm aware," Carter said.

I didn't understand. "But I thought you said you didn't know anything about Bruno?"

"That's not exactly what I said. I told you he was clean, from a legal standpoint. But his boy out in Worcester... he's talking now. The feds are involved, and he's probably gonna make some kind of deal."

"Wait," I said. "Then why'd you make it sound like you knew nothing about what's going on here? And when did you learn Michael Bruno is Johnny Bruno?"

Carter had his eyes on the body. "You're focused on the wrong thing. And, the problem right now is nobody knows where Bruno's gone. He and his wife were spotted at Logan Airport. They flew out last night."

"To where?"

"Miami. Like I said, Feds are involved now. This is a lot bigger than you and me."

"Bigger?"

He looked around.

I was thinking about how he was in the right place at the right time, firing his gun when this guy, Joey Carmelo, was about to put a bullet in me. "So how'd you know to go around back?" I had always been suspicious of Carter.

Something seemed a bit off.

"Shouldn't you be thanking me?" he said. "Instead of—"

"It's a fair question, isn't it?" I walked to the window. There wasn't much snow in the back compared to what there had been before it warmed up. I noticed the tracks coming from the woods behind the house, straight for the window.

"The tracks?" I said.

He nodded. "You know when you just have a feeling? That something's wrong?"

"You mean, like the one I have right now?"

Carter huffed out a slight laugh and reached into his inside pocket. I tensed up a bit, but all he did was take out a pack of cigarettes from his inside coat pocket. "You're one of those guys, never gonna trust a cop again, huh?"

"Probably not," I said. "And you don't have to smoke that in here."

He had the cigarette in his mouth, but hadn't lit it yet, shaking his head. "Nope." He looked at Joey Carmelo's body, and all the blood on the floor. "What a mess, huh?" He walked out of the room and past the fireplace, heading for the front door.

Sirens grew louder in the distance as Carter stepped outside and lit his cigarette, leaving the door wide open behind him.

Chapter 42

Raymond helped me move the table back to where my grandmother had kept it for at least fifty years. The blood-stained rug was already rolled up and out on the curb. I wasn't even sure the garbage men would take it.

I put the bloody mop inside a green garbage bag and stuffed the towels I'd used to clean up the mess inside with it. I tied the top, the wood handle sticking out, leaning it up against the house outside the garage.

The cops had all left, along with the Coroner who took Carmel away.

"I had the guy talking," I said to Raymond, sliding the last chair under the table, being careful not to scrape the hardwood floor.

"I've never met anyone as ungrateful as you," Raymond said. "Carter saves your ass, and you haven't stopped talking about it like he did something wrong."

I stared at Raymond, wondering if maybe he was right. It was like I had an idea in my head I couldn't shake.

The phone rang, and I rushed into the kitchen to answer it, being careful the way I took it off the wall, with blood dried on my fingers.

"Hello?" I said, placing it between my shoulder and ear. I walked to the sink, stretching the cord as far as it would go so I could wash my hands.

"Mr. Horn? It's Nathan Howell."

"I assume you spoke to Marilyn?" I said. I had called her soon after the police had left to tell her most of what had happened. But made it clear too many questions remained unanswered.

"I did," Howell said. "She's on her way back from New Hampshire now. And I was hoping you could come by my house?"

"Well, sure." I glanced at my watch. "I can fill you in on the details. But just so I'm clear, it's going to take more time."

He took a moment to reply. "I understand," he said. "But I believe Marilyn should be satisfied now. You've done all you can."

I had to make sure I heard him right. "I'm not sure I know what you mean," I said.

"Right. Well, how about this evening? Are you available?"

"You mean, now?" It was ten minutes after seven.

He said, "If at all possible, yes."

I looked down at my clothes, stained with the blood from Joey Carmelo. I'd need a shower. "I can try to be there by eight," I said. "Maybe eight-thirty, if that works?"

"That would be good for me," he said. "We'll see you then."

The next thing I heard was the dial tone.

I dried my hands and hung the phone up on the wall. Raymond came around the corner and went to the sink himself. "Who was that?"

"Nathan Howell," I said. I looked out the window toward the darkness on the street. It wasn't so quiet a few hours earlier, when there were cops from three different departments, a couple of rescue vehicles, a fire truck, and the coroner's van. "It sounds like he wants to end it. The investigation."

"Oh, well, isn't that good?"

I shook my head. "Why would it be good?"

"Won't you still get paid?"

I thought about it. "I'd like to think so."

"Then why isn't that good news?" Raymond stared back at me, as if he wondered if my head was screwed on straight. "If the feds can track down Bruno, what more is there for you to do?"

"He's just a middle man," I said.

"What's that supposed to mean?"

"What it means is if he had anything to do with Larry Green's death, he was nothing more than a middle man."

"Do you know that for a fact?"

I didn't have an answer.

Raymond went to the sink and grabbed the bottle of Palmolive, squeezing green liquid into his palm. "Soften hands, while you do the dishes." He laughed with his jolly deep-voice.

He could see it on my face that I wasn't in the mood.

"Come on," he said. "I'm just trying to lighten you up. You know how many times my father walked away from a case all those years, without having the answer?"

I nodded. "Yeah, of course I do. He had a drawer for them. He'd move them to red folders, told me he'd lay awake at night... they'd eat away at him." I paused, glancing out the window. "It's in the same red folder and drawer I keep Barbara's files in."

Raymond cleared his throat. "All right, well, you gotta remember, you've got a daughter who's depending on you to stick around for a while. It's not all about you."

"I get that," I said. "As if what I do for a living is ever without risks?"

"But you've gotta keep in mind, whoever sent this guy over here today—whether it's Bruno or someone else—could have someone else waiting around, to take you down if you keep at it."

I turned from the window and looked Raymond in the eye. "I'm not walking away. Not yet."

There was a long moment of silence between us.

"Well, it may not be your call. Your client, or her uncle... it doesn't sound like they even want it to continue. Am I right? To me, it sounds like the best outcome. As good a reason as any to wash your hands of this mess." He dried his hands on the towel hanging on the stove. "I hope you get something out of it, no? A buyout, at least?"

I didn't know what to think. For me, it was rarely about the money. If it was, I'd be working sixty hours a week chasing insurance fraud cases.

"You gotta learn to let things go," Raymond said.

I looked out the window again, as if I was expecting someone else to show up in the driveway. "I need to get in the shower," I said, and walked out of the kitchen.

Raymond followed and stopped at the bottom of the stairs as I headed up. "You want me to hang around?"

"The house?" I shook my head. "I'm not going to worry about it right now."

"That's brave of you," Raymond said, cracking a grin. "How about I just put the Bruins on. I'll call Beth, tell her I'll be home a little later. She's probably going to ask if you want to swing by later anyway, so you have something to eat."

"Well, I'm heading up to Newton. I don't know when I'll be back."

***

I parked behind Marilyn's car in the driveway at her uncle's house, seeing the two of them inside through the window. With the darkness around the house and the curtains open, the lights inside shone bright. Smoke rose from the chimney, filling the air outside. After a mild few days, the temperature had started to drop again. Last I'd heard, there was possibly more snow in the forecast in the coming days.

I watched the two before I went up the stairs to the door. They appeared to be arguing, or at least in a somewhat heated discussion. I couldn't hear—it wasn't like they were yelling—but I wish I knew what it could have been about.

The fact was, there was something about the two I never fully understood. They seemed to have a strange relationship, and I couldn't put my finger on why I felt that way. There were so many unanswered questions about everything—about everyone involved—it bothered me if I'd no longer be working on the case.

Of course, there was always the chance I'd have trouble putting it behind me. It happened more often than not, and I'd end up digging, obsessively looking for answers. I needed to work. But not only to put money in my pocket. Without it, I'd go back to spending my days trying to find Barbara's killer, trying to prove the man they had behind bars didn't do it.

I finally stepped up to the front door and rang the doorbell.

The way Marilyn opened the door, with the look on her face—a forced smile—I couldn't help but think something else was wrong. I wondered if maybe the two were at odds about whether or not it was time to close the case, unfinished or not.

"Hi," she said, stepping back from the door. "Come in." Her body shivered as she rubbed her hands up and down her arms. "Boy, this cold..."

We walked into the room where her uncle stood with his back to me, in front of the fireplace, taking his time—a moment or two—before he turned to acknowledge I was there.

He had a pipe in his mouth, but it wasn't lit.

"Mr. Horn," he said. "Can I get you a drink?"

A glass of red wine sat on the coffee table, along with a short rocks glass filled with golden-colored liquid I guessed was whiskey.

"Maybe a beer, if you have one?" I said, knowing I didn't need the kick of booze. Not right then.

Howell nodded and left us without a word.

I could feel the tension in the room.

"I understand my uncle informed you we've decided there's no need to continue the investigation?" Marilyn wouldn't look me in the eye. "I'm going to be leaving town soon. Perhaps as soon as tomorrow."

"For New Hampshire?" I said.

"Well, now. I've decided to leave New England. I think it's time for me to move on with my life."

Something didn't seem right, and I turned to the doorway as her uncle walked into the room with a bottle of Stroh's beer.

"We both agreed it would be good for Marilyn," he said. "To move past everything. It's caused more trouble than we ever expected, and, well..." He walked to the fireplace and took an envelope from the mantel, handing it to me. "This should cover everything you've done."

The envelope was thick, at least an inch. Maybe two, the top sealed with a rubber band around it. I didn't look inside.

"But we still don't know if this guy—his name's Michael Bruno—is the one who killed Larry. And I also believe someone hired him. And, without knowing who that person is..."

"Perhaps we feel it's no longer worth the risk," Howell said. But when the words left his mouth, he wouldn't look me in the eye.

"I don't understand," I said. "They had a man in custody who seemed willing to talk. And the feds are tracking down Bruno. This man in New Hampshire who was killed, he must've been paid by Bruno, or... I'm telling you, we're so close. If you just give me a little more time."

The uncle looked nervous. I could see it in his eyes. "Well, I'm sorry, but..." He cleared his throat. "I think you should go," he said, gesturing toward the doorway.

I hadn't even sipped my beer.

"I'm sure you'll find what's in that envelope sufficient," he said. "We do appreciate all you've done."

"All I've done? You mean, putting my life on the line?" I took a deep breath and let it out with a huff. "And don't forget, a young woman was killed in Boston." I gazed at Marilyn. "Are you telling me now you're no longer worried someone is going to come after you? You think leaving New England is going to make you any safer?"

Neither one responded.

I opened the door and walked out, slamming it closed behind me. I'd become enraged, and it crossed my mind to leave the envelope right there on the steps.

But I was no fool.

CHAPTER 43

HAWKER'S PUB WAS DIMLY lit with a light crowd, no more than six of us at the bar and enough seats between us nobody had to do any talking. All eyes were on the TV behind the bar, watching the Celtics get badly beaten out in LA. They were awful. But there was hope in the future with the Green drafting the six-foot-nine small forward, Larry Bird, a year earlier, in '78. But he stayed in college to finish his senior year at Indiana State, putting Boston a season away from seeing if the miserable franchise could be turned around.

I hadn't watched much basketball for the past couple of seasons. Nobody had. But it was the only thing on the TV in the bar, the sound up loud enough it's all you could hear, other than the couple in the back corner by the dartboards. The woman cackled, the two kissing like school kids.

I wasn't in much of a mood for any of it.

The door cracked open with a pop, and cold air filled the area around the bar. I turned as Maggie walked in with her thick, hooded parka covering most of her face and body. She removed the hood and pulled off her white knitted hat. The others at the bar looked her way, then went back to their drinks.

"How's it going?" she said, hanging her coat on the back of the stool next to me. She looked at the bottle of 'Gansett in front of me and gave Marty, the old man who owned the place, a nod. "I'll have one of those." She turned in her seat to face me, leaning on the bar with her elbow. "So, what else did they say?"

I sipped my beer and shrugged, arms folded on the bar. My eyes were still on the TV, even though I wasn't paying attention to it. "The whole thing doesn't make sense," I said. "All of a sudden, Marilyn's leaving the area? They just throw in the towel, after all that's happened?"

"How much have you told them? You're the one who's been in the middle of it. I know how you are, you don't want your clients to be any more involved than they have to, but..."

"She knows most of what's gone on," I said. "Don't forget, she's the one who bailed me out of jail. So it's not like there were any big secrets."

I had to think about it, but that's all I'd been doing. *Thinking*. I still hadn't come up with a good enough answer for any of it. "From the beginning, she told me she was afraid. That her life was in danger. Now she just wants to walk away, like nothing ever happened?"

Marty put the 'Gansett in front of Maggie, and she straightened up, taking a sip as turned to me. "Do you think she was lying about any of it?"

I took a moment to answer. "You know what? Nothing's ever felt right with this case. So much of it has never added up."

Maggie was still, with her gaze on the TV. "I wish I had an answer for you," she said, holding her beer with both hands.

I could tell there was something she wanted to say. I said, "What is it?"

She took her time, taking another sip. "What if someone got to them?" she said. "You've been threatened since day one. Who's to say they didn't go right to the source, to get you to back away for good?" Maggie was still, looking into my eyes like she could see what I was thinking.

I took a couple of moments. "I've thought about that," I said. "And, of course, the way they made it sound from the beginning was that she was worried. But at the same time neither one—Marilyn nor her uncle—ever seemed to show any kind of real fear. I mean, other than her taking off for New Hampshire, which seemed more like a weekend getaway than anything else."

"Did you meet the people she was staying with?" Maggie said.

I shook my head. "No. It was late, and in bed when I was there, the night she bailed me out."

I finished what was in the bottle and raised it to Marty with a quick shake to show him it was empty.

Marty came right over and put another on the bar.

"Thanks, Marty," I said.

He wasn't a man of words. Not unless you were the last one at the bar.

I said to Maggie. "As I told Raymond, I don't think I can walk away from this."

She cracked a small, crooked grin, her eyes on the TV now until she slowly shifted her gaze back to me. "Of course I know that. But..." The grin faded. "I think you should."

"You think I should what? Walk away? But that's exactly what they want me to do."

"Do you think it's worth getting yourself killed over? Just to find the answer?"

"My life is still in danger," I said. "This Bruno guy... I'm not sure how the hell he was... I don't know how he was off everyone's radar over there. But obviously, this guy's involved in something the cops never knew about. Not until now."

"It's a big deal," she said. The feds don't normally jump on a case just because a guy fired a gun in his driveway. Who knows if, or how long, they've been watching him."

I nodded, like I understood.

"This isn't just about some family squabble over a dealership," she said. "I'm sure you know that?"

I had to think before I spoke. "What about Carter? How come he's helping me now? Shows up in my backyard out of nowhere? Not to mention, his old buddy was working in New Hampshire at the time Larry Green's balloon crashed to the ground? And then there's the fact of Marilyn's first husband."

Maggie said, "Carter was watching out for you. You should be grateful."

"You sound like Raymond."

She rolled her eyes and sipped her beer.

"I appreciate it," I said. "Of course. I'd likely be dead. But, you have to admit I raise some reasonable questions, don't you think?"

"McCaffrey's not the first Boston cop to retire and finish his career somewhere else. But, that's beside the point. You have to get over this idea that all cops are crooked."

I laughed. "Do I?" I cleared my throat and kept my voice quiet. "I'm sorry. I'm on the edge here. I need sleep." I threw back my beer and emptied it, sliding it across the bar so Marty could see it.

Maggie and I both remained silent, our eyes on a game neither of us were paying attention to.

Maggie said, "Did Carter tell you Louie Ricci is likely going to be charged for that murder in New Hampshire?"

I shook my head, surprised, but wondered why Maggie hadn't started with that bit of news when she first showed up. Maybe it would've helped my mood. "Did he confess?"

"No. But they're trying to get him to cooperate," she said. "He's got a public defender, trying to work a deal. So he won't be talking until that's done."

I said, "No Mob lawyers?"

"I don't think so. He's smaller than small-time, from what I'm hearing."

Marty brought me over another beer and grabbed the empty bottle.

I hadn't spoken to Tony Guitieri since I went to see him, and wondered how much he knew had gone down since he pointed me toward Ricci. Partly, I was a bit nervous about telling him everything that had happened. I'm sure he hadn't expected the cops to get involved, and assumed I'd handle it myself.

I also didn't want to bring up his name with Maggie, even though she knew he was the one who sent me out to Worcester in the first place.

The truth is, Raymond and Maggie found it more than a little odd I had somewhat a relationship with the guy in the first place. But we'd done each other favors here and there. And as long as these favors were paid back, we were good.

That's how it worked with guys like Gautieri.

Maggie said, "Did Marilyn Green tell you where she was going?"

"No."

"Didn't you ask?"

"No. But I'm going to call her in the morning, see if I can get some kind of clarification."

"Do you think she's actually going to tell you? It doesn't sound like it to me," Maggie said.

We both sat quiet for a few moments, drinking our beers. I looked at my watch and thought it might be a good night to spend on the couch at the office. I had only had a few, but I wasn't in the mood for a drive back to Milton.

I glanced at Maggie, and could tell she was thinking things through.

She said, "Did you ever meet Mrs. Howell?"

"Marilyn's aunt?" I shook my head. "She's in Florida for the winter."

"And the husband's not with her?" she said.

"Maybe he doesn't like the heat," I said.

As much as Maggie had said she wanted me to walk away, she had a similar personality to mine, where she didn't like the feeling of not having an answer. If she wasn't a cop, I'd ask her to come work with me. Get her PI license. But she'd never leave the BPD.

After another couple of minutes with neither of us saying a word, Maggie changed the direction of our conversation. "How's Nancy?"

I didn't have much of an answer. "I have to call her," I said. "Last time I talked to her was when I told her to keep her eyes open, when I was starting to worry this case was heading down the wrong road."

"As it did," Maggie said.

"I should have called her earlier. It's just... the last couple of days I've been so wrapped up in everything. It's not like she's not on my mind every minute, as it is. I also don't like to bother her or make her nervous. She doesn't need me calling her every day to check up on her."

Maggie smiled. "I don't think she minds."

I looked at my watch, then glanced over my shoulder toward the payphone by the street. "You think it's too late to call?"

"Now?" Maggie shrugged. "I doubt she's in bed, if that's what you're asking. It's only eleven. But..."

Sometimes I hated to think of what she could be doing. Partying, I would guess. Although she was always such a good student, she always made her studying a priority. At least she used to.

"Have you talked to her?" I said.

"Not in a couple of weeks. She usually calls me or I try to call. But I'm like you, not wanting to bother her. She's got a big work load this semester."

"Good," I said. "Keeps her out of trouble."

I waited another half-minute before I stood up from the stool and reached into my pocket. I didn't have any change, and pulled out a dollar, holding it out for Marty. "Marty, can I get some change for the phone?"

"You're going to call her?" Maggie said.

I nodded, grabbed the change from Marty when he brought it back over, and headed out the front door. I left my coat inside, and felt how much colder it had gotten since I first walked into the bar.

It was quiet on the street. The only vehicle out there, besides the parked cars in front of Marty's, was a yellow cab, the smell of exhaust hanging in the frigid air.

I dropped three quarters in the slot.

The phone at Nancy's dorm rang five times before someone answered, the girl on the other end laughing. "Hello?"

"Hey, this is Nancy Horn's dad, I'm sorry if I'm calling too late, but—"

"Oh, hello, Nancy Horn's dad. This is Jessica." She giggled into the phone.

The name Jessica rang a bell. I'm sure I met her, but I couldn't remember all their names. There were at least twenty on Nancy's floor.

"Is Nancy around?"

"Let me go check."

It was quiet on the other end of the line.

It was taking a bit of time for Nancy to come to the phone. I'm pretty good at keeping my emotions under control and my imagination in check. But my mind was filled with panic.

I heard voices in the background on the other end of the line.

"Mr. Horn?"

It was Jessica again.

"I'm not sure where Nancy is. She's not in her room. Someone said she might've gone to the library, but I haven't seen her since this morning. Do you want me to have her call you?"

"You haven't seen her since this morning?" I said, as if I needed to repeat her exact words.

"We have different schedules," she said. "Do you want me to have her call you?"

I nodded into the phone. "Yes. Please. Tell her to call the office when she can."

"The office?" She paused. "Okay. Good night, Mr. Horn."

The phone went quiet, followed by a dial tone.

I hung up and waited, the raw cold cutting into my bones, considering I was out there without a jacket.

Maggie turned, sipping her beer, and glanced my way when I walked in. "Everything all right?"

I stood, grabbed my coat and tossed a ten on the bar. "Nance wasn't there. I think I'm going to head back to the office."

"Don't be worried," she said, as if I was able to hide it. "I'm sure she's fine."

"I know she is," I said.

Maggie stood from her stool and put her hand on my back. "You're a good dad," she said. "But you can't worry all the time."

"Well, considering the circumstances…"

Maggie didn't respond. She knew I was right.

I had reason this time to worry.

Chapter 44

I sat at my desk, the only light in the office coming from the lamp in front of me. With my yellow legal pad out, I made notes of the last few days to see if putting pen-to-paper would help me make some kind of connection to Michael Bruno, and all that had happened. I'd spoken with plenty of people. A lot had happened, and my brain was beyond the point of being able to keep it all together in my head.

My uncle Pat would often sketch things out in writing when he was having a hard time with a case. I felt like I could normally keep most of what I needed to in my head, but maybe as I got older, putting it in writing helped. Especially when a case got a little complicated.

Without a doubt, this one had. And it didn't help that Marilyn and her uncle had made a choice I didn't agree with or understand. But I wasn't quite ready to back down.

I went through each name, adding notes. I could find a reason to suspect each person on the list. But I could also come up with reasons *not* to be suspicious.

Karen Green.

Her daughter, Brenda.

Brenda's husband, Matt.

Jason Green and his friend Kip Rainier.

Richard Reagan.

I circled Reagan's name, but he wasn't talking.

I glanced over the names and had forgotten to write down the salesman from the dealership. Gary, his name was. I reached into my wallet and took out the business card he'd given me.

Gary Holden - Sales

I wrote it down and drew a line from his name to Larry Green's, at the top, and another to Jason Green.

Of course, I had no way of connecting anybody to Michael 'Johnny' Bruno or either of his goons.

But I knew any of the names in front of me could have hired them.

I wrote *dealership fire?* and circled it. Then underlined it. But it didn't fit. Why would someone kill Larry Green, and then burn down the building? And considering the conversation I heard between Rainier and Jason Green, it appeared it had only hurt Jason's chances of turning the business around as he had hoped.

But did he really want to turn it around? Did he really want to be in the car business? Was he trapped, especially when his father was still alive?

The question, of course, was the insurance money. But burning down a business for an insurance payment wasn't as easy as it sounded. There was a lot of risk involved, and a business already in trouble immediately raised red flags.

Healthy businesses rarely took a match to their buildings.

I know this because, until recently, I had a fairly solid client in the insurance business. I was already kicking myself for walking away from the steady flow of work, but for some reason I'd decided it wasn't exciting enough for me.

I couldn't help but think I'd made a mistake.

I had called Nancy's dorm again, and coincidentally the same girl had answered as before I left the bar. But Nancy still wasn't there. Looking at the phone next to me, I wondered if she was going to call at all. I was doing all I could to get my mind off of her, doing what I could not to worry.

But it had gotten to a point that I was tempted to drive up to her school, just to make sure she was all right.

Of course, that would be a mistake. It was almost 12:30.

I couldn't help but think about this guy Michael Bruno. Would he take his threats a step further and go after the person I cared about more than anything in this world?

I picked up the pad and tossed it to the floor in frustration. It was bad enough that I'd been fired by my client. On top of it, I couldn't just walk away, like a normal person would do. No, it was too late for that.

It felt personal.

I walked to the window at the front of the office and peered through the blinds to look outside. The Nova was parked right out front with a thin layer of snow covering it. I'd heard snow was a possibility, but I had hoped the weather guys had it wrong.

They often did.

The streets appeared quiet. The usual stragglers stumbling from the bars weren't out there. It was late. And it was cold. I didn't even see a car drive by, and wondered if I was the only one who didn't pay enough attention to the forecast.

I went back to my desk to turn on the radio on the shelf behind it. The phone rang, and the handset almost slipped from my hands when I answered it with such urgency. "Hello?"

"Dad?"

I breathed a sigh of relief and collapsed into the chair behind my desk. "Nancy. It's good to hear from you." I thought I was going to cry, and she must've heard it in my voice.

"What's wrong?" she said.

"Nothing. I... Everything's fine. I just got a little worried, that's all."

The line went quiet. "I was studying. I have a big exam in the morning."

"I'm sorry," I said. "It's this case I was working on. The one I told you about."

"The Larry Green case?" she said.

Nancy usually remembered all the details about my work. At least the details I shared with her. She was smart—something she surely didn't get from me.

"Jessica came to the library looking for me, told me you called. She said it sounded like something was wrong."

"I was just worried," I said. "There are some shady characters out there."

"You don't have to worry about me."

I smiled. She meant it when she said it—that she could always take care of herself. And sometimes I wish she needed me more than she did. That's just how things go as kids grow up.

"I was worried," she said. "So I'm glad you're all right. But why are you still at the office?"

I didn't really have a good enough reason. I only had a couple of beers. And there wasn't even any snow on the ground when I left the bar with Maggie. But I wanted to get to a phone as soon as possible to wait for Nancy's call. I also felt comfortable enough in the office. It was my home away from home.

I heard Nancy yawn on the other end. I said, "You should get to bed, if you have a test tomorrow."

"You should too."

The phone went silent again, then Nancy asked me about the case.

I told her how Marilyn had asked to stop the investigation.

"Why?" she said.

I thought I was going to be able to get off the phone without having to answer too many of her questions.

"I'm still not sure," I said. "She wouldn't really give me much of an explanation. She's moving away, so..."

"Moving away? She only hired you a couple of weeks ago, right?"

"Not even," I said. "It doesn't make sense."

There was a long pause between us. It was obvious we were both exhausted.

Nancy said, "So, do you have any other work lined up?"

I smiled. It was as if we had a role reversal, and Nancy was the parent asking me when I'm going to find a real job.

"Not right now. I still have some things I need to do."

"You mean, with the Larry Green case?"

I hesitated to respond, knowing she was going to come back at me with the same advice Maggie had given me.

"Yes. I still want answers," I said.

"Even though you were fired? Why's it matter?"

"I wasn't technically fired. They just... I don't know why they wanted to stop."

I didn't want to tell her all that had happened to me, from being arrested for the murder up in New Hampshire to having a man shot and killed in her great-grandmother's dining room. Or how I'd been threatened to stop the investigation.

And shot at.

Nancy said, "You must have some suspects though, right?"

It was as if I was talking to another investigator. As someone studying criminology at Plymouth College, and growing up with a father who's in the business, she couldn't help but ask questions. It was as if she was ready to jump in and solve them herself.

"There are plenty of suspects," I said. "Too many, in fact. But each one could just as easily be innocent as guilty."

"Isn't that the way it always is?" she said.

There was a knock on my door, and I reached for the Saturday Night Special. With the darkness inside and the blinds closed on all the windows, I didn't know who it could be. Especially with it being as late as it was. "Nance," I said. "Hang on, okay?"

"What is it?" she said.

"Just... Hang on. I'll be right back." I placed the handset on the desk and went to the door, staying off to the side and out of view, my back against the wall. "Who is it?" I held the gun in my hand.

"Jake, it's Maggie. Open up. It's cold out here."

I slid the lock bolt and unlocked the door, pulling it open. Cold air and snow blew inside as I pulled Maggie by her arm to get her inside. I slammed the door shut. "What the hell are you doing here?"

She had a large envelope in her hand. "I went by the station after we left the bar. I found something."

"Nancy's on the phone," I said, hurrying to the desk. "Nance? It's just Maggie."

"This late?" she said.

Again, acting like she was the parent.

"I'll have to let you go," I said. "You should get some sleep anyway, so you're well rested for that test."

"I'm probably going to study a little while longer. But, Dad?"

"Yeah?"

"Is everything okay?"

I nodded, my eyes on Maggie as she took off her hat and coat, both covered in snow, and hung them on the rack by the door. She shivered and rubbed her hands up and down her arms.

I said to Nancy, "Everything's fine."

The pause on the other end told me she didn't believe it.

"Tell Maggie I said hi," Nancy said. "And that I miss her."

"I will," I said. "I'll let you go."

"Okay. Be careful, okay? I love you, dad."

"Love you too," I said, and kept the phone against my ear for a few seconds listening until I heard the dial tone.

Maggie walked over to my desk with the envelope.

"Nancy said hello," I said. "And that she misses you."

She smiled and tossed the envelope onto my desk. "I guess she was okay?"

I nodded. Nothing made me happier and more relieved than knowing my daughter was safe. "I thought you were going home?"

"I was," she said. "But I know you're not going to let this thing go. So I went by the station to see if something had been overlooked."

"Overlooked?" I said.

She nodded at the envelope. "Open it."

I opened the flap and pulled out a stack of documents and a black-and-white photograph. It was a picture of a crowd sitting in what looked like some kind of stadium seating. One of the men's faces was circled with a pen, but I didn't know who the man was. He wore a Scally cap and sunglasses. "What's this?" I flipped over the photo. June 3, 1973, had been written in smudged black marker on the back.

"Remember Detective Carter mentioned the only trouble he knew Michael Bruno had gotten into had to do with taxes?"

I nodded. "Yeah, I think so. A few years back, right?" I looked at the photo, studying the men around the one whose face had been circled. They all wore Scally caps or fedoras and sunglasses. I didn't see any women in the photo.

"That's Raynham Dog Track," she said. "The man circled there is believed to be Michael Bruno."

I looked up from the photo, waiting for more.

"Boston PD had partnered with Raynham Police and Massachusetts' State Police on a potential gambling ring, involved in drugging greyhounds. But apparently the feds got involved, took it over." She pointed at the papers. "I don't even know if Carter saw these or not."

"Where were they?"

"Buried in some evidence files in the basement at headquarters. I honestly wasn't expecting to find them, but I was curious what else I could dig up on this guy."

I looked over the reports, one a hard-to-read carbon copy with *Raynham Police Department* printed across the top.

"It looks to me the only thing the feds were able to get on him was some kind of tax fraud. I still don't know what he's involved in. It's not clear. And I didn't find anything connecting him to any kind of Mafia, either."

I looked closer at the photo. The men around Bruno were all older. But then I saw him—the man I was looking for—seated two rows behind with binoculars up to his face. "It's him," I said.

"Who?"

"I'm almost sure of it," I said, as if talking to myself. I glanced at Maggie. "Richard Reagan."

"Reagan?" she said. "Larry Green's friend?"

I looked up from the papers I was looking over, trying to find Reagan's name. But he wasn't the main focus of the photo. It was hard to say if he was there with Bruno or not. "I'm not so sure I'd call him a friend."

CHAPTER 45

AFTER A ROUGH NIGHT of sleep on the couch at the office, if I can actually call it sleep, I was back in Milton making a pot of coffee. I drank half of it hoping to wake up, but it didn't seem to do much. I sat at the table and glanced over the Globe's headlines, but nothing of interest caught my eye, so I pushed the paper aside and grabbed the phone off the wall.

It was exactly 8:30 when I dialed Tony Gautieri at his home on the thirteenth floor of the Biltmore Hotel, next to City Hall.

Tony answered on the first ring. "Yeah?"

"Tony?"

"Who's this?"

"Jake Horn."

There was none of the usual excitement he normally had when he heard my voice coming from the other end. In fact, at first Gautieri was so quiet, I wasn't sure if he was still there.

I said, "Hello?"

There was another brief pause. "I was wondering when you were gonna call me," he said, his voice gruff with his Rhode Island-Italian accent. I could tell from the sound of his voice that something was up.

"You were expecting my call?" I said.

"Yeah, I was. You know why?"

I wasn't sure I should give an answer. "Uh, not really."

"I'm a little upset with you," he said.

"Oh, uh. Mind if I ask why?" I had a feeling I knew.

The phone went quiet until Tony cleared his throat. "When you asked me for a favor, you didn't tell me it was to help the pigs."

"Pigs?"

"You know what I mean," he said. "You got the cops involved."

"You mean, out in Worcester?"

"What do you think?" Tony said. "I'm a little concerned. You know there's a chance this could come back to bite me, don't you?"

But he said it like, *Don'chew*?

"Why would it come back to bite you?"

"Because, as I said, I did you a favor because I thought you were going to take care of things yourself. You never said the cops'd be involved."

"I'm sorry," I said. "But it was either him or me." I knew enough not to use any names on the phone. Gautieri had warned me about that once before.

Tony said, "You know, it ever gets back that I was the one who sent you out to Worcester... It's gonna cause me a lot of trouble. You know what I'm sayin'?"

"I do. But, it won't. I promise."

"Well, I'm just saying. If it does..."

I wasn't sure if that was a threat, but I brushed it off.

I needed his help.

I said, "Can you give me any details about this guy? And his buddies?"

"No."

"No?"

"Not right now."

Silence.

"Listen," Tony said. "I don't give a damn what happens to him or anyone else involved. As long as my name's never mentioned. You got it? I just want your word. Because the person I got the information from, initially, well, let's just say between the three of us, he's the only other person who knows anything. I trust the man, so he doesn't concern me, but..."

"I won't say a word," I said. "I promise. You can trust me. But, just so you understand, I did what I had to do. I had to clear my name."

There was another moment or two of silence.

I said, "What about the man he was working for? Do you know who he is?"

"I do."

"Can you tell me anything about him?"

"No."

"Can you tell me about him if you and I meet, face-to-face?" I said.

"I don't think so."

Tony wasn't going to budge.

I said, "Is he an associate of yours?"

More silence.

"Sorry, Jake. I'm going to pass on this one. I have to get to the office."

"Wait," I said, hoping he wouldn't hang up. "You can't tell me—"

"Good bye, Jake."

The phone clicked, followed by the dial tone. It was clear, at that point, there was something more to Michael Bruno. And Tony wasn't going to be the person to tell me what it was.

***

I parked in front of Richard Reagan's apartment building in Taunton, an uncleared coating of snow on the walkway from the night before. It didn't add up to much of anything.

I rang the doorbell for Reagan's apartment and waited a good minute without an answer, then tried the exterior door. It was locked.

I stepped back onto the walkway and looked up at the second-floor windows. With the sun shining and reflecting off the glass, it was hard to see if there were lights on in his apartment, or if he was even home at all. I squinted, using my hand to shield the sun, and saw that the blinds were closed.

I tried the doorbell again, but it didn't work. I had a feeling I was being watched, and shifted my gaze to the woman's apartment on the first floor to see her looking out at me, holding her enormous cat in her arms. She just stared at me, with no expression on her face.

I pointed toward the upper floors. "Is Richard upstairs?"

She shrugged, then disappeared from the window.

I thought she was gone, but the lock slid and the door opened, the woman standing on the other side in a nightgown and robe and scraggly white hair going all over the place, as if she'd just rolled out of bed. With a frown on her face, she looked me over. "What do you want?"

"Richard," I said. "Is he upstairs?"

"I have no idea. I haven't seen him." She opened the door to the building wider. "You can go up and look for yourself."

She didn't say much else, turning away and walking back into her apartment. She gently closed the door behind her.

I went up the curved stairway to Reagan's apartment and saw the door was closed. But I tried the knob, and it was unlocked. Stepping inside without knocking, I felt a chill right away. It seemed the heat was off. A powerful stench hit me hard, like a punch in the nose. With the blinds closed and the lights off, the only light came from the sun slipping through the sides of the closed blinds.

I headed into the kitchen. "Richard?" The table was covered in newspapers and dozens of empty beer cans, some tipped over and spilling onto the floor.

The odor had grown stronger, but when I looked in the sink, I saw a large pot with what looked like beans. But they were mostly burnt, and when I pulled the pot closer to sniff it, I realized the odor's source.

I pushed open a door that was slightly ajar and looked in the bathroom.

I turned and saw another open door and could see a glimpse of a mattress on the floor, with someone—I assumed Richard—fully clothed and face down, sprawled out on top of it.

My first guess was that he was dead. But once I stepped in the room, I could hear a soft, rumbling snore. There was no sheet on the brown-stained mattress, only a blanket bunched-up between it and the wall. A plastic milk crate with a worn leather wallet was next to the mattress. Richard seemed to be out cold and didn't appear to be close to waking up. I looked through the wallet and found it stuffed with business cards and a dozen or so paper ticket stubs from Raynham Dog Park.

I flipped through the business cards; most of them old and worn and a few faded to a point of illegibility as if they'd gotten wet. There was a card for Green Chrysler. Larry Green's name was on it.

Two other cards were stuck together, one for a lawyer in Boston on top. I peeled them apart, and the one underneath was one I wasn't exactly surprised to find. It had the name Bob Pearson on it, and what looked like a hand-drawn sketch of a logo with Pearson Woodworks printed across the card.

I noticed one of the ticket stubs had numbers scribbled on it. I flipped it, and on the other side was a phone number with a local 617 area code. I didn't recognize it at first, slipping it into my pocket.

There was a phone on the floor next to the mattress, with the handset off the hook. I picked it up and listened to nothing but a dial tone.

"Reagan!" I said, kicking the side of the mattress hard enough his body shook.

He grunted, and turned over to his side facing the wall.

So I gave the mattress another good nudge with my boot and yelled louder, "Reagan!"

This time, he woke up. Turning to look at me, his eyes barely opened. He stared at me, on his back now, elbows propping him up. "What the..."

"Get up," I said, then tossed the photo of him and Bruno on his chest.

Reagan took the photo, then reached for a pair of glasses on the floor and slipped them on. "What's this?" He looked over the photo, straightened his glasses, then raised his gaze to me. "Where'd you get this?"

"It doesn't matter," I said. "You know Michael, AKA Johnny, Bruno? You know what that means?"

He shrugged, shaking his head. "It doesn't mean nothing."

I said, "Bruno is likely behind Larry Green's death. And the only missing piece to the puzzle is how he was connected to Larry Green. And who had hired him." I pointed at the photo. "On top of all the other reasons you had for killing your old friend, this just about ties you directly to the man the Feds are out looking for."

Reagan let out a wheezing cough, pushing himself up from the mattress like a baby deer taking her first steps. I caught him when he stumbled.

"Waking up drunk's a good sign you've got a problem," I said, grabbing his arm as if he was about to fall.

He took off his glasses and walked from the room with the photo still in his hand. "I gotta pee." He went into the bathroom from the kitchen and closed the door behind him.

"Don't bother trying to destroy that photo," I said. "We already have a duplicate."

Reagan didn't answer, but I could hear him doing his business, and stepped away from the bathroom door. I quietly opened the kitchen drawers, but most were empty other than one filled with what looked like unopened mail.

I jumped when a gunshot rang out from the other side of the door. Rushing to the bathroom door, I didn't hear another sound.

"Richard?"

He didn't answer. I tried the knob, but it was locked. I pounded on the door, then drove my shoulder into it. The door swung open and stopped when it hit the bathtub behind it.

My eyes went to Reagan, seated on the toilet with his pants at his ankles. His body leaned against the wall, his chin on his chest. Blood dripped on the green tiles on the wall and onto the roll of toilet paper.

A .38 sat on the floor, at Reagan's feet, his hand hanging over it.

I checked his pulse, but had no expectations of finding one.

Richard Reagan was dead.

***

By the time the Taunton Police showed up, I'd opened all the windows to get the stench out, but it didn't seem to make much of a difference.

I wasn't sure it was the right thing to do, but I'd kept the business card and ticket stubs I took out of Reagan's wallet. After about an hour of being questioned and waiting outside for Nick Carter to make it out from Boston, I walked down the driveway toward the street when I saw him walking from his car, parked three houses down.

Two additional officers showed up just as I stopped to talk to Nick, and I waited until they all went inside to start talking. My voice low, I said to Carter, "Reagan told me he didn't know who Bob Pearson was." I handed Carter the card. "He lied."

Detective Carter took the business card from me and looked it over. He kept his voice low. "Did you show this to anyone inside?"

I cleared my throat, shaking my head. "Not yet."

He looked around, like he wasn't sure what to do with it, then handed it back to me. "This is a crime scene, Jake. You need to give it to the officers." But the look he gave me said otherwise, like he expected me to keep it. At least that's the read I got from his gaze.

I slipped the card into my coat pocket. "I don't know if Reagan is directly responsible for Larry Green's death, but he clearly had something to do with it."

Carter nodded, as if he agreed. "I should go in and talk to these guys."

I grabbed his arm as he started to walk away. "Wait. Don't you see the connection?" I wasn't sure he did. "Larry Green's balloon allegedly landed on Pearson's property. But I'm not even sure it was ever actually in the air."

"You're basing your theory on *what*?" he said.

"There was one witness who saw it in the air, and one who saw it land. One witness is dead, the other's missing."

"That doesn't tell us anything," he said. "But, if it'll make you feel any better, I'd be willing to go along with the fact that Reagan was involved."

I was hesitant to tell him the rest, considering the photo Maggie shared with me could get her in trouble. I'd already put it in my car.

"I'm almost certain Reagan knew Michale Bruno," I said.

Carter's eyebrows rose. "How do you know this?"

"I can't say. Not yet."

"You can't say? Who do you think you—"

"Just give me some time," I said. "I can get the answer." I looked toward the door as the coroner and one of the paramedics carried Reagan's bagged body to the doorway. The two lifted it onto the stretcher at the bottom of the steps.

The old woman was in the window watching me, the dog-sized cat in her arms.

I said to Carter, "There's someone else out there who is behind everything," I said.

"Yeah, Michael Bruno," he said.

I shook my head. "No, but I mean somebody hired him."

"Reagan?"

"He didn't have two pennies to rub together. And I can't imagine he had that kind of pull without someone else's help... Someone who had the means to pay to have Larry Green killed."

CHAPTER 46

I STOPPED AT A payphone on the way back to my office, but had to get out and dig in my seats and lift the floor mats to look for a dime. But by the time I found one under the driver's side, someone else had slipped into the phone booth and closed the door.

I waited in the front seat of the Nova, waiting, and leaned my head back. I felt guilty about what had happened to Reagan, even though I had little doubt he was either partly responsible for Larry Green's death, or knew the person who was. It's easy for any man to fall from grace. Money, like life, can be taken away in a second, and change the person, or those left behind, in a matter of seconds.

Whatever his tie to Michael Bruno, if that photo was enough evidence to show a connection existed, it would be impossible to prove any of it without the Feds somehow capturing Michael "Johnny" Bruno. The chances were good that he'd already fled the country.

I'd made mistakes. I should have leaned into Reagan harder. I couldn't have known he'd left a gun in his bathroom, or that he'd take that moment to end his life. But I likely could have stopped it. At least that's what I kept telling myself.

And if Reagan was indeed involved in Larry Green's death, what was his reasoning? Revenge? I didn't see what he had to gain from killing a man he once called his friend.

The more I thought about it, the more I wondered if I had it all wrong.

It had been a good five minutes before the woman finally stepped out of the phone booth. And by the time I got in there myself and dropped a dime in the slot, darkness had taken over the sky. The sun that seemed to fight to break through the clouds all day had finally set.

I watched the woman get in her car. She put on her headlights and turned the car. The long beams of light cut across my face.

I took my wallet out. I'd written Nathan Howell's number on the back of my own business card, and when I pulled it out to dial, I felt my heart begin to race. My mouth went dry.

I took the ticket stub I took from Reagan's apartment out of my coat pocket. With my business card and Howell's number in one hand, and the ticket stub in the other, I compared the two.

The number written on the ticket stub was Nathan Howell's.

I pulled the lever, and a sharp clink echoed as the dime dropped and bounced down the metal chute before rattling into the coin return with a ping. I took my dime and threw open the phone booth's door, rushing to the Nova.

I jumped behind the wheel and turned the key to start the engine. I slapped the shifter and slammed my foot on the gas, tires squealing as I cut across the parking lot and onto Route 2.

***

No cars were parked on the street in front of Howell's house, but I could see light from inside slipping through the closed curtains on the windows. As dark as it was, there were no lights on over the porch.

I hurried through the frigid air and tried not to slip on the snow-covered walkway. It had not been cleared.

It made little sense to me how either Marilyn or her uncle would have anything to do with Richard Reagan, or why he'd have the uncle's phone number written on an old ticket stub from the racetrack.

Clearly, there was a reason. I hadn't convinced myself that either Marilyn or her uncle had something to do with Larry Green's death. The simple fact that they had hired me made it impossible.

I knocked so hard on the door it hurt my knuckles. I waited as a cold breeze came up from behind me. My mind was going a hundred miles a second with so many thoughts I couldn't get them all straight.

I tried to think back to that first night, how the uncle had stopped Marilyn from meeting with me. He was never on board with an investigation. But he didn't seem to stop it, either. It made no sense.

Standing for at least half a minute, I didn't have the patience to wait. I pounded on the door this time, and within a few moments the porch light came on.

The door finally opened.

Nathan Howell stood on the other side. I couldn't tell if he was surprised to see me or not, his face without expression. "What are you doing here?"

"Can I come in?" I said. I wasn't sure what his answer would be.

The uncle glanced over his shoulder as if someone else was there. I assumed it was Marilyn, but it seemed to me he wasn't quite sure how to answer. "I'm in the middle of something."

I said, "Is that a no?"

"Perhaps another time would be—"

"You really think I'm here making a social call?"

His Adam's apple jumped as he swallowed. He stepped back from the door and gestured with a nod for me to come inside.

I stepped into the warmth and the smell of burning wood. The glow from the fireplace came from the room to my left, by the front door.

"Where's Marilyn?" I said, looking up the stairs and down the hall. I hadn't moved from just inside the front door.

"She's resting," he said. "She's flying out in the morning."

"Oh yeah? Where's she going?"

He stared back at me without a response. "What is it you want, Mr. Horn?"

"Is there a chance you can get Marilyn?" I glanced up the stairs again, but it was dark. "I'd like to speak with you both, if—"

"Why don't you tell me what this is about," Howell said. "This has all taken a very emotional toll on her. On both of us. So, if you don't mind, please tell me why you are here. As I mentioned, I'm in the middle of something."

I followed him into the room with the fireplace.

He had a drink on the side table next to the wingback chairs facing the fireplace and a paperback open, page-side down on the same table.

"What are you reading?" I said.

He looked at me as if he wasn't sure why I'd asked such a question. Or maybe he didn't know what I meant.

"The book?" I said, nodding toward it. "What book are you reading?"

He didn't answer. He instead crouched in front of the fire with the steel poker, prodding the glowing embers until they sparked back to life. Flames wrapped around the logs, which were quickly engulfed in flames. Howell didn't move, still crouched with his back to me, and continued shifting the burning logs around the open fireplace.

Reaching for a fresh split piece of wood from a small stack on the hearth, he placed it on the fire. He still hadn't turned to face me.

I walked closer to him and over to the table with the paperback. I lifted it and read the cover. The title was *Eye of the Needle*.

"You like Ken Follett?" I took the ticket stub I took from Reagan's wallet and stuck it between the pages, using it as a bookmark. I closed the book and dropped it on the table, but also made sure Nathan Howell had seen what I'd done.

"What was that? he said.

"What was what?"

"What did you just put in my book? What are you up to?"

"Oh, I didn't want you to lose your place," I said.

Marilyn's uncle used the poker to support himself as he rose from his crouched position. He stepped toward me and reached for the book. He opened it to the page where I'd placed the stub. "What is this?" Looking at both sides, he froze when he saw his own phone number. He raised his gaze to mine. "What the hell are you trying to do?"

"What am I trying to do?" I shrugged. "You told me you didn't know Richard Reagan. But that ticket stub was in his wallet."

He kept his eyes down on the stub, and took a moment before raising his gaze. "I have no idea why he would have my number. There must be some sort of mistake. Maybe he... Maybe Larry was over here at some point. He must have given it to him. In case he needed to reach him here." He turned to face the fire.

"You're lying," I said.

Howell turned to me. "You can believe whatever you'd like." He picked up his drink. His hands were shaking. He took a sip but had trouble getting the glass to the right place on his lips. A drip came down his chin, and he wiped it with the back of his hand. "I want you out of my house!" he said, gritting his teeth. He pointed toward the doorway. "Get out of here right this moment, before I call the police." He took the ticket stub and threw it into the fire.

But I reached into my pocket and showed him the real ticket stub. I'd written the number myself, on the one I'd put inside the book. "Just in case you think burning that ticket helps you. The number on this one matches your handwriting."

I stepped toward him, keeping my eye on the steel poker in his hand. I could see from the way he was shifting his grip, he was getting ready to take a swing. I held up another piece of paper, this time the one with the number he'd given to me for New Hampshire, when Marilyn was first going up there. He'd written it himself.

"I'm not a forensic document examiner," I said. "But this handwriting is a damn-near perfect match." He had a way of writing the number seven, with the line through it, the way they did in Europe to distinguish the number seven from a one.

Howell came toward me and tried to grab the stub from my hand.

"I don't think so," I said, holding it out of his reach. I stuck both pieces of paper in my pocket.

Howell placed the poker down and went over to the secretary's desk between the two windows facing the front of the house.

He opened a drawer, as if trying to hide whatever it was he was doing. When he turned, he was holding a gun.

I remained calm. I wasn't going to let this old man intimidate me. I didn't take him for a murderer. At least not the type to do it himself.

"Why'd you do it?" I said.

"I don't know what you're talking about," he said.

I grinned. "The game is over. Just tell me why. I can come up with a few reasons you wanted Larry Green dead. But, it seems to me you went through a lot of trouble to make it happen the way it did. I just want to know why."

The uncle took another step toward me, the gun still raised. "How much do you want," he said. "We keep this between me and you. I'll give you whatever you want."

I said, "You think you can bribe me? After all I've been through?"

"Don't make me shoot you," he said. "Please. I'd hate to—"

"Was it because he married Marilyn? Were you upset about them being together all these years? Until you couldn't stand it anymore?"

He didn't respond.

I eyed the gun. "I assume you decided to go to Reagan with your plan, knowing you weren't the only one who had something against Green. Am I right? And then he told you he could make it happen, for the right amount of money? Is that right?"

Howell pulled the hammer back on the pistol, his voice in a whisper. "I did it for Marilyn," he said. "But it was all a big mistake. I don't know what I was thinking. I thought I could trust Reagan. But these men he hired... They weren't even supposed to know I was involved. He gave me his word, my name would never be mentioned. But there were too many people involved. And when I tried to back out, it was too late. Then they wanted more money. More money than I had."

"You tried to stop it?" I said.

He took a moment before finally nodding.

"Does Marilyn know any of this?"

He shook his head and put his finger to his lips. "Please, keep your voice down." He had tears in his eyes. "All this time, I've been paying them. But it was never enough. And then they wanted more. If I didn't come up with a way to pay them, they threatened me. Not only my life, but..." His eyes went to the doorway.

"They were going to kill Marilyn? So, her life was really in danger?"

"I don't know for sure, but I do believe that evening she tried to find your office, if I didn't pick her up, it would have been her."

"You mean the girl? The one in Boston? They believed they killed Marilyn?" I stepped closer to the fireplace.

"They told me it was her. But she was already with me, after we got back here from Boston. I knew they'd made a mistake. And I figured, at the very least, you could protect her. I never imagined you'd..." He took a deep breath and let out a sigh, the gun still pointed at me. His voice in a whisper, he said, "I'm sorry. But I'll need you to come for a ride with me."

I turned to the fireplace, and could feel Nathan Howell stepping up behind me. I grabbed the steel poker leaning against the bricks by the fire and swung it as I turned, striking his wrist with such force he screamed.

He dropped the gun to the floor and fell to his knees, holding his wrist. He cried out in pain. "You broke my wrist, you son of a bitch!"

By the looks of it, I don't think he was wrong.

I turned to the doorway when I felt someone's presence.

Marilyn was standing there, tears in her eyes. She glared at her uncle on the floor and clearly in pain, but didn't move to help him. "Why?" she said. "How could you?" She stepped into the room.

"You heard it all wrong," her uncle pleaded. "He's lying. This man had no idea what he's talking about." He tried to get to his feet, but stumbled and stayed seated on the floor, his back against the couch.

"You didn't want me to hire him," she said. "And I couldn't understand why. But it all makes sense now. You're the one who convinced me not to bother the police, and that they would never help me." She was standing over him now. "Why? Why did you do it?"

"I didn't do it!" Howell yelled.

"Well, actually he *paid* someone to do it," I said. "Just so we're all on the same page."

Howell gave me a look, then closed his eyes and lowered his chin to his chest. He held his wrist.

"You might want to get that looked at," I said.

Howell finally raised his gaze. "You really want the truth?" he said, looking from me to Marilyn. "Your aunt. She's the reason. And Larry Green is the reason she now lives eighteen hundred miles away from here."

Marilyn's mouth hung open, watching her uncle. She gave me a quick glance and said to her uncle. "What are you talking about? I don't understand."

Howell let out a sigh. "She had an affair with Larry. It was not long after you started working for him."

Marilyn gasped, and had to grab onto the chair to keep herself from collapsing to the floor. I stepped over to help her keep her footing.

I said to Howell, "You had him killed, because he had an affair with your wife?"

Marilyn seemed unable to speak. Her breathing was heavy. She appeared to be hyperventilating.

Nathan said to her, "I swore to your aunt I would never tell you. But I was never going to forgive her. And I certainly could not forgive him. Over time, my rage only grew. I despised him for marrying you. But this... I could not handle it."

Marilyn let out a yelp, like a small dog's bark, and started to cry. She sobbed like a child. And then she let out a loud scream that cracked my eardrums.

"Marilyn," he said. "I couldn't watch it any longer. The way you loved him. It made me sick to my bones. And I thought, at the very least, you would be better off with him dead. But the fool..." He tried to get to his feet while still holding his wrist. "The fool couldn't even afford to continue paying for his life insurance. You would have been taken care of financially. At least for a while."

"And what would you get out of it?" I said. "Revenge?"

Howell was on his feet now, then sat in a wooden chair against the wall. "You know how much money I had to shell out for these two?" he said. "I paid for their apartment. I paid for their food. Like a couple of kids. But once my wife confessed..." He shook his head. "I knew it all had to come to an end."

Marilyn hadn't said a word, sobbing almost uncontrollably in the chair facing the fireplace.

"Does your wife know what you did?" I said.

"We haven't spoken a word to each other since she left," he said. "But she doesn't know our condo down there is about to be foreclosed on. As is this house. I'm broke. I don't have a dime left to my name."

Marilyn turned to look at her uncle. Her lips moved, but no words came out.

Howell gazed at his niece, his voice soft now. "If I didn't pay them everything I had, you would have been dead. Plain and simple."

Marilyn got up, ran out of the room and up the stairs.

"I need to use your phone," I said. "I'm sorry, but I'm calling the police."

"For what?" Howell said. "You have your answer. What good does it do calling the police?"

I couldn't believe what he was asking. "Well, I wouldn't accept a bribe either way, but it sounds to me you can't afford one either way, so..."

"Don't," he said. "I'm begging you." He stood up from the chair. "Besides, all you have is a piece of paper with my phone number on it. You think that's evidence? I know how these things work."

"I have plenty," I said. "And Marilyn knows the truth now, so you're going to—"

"You really think she'd do that to me? I guarantee you, she won't turn on me like that. She has a good heart. Marilyn will learn soon enough what I did was right."

We both looked toward the windows when red and blue lights lit up the darkness outside the house. I went to the window and saw three Newton Police vehicles in the driveway. Six officers ran toward the front door.

I turned to the uncle and the panicked look on his face. "Who called the police?" he said.

We both turned to the doorway, where Marilyn stood watching us. "I did," she said, then disappeared.

The front door opened, and the officers charged into the room.

CHAPTER 47

Maggie and Detective Carter walked into my office, each holding cups of Dunkin' Donuts coffee. Maggie had two, and placed one on my desk. "Black. No sugar."

"Thanks," I said, and peeled off the plastic tab.

Raymond came out of the bathroom from down the hall, wiping his hands on his pants. He gave the two each a nod. "Maggie. Detective. Good to see you." He glanced at the coffee. "Where's mine?"

"I didn't know you'd be here," Maggie said. "I'm sorry."

Carter said, "Don't tell me you're working with this guy now, are you?"

Raymond laughed. "Nah, Jake can't afford me. Not when his client's up on murder charges."

"My client's uncle," I said, correcting him.

Carter turned to me. "Wait, so you didn't get paid?"

"I gave the money back to Marilyn," I said. "Nathan Howell's broke. And Marilyn has nothing."

I didn't either, and certainly could've used the money. But I felt I did what I thought was right. I picked up my coffee and took a sip.

"I'm thinking of calling some of my old insurance clients. At least it's steady work."

"But you hate it," Maggie said.

"Yeah, but not as much as I hate being broke."

Raymond went over to the coffee machine. "I guess I'll make my own coffee." He cleared his throat. "Since nobody brought me one."

"I said I was sorry," Maggie said.

Detective Carter laughed.

I went to the window and looked outside. The sun was finally shining, and a lot of the snow we'd gotten had started to melt, creating puddles all along East Broadway. "So, what's the latest on Michael Bruno? Still no luck?"

"US Marshals are involved now. They think he's either in Cuba or Mexico."

"If you find him, is there enough to get him for Trudy Bailey's murder?"

"We should be able to. But finding him is a big if. He'd been able to keep a low profile all these years. I can't say it'll be any more difficult for him now, if he's gotten out of the country. But at least between Louie Ricci and Nathan Howell, we've got two willing to say what it takes for lighter sentences."

"But until you find him," Raymond said, sipping the coffee he'd made, "I guess it'll be more added to the pile."

We all knew what he meant. There were thousands of open cases either unsolved or unresolved each year in Boston alone. And close to a third of homicides were never solved. It was the reality of police work. Sometimes it was a lack of evidence. Or in plenty of cases, a lack of witnesses.

I wasn't going to mention the corruption in the department. Not in front of Carter, Maggie, or Raymond. They were good cops, but often preferred to pretend the problem wasn't as bad as it was.

Carter turned to me. "I assume you heard about the arson charges?"

I was about to sip my coffee, but stopped. "The dealership?"

He turned to Maggie. "You didn't tell him?"

She shook her head. "Tell him what?"

"Oh, right," Carter said. "Norwood police are pressing charges against Kip Rainier. For arson."

"The rich kid?" Raymond said, looking from Carter to me. "Did you know this?"

I shook my head. "Not at all. I would've suspected him, but..."

"Apparently he spoke with a real estate agent a few months back, looking for property so he could open a dealership. But there was nothing available. When the agent suggested he try to buy an existing dealership, especially one that could be struggling, he made a joke at the time. He told her he had one in mind, but he'd have to burn it to the ground to get it in his price range."

"That's enough to make him guilty?" Raymond said.

Carter shook his head. "No, but apparently his father had been investigated for arson a few years back. He had bought a struggling restaurant and it burned to the ground a month later. The insurance company determined it was arson, but were never able to prove it was the father."

"Does anyone with money do it honestly anymore?" I said. "I knew there was something off with the kid. But hopefully they can find something more to pin it on him." I looked at my watch. "I have to head up to New Hampshire," I said. "Nancy's coming home for the weekend." I had plenty of time, but couldn't wait to get up there to get her. There was nothing that mattered more to me.

Carter reached out and shook my hand. "Good work," he said. "I'm sorry I doubted you."

"I'm sorry I thought you were a crooked cop," I said.

His eyes widened. "You what? You thought I was—"

"Don't take it personally." I laughed.

Maggie gave me a quick hug, then pulled Detective Carter by the arm and toward the door. She shoved him outside before I said something else in my attempt to ruffle his feathers. Stopping before she closed the door, she gave me and Raymond a wave. "I can't wait to see Nancy. I'll see you tonight."

She pulled the door closed, and Raymond grabbed his coat from the rack. "You know, what I said about me not working here. I hope you know, I'm always going to help you out, no matter what. I owe it to my father." He looked around the office, taking a moment before he opened the door and walked outside.

I went to the thermostat to lower the heat. I had no plans to come into the office while Nancy was home. I grabbed my coat, but before I killed the lights, the phone on my desk rang. I was tempted to let it go, but hurried over and picked it up.

I said, "Horn Investigations. This is Jake."

***

Thank you for reading *When the Smoke Clears*. I appreciate you for giving my stories a try.

If you enjoyed the mystery, I'd love to stay in touch. Head over to GregoryPayette.com to sign up for my newsletter — you'll get a free crime story just for joining, plus early updates on new releases.

And if you have a minute, an honest review on the store where you purchases *When the Smoke Clears* makes a real difference for an author. Even a line or two helps other readers find the series.

If you enjoyed getting to know Jake Horn, I'd like you to meet Charlie Harlow. He's a deputy U.S. Marshal with a good heart and a will of steel. The first book, *Shake the Trees*, is fast-paced and loads of fun!

Learn more at GregoryPayette.com

Visit GregoryPayette.com for more stories
HENRY WALSH MYSTERIES
Dead at Third
The Last Ride
The Crystal Pelican
The Night the Music Died
Dead Men Don't Smile
Dead in the Creek
Dropped Dead
Dead Luck
A Shot in the Dark
Dead or a Lie
JAKE HORN MYSTERIES
A Ring and a Prayer (Series prequel)
A Good Time for Goodbye
The Silence of the Sand
When the Smoke Clears
U.S. MARSHAL CHARLIE HARLOW
Shake the Trees
Trackdown
Half Moon Rising
JOE SHELDON SERIES
Play It Cool
Play It Again
Play It Down
STANDALONES
Bicayne Boogie
Drag the Man Down
Half Cocked
Danny's Womack's .38
We're Not Down (summer 2026)